Universal TRUTH

Universal Truth

The Austen Chronicles book 3

4 Horsemen
Publications, Inc.

A.R. Farina

Published By: 4 Horsemen Publications, Inc.

4 Horsemen Publications, Inc.
PO Box 417
Sylva, NC 28779
4horsemenpublications.com
info@4horsemenpublications.com

Cover by J. Kotick
Typesetting by Autumn Skye
Edited by Jen Paquette

Library of Congress Control Number: 2024950850

Paperback ISBN-13: 979-8-8232-0763-8
Hardcover ISBN-13: 979-8-8232-0764-5
Audiobook ISBN-13: 979-8-8232-0766-9
Ebook ISBN-13: 979-8-8232-0765-2

For Lea,
It is a truth
universally acknowledged
that I couldn't have done
any of this without you

Table of Contents

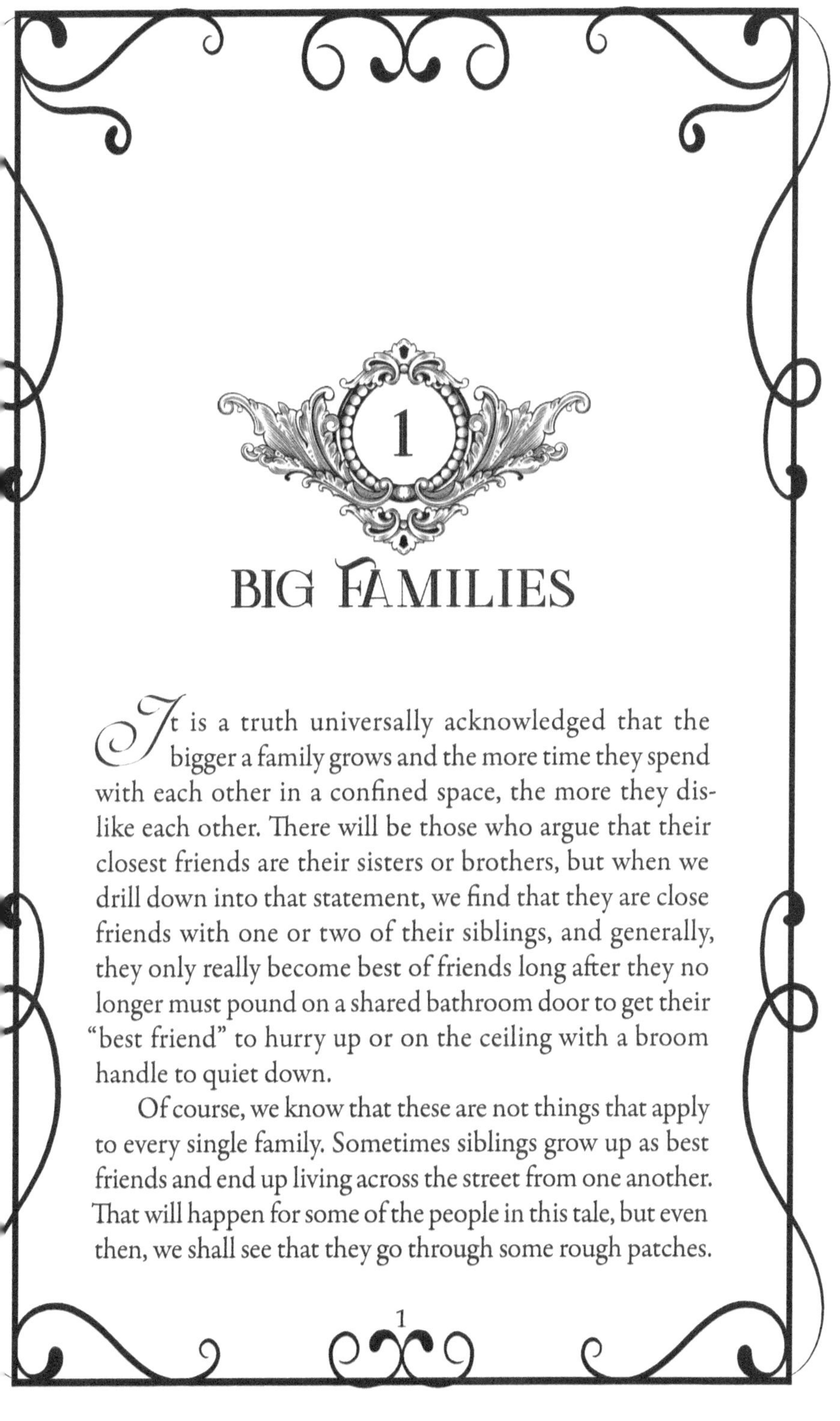

1

BIG FAMILIES

It is a truth universally acknowledged that the bigger a family grows and the more time they spend with each other in a confined space, the more they dislike each other. There will be those who argue that their closest friends are their sisters or brothers, but when we drill down into that statement, we find that they are close friends with one or two of their siblings, and generally, they only really become best of friends long after they no longer must pound on a shared bathroom door to get their "best friend" to hurry up or on the ceiling with a broom handle to quiet down.

Of course, we know that these are not things that apply to every single family. Sometimes siblings grow up as best friends and end up living across the street from one another. That will happen for some of the people in this tale, but even then, we shall see that they go through some rough patches.

Exceptions are exceptions. They don't prove the rule as the common parlance goes. They are just exceptions.

There is never really space equity in any family even if they are all crammed into an apartment or spread out in a mansion. Someone feels slighted. It is much worse for a big family who is confined to a small space. The eldest children, simply because they were born first and won some sort of genetic lottery, generally get to have more space as they grow. The argument is that that child needs "space and privacy." Those elder siblings may be moved to an attic room or have part of the basement partitioned off for them where they hang their clothes on exposed pipe and may have to run a cooling or heating device depending on the seasons. Their mattresses may be on the floor and their shelves may be crates turned on their sides or planks put across concrete blocks. It may smell like mildew, and a critter or two may find its way into the living space, but it will be space. Room to move about and dance or talk on the phone or just to be alone, save for the critters who, generally, don't have much to say anyway. The two siblings who stay close in this story are the eldest two of five, so it is likely these accommodations played a part, or it could be that one of them is just a nice, forgiving type, and it is because of her disposition that the two stay friends. That will be up for debate as we move on, but we shall not linger on the question of why. It just is.

Meanwhile, in the main part of the house, there is a large living room with several mismatched couches, chairs, and tables situated in a way that almost everyone in the room can sit somewhat comfortably while watching TV. There is a kitchen that was made for cooking and not eating, but there is still a small table because sometimes someone just wants to eat a quick meal away from everyone else who is seemingly always in the way. It is possible that three other siblings share a 10 by 12 room, and each of them has one drawer in a dresser designed for a toddler. Fear not though because each of them has one-third of the closet even though one of them most assuredly has an affinity for clothes while the others do not, and what is the big deal if she just put her clothes over the Sharpie marker line drawn onto the rod in the closet? "This is so unfair!" is likely shouted, and feet are stamped, hair is pulled, arms are pinched, and dirty socks are passive-aggressively left on clean pillows. Any one of those children would happily snuggle up with a rabid opossum at night in the cold and breezy attic to not have to hear their siblings talk in their sleep, or through night terrors, or smack their lips together, or just breathe. This is the case for our tale here. Three siblings, all within a few years of each other, are forced to share living space for much, much longer than they would like or was, as we shall see, absolutely necessary.

Likelier still, there are several rooms in the house that are off limits to the children, which could have been easily converted to a much larger bedroom for multiple siblings while the smaller room was reserved for one or both parents to do whatever it is the parents do in there. The parents already have a large bedroom with their own bathroom. Why then, if parents have a warehouse-sized bedroom that could have two adult-sized dressers, a tall skinny one and a shorter, longer one in addition to a walk-in closet that has not only empty shelf space but has room to store empty emergency hangers for those times when hangers are broken due to accidents or rage or both, do they need one or more other rooms in the house that are just for them? Do they really need a guest room? Really? A guest room! For guests? The family is already big enough. They don't need guests, do they? As though having more people stay over is a good idea. There are already five woman-sized "children." Is the comfort of a potential guest more important than the comfort of an actual child? Seems unlikely. Does the mother really need an office inside the house when there is already an office for the family business in an outbuilding? Besides, what does she even know about the family business? Does he need a library? Shouldn't he be more concerned with the family business? You know, the one he started on his own but upon which the fortunes of all of them hinge? Why would they let their oldest children move into an unheated part of the house with things that crawl or slither or fly and sting? Why would they leave multiple children crammed into a tinderbox of hormones and angst? Why indeed did the parents in the tale that is about to unfold do just that?

These questions have no satisfactory answers. Things happen because they happen, and if the parents in this story were asked, which they are not within these pages, but if they were, they would likely say that is how it was done. The parents had parents who treated them thusly, and so they did the same. They didn't really even think about it as many parents of a certain era didn't. The parents in this tale are of the Baby Boom generation, and they did things the way they did because it is what people did. Appeals to antiquity are problematic, and they shall be tackled in this tale of a large family who certainly love each other, but who do not like each other very much for reasons we shall soon see. Maybe it is that not all truths that are universally acknowledged are universal truths.

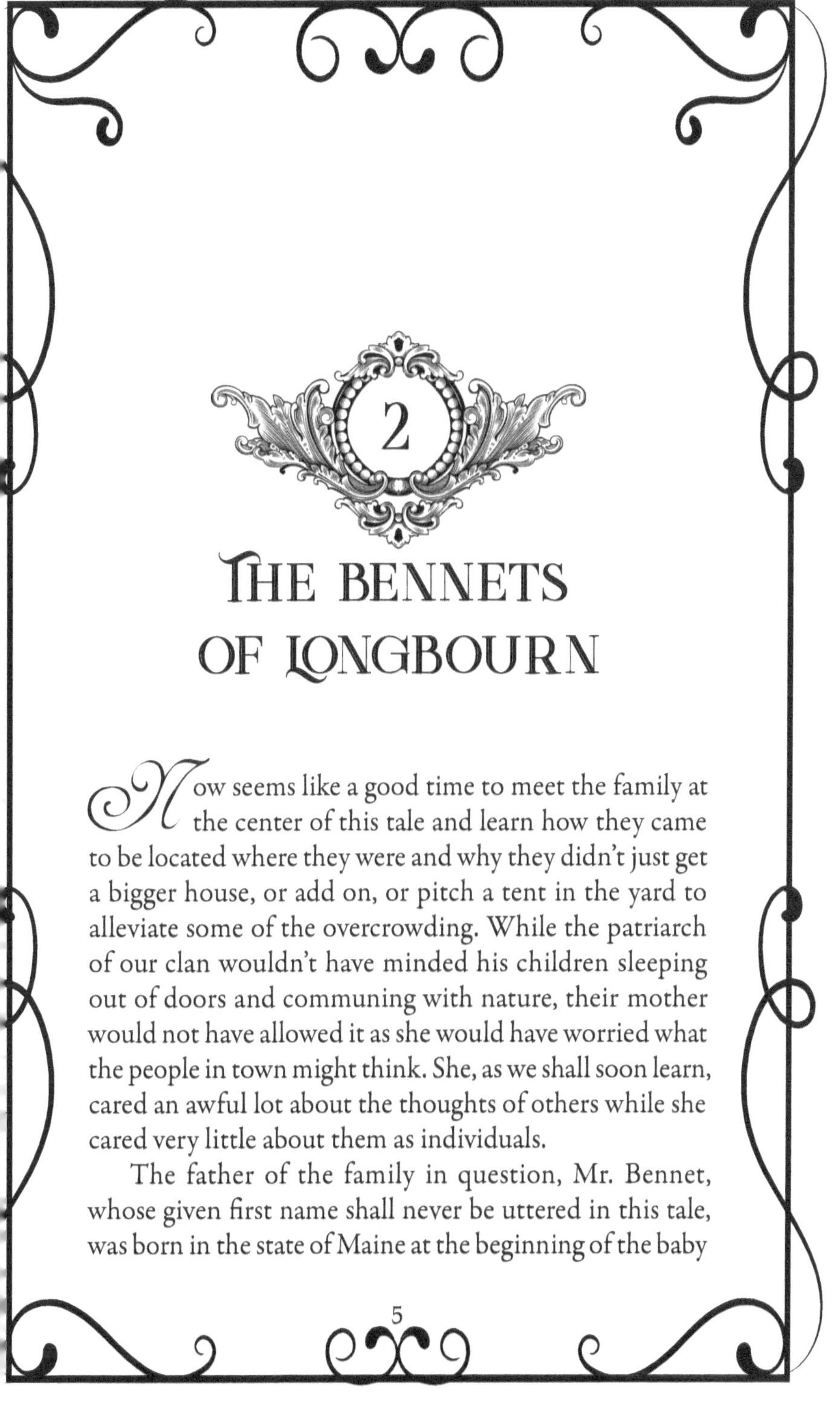

2

THE BENNETS
OF LONGBOURN

Now seems like a good time to meet the family at the center of this tale and learn how they came to be located where they were and why they didn't just get a bigger house, or add on, or pitch a tent in the yard to alleviate some of the overcrowding. While the patriarch of our clan wouldn't have minded his children sleeping out of doors and communing with nature, their mother would not have allowed it as she would have worried what the people in town might think. She, as we shall soon learn, cared an awful lot about the thoughts of others while she cared very little about them as individuals.

The father of the family in question, Mr. Bennet, whose given first name shall never be uttered in this tale, was born in the state of Maine at the beginning of the baby boom. His family did what many families did in Maine. They caught and sold fish. Unfortunately for him, an ear infection at a young age caused him to have balance issues and made him incredibly prone to motion sickness. Thus, he was unable to work the boats with the rest of his family. Working families often have progeny to lock down a free labor force and to have someone to care for them in their old age. Since young Mr. Bennet was all but worthless to them, at age ten, he was loaned out to a family acquaintance, a twenty-year-old self-starter called Mr. Collins, to work on his farm. He learned a lot about life and death on that farm from the work he did on the land while figuring out the rest in Mr. Collins' well-stocked library.

Mr. Collins, who was like an uncle to Mr. Bennet, wished to see his young charge succeed and so, for his 18th birthday, he purchased Longbourn Farm in Connecticut, just outside of a town called Meryton. Mr. Bennet's formal education ended in 8th grade, but he was considered a good worker and very bright, being a self-educated, voracious reader. While no bank would give anyone of that age a loan based on those qualifications, Mr. Collins, a religious man who had faith in God and faith in his protégé, sold Mr. Bennet the property on a land contract. Much more on that choice to come. Mr. Bennet bid his birth family goodbye and moved south, bringing with him only his grit, a collection of books, and his Maine accent. They didn't notice his absence, and we shall think nothing more of the elder Bennets save for one quick reference to them. If you blink, you may miss it. Don't worry. It isn't that important.

Meryton was close enough to several major cities in four different states; thus, it saw a variety of people come through as tourists wishing to breathe fresh air or rich investment banker and insurance broker types who wanted a second home in the country. There was, due to its prime location on train lines to major hubs of activity, an army reserve base situated there. Those in the reserves would drop into Meryton from one of the many surrounding major cities one weekend a month and several weeks a year to train and stay in shape should the need arise to be called upon to active duty. The base was a constant hub of economic activity upon which Meryton thrived.

Edward Gardiner, a local attorney who spent most of his time dealing with wills, contracts, and other business-type legal matters was Meryton's most eligible bachelor for years. He was affable and pleasant but worked hard running his practice and didn't think about much else. However, one day, a woman 10 years his junior hired him to help her brother, a reservist, who had gotten himself into a scrape while in town. Quite unexpectedly, sparks flew. He got the young man off with community service and a small fine and married the woman.

They had three children all of whom factor into this tale. The eldest, a girl, went on to marry a man, Mr. Phillips, ten years her senior. He was a junior partner of her father's, and while Mr. Gardiner didn't like the arrangement at all, he was reminded by his own wife of their age difference while she patted his ever-expanding mid-section. Mrs. Phillips would earn her paralegal certification and work in the office with her husband. We shall see her again. She is very important to this tale.

The youngest, Teddy Gardiner, had no head for law, but numbers made perfect sense to him. He went to one of the many state universities near him where he studied economics. He moved to New York where he toiled away on Wall Street while amassing a small fortune. He fell in love with and later married a bartender who was, shockingly enough, 10 years his junior. They would have four children in quick succession. They will all appear in this tale much later. Don't forget about them.

So, we land on our matriarch, the future wife of Mr. Bennet. She will be called Miss Gardiner, Miss Connecticut, Mrs. Bennet, sister, wife, dear, Mother, or Mom in this tale. She too has a first name, but it shall not be used as no one in her orbit used it. While her sister was pretty and her brother was handsome, she was stunning in the way that Hollywood starlets of the time were stunning. The only real difference between Ava Gardner and Miss Gardiner was that Ava Gardner knew someone who knew someone who took her picture when she was 18, and the right person saw it at the right time. Luck often wins the day.

Being born female in the middle of the baby boom, no one expected much from her and so, she expected nothing from herself. Gender politics and the patriarchy had been going strong for generations, and they would be on full display. She dated boys, won several local beauty pageants, and parlayed that into a year as Miss Connecticut where she was not a finalist in the Miss America Pageant as she didn't have much of a talent, and her answers to the interview questions were atrocious. She was nervous as anyone in her place would have been. Still, she wore her crown proudly and was wearing it during a ribbon cutting event at the new library in Meryton when she caught the attention of a local gentleman farmer who had donated money for the new building. He stood next to her in the official photo of the event. He leaned over just as the picture was taken and whispered into her ear one sentence that won her heart and set this tale in motion. That one sentence meant the world to her. It didn't hurt that he was 10 years her senior, ruggedly handsome, and somehow single.

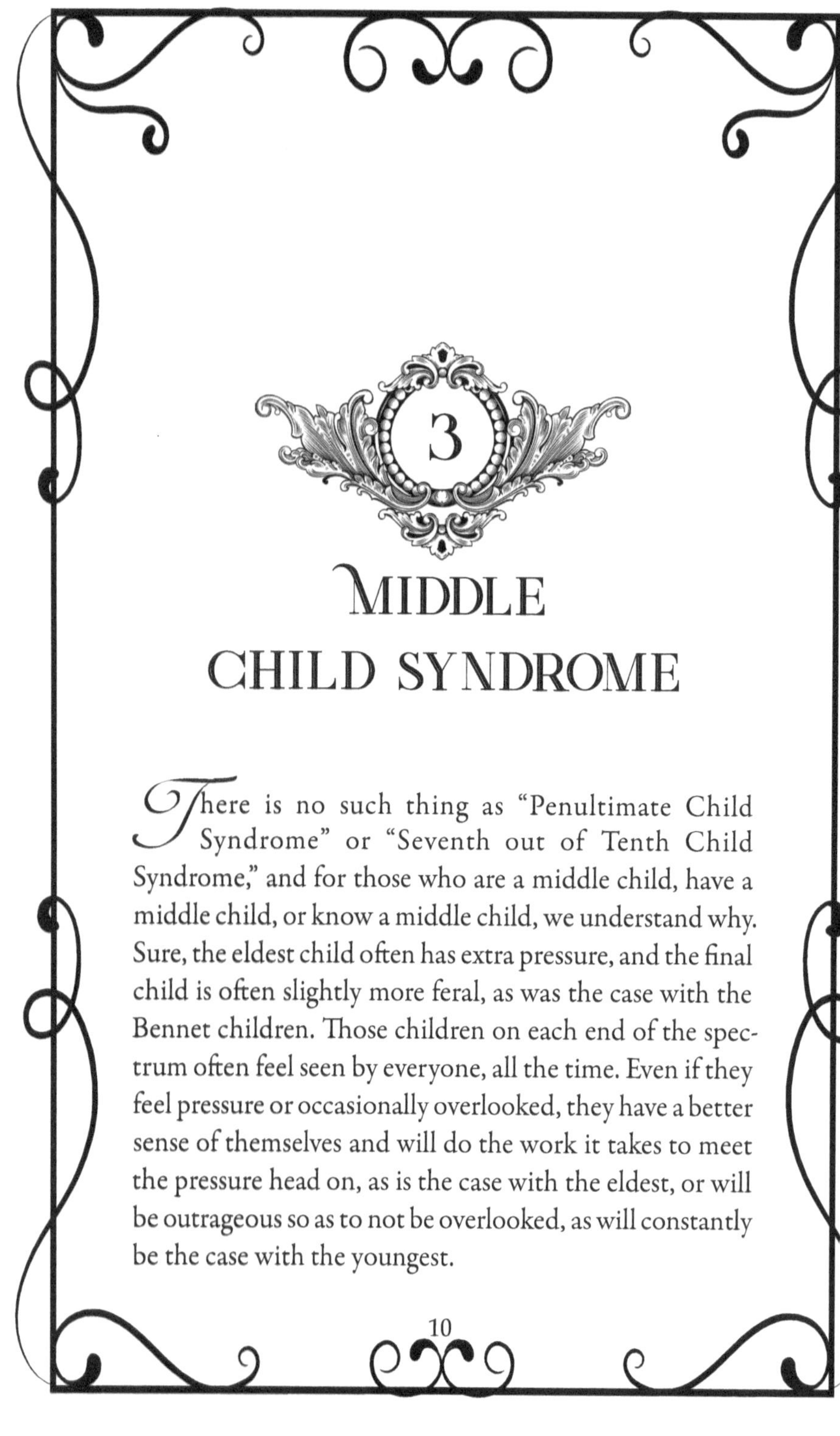

3

MIDDLE CHILD SYNDROME

There is no such thing as "Penultimate Child Syndrome" or "Seventh out of Tenth Child Syndrome," and for those who are a middle child, have a middle child, or know a middle child, we understand why. Sure, the eldest child often has extra pressure, and the final child is often slightly more feral, as was the case with the Bennet children. Those children on each end of the spectrum often feel seen by everyone, all the time. Even if they feel pressure or occasionally overlooked, they have a better sense of themselves and will do the work it takes to meet the pressure head on, as is the case with the eldest, or will be outrageous so as to not be overlooked, as will constantly be the case with the youngest.

Middle children are often, according to the aforementioned syndrome, loners. They don't feel as though they can compete with the elder siblings as they are "not old enough to understand" nor do they wish to compete with their younger siblings so as to not seem "childish." They have big dreams but don't know how to express those dreams in a way that anyone will hear them. They often find one good thing about themselves and decide that is what they are. They become fixed on that thing simply because at one point in time someone said, "You are" whatever that thing is, or someone may say, "Good idea" to something they said once. They wanted the attention, and they received it. It could've been a one-off thing, or it could have been well-meaning. Either way, middle children, in their need to be seen and recognized, will form strong opinions about that thing for which they were given attention.

We already know that the matriarch of our story was a middle child, and someone told her she was pretty and, to be fair, she was, but that became the thing that mattered most to her. Her own looks never did fade. Yes, she aged as we all do, but she was a head-turner right until the end. People often wondered how it was that Mr. Bennet, who wore signs of age, managed to end up with Mrs. Bennet. Even if they did know that all those years ago, he was a ruggedly handsome young man, that still didn't explain how, on his best day, he was a New England six and a half, he could end up with Miss Connecticut, a New York ten. Lots of people told her she was "hot," and they asked her to put on swimsuits and cut ribbons. They told her she was "pretty" and asked her to walk in heels. They called her "sexy" and asked her to do things she did because they gave her attention for doing it. Being Miss Connecticut put her in the spotlight, but she still felt alone in a family full of self-serious studious types.

However, Mr. Bennet, that day on the steps of the library whispered in her ear, in his thick Maine accent, that she was the most beautiful and elegant woman he'd ever seen. If one visits the Meryton Library, one can see the still of the photo today where Mr. Bennet is bent over instead of standing straight, mouth just inches from her ear, her hair covering part of his face. His eyes are closed, and she is smiling the most real, perfect smile anyone in Meryton would ever see. She is radiant. If Ava Gardner's brother-in-law hung that picture up in his window in New York City, we would have no story to tell.

So it was, that between nameless, faceless judges in the years of beauty pageants, the constant reminder from almost everyone she'd ever known how great she looked for having whatever number of children she'd had up to that point, and most of all because her husband told her that no one would ever be more beautiful than she was, she assumed that looks were all that mattered and were the key to having the best life. She was convinced that it was her outward appearance that drew Mr. Bennet to her and kept him loyal to her for all the years of their marriage.

It was true that her looks interested him at first, and her looks kept him interested for the years of their life together, but it wasn't her looks that kept him loyal. No, Mr. Bennet was simply a man of his word. He gave his word to her, her family, the rest of the congregants, and the deity of his choice on their wedding day, and that was that. There was no further discussion to be had. She should have known that was the case, and he proved over the years in all things he did that he was never willing to back down from his word regardless of the consequences, and no word could be more important than the word one gives on one's wedding day. Still, she was convinced that her looks were the key to her happiness, and thus it was, she assumed looks were the key to happiness for her children. She was a middle child with a sense of self that made sense to her and, like her husband's word, it couldn't be shaken.

Thus, when her first child Jane was born in the back half of the 1960s, no one was more relieved that she came out adorable. Some babies are born adorable and manage to stay that way forever. Jane Bennet was one such child. While there were subtle differences to those who knew them both, strangers and distant relatives went on and on about how much Jane looked like her mother. They just meant she was beautiful but couldn't find a way to artic-ulate it. Jane was not hot, nor pretty, nor sexy. She was an elegant beauty with an elegant, beautiful personality to match. She looked for the good in everyone and managed to find it.

Eighteen months later, just as the 1960s were ending, a short time after Neil Armstrong did his one small step for all mankind, Elizabeth Bennet came screaming into the world. She was colicky and could only be soothed by the touch of her older sister. Had Lizzy, as they came to call her, been born first, many people would have commented on her looks as well, but she was born second, and her sister, the yin to her yang in many ways, was always there for comparison, and so, she was cute enough.

There was a time for three years when the Bennet girls ruled the roost. Kind and cherubic Jane and wary and devilish Lizzy were the princesses of Longbourn. They ran around mostly unsupervised, got dirty, and brought joy into each other's lives. These are the two siblings who were the aforementioned exception. Lizzy bypassed the terrible twos and had landed firmly into the tyrannical threes as Mrs. Bennet called them. Lizzy and her mother didn't see eye to eye on almost anything, a trait that would continue for the rest of their lives. Jane could always find a way to bring Lizzy back from the brink of a tantrum with a whisper or a touch.

Truth be told, there are few people in the world who don't feel better when Jane Bennet is in the room. Lizzy could easily be soothed by Mr. Bennet, of whom she'd grown quite fond. In the evenings, after their dinner, he would let her sit on his lap in his reading chair in his library. He would read aloud whatever it was he was reading, and she would sit and try to follow along with the words on the page. To be clear, most of this was not incredibly appropriate for a child of that age, but as was the case for Boomer parents and their Generation X children, they didn't think about the effects of media on their children in any way as long as whatever it was kept the children quiet.

So it was that Mrs. Bennet found herself ready to give birth to her third child just when they needed to enroll Jane into the half-day kindergarten at the public school in Meryton. She feared having an infant and, for all intents and purposes, being alone with an angry, questioning, inconsolable Lizzy all day. As Mr. Bennet was either out on the farm overseeing whatever he oversaw or in his library "having a one quiet moment to myself," times when even his darling Lizzy was not permitted behind those doors until after dinner, the decision was made to keep Jane out of school for one more year to "be a help."

Problematically, when the time came for Jane to go to school the following year, Mrs. Bennet found herself once again pregnant with her fourth child, Catherine called Kitty, a pixie-like child who would grow to be easily led and wanted so desperately to be liked by everyone. With a fearsome four-year-old and a one-year-old, there was no way she could "do it without Jane."

The following is language from an actual law that was in place in Connecticut in the early 1970s. The law set forth in 1872 read:

> All parents and those who have the care of children shall bring them up in some lawful and honest employment and instruct them or cause them to be instructed in reading, writing, spelling, English grammar, geography, arithmetic, and United States history and in citizenship, including a study of the town, state, and federal governments. All [children] between the ages of eight and fourteen years should attend some public or private school for at least three months each year, unless instructed at home or prevented from attendance by mental or physical disability.

The law said that Jane need not begin schooling until she was eight, and between Mr. Bennet's library at Longbourn and the Meryton Public Library, which he knew intimately, he was sure his children would learn all of those above-mentioned skills before they turned fourteen. He knew that Jane could already read, write, and spell many words, and Lizzy was her equal in every way. Learning about the local and federal government was easy enough as he had a copy of the state and federal constitution, and the library had, as all libraries do, an entire section dedicated to history. He purchased some basic, intermediate, and advanced math books after conferring with his brother-in-law, math whiz and stockbroker Teddy, and the Bennet home school began in earnest. The school Marm even had an office.

Later, when the younger Bennets were "starting school," the state of Connecticut added some more requirements about parents having high school diplomas and the kids taking bi-annual standardized tests in certain subjects, but by then, with the help of their aunts and uncles, as well as the local library staff, the Bennet girls were academically years ahead of their peers.

Back in 1974, however, when the fifth Bennet daughter Lydia, who would grow to be the tallest, most impatient, and overly impertinent, typical youngest child, as we shall see, was born, Jane and Lizzy were teaching themselves grammar by copying longhand from their favorite novels and short stories. This also taught them penmanship, which was, believe it or not, an actual skill people used to learn. They read aloud to the other children from the collection of historical biographies and social commentaries. So it was that they learned far more about history than was ever required of the children who attended "normal school."

Eagle-eyed readers will notice that we skipped over the third Bennet's birth name and personality traits. Of course, that should have been expected as the title of this chapter indicated. It was done to be cheeky for sure, but it was also done because the third Bennet child, much to her own surprise we are sure, is the heroine of this story. It is with her we shall spend most of our time. None of the big Bennet-changing events that happen in this story happen *to* our heroine. They never happen *because* of her either. Sometimes, she sat in the room when the thing happened, and no one even noticed she was there. Sometimes she heard the thing happen from another room, or via letter, or from a dramatic retelling done by one of her siblings or her mother. Thus, being removed from the story, she has the best opportunity to be objective. Someone must. It would seem then, knowing all of that about her, that she would be a bad heroine. What kind of heroine does nothing? This is a good question. The way to find the answer is to turn the page and see where this story goes.

4

MARY

*T*he third Bennet girl, for they did have five girls and only girls because that is just the way of some families, was called Mary. She was, according to her mother, plain looking and, according to her father, self-serious to the point of ridicule. Notice he didn't say ridiculousness. He didn't think she was ridiculous, but he knew that was how her sisters, her mother, and pretty much everyone except for his sister-in-law, Mrs. Phillips, saw her. They each saw what they wanted to see. Her siblings, when they did bother to see her at all, besides as an often-hysterical know-it-all, each saw something different.

Jane, who never said a cross word about anyone ever, thought of Mary as a loving sister who caused no drama, wasn't a gossip, and was the smartest of them all. The first two were, and still are, absolutely true. "Smartest" is a bit of an objective term. What does that mean really? Did she score the best out of her sisters on the standardized tests when they were administered? Yes. Did she study past tests and train herself to take standardized tests once she realized that was the metric? Yes. Did she always carry a notebook with both a pencil and a pen just in case she needed to make notes about anything that she might deem useful? She did. Sometimes more than one notebook just in case.

Lizzy, who said plenty a cross word about plenty of people but hardly any for Mary, thought she was "book smart, walking dumb," a phrase that has likely gone out of favor at the time of this writing, but that was used extensively. It wasn't always the put-down that it sounds like, and Lizzy didn't mean it as one. It is hard to read the word "dumb" and not think the person is being harsh, but Gen Xers said a lot of things as children that they thankfully left in the past. For those not in the know, that phrase simply meant that due to Mary's proclivity to stay home and read, she didn't know much about how to interact with humans. Lizzy assumed that Mary didn't understand people very much. It was a reasonable suggestion based on bad information. As we shall soon see, she understood way more than anyone knew.

No one knew Kitty's opinion of Mary because Kitty was so malleable that everyone assumed she agreed with whomever she was with. She would nod when Jane would say, "Oh, yes, Mary is so very smart. If only we could all remember things like Mary, we would all be geniuses." She never said a word of disagreement when Lizzy would say, "Oh yes, she will have a terrible time when she *finally* leaves home." When Lydia would say, "Mary's such a bore and a tattle-tale," Kitty offered no objections. Of course, it isn't really possible to be a boring tattle-tale. Tattlers, for the most part, tattle because they get a rush of excitement out of it. Mary never tattled on anyone. She simply reported the facts as she saw them. Lydia was behind on her studies because she snuck off behind the library to make out with that terrible boy. Mary gained no pleasure in reporting these facts to their mother when she asked, "How was your trip to town, girls?" If Lydia had called Mary a boring reporter, that would have been accurate.

While this gives us a hazy picture of who Mary Bennet was, that picture is based on observations by her sisters and parents but not on facts. There is no complete truth there, and one thing we know for sure is that Mary Bennet was always looking for the truth, even though she knew that sometimes, the truth was a moving target. Some truths that people hold at age fourteen might be different by eighteen and different again by twenty-eight. She was always trying to find the pattern. Because of that, she loved history better than all of them, but Kitty often had the best head for dates. It could have something to do with the fact that she didn't form any opinions of her own, and so, if all she had to do was recite back when something was done and by whom, she could do it. She couldn't tell you *why* it mattered that the British defeated the Spanish Armada in 1588, or what it was that Elizabeth I did to make that happen, but that wasn't on the test. Mary wanted to know when, but she more importantly wanted to know why.

Mary was not the earliest to read; that was Lizzy. Mary started at four, and Lizzy, as we've seen, was reading by three. While Mary was almost always upstairs or downstairs or outside reading, she never, ever, caught up to the number of pages Lizzy read. Mary was slow and methodical; Lizzy could zip through a book in a day. She learned to skim, scan, and absorb because by age 13, she had become the de facto school Marm when it came to keeping Lydia, and by extension Kitty, in line and on task. Jane was the eldest but was far too nice. So as not to cut into her pleasure reading or her own studies, Lizzy learned to speedread and thus her books read tally forever stayed ahead of Mary's who was not in charge of anyone or anything whose name was not Mary Bennet. Because of that, she could take all the time she liked to read slowly and deeply, while often taking extensive notes.

Mary had excellent penmanship, and she was a very good writer. She could diagram the life out of a sentence. When asked to write a 500-to-700-word essay, she always had 600 words. If asked to write a formal poem, her pentameter was always iambic. However, her sister Lydia, who was a fabricator, fibber, and falsifier, was the best of them when it came to the written word. She used her magnificent calligraphy skills to forge notes in both of her parents' hands. She used what her mother called "big imagination," and what Lizzy called "lying heart," to make up the most amazing stories that were always rooted enough in reality to be believed. Her poker face was legendary. She never broke. She never backed down from a lie. If she cared enough to enter fiction contests, she would have always won. Lydia didn't care for that because school "was for nerds like Mary."

Mary was not the best at math; that was Jane who had her uncle's head for numbers. However, Mary was excellent at solving story problems. Unlike her peers all around The Nutmeg State, she was never timed whilst sitting in a classroom. She could spend as long as she wanted working through a story problem until it was done. It was her preference to give things time and space and come to the right answer. She was rarely first, but she was rarely wrong either. Better to be last and right than first and wrong.

There was one thing in which Mary had no skill, and no amount of practice could solve the problem, and that was in musical ability. There was a small upright piano in the house, and Mrs. Bennet could play. It was her talent, and while we know she wasn't good enough to make a dent at the national level, she did win Miss Connecticut, thank you very much. Still, she taught all her children how to be proficient enough that they didn't sound like they were stepping on broken xylophones. Sadly, Mary, who loved to listen to music, and think about music, and feel music in her heart, and believed that music was a beautiful form of communication, couldn't play at all. If the sisters were ranked by musical skill, which Mrs. Bennet did, the ranking was Lydia, Lizzy, Jane, Kitty, all of her nieces and nephews, the cat when he walked across the keys at night when Lydia failed to close the lid, and then Mary. Lydia was good enough that she played in several talent shows and was even asked to join the school band, even though she wasn't part of the school. Band seemed like a thing for nerds as well, and so, she passed, but she still played all the time and was, as we shall see, exceptional.

We can't know if any of the Bennet children were good at drawing, painting, or any other visual art. None of them were so inclined to take it up. Likely because Mrs. Bennet didn't want to have to clean up the mess that painting, drawing, and other arts and crafts entailed. It was enough that they lived on a farm and that her girls were always tracking mud and dirt and whatever else into the house all the time. She didn't want to have to worry about glitter as well.

Would Mary Bennet ever consider herself "the anythingest"? She would not. Unless "middlest" was a thing people called people, which, as of this writing, no one has. Still, because she was second best at everything that was on the tests, she managed to earn the highest score. While she was proud of those scores, it wasn't a competition with her sisters. She never felt like she could compete with them, so she didn't try.

She was competing with everyone else for her place in the world against people who didn't even know she existed. Yet, she needed for *them,* whoever they were, to notice her. She didn't believe that those tests she took were the only way to measure intelligence, but she understood they were the way it was done. Her parents were essentially rogue educators. The only way the state of Connecticut kept tabs on the children was to make them be like the rest of the children in the state and take the tests. Tests were not a measure of much beyond information. Mary knew the difference between information and knowledge at an early age, and so while she understood that she was the best test taker and the most "standardized" of her sisters, she did so because she had a plan. Those tests were just a way to get a foot into an educational door, but once inside the door, it was up to her to stay there.

If there were many people around with whom she could discuss theories, she would have discussed them. We shall see that she did seek out some outside input on certain subjects, but for the most part, when she would have the chance, she spoke with her father, who had lots of opinions, but his time was often consumed. However, on some evenings and weekends, when the rest of the family was out doing something or while they watched something on TV that they considered frivolous, the two of them would talk for hours. She read a lot of theory. She liked to find one theory to contradict the other so while her mouth wasn't in conversation with someone, her brain was having a salon. Still waters run deep indeed.

Mary knew that she was a middle child from a small town, built on the back of the military industrial complex and tourism, that most people in her own state couldn't find on a map. She knew she was a person who had no extracurricular activities, official school records, or anything that people needed to go on to a residential college, which is what she wanted most of all. Mary, who shared a tiny room with two of her sisters whom she knew all too well but who didn't take the time to know her at all, wasn't afraid of living in a tiny dorm with a stranger that could possibly turn into a friend.

She didn't know where she wanted to go, just that she wanted to go somewhere full of other people all seeking the truth. People looking to discover the human condition. People who had real debates about which American novelist was the best. We shall see soon enough on which school she will finally set her sights, at which point this tale gets moving and unfolds to a rollicking and triumphant conclusion.

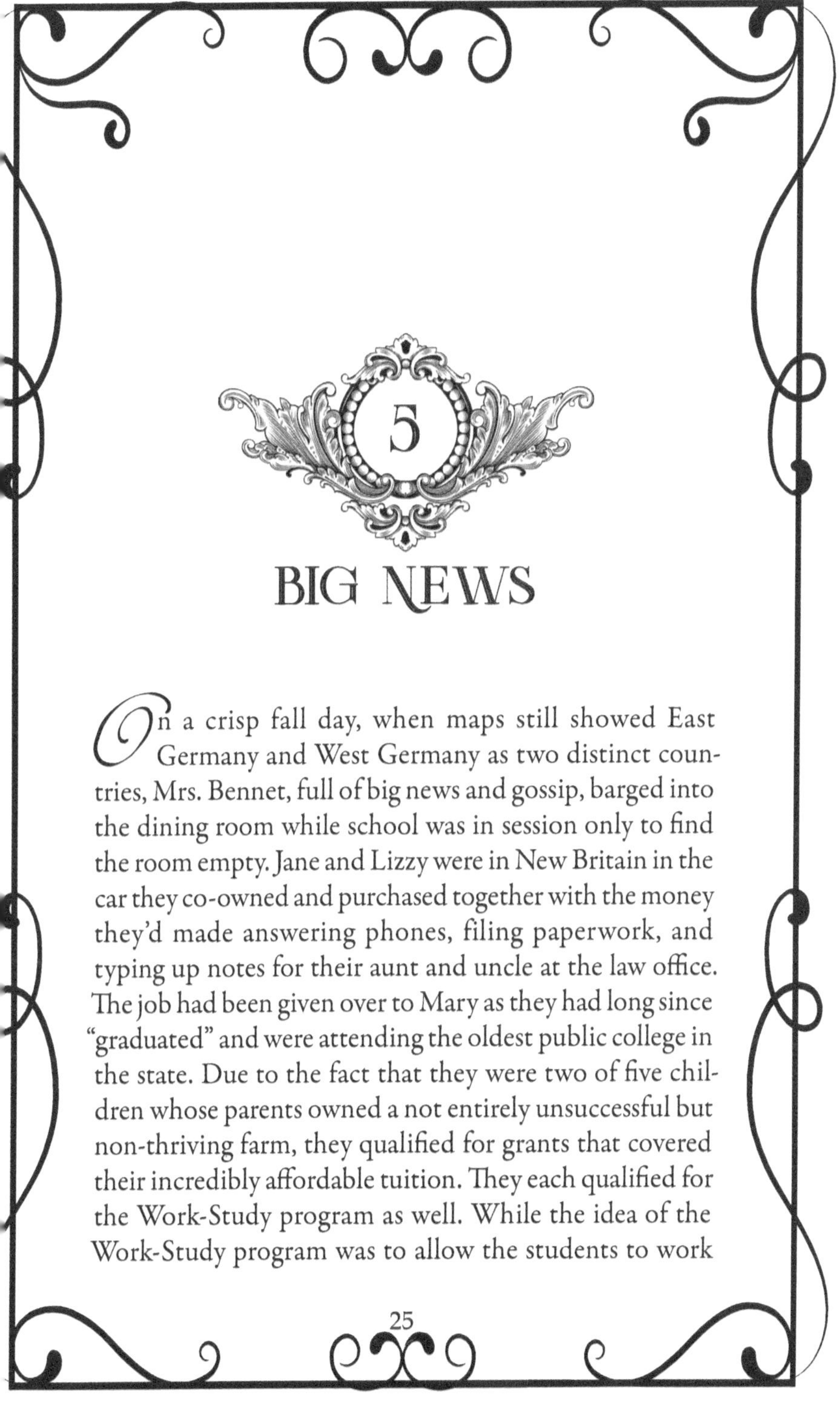

5

BIG NEWS

On a crisp fall day, when maps still showed East Germany and West Germany as two distinct countries, Mrs. Bennet, full of big news and gossip, barged into the dining room while school was in session only to find the room empty. Jane and Lizzy were in New Britain in the car they co-owned and purchased together with the money they'd made answering phones, filing paperwork, and typing up notes for their aunt and uncle at the law office. The job had been given over to Mary as they had long since "graduated" and were attending the oldest public college in the state. Due to the fact that they were two of five children whose parents owned a not entirely unsuccessful but non-thriving farm, they qualified for grants that covered their incredibly affordable tuition. They each qualified for the Work-Study program as well. While the idea of the Work-Study program was to allow the students to work and pay for tuition, there was an option for students who qualified for the program to be paid, and so they did.

Because neither of them really started school at a particular time, they both went off to college when they felt the time was right. Jane made sure that all of them registered and took the SAT by the time they turned 17. Kitty was going to take it that year, and Mary took it the previous year, once again earning the highest score. Lydia, for reasons that will become obvious, never took the test. While Jane was two years older than Lizzy, she started college just one year before her because the general rule about school was, "We can't do it without Jane." While it was Jane who did all the paperwork and jumped through all the hoops with the state, and who did all the leading when the girls were still little and learning the basics, we know it was really Lizzy who kept the younger two in line as Mary needed no such encouragement. So, Jane felt free to head off to college having loved the experience so much that she majored in early childhood education. Her student teaching will begin and end in these pages.

Lizzy did not enjoy the experience of being a teacher of young children very much, but she did love words and learning and so, as it will surprise no one, majored in English with a concentration in Women's Studies. She used her own money to pay for some summer classes because for some reason, at that time, financial aid was not available during the summer even though courses were offered, so Lizzy too was in her final year. She and Jane spent a lot of time on the drive to and from New Britain and Meryton discussing what they would do next.

Mary was at the law office. Lizzy and Jane had often counted the time there as their reading comprehension, penmanship, typing, and grammar assignments and so, Mary too used her time there to practice her skills. They did not just type the words their aunt and uncle gave them, but they took the time to read them and process them. Of course, revision was out of the question as they were not lawyers or paralegals, but they did the final proofreading and edits. In the law, a misplaced comma can be dangerous. All told, the three eldest Bennet sisters saved their aunt and uncle far more money than they ever paid out by double dipping work with school, and all three of them found that they were well versed in how to construct an excellent argument, but only two of the three of them ever employed that skill aloud.

Lydia and Kitty, listed in reverse age order on purpose because it is always "and Kitty" when she is included in a pairing, were at the library. Kitty was taking a practice SAT test, and Lydia was staring out the window watching this week's Army reservists run by. She sighed loudly in hopes of distracting Kitty from her studies, but Kitty was more scared of what Lizzy would say if she didn't finish the practice test than what Lydia would say about not caring enough about men running through the streets. To be fair, Lydia had plenty to say, and the teasing was relentless. Lydia, who was the boy craziest of them all, couldn't understand why everyone else wasn't, and since Kitty was an easy target for emotional bullying, she shot her emotional arrows. They struck home and caused a lot of damage. Some siblings mean well, and some are mean.

Back in the dining room, Mrs. Bennet said some curse words about the girls to the cat who flicked his whiskers and swished his tail to let her know that he didn't care much for that kind of language. We know that two of the Bennet children were, at that time, women in their 20s, one was about to legally be a woman, and one of the other two was often mistaken for a woman by the soldiers in town, just as she hoped they would, but Mrs. Bennet always referred to her children as "the girls." Stymied by their educational endeavors, she had to choose between putting on her jacket and going to find her husband out on the farm to tell him the big news or calling her sister or sister-in-law to tell them.

She opted for the former because it was a local call. More on phone calls later. Seriously, there will be a whole section about it. It won't be terribly boring and will be important and an actual plot point. Just know for now that the Bennets kept to local calls when they could, which kept their social circle local as well.

When the phone rang, Mary turned down the radio. When she was in the office by herself, she listened to music on the office radio. The bass solo in Fleetwood Mac's "The Chain" was just getting started, and while she loved that song in general, and that album in particular, she turned it down without regret. She was at work and Mary believed in being a professional. Now, if she'd been at home, she likely would have waited for the song to finish before she did anything else even though Lydia would certainly comment on the fact that Mary owned the tape and had a Walkman so she could listen to it any time she wanted. Lydia didn't understand the joy Mary felt when a song she loved came on at random.

"Gardiner and Phillips Legal Services, this is Mary speaking," Mary answered with the practiced phone-answering voice her aunt taught her. While Mr. Gardiner had long since retired and passed away, they kept the name because it was often the way with small businesses in small towns.

"I need my sister."

"Hello, Mother. Good to hear from you," Mary deadpanned in the voice she reserved for her mother. While her speaking voice could have been called droll when she was that age, it had much more to do with the way her family expected her to be as opposed to what her inside voice was dying to say.

"Don't be childish, Mary."

Mary pulled the receiver away from her face and took a deep breath. She exhaled and brought it back to her face. "Yes. My fault, Mother."

"Yes, well, it is very important, and I must speak to her directly."

"She and Uncle are in court today. Can I take a message?"

She mumbled something about Mary being worthless and hung up on her middle child.

"Guess not," Mary said to no one. Before she could hang up, the rollover line lit up. She pressed the button switching the call to line two, and before she could start her practiced greeting, her mother was already talking.

"If you must know, Netherfield Park has been rented by Charles Bingley and his sisters."

Mary, who actually didn't care why her mother called in the first place, sat in silence on her end of the phone. Part of it was because when her mother made wild claims, she found it best to let her silence do the talking for her. Her sisters all handled the wild allegations differently and the result was never pleasant. The other reason for her silence was that she was curious about the news.

Firstly, she wondered about the library at Netherfield Park. There was a rumor that it was the most well-stocked private collection in New England and that due to the elusive nature of the property, the furnishings, including the books, were shrouded in mystery. She would have loved to spend some time in there.

Secondly, she did know who Charles Bingley was because she'd seen his name and face in the paper. Every morning for years she read the *The Hartford Courant,* including the sports section, the public notices, and even gave the classified ads a glance while she and her father had their coffee. They were early risers and were happy to sit quietly while they read. When they finished the paper, they would eat a light breakfast and have discussions about the contents. When they disagreed about something, Mary would jot that topic down so that they could explore it later when they had some time alone in the library. Lydia was baffled by this morning ritual. Why would anyone want to be up so early, and who would wish to spend an hour alone with Mary each day?

Due to her years-long morning ritual, she was all too aware of who the Bingley family was. They owned a brokerage firm in Hartford that handled a lot of the insurance money that was, as Mary saw it, inappropriately being invested into the market. The money was supposed to be there when the emergency happened, not tied up in some risky thing like the ever-volatile market. Still, it was legal and the Bingleys did it. They didn't handle individual portfolios. They strictly invested on behalf of companies, so that made it less problematic and more profitable. Hartford was, and is, essentially the insurance capital of America. There is a lot of money to be made there. One week prior to this big news, the Bingley patriarch died suddenly. He and his wife had long since divorced, and thus, Bingley Investment Strategies was in the possession of his three children, none of whom sat on the board of the company nor had much to do with it.

Louisa Bingley Hurst, the eldest and least public of the family, was reported to be the secret brains behind the organization. Mary hoped this was true. A massive multi-billion-dollar company being run by a woman would be life-affirming. We shall find out later that this was all conjecture. She was an excellent manager and could have been excellent if she had a seat on the board, but she spent most of her time managing to keep her louse of a husband out of the tabloids.

Caroline Bingley was the most public of the siblings, and so while her brother-in-law was being kept out of the tabloids, she was in them. She studied music composition at a school of some renown in New York, but she became famous for being born Caroline Bingley. She was tall, angular, and rich. Regardless of the facts of the matter, she was dubbed "The Bingley Beauty" by several of the New York tabloids during her time there, and it followed her everywhere she went. Most people, simply because they were told she was beautiful, believed she was. Mary had almost no opinion on her looks but often wondered what it would be like to be skilled enough to earn a degree in music composition.

Charles, the youngest, was fresh from earning his Bachelor's degree in business from a small Midwestern college. He was back in the area and enrolled in an MBA program at Connecticut's own Ivy League school. While it was true that money opened doors at Ivy League colleges,

Mary was impressed that he had the ambition to go even if he didn't have the smarts to get in on his own. There was, of course, speculation on both sides of this. He was seemingly charming and delightful, which made people question his intellect. Mary, having no knowledge of him as a person, reserved judgment on that accord. It was reported though, that because he was the one in the family to go to business school, he was positioning himself to take over the company. Mary had to agree that, on paper, it made sense. What made no sense was why they would wish to rent an empty farm in Meryton.

"Hmmm," was Mary's chosen response. She wanted to ask why her mother chose to mention only Charles Bingley by name. She didn't because it would have angered her mother to rage levels which would have turned into a lecture about the "feminist garbage" that she and Lizzy uttered. It could have been worth it; Mary had a lot of work to do.

"You're no fun," Mrs. Bennet said as she slammed the receiver down. At least she hadn't called her worthless.

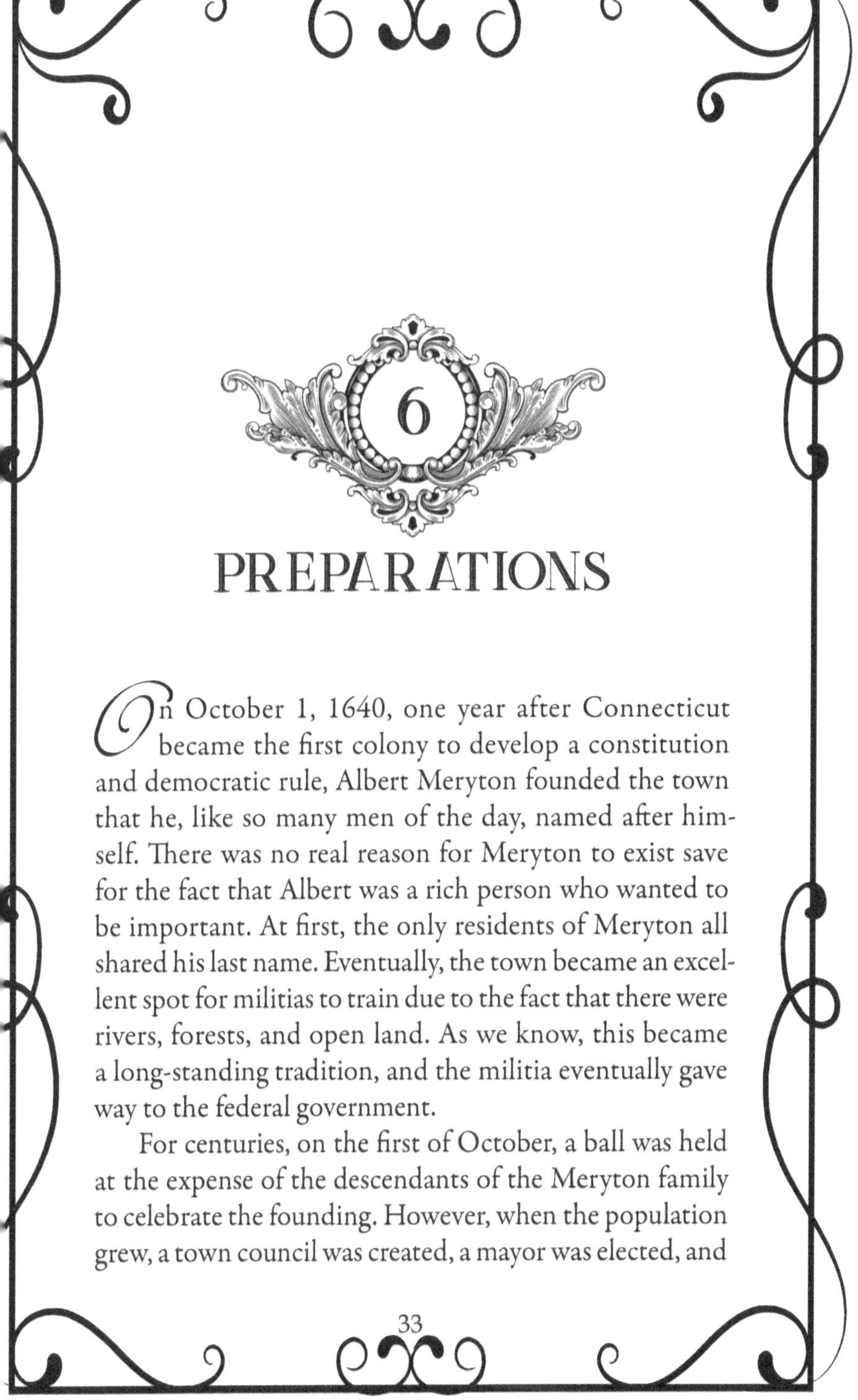

6

PREPARATIONS

On October 1, 1640, one year after Connecticut became the first colony to develop a constitution and democratic rule, Albert Meryton founded the town that he, like so many men of the day, named after himself. There was no real reason for Meryton to exist save for the fact that Albert was a rich person who wanted to be important. At first, the only residents of Meryton all shared his last name. Eventually, the town became an excellent spot for militias to train due to the fact that there were rivers, forests, and open land. As we know, this became a long-standing tradition, and the militia eventually gave way to the federal government.

For centuries, on the first of October, a ball was held at the expense of the descendants of the Meryton family to celebrate the founding. However, when the population grew, a town council was created, a mayor was elected, and standard business hours became a thing; it was impractical to have a ball on a random Tuesday in October. Thus, it was decided that on the first Saturday in October, the town of Meryton would have, at the expense of the taxpayers and buoyed by donations and fundraisers, a Founder's Ball.

As the years went on, the ball progressed from a much more traditional ball with gowns and corsets and suits with tails into what other villages might call a festival. As technology changed and carnival games advanced and rides evolved to include some carnival-style attractions, there were still pony rides, a petting zoo, a corn maze, and bobbing for apples. At 6 in the evening, a community-wide dinner was served. It was still buffet style but was no longer a potluck because cooking for 50 people is different than cooking for thousands. The dinner was immediately followed by a public dance complete with a live band. The only cost of admission was to be a resident or the guest of a resident. To be a resident of Meryton, one must own land, rent land, own a business, or be a member of the Army Reserve Unit who trained in the town. So, essentially, anyone was welcome, and people came from miles around. For one day a year, Meryton had enough people in it be called a city, not just a village.

There were less than 2,000 year-round residents in 1989, and there are not many more as of this writing. The population does swell a bit during holidays, and the steady stream of reservists keeps the average number of people in town at any given time to just over 2,000. As is the case with many towns of this type, there is a main street that is often called Main Street, as was and is the case in Meryton. The business district ran for about half a mile, roughly five city blocks long. Each crossroad on Main Street was named for one of Albert Meryton's children.

It was on these five blocks, from Veronica at the east to Victoria at the west, with Victor, Vance, and Vincent in between where the Ball took place. The roads were blocked off. Multiple tents were set up at the Veronica end of town, and that is where the buffet was served. People would grab plates, take their fill, and wander back down where people ate wherever they could find space. People were generally courteous enough to leave the tables for older folks and those with disabilities. Some people brought their own folding chairs. Others brought blankets and sheets and spread them out wherever they could for makeshift picnics. The Bennets and Phillipses set up tables on the sidewalk outside of the law office for family and friends.

On the Victoria side of town, the stage was set for the band to play. There was no need for a dance floor as all of Meryton from 8 to midnight was a dance floor. The music was loud, and it bounced around the two- and three-story store fronts that lined Main Street. When the final note of "Yankee Doodle," the state song of Connecticut, played, the street lights would come on, and for the next few hours, most able-bodied residents of Meryton helped clean up. The sanitation department backed in the garbage trucks, and residents started picking up detritus that was strewn about. People helped take down the tents and the stage and get them back into the storage barn behind the high school, which was two blocks down on Vance. The carnival rides were taken down and loaded onto their trailers and were off to the next event. By sunup on the first Sunday in October, if a stranger rolled into town, that person would have no idea what transpired the evening before.

On the particular Saturday in October when we set our tale, as the town was setting up for the big event, three days after Mrs. Bennet's big news, Longbourn was full of life. Charlotte and Maria Lucas, descendants of Albert Meryton himself, daughters of the Mayor, Bill Lucas, were there getting ready for the big day as well. Charlotte was the administrative assistant to the mayor, her father, in whose home she still resided. And while she was several years her elder, she was Lizzy's best friend. She was brought in during the early days of the "Bennet school" to help as a math tutor, but when it was discovered, not by Mr. Bennet but by Charlotte herself, that Jane had already surpassed her in skill, she used the time at Longbourn to do her homework and get to know the girls. She and Lizzy clicked in the way that people do sometimes, and the six-year age difference mattered not at all. Maria Lucas was the same age and had the same temperament as Kitty. They liked each other very much. Lydia tolerated her because, like Kitty, she was easily led.

The Lucas sisters came over just after lunch, as was the tradition, on that particular Saturday because it was always difficult to decide how to dress. The festivities began at 2 and consisted of a lot of time on one's feet. Thus, one wished to be in comfortable shoes and comfortable clothes. As is often the case in that part of the country at that time of year, the weather was often volatile. The Founder's Ball was a rain-or-shine, snow-or-heat kind of event. While considering all of that, there was the dance to think of later, and of course, one wished to look one's best while on the dance floor in case there was some romantic interest there from out of town whose eye might be caught. There were young women in various states of undress all day throughout the house, and so Mr. Bennet locked himself in his library after lunch until he was told it was safe to come back out.

Mary, who had no concerns about what to wear except for her choice of eyewear on a night like that, joined her father behind the locked door. She put on a pair of blue jeans and some work boots, for all the Bennets had work boots; they lived on a working farm after all. She slid one of her smaller notebooks into her back pocket as she never left home without one. She wore a long black tee shirt and tied a sweatshirt around her waist as it always got cold by the end of the evening. She put her hair up in a high ponytail and ran a pencil and a pen through in opposite directions making an "X" on the top of her head. She made sure to wear her thick, plastic-framed glasses, as her wire frames, which were better suited for work and study, were not sturdy enough for the inevitable bouncing off people all day long and being flung about on mechanical death machines. While she didn't often go on rides or dance or do much but sit with her aunt at these events, she could sometimes be persuaded to join the fracas. Her father always called her "Buddy" when she wore those frames. It wasn't because he was being particularly friendly or that he felt she was his pal; it was because they reminded him of the glasses early rock pioneer Buddy Holly wore.

Whether he meant it as an insult or a compliment she didn't know, nor did she mind the Buddy Holly moniker because she happened to like his music quite a bit. While most people heard his songs and thought of love and happiness as the music was so catchy and made one want to dance, Mary heard the longing and sadness that wasn't really buried that deep at all. He constantly sang about "being blue" and "maybe" and having to be reminded to "not be lonely." The truth was right there for anyone to see, but instead, they often focused on his tragic death, which it was indeed, but Mary wondered why no one wanted to investigate what must have been his tragic life as well.

At the crack of 3, Mrs. Bennet barged into the library, for the door was not actually locked, nor did it have a lock, but the rule was if the door was closed, Mr. Bennet was locked in and not to be disturbed. We shall see that Mrs. Bennet came up with all kinds of reasons to disregard that rule. It was time to leave for The Founder's Ball, and while Mr. Bennet had intercoms installed all around the house and the grounds, and she could have pressed the button on any one of the boxes and made the announcement that it was time to go, just as she did most nights when dinner was about to be served, she barged in that day because she had "urgent private matters" to discuss with her husband.

He was sitting behind his desk with his chair tilted back and his feet up on the desk. He held a book in both of his hands that was inches from his face. Would it have been better for his eyes, his posture, and his desk if he sat with his feet on the floor, book on the flat surface while wearing his glasses? Likely. Did he care about any of that? Not remotely. Mary, whom her mother had forgotten was in the room, sat with her feet on the floor, glasses on and book in her lap. Had her mother realized she was there or paid attention to anything at all, she would have noticed that he and Mary were both reading Amy Tan's *The Joy Luck Club*. Had she noticed, she might have asked why they were both reading the same book at the same time. Why not just wait until one or the other was done, and did they each buy a copy, and was this something they did often? She didn't notice and so she didn't ask. Had she noticed, would she have taken the time to ask? Not likely.

"Husband!" She was shouting as the door opened. Another reason we shall not know their first names is that no one ever used their names. The children all called them some variation of Mother and Father. They sometimes, to both Mary and Lizzy's chagrin, called each other those names as well. Not in the "ask your mother" way, but in the "Mother, can you get me some toothpaste when you go to the store?" way. They jokingly called each other Mr. and Mrs. Bennet, they sarcastically called each other Husband and Wife when the person in question wasn't doing a thing the other wished they would be doing, or they lovingly called each other "Dear."

Without putting his feet on the floor or looking up, he responded, "Present."

She walked forward and knocked his feet off the desk, forcing him to sit up. "Your daughters need you to do them a favor today."

He folded the top corner of his book over, something that made Mary cringe, and he closed it. "Do they? Why then, pray tell, are you here doing the asking? Why not send the leader to ask herself on behalf of them all?"

"Pffft. They're all busy getting ready for the ball." She walked past him to the window and tried to open it. "It's stuffy in here." The window was hard to open, and it often took some banging, and oftentimes one had to stick a flat head screwdriver between the sill and the bottom of the window to get it started. There was just such a tool sitting there for that purpose, but Mrs. Bennet always unlocked it and pushed up first just to see if she could do it. She couldn't and so she stuck the screwdriver in and started to lever it open.

While she was doing that, he looked at his middle child, who was still in the room, ready for the ball, not remotely looking like she needed a favor. He winked. "Are they now? Well, that is certainly a time-consuming task. Those Lucas girls arrived what, three hours ago, and they are still not ready?"

She turned back to him, once again, not looking at her daughter in the high-backed chair in the corner. "It's about them, actually."

"Our daughters need me to do them a favor regarding the Lucas girls? Has war been declared? I thought we liked the Lucas girls. I certainly like that older one a lot. She is very bright and…"

"Make fun all you like, Mr. Bennet, but it could easily turn to that if you don't do what I need you to do."

He opened his middle drawer and pulled out his already-packed pipe. He bit it between his teeth, struck a match, closed his lips over the stem, and inhaled, getting the tobacco burning. Mary, who read enough to know that smoking was bad for her father but wasn't comfortable enough to have that kind of conversation with him, had fond memories of the cherry-scented tobacco he used. Once the pipe was going strong, he waved out the match and dropped it in the ashtray on his desk. He let the nicotine do its work. He took another puff. "What is the favor?"

"I thought you'd never ask," she said as she sat down in the chair on the opposite side of his desk. While it is true that there was an official office for the business of the farm, and his library didn't need a desk, nor a chair for a visitor, he felt that his library was his "personal office" where he conducted "family business."

"You would have told me what the favor was had I asked or not."

"Yes, well." She ignored the truth he spoke. "When we get to The Founder's Ball today, I need you…"

"You need or they need, Dear?"

"What did I say?"

"You said 'I need' just now."

"Well, yes, I need, I need because it is for their own good, so it is me asking you to do a favor on their behalf. You should know that when I say 'I,' I really mean 'you all.' Everything I do is for the betterment of this family. You shouldn't tease me."

"Yes, of course, Dear. I know. You hate to be teased, and you are selfless."

"Well, thank you for understanding. Anyway, *they* need you to make sure you introduce yourself to Mr. Bingley while they are there so you can introduce them as well."

"They need this, do they?"

"Why yes. Of course. Mr. Bingley is now one of the richest people in the state. He is young, handsome, and obviously in need of a wife. People don't take titans of industry seriously when they can't manage their personal lives."

"Titan of industry?"

"You know what I mean." She waved off the intended barb.

He took a draw on his pipe. "I do know just what you mean. You would like me to make sure that Mr. Bingley chooses from our crop of girls instead of someone else's."

"Why yes, of course. If one of our girls catches his eye, and what kind of young man wouldn't be drawn to Jane, then we needn't worry about that blasted Collins man and his claim to Longbourn."

Mr. Bennet, who was aware that Mary was in the room, and who didn't like to talk about the family finances in front of the children, even though they were all aware of them as their mother never stopped talking about the defaulted land contract and the fact that while they still lived in Longbourn and worked the land and paid the bills, Mr. Collins' son, William Collins, technically owned the property and could, at any time he wished, put them all on the street.

"Yes, of course, Dear. I will most assuredly introduce Jane to Mr. Bingley."

"Thank you, Husband." She was up and heading toward the door. "Girls!" she shouted.

"Just as long as it is you who explains to her what her duties are regarding treating herself as a commodity and all of that."

We can't know if Mrs. Bennet was able to hear that final comment over the shouting and effusive praise she was heaping on their father for being so great of man to be able to offer such great opportunities to them by way of introduction to Mr. Bingley. It is safe to assume that whether she heard it or not, the results would have been the same.

Mr. Bennet rose and went to the door she left open, for she always left the door open when she came in and went out. He looked over at Mary who had been sitting still and remained silent the whole time. She often wondered if she banged on a pan and did jumping jacks if her mother would notice her when she was talking about "the girls" to her father. She knew that "the girls" really meant "four of the five girls." Mary did like to be included, but she knew the things being discussed, things like, boys, parties, social engagements, clothes, or any of the other materialistic things, were things that only her mother, Lydia, and Kitty by proxy, cared about. Jane and Lizzy didn't go out of the house looking like hobos, but they were farm kids. A bit of dirt and a sweaty upper lip didn't bother them one bit.

He sat back down and gestured to the chair his wife had just vacated. Mary placed her bookmark in her book and closed it. She came over and sat down, back ramrod straight, as was her way. Had it been a normal Saturday, she would have found herself in the same room but dressed in her house cardigan and wire-rimmed glasses still sitting up perfectly straight. She loved the high-back chair in her father's library as it was designed for people with excellent posture to sit in perfect comfort. If there was one thing where Mary excelled above all her sisters, it was that her posture was excellent. She placed her book on the desk and rested her hands on her lap. "Yes, Father?"

"Three things."

Mary nodded.

"First, don't think those things about your mother. She means well." He need not express what thoughts it was that she was having. All of them had similar thoughts about their mother. They thought her overwrought, melodramatic, short on thought, and long on action. Asking her husband to offer his eldest daughters up to a rich stranger for financial gain came with some terminology that we shall not include here, for it is not that kind of book, but readers can fill in the blanks.

Lydia or Kitty would have responded with something akin to "What thoughts?" Jane, who couldn't lie to save her life, would have sat tight-lipped and nodded her head. Lizzy would have launched into an argument about why keeping her thoughts to herself wasn't going to help anyone. Mary Bennet said, "I know she does, Father, but they are my thoughts, and they are based on measured observation. I'm not speculating."

"Yes, I know. Still, I wish you could give her the benefit of the doubt."

"I shall not, Father. She has not earned it."

He nodded, knowing the answer he would get, but feeling better for having defended his wife nonetheless. "Second, I already walked over to Netherfield and introduced myself to our neighbors yesterday. He is a fine young man. His siblings seem, well, I don't wish to cast aspersions without knowledge, but let's say less friendly. Bingley told me that he would love to meet my family, and so, I've arranged with your uncle to set up extra tables outside of the law office, and we shall all meet there to share a meal. He will have a party of five. His brother-in-law and a college friend will be joining them. I promise not to offer your sisters up for trade. Should Mr. Bingley wish to fall in love with Jane, that will be a happy accident, but there shall be no expectations from me."

"Thank you for the clarification, Father. Why didn't you just tell Mother that news?"

He laughed. "What is the fun in that?" He lit another match and stoked his pipe which had gone out as pipes do.

"If you say so."

"I do. One of the things I love most about your mother is how easily I can get on her nerves. Her nerves and I have been well acquainted these past twenty-three years."

"If you say so," she repeated. She and her mother's nerves were also well acquainted, and Mary preferred to not get on them. "What was the third thing?"

He blew out some smoke. "Yes, well, the third thing is that I don't want you to concern yourself with the property or our financial situation. Things are not as I would like them to be, that is for sure, but so far, the young Collins has honored his father's deal with me. Technically, yes, we are behind on some payments on the land contract, and technically, yes, he could take the land, legally, but his father wanted me to have this land, wanted *us* to have this land, and he told me that he believed I would find a way to pay things off and own the land outright. I have some irons in the fire, and I don't wish to worry you. It might take a few years to see them through, but we will not be out on the streets any time soon, and we won't need your sisters to marry well to keep the place."

"Of course, Father," Mary said. She had some plans that were somewhat reliant on the fact that her parents' financial situation was dire. If he thought it would take a few years to right the ship of Longbourn, all the better for her.

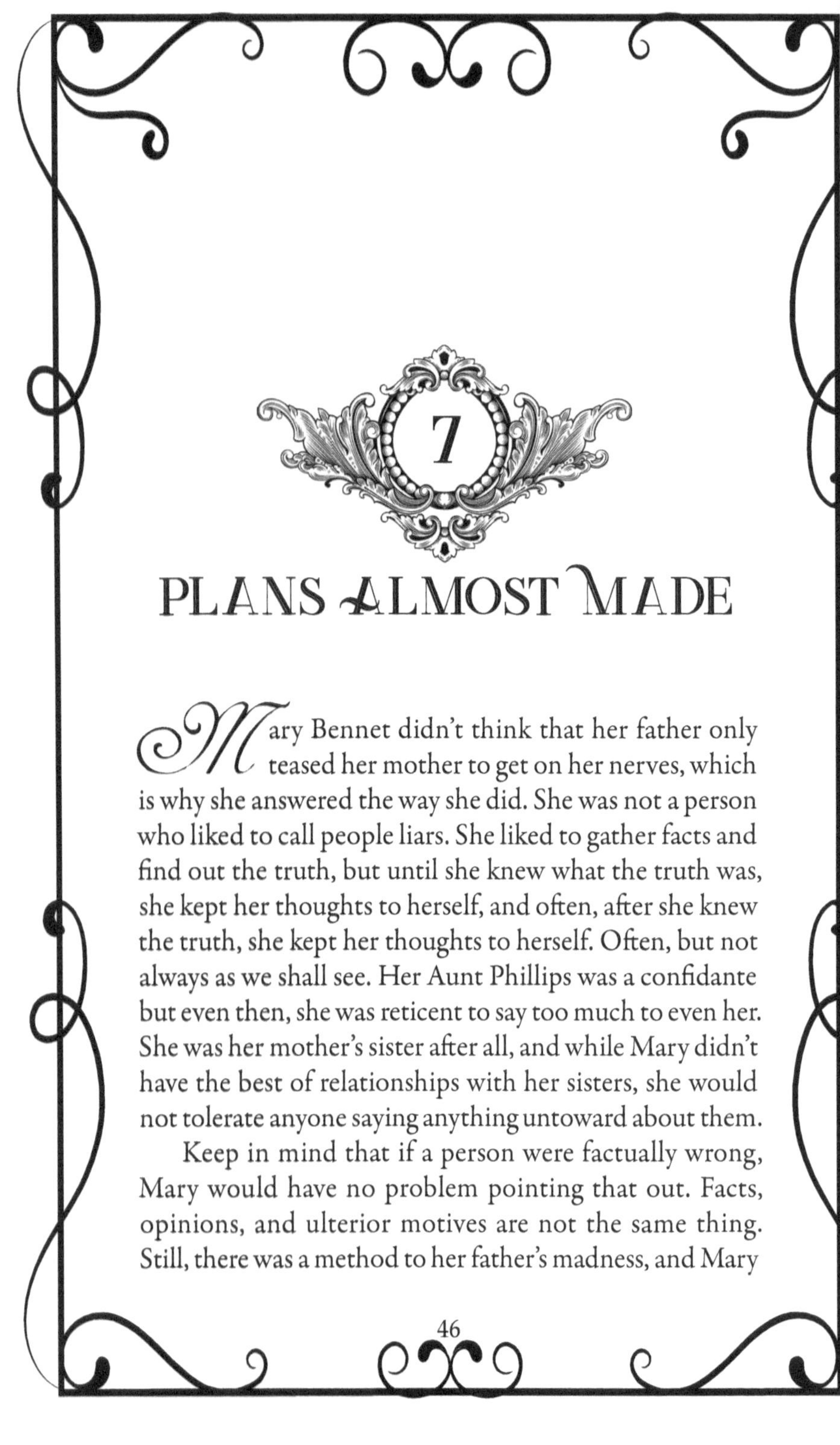

7

PLANS ALMOST MADE

Mary Bennet didn't think that her father only teased her mother to get on her nerves, which is why she answered the way she did. She was not a person who liked to call people liars. She liked to gather facts and find out the truth, but until she knew what the truth was, she kept her thoughts to herself, and often, after she knew the truth, she kept her thoughts to herself. Often, but not always as we shall see. Her Aunt Phillips was a confidante but even then, she was reticent to say too much to even her. She was her mother's sister after all, and while Mary didn't have the best of relationships with her sisters, she would not tolerate anyone saying anything untoward about them.

Keep in mind that if a person were factually wrong, Mary would have no problem pointing that out. Facts, opinions, and ulterior motives are not the same thing. Still, there was a method to her father's madness, and Mary assumed she knew what it was. She knew that he would tell her if he wished and wouldn't if he didn't wish. There was no reason to cause any unnecessary consternation.

So it was that she and her father exited his library and joined the rest of the group as they piled out the front door for the walk to Meryton. The Bennets had vehicles. We already know that Jane and Lizzy shared a car. Mr. Bennet had several trucks for farm work that were more than safe enough for use on the roadways that the Bennet girls could use at any time they saw fit. Mrs. Bennet had a Jeep Wagoneer. It had 4-wheel drive, which made her feel safer in the winter, and it was made of steel, which made Mr. Bennet feel safer. He was not a man who thought that women were bad drivers. His daughters, for the most part, chose not to drive a steel box on wheels, and he was just fine with that. He was a man who knew his own wife was a terrible driver, who was often distracted, and so, he wanted her to be safe when she traversed the roads.

They could have, if they wished to, driven the two miles to Meryton. They could have parked in the employee lot behind the Phillips' law office and been in the heart of the action, but they liked to walk. Many of the Meryton residents walked where they needed to go. There was a small market that was a butcher shop and had most of the essential groceries anyone could need. There was Jones' pharmacy, a hardware store, several shops that sold gifts of all kinds to locals and tourists alike, and a five and dime that had a cornucopia of items that people didn't think they wanted or needed. There was a bakery, a 24-hour diner situated between the two bars, two clothing stores, and three fine dining establishments. The Long family owned a small motel. That part of Connecticut brought enough year-round tourism and "season watchers," that there were even a few Bed and Breakfasts that managed to do a year-round, robust business.

The most popular place in town and the entertainment hub of Meryton was a small theater that showed second-run movies. The fact that these films had been released one to two months prior didn't deter most of the residents of Meryton from packing the place on the weekends. The owners turned the living quarters above the theater into a store that offered new and used books and music while renting videos for home use. If one wanted to be seen or see anyone, The Theater, which was both what it was and what it was named, was the place to go. Of course, when one wanted to shop in bulk, see new movies, have a wider selection of books and music, or have more options for VHS rentals, Meryton wasn't too far away from many cities that had it all. However, most residents of Meryton felt that what they had was good enough. If they didn't have to leave town, they didn't.

There were walking paths all around town, and where they were not paved, worn paths appeared, like those that happen in every town in the world. Longbourn was situated not too far from the river. Years ago, in conjunction with the reserve base, the village commissioned a walking path that ran alongside the river. For years, the trainees simply ran along the river and wore down a path, but it often became unpassable during wet weather. It wasn't paved in the traditional sense that there was asphalt poured over compacted dirt, but rocks were poured there, and over time, with the running soldiers and the residents of Meryton, the path became passable in all kinds of weather. One couldn't walk it in wet weather without getting a bit of dirt on one's shoes, but in dry weather, it was firm and easy going. In the winter, it was harder to travel, but enough people in the area had snowmobiles, and within an hour or two of fresh snow, anyone with the proper footwear could walk along the path.

Mrs. Bennet, Lydia, and Kitty led the pack. Each girl flanked her mother, and to an outside observer, and much to the delight of Mrs. Bennet, they looked like sisters dolled up for a night on the town. We know the phrase "dolled up" is sexist and outdated, but in 1989, it was only considered one of those two things to the public in general, and neither of those things to Mrs. Bennet or Lydia. Kitty, as far as we know, had no opinion on the matter.

Jane walked next to Maria Lucas, who, like everyone who met Jane, either wanted to be her or be known by her. She didn't really have any questions of import for her, but she asked anything and everything that came to her mind. Jane answered them all as best she could and when she didn't know, she simply said that she didn't and would say, "We can find out together." It was the use of the word "together" that always made people weak in the knees.

While Mrs. Bennet was the only real local celebrity Meryton ever had, it was Jane Bennet who got all the attention, and she didn't even try. Having a perfectly symmetrical face with high cheekbones, seemingly flawless skin, and rolling wavy hair along with a pleasant disposition drew people in like moths to a flame. There are plenty of really, really mean and horrible good-looking people that repel everyone around them. One is about to arrive.

Mr. Bennet and Mary followed in the third grouping. He puffed away at his pipe, and she kept pace with his long strides by walking briskly. They spoke of the weather and pointed out things in nature as they passed. As was the way with Mr. Bennet, his public relationship with his family was markedly different than his private one. As we know, he and Mary shared a lot of ideas in private, and we can assume, rightly so, that each of his daughters, yes, even Kitty, had a private and unique relationship with him. Publicly, he presented himself as the charming country gentleman who was a patron of the library and pillar of the community. He wasn't so much cold to his children in public as he was aloof. He had his reasons, and the girls all understood them, yes, even Kitty, without having to have them explained. Understanding and liking are not the same, and they should not be conflated here.

Lizzy and Charlotte took up the rear as they walked arm in arm, heads nearly touching as they talked to each other about all the things in the world at a volume meant only for each other as they often did. The phrase thick as thieves was not written about Lizzy Bennet and Charlotte Lucas, but it may as well have been. While Lizzy and Jane loved each other and would remain committed sisters and excellent friends for the rest of their lives, Lizzy and Charlotte Lucas shared something different. They chose each other. It was always love that led them. Were the rest of the Bennet sisters jealous of their relationship? Of course. Would they admit it? Of course not. At least not aloud.

Two miles may seem like a long walk, but to a family who had always lived two miles outside of town, it was just a jaunt, and before they could complete any real conversations, they arrived. Once they were in sight of the festivities, Lydia, Maria, and Kitty bolted to join the melee.

While they were all fully grown in body, they were still close enough in age to 10 than to 25, and so that part of their lizard brain took over. Charlotte, Lizzy and Jane, who were in their 20s, still felt the joy of the carnival, and they scampered behind their younger sisters to find some fun. Mary, who was also closer to 10 than 25, was, as her father often said, born 40, so she did not bolt, nor scamper. She strolled deliberately with her parents to the law offices where she would sit and people-watch while chatting amicably with her aunt, uncle, and parents as well as anyone who stopped by. Mary was polite to everyone. They rarely said more to her than "hello," so she managed to sit and absorb the conversations as they unfolded.

The Mayor and First Lady Lucas arrived several hours after the party had already started, and they settled in at the tables in front of the law offices and sat with the Phillipses and Bennets. Mrs. Lucas thanked Mrs. Bennet for allowing the girls to come to Longbourn to ready themselves for the day. Mrs. Bennet found a way to sound magnanimous when she assured her *friend* that it was no trouble at all. She then launched into a soliloquy about how lovely Jane looked and how she was surely turning heads all around town at that very moment. Everyone agreed that this was happening because everyone had eyes and had been in public with Jane.

Mrs. Phillips loved her sister very much, but she could only take her in small doses, and while she too knew that Jane was a great beauty, she didn't need to be reminded about it every five minutes. She hadn't forgotten nor would she ever. She turned to her niece and asked, "Walk with me, Mary?"

"Gladly, Aunt." Mary stood. She held out her hand and helped her aunt up. Granted, she didn't need the help at all, but she appreciated the effort, so she took it. They stood, straight-backed and shoulder-to-shoulder. They were the same height, had the same sensible haircut, and had the same slope of the nose.

"Oh. Look at you. If Mary had worn her normal glasses instead of those monstrosities, people would think the two of you were twins," Mrs. Bennet said. We shall leave it for each reader to decide if she was saying it just to say something or if she meant it as a compliment to her sister for looking like a 17-year-old or a dig at her daughter for looking like a 50-year-old.

"Yes, Mother, it's the glasses that do it," Mary said in the flat and emotionless way she often spoke to her mother.

She was drowned out by her aunt who was saying in the loud and sometimes shrill way she often spoke to her sister, "I love those glasses."

"You would," Mrs. Bennet said.

"Yes, well." Mrs. Phillips looked at her identical niece. "Shall we?"

"Let's." Mary held out her elbow, and her aunt locked arms with her.

It might be shocking to know that they didn't discuss the comments made by Mrs. Bennet at all. Most people would. They both had just grown so accustomed to her that they didn't feel the need to discuss her actions or words or much about her at all. Later in this tale, we shall see that they will be forced to talk about her at some length, but let's not skip ahead too far.

They did talk about all kinds of other things. Mary was not just a dead ringer for her aunt, but she shared much of the same sensibilities. They were practical. They believed in the truth. They genuinely thought it would set one free. It is partially why they didn't bother talking about the comments Mrs. Bennet made. There wasn't much to say really. She was uninformed most of the time and pigheaded the rest of the time. Being wrong wasn't an issue. They both admitted to being wrong all the time. It was the unwillingness to admit to being wrong or doing anything to correct it that irked them both.

However, it didn't irk Mrs. Bennet at all because she didn't know, or care, if, or when, she was wrong. None of that mattered. She knew what she knew and was dedicated to those few things. She was not naturally curious. She had most assuredly been outside of the town limits of Meryton, but she found that being within those friendly confines swaddled her with comfort. Mary thought it was willful ignorance. Her aunt knew it was much deeper than that but also knew it wasn't her place to say. Children need to figure out their parents in their own time. Rushing it can only lead to drama or trauma, and Mrs. Phillips wished neither on her niece.

"Have you finished *The Joy Luck Club* yet?" Mrs. Phillips asked as they reached the end of town where the stage was being erected.

"Not yet. Father wished to read it as well, so I am pacing myself."

"Really?" Mrs. Phillips raised her eyebrows. "Although I don't know why I am surprised by anything that man does. He contains multitudes as they say. That should lead to an enlightening conversation."

"I suspect it will." Mary chose to respond to the final comment first. "Whitman is one of Father's favorites as well, so the multitudes thing would please him."

"Yes, well, if you feel so inclined, I would love to hear your final thoughts on the book and your thoughts on the conversation you have with your father regarding it."

"I see no reason why I couldn't share both." Had anyone else asked, Mary's response would have been much different. Her father did, in fact, contain multitudes, and as we've seen, he didn't always choose to share them, but she knew speaking about her personal conversations with her father to her aunt was like shouting into a locked vault.

"Let's sit," Mary's aunt said to her as she nodded her head toward the unoccupied bench. Being at that end of town, near the construction of the stage but away from the fun and games afforded them a bit of privacy in a public place. She turned to face Mary, so she looked like she was riding the bench side saddle. Mary followed suit so that the two women faced one another, clearly indicating to anyone who happened by that they were not invited. Mrs. Phillips put her hands out palm up, and Mary took them.

"Is all well, Aunt?" Mary asked, sounding calm but feeling sick.

"Oh yes, dear." She laughed. "I suppose I am being a bit melodramatic. No need to cause consternation."

"Yes, well…" Mary did not finish her own thought as she wasn't sure what she could have said that would have sounded appropriate.

"We should make a plan."

"Should we?" she asked with a bit of glee. Mary was always on the side of making a plan. Her middle name

could have been Plan if it were not already Josephine. "Whatever for?"

Her aunt squeezed her hands and leaned forward in a conspiratorial way. Mary leaned forward so that her aunt's mouth was right next to her ear. It wouldn't have mattered as she could have shouted her response, and no one would have paid them any mind. To be fair, they could have likely had this same conversation at the tables in front of the law offices and hardly anyone would have paid them any mind. However, Mrs. Phillips was worried that the one person at the tables who contained multitudes might care very much, and she wanted to start this conversation without him.

She whispered into Mary's ear, "College."

Mary, who very much wished to discuss this with her aunt, felt a surge of adrenaline rush through her body. She sat back from her aunt but clutched her hands tighter and looked deeply into her aunt's matching eyes. She knew she would only find honesty and earnestness there, but since it was a dream to go off to college that she kept to herself for so long, she was afraid to actually discuss it aloud, even with the person she trusted most in the world.

"Well," she began, "I've actually been..."

"There you are! Finally," Lydia's voice boomed. "We've been looking for you for *ages*." She said the final word as though it weighed a ton, and she struggled to get it out. "Mom says that you need to come back and eat now; there are some guests she wants *everyone* to meet."

Kitty did what backup dancers do. She nodded along while trying to stand in the same pose as Lydia. Her arms were crossed, and she was angry with the weight of the task and put out at having to be seen in public with Mary. She wasn't convincing.

"Thank you, girls," Mrs. Phillips said to her nieces. "Run along and tell my sister we will be there shortly."

Lydia stamped her foot as though she was trying to kill a bug. "She said you'd say that," she said through ground teeth and sudden rage. "She said if we returned without you, we can't eat dinner."

Kitty nodded in agreement, trying to look hungry and malnourished. She was the smallest of them in general and shorter by half a foot, but she didn't look remotely malnourished. She was a top-flight athlete who was a ball of muscle; additionally, the Bennets were farmers, after all. They would never go hungry.

Lydia, who could code switch better than almost anyone, said in a syrupy sweet voice, "You won't let your nieces starve to death will you, Aunt?"

Mary exhaled a breath just as their aunt inhaled one to retort. "It's fine." She looked her aunt in the eye and nodded. "We're coming." She stood up and pulled Mrs. Phillips up to standing in one fluid motion. "See. We're up. You win. We're coming. It's fine."

"Pfft," Lydia said as she turned back into the little monster Mary thought she was and turned her back on them. "As if I care." She held her hand out behind her with the implication that Kitty should take it.

Kitty reached for it as she looked over her shoulder at her sister and aunt and tried to make eye contact with them. The former's hands were shoved into her pockets, looking down at her feet, seemingly willing them to move away from that bench and the conversation she was, it turned out, dying to have, and the latter was looking directly at Kitty with love and compassion and a dash of understanding as a person who had an overbearing and emotionally difficult younger sister whom she often tried, and failed, to please. They made eye contact and nodded at each other in recognition.

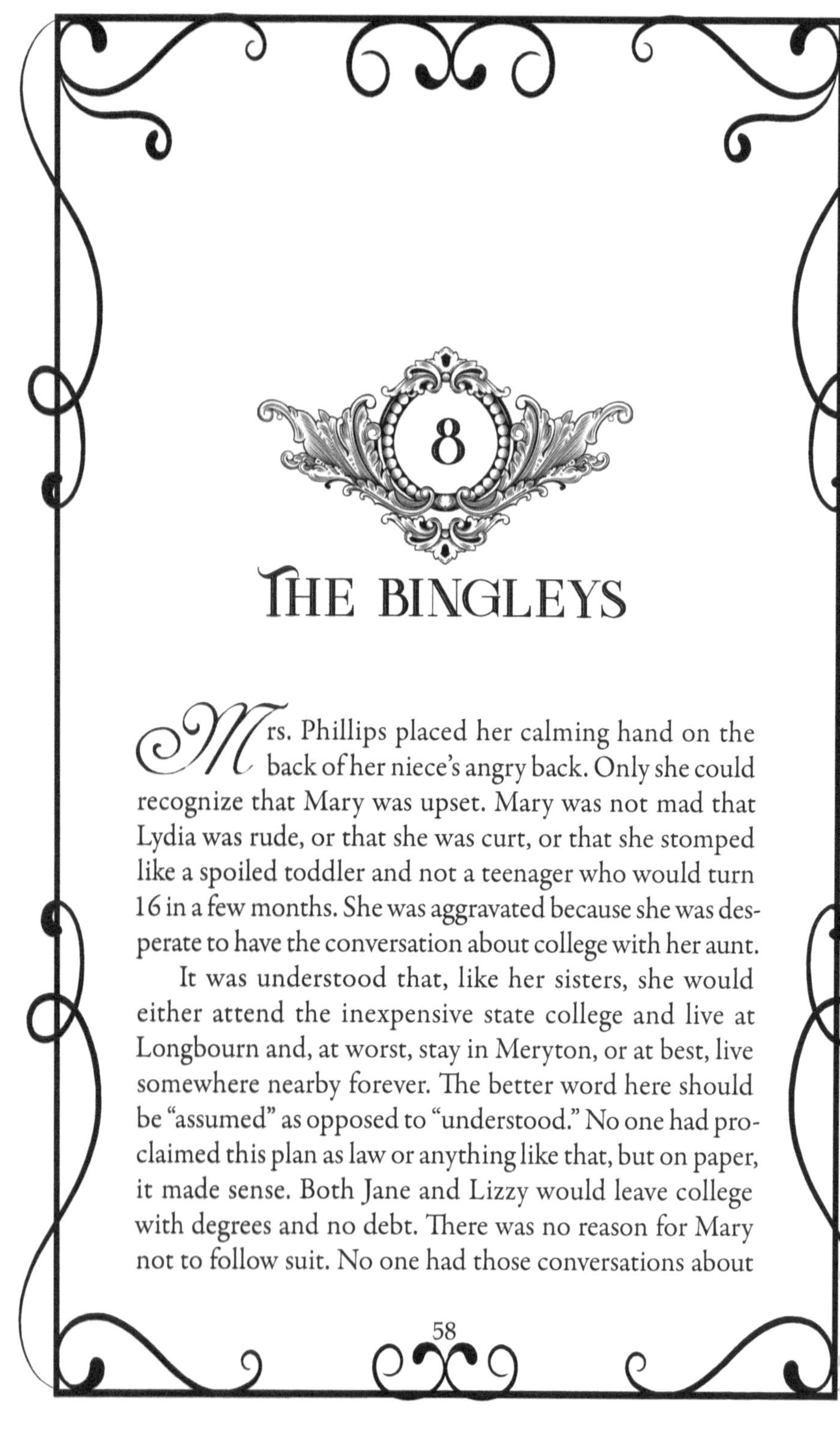

8

THE BINGLEYS

Mrs. Phillips placed her calming hand on the back of her niece's angry back. Only she could recognize that Mary was upset. Mary was not mad that Lydia was rude, or that she was curt, or that she stomped like a spoiled toddler and not a teenager who would turn 16 in a few months. She was aggravated because she was desperate to have the conversation about college with her aunt.

It was understood that, like her sisters, she would either attend the inexpensive state college and live at Longbourn and, at worst, stay in Meryton, or at best, live somewhere nearby forever. The better word here should be "assumed" as opposed to "understood." No one had proclaimed this plan as law or anything like that, but on paper, it made sense. Both Jane and Lizzy would leave college with degrees and no debt. There was no reason for Mary not to follow suit. No one had those conversations about

Lydia and Kitty. It wasn't that they were not capable; they were just, as far as anyone knew, not interested. Well, Lydia wasn't interested. No one asked Kitty.

It wasn't what Mary wished to do at all. She had a plan that she'd only shared with one person so far. She was keen to know how her aunt knew or if she just could tell that Mary was bursting at the seams of Meryton. She knew that Harriet Harrington, the reference librarian who helped her do some investigating into her collegiate options, wouldn't say a thing. She believed in the librarian-patron privilege and had strong opinions about the practice of keeping records. In 1989 in Meryton, they still used checkout cards that were signed by the patron and replaced back in the book on the shelf; thus, anyone could see who most recently checked out the book or who checked it out five years prior. Many of the residents of Meryton cast aspersions based on those all too public checkout records, and as Miss Harrington knew, it meant that oftentimes, people wouldn't check out books or ask for help for fear of becoming the victim of Mrs. Long and the other town gossips.

Mary needed Harriet's help to find college guidebooks. The Meryton public library had just one, *The Barron's Guide*, which was the gold standard to be sure, but it was limited in scope. It only had around 1500 options, and Mary knew there were many more options than that. While she and her father read *The Hartford Courant* every day, she spent plenty of time reading the subscriptions to national papers both in the library and at the law offices. A few years earlier, she ran across an article in *The Washington Post* that went into graphic detail about the other college guides. She discovered there were guides that could offer more insight beyond just cost and admission requirements. She took notes but wasn't sure what to do with them.

She was just beginning to consider that her future might not be relegated to the friendly confines of Meryton when Harriet arrived in Meryton fresh from earning her library degree at St. Johns University in New York. She was only slightly older than Jane and so quite young for Meryton's standards of working professionals. Mary wanted all the information she could gather; the library was the place to get it, and she found an ally in Ms. Harrington who managed to find all the books Mary needed using the magic that librarians have.

In 1989, there was no way for one to search for college options. Sir Berners-Lee, who was not yet Knighted, wouldn't release the World Wide Web until 1990, and it wouldn't significantly affect the residents of Meryton for many years after that. Due to having a military base near town, Meryton would be a bit of a unicorn when it came to connectivity in relation to other small towns. When it comes to the internet, as of this writing, many small towns lag. Forgive the pun. Eventually, Harriet would go on to digitize the library and keep those records private while wearing a pin to work each day that read "another hysterical librarian for privacy."

Mrs. Phillips tried, in that gentle touch, to put Mary at ease and convey that they would continue the conversation. Upon feeling her aunt's hand between her shoulder blades, the message was received, and Mary pulled her hands out of her pockets. She allowed her shoulders to drop from her ears. She cocked her elbow back out, and her aunt slipped her arm back through it. They didn't need to say more, and by the time they arrived in front of the law offices of Gardiner and Phillips, one of them was smiling, and one of them wasn't grimacing.

"We *found* them," Lydia announced.

"*Finally*," Mrs. Bennet said back, leaving no person gathered around to wonder why Lydia was the way she was.

While her father prepared her for the guests, Mary was still a bit shocked to see the Bingley siblings in person. While she'd seen plenty of news clippings with her mother in them, as she kept them all and had scrapbooks that she flipped through more often than Mary thought was healthy, it was different to see someone in person whom she'd only known from the papers. Presidents and Prime Ministers were on the same pages as Louisa, Caroline, and Charles Bingley. She would have been equally surprised to show up and see Margaret Thatcher sitting there. She knew she was real as well but didn't expect their paths to cross. It made her slightly nervous, but she was a person who liked to rise to a challenge. She believed that running from feelings solved nothing. She was determined not to let them know they unnerved her in any way. They were just people after all. Rich and powerful people who could buy Meryton and burn it to the ground just for fun, sure, but people.

Charles Bingley, who was sitting next to Mr. Bennet, stood up to greet them as though he was a gentleman from a bygone era. We shall see he was just that, and standing up when ladies entered or exited his area was something he did. Putting his old-timey good manners on display, he spoke directly to the eldest of the recently arrived quartet. "You must be Mrs. Phillips." He walked around the table and came to shake her hand. "This is your establishment I understand." He said it as a statement, but it sounded like an invitation for her to talk. He stood a good foot taller than her. Mary couldn't tell how much of it was actual height and how much was his thick, messy strawberry blond hair, which sprouted from his head and seemed to defy gravity.

Mrs. Phillips took his hand, and he shook it. He bowed his head to her. It brought him closer to her, and thus Mary's, height. "Well, yes, it is. It was my father's and now..."

"Our father's," Mrs. Bennet interrupted. Everyone turned to look at her, which was just what she wanted. She smiled brightly. Her perfectly straight white teeth shone in the waning sun. "He was my father as well, Mr. Bingley."

"Please just call me Bingley. Everyone does. I don't care for Charles, and Mr. just seems too formal. I've just graduated from college, after all. We all called each other by our last names in my fraternity, and I've grown accustomed to it. Besides, I can't possibly be a 'mister' just yet." He smiled brightly back at her and looked around the gathered group to let them all know that this invitation to just call him by his last name was for all of them. His not nearly as white nor remotely straight teeth were not conventionally pretty but added to his charm. "And of course, Mrs. Bennet. I didn't mean to offend. I didn't mean to imply that Mrs. Phillips started the business all on her own. I just knew that she and her husband ran it now."

"Yes, well..." She trailed off as she often did when she wanted to have the last word but didn't know what she wanted those words to be.

Mrs. Phillips cleared her throat just to be doing something and break the awkwardness. Everyone turned back to her. "It was our father's business, but my husband and

I run it now. Our niece, Mary," she pointed with her head, "works for us now."

"Jane and Lizzy worked there first." Mrs. Bennet just couldn't help herself.

This time, Bingley, for we too shall adhere to his wishes and call him that going forward, didn't respond to Mrs. Bennet. Instead, he looked from Mrs. Phillips to Mary. "Will you be following the family tradition? Will it be Gardiner, Phillips, and Bennet one day?" Bingley's thousand-watt countenance turned to Mary who actually smiled at him for just a brief second.

While it is true that Bingley had made many a person swoon, he'd met his match that day. The fact was, Mary Bennet didn't swoon. There wasn't a man nor woman in the world who could make her cheeks flush in that way. Her mother could make her cheeks flush in a different way as we've seen.

Still, he was smiling his big friendly face at her, and that reached her. She wasn't romantically inclined, but that didn't make her an automaton. She didn't dislike people. She just knew that most people she knew in her small community were irritating. She made eye contact with him as she was inclined to do when speaking to people. "No, I don't think that..."

Her mother saw a smile coupled with direct eye contact, and she sprang into action. She couldn't have Mary falling in love with him. While she wasn't opposed to a woman fighting with another woman over the attention of a man, she was opposed to the brawl happening under her own roof. Had she known her middle child at all, she would have known that this was not a concern. "Our Jane is going to be a teacher!" she shouted.

Mary closed her eyes and bowed her head, mentally removing herself from the moment. She felt that same hand on her back again. She breathed in deeply. She let her aunt's calm wash over her. When she looked back up and opened her eyes, Bingley had turned his attention to the aforementioned Jane who was sitting next to Lizzy and their uncle at a different table. What she didn't see with her eyes closed was that he paused and waited for her to look back at him. When he recognized that she wasn't going to reengage with the conversation, he moved along. He loved to make nice.

"Is that right? What grade?"

"Early Childhood. So, I could run a preschool or teach up to third grade."

Their eyes were locked together as though they were really seeing each other for the first time, which isn't technically true as they had been introduced, but they hadn't actually *seen* each other. Eyes are the windows to the soul and all of that, and so had anyone stood up between them at that moment, they might have been cut in two by the intense heat that radiated in the space between. Mrs. Bennet saw it, and feeling that her mission had been accomplished, smugly sat back in her chair and smirked.

Mrs. Phillips saw the smirk and felt the anger ripple through her. Even though she knew Mary was not in competition for Bingley's affections not because she wasn't worthy of them, but because she knew, in the way that people instinctively know things about people they love, that Mary wasn't interested in any of that, she was still outraged on her niece's behalf. She knew her sister valued beauty above all else in the world, and that was why Jane and Lydia were her favorites, but her blatant favoritism wasn't good for Kitty, it hardened Mary, and it pushed Lizzy away from her. Of course, Mrs. Phillips only ever said this to her husband because she was not the kind of childless person to chime in on how to raise children. She felt it was wrong, and she did her best to give value to the other three girls as best as she could without playing favorites. They noticed and appreciated it, even Kitty.

Bingley sat down next to Jane, and the dome of smitten settled down over them. They ignored everyone else for a while, so we shall ignore them as well. Mary sat in his vacated seat between the other Bingleys. "Hello. I'm Mary. I'm so sorry for your loss."

This caught the attention of both women. They glanced at each other out of the corners of their eyes before they turned their attention to Mary. No one had thought to say that to either of them. There had been lots of questions about how they were finding Meryton and how long they would stay and if they were going to try to buy Netherfield and other gossipy things that people heard about them. The eldest spoke first as eldests often do. "Thank you. It's been difficult as you can imagine. I'm Lou." She extended her hand across the table.

Mary leaned forward and shook it. It was a firm shake that could have looked like they were closing a business deal: locked hands, one pump, and release. "Lou," Mary said aloud, trying it out. Mary knew all about family nicknames. She just wasn't expecting to be let into them so quickly with strangers. She turned to Caroline and extended her hand. She was met with three fingers. Mary was certainly not going to kiss the back of her hand, so she shook them up and down a few times before letting go.

"Caroline," she said with a soft British accent that neither of her siblings had.

Considering they all grew up together and Caroline was the middle child, Mary knew it was a ruse. While the Bingleys didn't have the harsh and distinct New England accent that she and her family had, they were certainly not British. No middle child would suddenly sound different than the other two unless it was intentional. Caroline sounded like an unskilled American who attempted what she thought a British accent was without having actually met a person from England. "It is my pleasure to meet you, Caroline, although I wish it were under better circumstances."

Caroline nodded and shrugged her shoulder, indicating that she heard Mary but didn't have anything else to say.

"That's kind of you to say," Lou chimed in, recognizing that Mary was being sincere and that her sister didn't know what that looked like.

"It's true." Mary turned her attention away from Caroline, who looked over at her brother, who seemed to be chatting amicably with Lizzy as well as Jane. Mary pushed the center of her glasses to secure them high on the bridge of her nose. They hadn't slipped down, but it was something she did when she was slightly uncomfortable. Rising to a challenge is one thing, but being able to shut her feelings down completely was something else. She didn't play poker, which was good because she would have lost all of her money. "I've read about your family circumstances in the paper, and I can't imagine going through something so painful and having to do it in public."

Lou leaned forward in a conspiratorial way. "It is why we are here, actually. I mean, not here," she waved around at the events, "but here in Meryton. We needed a place to be out of the way to figure out what to do."

Mary leaned forward in response. "Well, the paparazzi will certainly be off your lawn out here, but you won't be able to run from the small-town gossip. My mother knew you were coming almost immediately. Someone knew someone who knew someone from Morris' real-estate agent's office who brokered the rental, and by noon that day, everyone knew." Mary was easing into the conversation with Lou and thought it was going well.

Lou also thought it was going well, but Caroline, who heard it all but was pretending not to, couldn't help but chime in at the mention of paparazzi. "That's how it starts though. What's to stop your mother and her *friends* from making one call to those horrible people?"

Mary, not normally in a mood to defend her mother, didn't like Caroline's tone. So much for middle-sister solidarity. "Why would they? What do they have to gain?"

"Really?" She rolled her eyes and held her hands out. "Those papers pay a lot of money for tips and even more for pictures. I wouldn't be surprised if we were being scandalized right now."

Mary felt the insult like a slap. She sat back hard in her chair as though she was pushed. She looked from Caroline, who seemed to be genuinely waiting for a response, to Lou, who was looking at her younger sister with her mouth agape. She felt Mary's eyes on her, and she turned to face her.

She licked her lips as an indication she was going to start talking while her brain figured out the best way

forward. "Please forgive my sister. She's been through a lot. People jump out of bushes and hide in bathrooms to get any pictures of her they can. She didn't mean that sitting here with you and your family was a scandal. Right, Care?" She turned and looked at her sister with a pleading look that Mary knew all too well. She'd used it on Lydia thousands of times. It was the look that said, "Please don't do this to me."

If Caroline was anything like her sisters, which Mary suspected she was very much like Lydia, then the look would go ignored. Mary turned over what Lou said. She was willing to consider it, and maybe it was a reason, not just an excuse. She couldn't know what it was like to be Caroline Bingley, or any of them really. Just a few minutes prior, she'd had to get over the fact that there were famous people sitting at her family's table.

Both Mary and Lou looked from each other to Caroline to see how it was she would respond. Would she take her sister's rope, or would she swim farther out? She sat with her arms crossed, chin jutted out, teeth clenched as though she was the one who'd been insulted and not the person who just insinuated that sitting with the Bennets and Phillipses was scandalous. We can't know for sure how Caroline would have responded because, at that moment, the sun was blocked out by a walrus of a man with a booming voice. "There you are my dear. I apologize for my tardiness. Business and all."

Lou rarely looked relieved when her husband arrived and interrupted a conversation, but she could not have planned it better. She looked to Mary, and they shared a brief look. Mary, who knew all too well about being interrupted and having little agency, nodded. Lou smiled an apologetic smile and then looked up to her husband. "Hello, darling." Lou beamed up at him. She stood and gave him a peck on the cheek.

"You can have my seat," Caroline said as she stood up and started walking away. "I need to stretch my legs."

"Thank you, Care Bear," Mr. Hurst shouted much too loudly.

Caroline stopped with her back to the group at the sound of the nickname. She clenched her fists and took a deep breath. She unclenched her fists, pulled her sunglasses down from the top of her head, and put them on her face. She walked away without a word and disappeared down Vance Street. She walked with purpose, so Mary assumed she was heading back to wherever she parked her car.

Mr. Hurst continued without noticing any of that. "Who do I have to thank for the prime real estate at this shindig?"

Lou took him over to Mr. Phillips and introduced him to everyone else, leaving Mary to sit and ponder. She walked through it all again. She tried to picture the look on Caroline's face as she said what she said. Was it fear? Was it disdain? Could it be both? Did she care? Should she care? What would it matter either way? Was there something about her and her family that was particularly scandalous? What could that possibly be? The answers had to be there. She didn't really know the Bingleys beyond what she'd read in the papers, but she had new data, and her mental notes were not going to do it. She needed to figure it out. She looked at her parents and her aunt and uncle who were having an excellent chat with the Hursts. She looked at Lizzy and Jane entertaining Bingley. She didn't expect Caroline to come back. That meant her obligation to being sociable was over, and so, she pulled the pencil out of her hair and withdrew the notebook from her back pocket.

Mary had the ability to laser focus on her ideas to the point that she could block out all the noise of the world around her. She could sit with a book while Lydia worked on a new song and missed notes that could rattle the dishes in the cupboard and not flinch at all. It was a skill she picked up early on in life. Being an introspective introvert in a house too small for seven people while sharing a room with an extrovert who spoke without thought meant that the only way to be alone was to create a safe space within her own mind. Once she started chasing down her most conflicted thoughts, or when she was concentrating on the notes she took while she read, or when she was editing a document for her aunt and uncle, she could crawl inside her own mental palace as soon as her writing instrument connected to paper. Her good posture forgotten, she would hunch over her notebook, start scribbling, and lose track of time.

The notebook was small, and while she had excellent penmanship when she was in the zone, she scribbled with wild abandon. So it was that she filled several pages more than she intended when she was interrupted for the third time since she arrived at the Ball. This time, it was Jane who placed a gentle hand on her shoulder. "You should really get something to eat soon. The dance is about to start."

Mary looked up at her sister's perfect face. She was the human embodiment of the Fibonacci sequence. The golden ratio could have been called the Jane Bennet ratio. The street lamps had come on, and the fairy lights that had been wrapped all around the lamp posts were blazing. The sun had set, but Mary had missed it. She smiled up at Jane who, like Bingley, had a face at which other people wanted to smile. "Wow. I was really out of it huh?" Mary looked back down at her notebook and flipped through all the pages she'd written.

"Yeah, you were in the zone. Lydia, Maria, and Kitty even sat at the table with you and talked and ate and were, well, loud teenage girls, and you didn't even flinch."

"Well, there is a particular register of sound that Lydia makes that makes me pull my head into my shell even more."

"Yeah, well she was hitting it. It annoys her when she can't annoy you. I explained it to the Bingleys so no need to worry about them."

"Explained what exactly?" Mary pushed her glasses up. She never expected to be, nor did she want to be, the topic of any conversation that had to explain her behavior in any way.

"Oh, you know, that you just sort of get interested in stuff so intensely that you disappear until you figure out whatever it is you are looking for. I've seen you read a history text at the dinner table while Kitty was kicking a soccer ball against the wall for an hour while Mom screamed at her to stop for 59 minutes, and you didn't move. Lizzy said you were like a terrier for truth."

Mary was torn on how to feel about the dog comparison. She thought she knew Lizzy well enough to know she wasn't calling her a dog, and she also knew that if Jane thought Lizzy was being mean about it, she wouldn't have shared it with her. "Lizzy said that about me?"

"Sure. She's not blind. She likes you. She respects you. She sees you."

"Hmmm."

"No. Really."

"Well, you would know best. You'd never lead me a… *stray*," Mary punned.

Jane laughed in her angelic laugh that actually made two people who were walking by stop their conversations and look over. In another time, Jane Bennet would have been called a Siren. "Yes, of course not. So anyway, we just left you to it after we explained it to Bingley. He asked why you were hunched over like that since you had such perfect posture when you were talking to his sisters. Your posture is so good that strangers notice. That is something special really. When everyone got up to head to the dance, Mom wanted to just leave you here all night and let you starve to teach you some kind of lesson, but, well, she's gone now, and I don't think you need to learn a lesson or starve."

Mary stood and stretched. The mention of the hunch in her back caused her to want to shake that out. Jane was slightly shorter than she was. Mary was the middle child in age and height but, except for Lydia who took after their father, none of them were particularly tall. She looked down at Jane and said, "Thanks."

"Do you want me to sit with you while you eat, or do you need more time with that?" She pointed at the notebook. "Need to talk about it? You were still writing so hard that I wonder how you didn't break the pencil lead." Mary looked at her pencil that was pointy sharp when she first stuck it in her hair that morning to see that it was a rounded nub and would need to be sharpened soon.

Mary knew her sister well enough to know it wasn't an empty gesture. "That would be nice, but I don't want to keep you from the dance. You and Bingley seemed to be hitting it off, and I don't want to get in the way of that."

"Oh, well, yes, he is quite lovely, but you know, I don't like to be too forward *and...*"

It was Mary's turn to interrupt, having been thrice the victim. "I think that maybe this is a time to be forward. How long is he going to be around? Do we even know?"

"He didn't say for sure. They signed a lease for a year, but that was because it was the only option they could get. They are waiting for his friend Darcy to arrive so they can work on plans. I guess he has already gone through something similar with his family estate, and so they want him here to help them work through their options. They needed to be close to Rhode Island, where Darcy lives, and close to the city for Caroline and Louisa, so they picked here. I suspect they will be in and out a lot."

"So, maybe this is the time to find out if you like him. I mean, you seemed totally into him, and the feeling looked mutual. I don't know much about it, but I've read books."

Jane's face flushed a bit. "It's true. It isn't just that he's handsome because he objectively is, but he was so nice and funny and patient when Mom would interject with her comments. He asked Lizzy lots of questions about her Women's Studies degree, which no one but you and me do, so that was a bonus too."

"I don't hear a reason for you to not be over there then."

Jane looked over at the crowd as they gathered on that side of town. The band was still tuning up and noodling around. "I just wanted to be sure that you're okay." She said it and meant it because Jane Bennet never said what she didn't mean, but the rest of her body was clearly being swayed as she didn't look back at Mary as she said it.

"I'm fine. I still need to process everything anyway. We can talk later if you want to."

Jane did look back at her finally. "Yeah?"

"Yes, of course."

"OK then." She nodded as she said it. She leaned forward and kissed Mary on the cheek. "Go get some food and come over and join us. Yes?"

"I will," Mary said. "Promise."

That was all it took because Jane knew if Mary said she promised, then Mary would follow through. Mary didn't promise to dance or to have fun; she just promised she would eat and come over to join them. That was something she could easily do. Jane walked in one direction and Mary in the other.

She hadn't really intended on getting so wrapped up in her thoughts like that, but since no one was paying much attention to her, and her mother made sure that no one would, it only made sense for her to go to her happy place inside her own mind. She wasn't the last person there to get food, but she was thankful that Jane nudged her when she did. They were starting to break things down, and the options were much more limited than she knew they would have been earlier in the day. She got a dried-out burger that would need lots of ketchup and mayo to bring it back to life, some chips, and a brownie to eat, grabbed a can of Mt. Dew, and wandered back to the family tables determined to make sense of her notes and the conversation she just had with Jane.

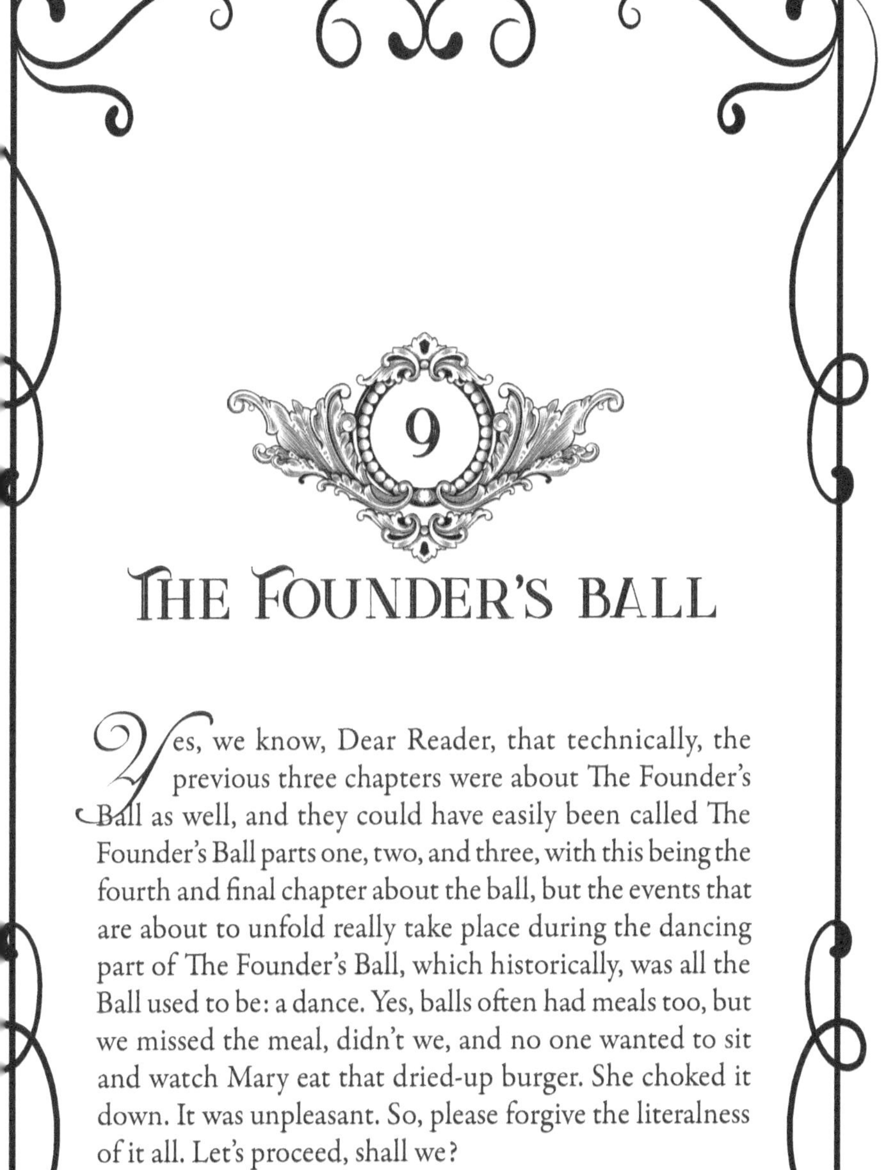

9

THE FOUNDER'S BALL

Yes, we know, Dear Reader, that technically, the previous three chapters were about The Founder's Ball as well, and they could have easily been called The Founder's Ball parts one, two, and three, with this being the fourth and final chapter about the ball, but the events that are about to unfold really take place during the dancing part of The Founder's Ball, which historically, was all the Ball used to be: a dance. Yes, balls often had meals too, but we missed the meal, didn't we, and no one wanted to sit and watch Mary eat that dried-up burger. She choked it down. It was unpleasant. So, please forgive the literalness of it all. Let's proceed, shall we?

As Mary was throwing her plate away and finishing off the last sip of her soda, the band, who had plenty of original music but who knew the assignment and played only covers at The Founder's Ball, kicked the dance off with a banger. Even people who don't like The Rolling Stones could admit that starting a party with "Start Me Up" was a good call. Even Mary nodded her head with approval when she heard that opening lick and was bobbing her head along by the time she walked into the fray.

Mary's version of joining the fray and other folks' version of joining the fray were, unsurprisingly, quite different. It wasn't that Mary was opposed to dancing or fun in general. She was actually a decent dancer, and for having absolutely no musical ability, she had rhythm. Maybe Mrs. Bennet should have allowed her to try out the drums, but you know, her nerves. As of this writing, Mary Bennet never picked up a drumstick. Still, dancing alone or in a room with her sisters was much different than going to "a dance." She didn't really enjoy very large groups of people all touching her at the same time from all directions. Large groups of people who sat in seats and looked at the film on the screen or the band on the stage were something different. Even then, a touch or bump was accidental and came with apologies. At a dance, when the masses were uncontrolled, and they moved with reckless abandon, Mary felt vulnerable. She tensed up. She preferred to move with cautious reservation. She knew though, that cautious dancing was from a forgotten time with corsets made of bones, and gloves, and furtive glances between suitors as opposed to people being able to breathe freely whilst touching the person they wished to touch during a slow dance and dancing without a dance card. While she didn't wish to be held that way, she knew most people did, and she did not wish to stop people from expressing themselves how they saw fit. Thus, having to choose between the two, she chose the thick glasses and tense shoulders all day long.

Many people accused Mary Bennet of being a buzz-kill, but she was no such thing. When a person chooses not to participate in certain activities, that person is often wrongly labeled as a killjoy. That is almost always a projection of guilt. Joy just looks different for some folks than it does for others. The truth is, Mary Bennet loved nothing more than watching people, collecting data on them, and coming to conclusions that she could then test out later by further observations or through direct questioning of that person. She was a bit of a sociological Sherlock Holmes.

By the time the band launched into song two, which was a rollicking version of Carole King's "I Feel the Earth," a song that Mary loved and made her feel pangs of regret for being so, so bad at the piano, she started her walk around the dance floor. To call it a floor is a bit of a misnomer, but calling it a dancing area that was a dense mass of bodies in the center that slowly filtered out to a less dense mass of bodies on the edges ending with some stragglers who were unsure of themselves on the outside of the allotted dancing area sounds admittedly terrible, even if it is accurate.

She saw her mother and aunt doing some kind of shoulder dance that would have certainly made Lydia cringe in embarrassment. Mary saw it for what it was: two women, who were not old by any stretch of the imagination, but who, due to marriage and circumstance, had been treated as old maids for far too long, reliving some childhood joy. The song, which was released just before Mary was born, was not a reminder of a time when they were still young girls but was a reminder of a younger time. King had, after all, gained fame as a songwriter when the two women both could have been called Miss Gardiner. The band, clearly aware of this fact, transitioned into King's first big hit as a songwriter, "Will You Still Love Me Tomorrow" by the Shirelles. No longer Miss anything and not women who advocated for being called Ms. instead of Mrs., Mrs. Phillips and Mrs. Bennet launched into a dance that Mary had never seen but was obviously something they'd done thousands of times as children. There are some siblings who have secret dances and some who don't. Mary smiled at her mother and aunt who, like her, had dances imprinted on her that she would never, ever forget.

Mary saw her father, who like her, was on the edge of the dancefloor, watching his wife and sister-in-law inadvertently clear a space around them as they launched into their arm and hip-swinging routine. Mary could see how happy he was just to watch her, and she understood more about them from that distance. She was seeing them as strangers saw them. They were all the things for each other that the other one was not. Carefree and fearless. Careful and cautious. They balanced each other out in a way that few couples did. They were not jealous of each other. They bickered and quarreled all the time, but it was, Mary understood, all part of the way they loved each other. It wasn't for her; that was for sure. Bickering and quarreling could be good fun if, after the arguments were over, she could go be alone and reflect on it. Her parents were seemingly in each other's space all the time. It seemed overwhelming, but she saw the way he watched people watch her and how he stood a little taller seeing people see his beautiful wife's beautiful spirit on full display. He wasn't proud of her per se as she wasn't doing anything in particular that was worthy of pride, but he was proud to be her husband because she was just who she was.

Mary circled the dance floor for another hour. She spent some time standing next to her father just so he knew she was there, so she could report back to her mother later that in fact, she put in an appearance even though she would continue to be belittled for her choice of attire. They didn't speak as they watched their family and towns-folk jump and dance and twirl about. They stood shoulder to shoulder, arms crossed, heads bobbing in time to the music. It appeared that while they were not totally joyful, they were at least having a good time. One of them certainly was not miserable and the other was actually having a good time. Joy is relative.

Having grown disgusted at watching Lydia, Maria, and Kitty throw themselves at men and boys and turning songs that Mary had never found remotely suggestive into slobbery make-out sessions complete with groping and gyrating, Mary found a place just next to the stage where she could be part of the event without having to be part of the event. At some point, her father walked by, as though he knew he'd find her there, absorbed in the music while studying people, and handed her a soda. She doffed an imaginary cap to him, and he bowed to her. They both smiled. He moved around the edge of the proceedings, keeping his eye out for his wife because of all the people to watch, she was his favorite. No matter how many times a day he saw her, he always wanted to see her one more time.

From her vantage point, Mary spotted Jane and Bingley dancing with a group but clearly only having eyes for each other. Included in their little circle were Lizzy, Charlotte, Lou, and her husband as well as Caroline Bingley, who reappeared about 30 minutes into the festivities with a massive, square-shouldered, square-jawed man who must have been the friend, they were waiting for, who, according to Lou, went by Darcy. He stood and took up space while Caroline tried desperately to get him to dance with her. He would not be persuaded into actual dancing, but he did occasionally make eye contact with people and bend over to talk directly into their ears and placed his ear next to their mouths so he could hear that person talk. Of course, Mary couldn't hear anything over the sound of the band, but she could tell that whatever it was anyone was saying to him, he was desperately trying to listen. He didn't seem to be much of a party person, but he was there, obviously, at the behest of his friend to help his family, so that said something about his character.

When there are live bands at dances, they, for the most part, start hard and play upbeat fast numbers for an hour or so, at which time, they will play a few slow numbers and take a break. It is all about the pacing, and considering that the band that was hired to play The Founder's Ball each year played for roughly four hours, those breaks were crucial.

So it was, that after the band cycled through hits from modern day and the previous three decades, the singer leaned into the microphone and said, "We're about to slow things down now." The crowd applauded and wooed. She took a big drink of water while the saxophonist belted out the opening riff of Wham's "Careless Whisper." Couples paired off. Mr. Bennet sought out Mrs. Bennet, whom he knew would be waiting for him somewhere on the dance floor as they had an arrangement that he would be allowed to forfeit any and all fast songs that were not swing numbers as long as he sought her out and danced closely with her during all slow songs. He was willing to make the agreement as there were rarely any swing numbers during the Ball, although the inclusion of the saxophone this year gave him pause.

Jane looked up at Bingley, who had his right hand outstretched as soon as the singer spoke about slowing things down. She slid her hand into his and stepped close to his chest. She put her other hand on his hip, and he put his on her back. They seemed oblivious to anyone and anything, as though the band was playing just for them. Lou and her husband fell into each other, laughing and smiling. Lizzy and Darcy made eye contact. She started talking. He leaned forward to hear her. He stood up straight, seemingly frustrated at whatever she said. He turned and walked away. Caroline chased after him. Lizzy, seemingly equally frustrated by whatever the interaction was, stormed off the dance floor and walked away from the festivities. Charlotte chased after her.

Mary, who wasn't one to chase after anyone, but who was a person who was curious enough to know what was going on, and who saw a way to get away from the party, walked, deliberately and with purpose, after Lizzy and Charlotte. She walked to the edge of the dancefloor that faced the town and spotted her sister and her best friend back at the tables in front of the law offices. The band switched over to "Faithfully" by Journey. Mary considered this to be a strange choice as the first slow song was about cheating and begging for forgiveness, and the second was about remaining faithful. She had no one to speak to about it, so she quickly pulled out her notebook, slid her blunt pencil out of her hair, and jotted down a note for later.

When she arrived at the table, Lizzy was swearing and fuming and saying some unintelligible things. Mary made out the word "arrogant" for sure. Charlotte looked at Mary and smiled.

Unlike Jane, who just smiled at everyone and who genuinely put everyone at ease, Charlotte was nice to people she felt deserved it. She and Mary were not nearly as close as Lizzy and Charlotte were, but they were more than friendly. They had a mutual respect. They were both practical people who understood their place in Meryton while wishing to find themselves outside of it. However, while there, they did their best to make it bearable. Of course, readers of an earlier book in this series know neither of them stayed in Meryton, but that they took different paths altogether. More on that to come here though. Just because we know the end results doesn't mean we know the path. Reading the final page of a novel isn't the same as knowing what happens.

"So," Mary said as she sat down, "you didn't hit it off with the new guy."

"Yes, well," Charlotte began, "he, um, rejected our Lizzy here."

"It isn't that. I can take being rejected. Not everyone has to like me or find me attractive; I'm not my mother. It was how he did it."

Most people in this situation would follow up with a "Dare I ask?" or "Would you care to tell me?" or some other indirect question. Mary Bennet didn't like those. What purpose did it serve to ask the question only to have to ask it again? It was much more honest to just come out with it, and if the person wished not to talk about the thing, the person need not respond or could respond with a firm, "No."

Thus, Mary asked, "How did he do it?"

"I said, 'You don't seem to be enjoying yourself with the upbeat numbers. Maybe you would enjoy a slow dance with me?' Which I know sounds desperate, but I promise it wasn't as bad as all that. He was having a terrible time, and that Caroline woman was all over him, making him and the rest of us in the circle very uncomfortable."

Charlotte chimed in. "It reeked of late night on pay cable for sure." While the Bennets didn't have cable television, they knew the Lucases did as Mayor Lucas was on the committee that brought it to Meryton in the first place. His argument was that he didn't want everyone's yard mucked up with those gigantic satellite dishes. So, while Mary hadn't spent any nights at the Lucases to watch any steamy late-night cable movies, she'd heard about them plenty from Lydia and Kitty who went over there at least once a week.

Lizzy, who had clearly seen plenty of those films as well, nodded in agreement. She closed her eyes and clenched her fists. "Yeah. I mean, I am all for women owning their own bodies, and if they want to throw those bodies at gigantic, classically attractive, emotionally distant, and obviously stunted men, that's fine. I just don't want to see it. I mean, there's a reason we don't see Catherine get with Heathcliff, you know?"

Mary heard what she'd said and looked to Charlotte, who clearly heard it as well. They nodded. No further conversation was needed. Mary liked to think that part of the conversation added the fact that *Wuthering Heights* was a Victorian novel, and Catherine and Heathcliff were terrible people, so maybe that was a terrible example. We can report that Charlotte did not think that at all. The truth is there are three groups of people in the world: those who give up on that book because they hate it, those who read it through to the end and dislike it but get what Bronte was doing, and those who know it is full of problematic people doing terrible things and love it anyway. Charlotte was the first, Lizzy was the second, and Mary was the third.

The fact was Charlotte heard what Lizzy said and thought, "Oh, no" which is what she thought Mary was thinking so, maybe they needed to have a conversation after all. Still, they both knew that it meant that Lizzy was in trouble with this guy. She'd found a challenge, and she was not one to back down from a challenge.

In a different story with a different lead character, the sister would ask something like "Do you really want to know?" or some such nonsense, but in this story about Mary Bennet, whose older sisters apparently knew her better than she thought they did, Lizzy wouldn't bother with that. She continued, "After I asked if he wanted to dance with me, he said, and I'll never forget this as a long as I live, 'I can't be tempted.' Really? As though I'm a temptress? How dare he? Especially after that tart was, well," she waved at the air, indicating the past conversation, "you know, obviously trying to tempt him."

"Tart." Mary nodded and snickered a bit. "Good one. Don't really hear that one much, but I like it, so much more refined and upscale as opposed to lots of other words people have used about Caroline Bingley, I am sure." She hadn't meant to say it aloud, but it just came out. There was something about Lizzy's choice of words that got Mary's mind whirling about Darcy's choice of words in relationship to the rest of the evening, both what she observed and what they said happened.

"Glad you approve of my vocabulary choices."

"Well, yes, words matter, don't they?" Both Charlotte and Lizzy were staring at her now. She'd accidentally gained their full attention, which she thought would be something she liked, but it turned out that maybe she didn't. She would need to think about that later. She pushed her glasses up on the bridge of her nose and cleared her throat. "He said, 'I can't be tempted,' not, 'You can't tempt me,' and while they sound like the same thing, they actually aren't. You were not calling Caroline Bingley a tasty, albeit fatty, sugar-filled, and one may say, tempting pastry, were you? You were calling her a strumpet."

Charlotte snorted a laugh. She clamped her hands over her mouth. She looked down and tried to get herself together.

Lizzy, who if the shoe was on the other foot, would have been laughing as well, didn't find it as humorous. "While, yes, I was, I most certainly would not say strumpet unless I was in a play."

"Yes, well, most people wouldn't say tart about a person either."

"I was just doing a character defense of Curley's wife for my Sex Roles and Sexism class. It was on my mind. I must have written it fifty times this week."

Mary nodded. She looked up and processed the information. She nodded more. "Makes sense."

Charlotte, who'd comported herself, looked up confused. "Who's Curley? What makes sense?"

"He's the boss in *Of Mice and Men*," Lizzy explained. "His wife doesn't have a name and there is a whole conversation about her being a 'tart.'"

Charlotte nodded at Lizzy. She'd read the book as well but just one time. She cried on and off for a week after reading it, and she did her best to never think of it again. She turned her attention to Mary. "And you just knew this?"

"I did." She didn't say it like it was a big deal because it wasn't a big deal to her. She wasn't showing off. She just so happened to have read the book enough times and had quite a lengthy conversation about it with her father. He asked her what she made of that word at the time. Mary wondered if that meant he had a similar conversation with Lizzy at one point. She wouldn't ask because she never wanted to come across as jealous of the time her father spent with her sisters. We can confirm that he did, in fact, have that conversation with Lizzy as well but not the other three of his daughters. He thought it would make Jane blush, he thought Lydia would take it personally, and he was afraid Kitty wouldn't have an opinion on the matter.

"Hmmm," Charlotte said and shook her head. "And to think your parents thought you would need me to be your tutor."

"Well, I for one am glad they thought that." Lizzy placed her hand on top of Charlotte's. "Best friends are hard to come by in any part of the world, but in Meryton, they are even more scarce."

"And I respect and admire you very much," Mary said.

Charlotte touched her heart with her free hand. She knew Mary well enough to know that it wasn't as cold as it sounded. "Anyway, what were we talking about?" She wiped a stray tear from her cheek.

"Tarts?" Lizzy asked and looked at Mary.

"Not exactly." Mary continued her thoughts from before, "He didn't call you a temptress. He didn't say anything about you at all, in fact. You just took it that way because he rejected you. Here he was, clearly uncomfortable the whole time..."

"How do you know?" Lizzy interrupted.

"I was up by the stage, people-watching. I saw the way she was acting and how rigidly he stood whenever anyone touched him or tried to get him to do anything. He looks like a guy who is likely pretty tightly wound in any circumstance, but he showed up late to a party where he knows only four people. One of them, his best friend, is making eyes at the prettiest girl in the universe who is making eyes right back at him. One person is drunk. One person is trying to keep the drunk person occupied to stop him from becoming more drunk, and the other is clearly throwing herself at him. There must be something more going on there. Not sure if Bingley encourages it or if he is oblivious. Either way, Darcy doesn't like it. He isn't interested. So far so good?"

Lizzy and Charlotte both nodded in unison.

"Yes, well, he spent a lot of time bending over and talking directly into everyone's ears. I assume that means when he did that, you had no idea what he was saying to those people, nor does anyone know what he said to you."

Lizzy and Charlotte looked at each other to confirm this was true for each of them. They both nodded and looked back to Mary.

"So, we might assume, and I don't like to assume, you know, but all I have is the observations that I made of the man for what, 30 minutes, and the little bit of knowledge I have of Caroline, but I assume he told her that he wasn't going to dance no matter what or something like that, and she should quit trying to tempt him. Thus, when you asked when the music was a bit quieter, he likely used that same language to make sure Caroline heard it."

By the time Mary ended her argument, they were both nodding.

"Or, you know, he thinks you are a succubus."

10

SLEEPOVER

The sleepover is a time-honored tradition that popular culture has all wrong. There is an understanding, for some reason, that sleepovers do not begin until children are around 7 or 8, and they end by the time a child becomes a teenager unless it is a horror movie or a story about mean girls, and then sleepovers happen as a plot point for terrible things to happen. This is false. Regular people have sleepovers all the time, and the fact remains that sleepovers happen well into adulthood. Sometimes it is out of necessity as one is a bit too intoxicated, and sometimes it is planned because one plans on staying up too late and becomes intoxicated. Other times, people just want to stay up late sans alcohol and be near people they love and admire. It is time, here and now, to end the trope. Sleepovers are not just for children.

The fact is, sleepovers begin and end when the people wish them to. Lydia and Kitty would often, much to Mary's relief, spend nights over at Maria's house. The Mayor and his wife found having kids over made their lives easier. Their kids were always on their best behavior when guests were over, and the kids entertained themselves. If the sleepover was planned in advance, one of them would take Maria to The Theater and allow her to rent some movies for her and the Bennets to watch, and they would rent some for themselves. While the Bennets still only had one TV and one VCR, the Lucases purchased a portable TV/VCR combo that either of their children could use. Because when Lydia and Kitty were at the Lucases, more often than not, Charlotte was at Longbourn in what Mary called "The Prisoner Swap" so there was never any fighting about who would have a turn, and to be fair, even if Charlotte was home when Maria had overnight guests, she often found herself in the living room with her parents watching whatever they watched. She was an adult, after all, who would still sleep over at her friend's house and watch movies with her parents. Living at home into adulthood can create some confusing family dynamics as we shall soon see.

Exactly one week after The Founder's Ball, the Bennet girls found themselves once again in downtown Meryton. This time, they were not attending a dance but going to see *Uncle Buck* at The Theater. It had been released in August of that year and was finally making its way to Meryton. It was rare that they were all excited to see the same film, and that second weekend in October was no different. Mary, who was a fan of John Candy because he seemed to be an actor who knew who he was and wasn't embarrassed by that, was excited to see him lead a film. She enjoyed his turn as Barf in the Mel Brooks' *Star Wars* knock-off *Space Balls*. It was not Brooks' best work, and she felt he was slowly becoming a master of farce instead of satire, but he still was trying, and Mary respected someone who tried.

Lizzy was always interested in seeing a new John Hughes film. She found them equal parts feminist and misogynistic. Clearly, Hughes liked to have female protagonists, but he didn't always know how to treat them respectfully. Jane thought it looked "cute." Kitty, who'd seen the commercial for it with Jane when they were watching some TV show, agreed, and thus, she was locked in as a vote for cute. Lydia, who secretly thought it looked funny, but who wanted to be contrarian, was making a big stink about it. She had been told in no uncertain terms by Lizzy, using words that we shall not share here, that no one was making her come with them, and she could happily stay home and watch *The Golden Girls* with their parents.

The sisters sat in age descending order from left to right in the center of the back row of the theater. They bought five drinks and three popcorns, two mediums that sat between Lizzy and Jane and Lydia and Kitty and a small that Mary held on her own. They tried a variety of different combinations of where to situate two large popcorns when it was just the five of them, but Mary ended up having to reach in front of Lizzy or Kitty the whole time, and it was problematic. When Charlotte or Maria came along, it was easier, and Mary would share with Charlotte who would sit between her and Lizzy, even though she was the oldest.

The lights turned down, and the Bennets were settled in to watch the previews, which were technically for movies that had already been released in the wider world, but that would be coming to Meryton soon. They whispered to each other as the previews rolled, discussing if they were going to come see those pictures or not. The whispers were low and in the ears of sisters out of respect for the rest of the theatergoers because being rude to each other wasn't an issue for the Bennet girls, but being rude to strangers wasn't something they did. Even Lydia was respectful to strangers, and when people got to know her and found out what kind of person she really was, they were generally shocked. Lydia didn't even know it was happening. Sometimes we learn by example. Of course, Lydia had other ways to embarrass herself in public.

The final preview rolled for a thriller with Michael Douglas and Andy Garcia called *Black Rain*, which Mary and Lizzy agreed they would see as a duo. Jane thought it looked too gritty for her tastes, which surprised no one. If Kitty was unattached at the time they left the house, she would likely come too, they knew, so they didn't bother to ask her. Since Lydia had decided she wasn't interested and leaned to whisper it to Kitty, that was likely the final word on the subject. Alas, poor Kitty.

The doors of the theater were kicked open, and a group of people who were not taught the same good manners about being rude in public came in. Three of the five members spoke at full volume as their eyes adjusted to the dark, and they continued to speak as though they were in their own home until they finally settled down just as the movie began with the jangly piano playing as a teenage girl walked down the sidewalk. The loudmouths kept on loudmouthing until a chorus of shushes rained down on them from all quarters. The group, who readers likely have guessed the identities of, were shocked into silence.

Other than plenty of laughter and quite a few "awws," mostly from Jane and one member of the party who arrived late, there were no more outbursts during the film. When it was over and the final scene of Uncle Buck and Tia Russell waving at each other with the freeze frame on Buck's smiling face, designed to pull on viewer's heart-strings, pulled on Jane's, and the lights came up halfway. While the end credits rolled and Jane was wiping tears from her face, she looked up to see Bingley who, unsurprising to anyone, was one of the silent members of the latecomers, unabashedly doing the same thing. They made eye contact, they both froze for a second, and then they laughed through the tears.

Darcy, whose opinion of Lizzy being a succubus had yet to be determined, looked directly at her and nodded in a way that looked like a solemn bow. Lizzy, whose face flushed at the gesture, turned away from him so that when he looked back up, she was nudging Jane out of the theater. Mary saw it all and resisted the urge to reach for the pencil in her hair.

Lydia and Kitty headed upstairs to look around the other part of The Theater. Because of the nature of the business, the stock was constantly rotating. They didn't really have the pocket money that the rest of the sisters had although they did earn some from doing work on the farm. They really just liked to look at people more than anything. They had not gotten to the point yet where they would like to sit at the 24-hour diner and drink sodas or coffee and see and be seen by people, nor did they have a car where they could prowl around with the windows down just seeing who was out and about, so they relied on hanging around The Theater. It had been a safe bet up to that point in their lives, so it made sense to keep doing it.

Jane, Lizzy, and Mary bid them adieu and started the walk home. It was 1989. No one thought twice about leaving two teenage girls with no means of communication and little pocket money alone in town. There was no plan in place to have them collected or brought home. They would simply arrive when they arrived. That may sound like an insane proposition to some readers, and to others, it may sound like a simpler, more enjoyable time. We are not here to judge on that score except to say that Lydia could have done with some supervision in general.

As the three of them started the walk back to Longbourn, a sporty little Dodge pulled up next to them into an open, on-street, parallel parking spot. Caroline Bingley was in the driver's seat. "Jane!" she shouted even though she was only a few feet away from them. "I thought that was you back there."

Mary thought it was a ridiculous thing to say. Of course, Caroline knew it was Jane back there. Her brother and Jane made eyes at each other, and had Lizzy not been in such a hurry to avoid Darcy, and had Jane been a person who knew how to use any force whatsoever, they would all still be standing around outside the theater talking with each other. Mary reached for her pencil now and pulled out her notebook to scribble a quick note. The pencil was back in her hair, and the book was back in her pocket before Jane had approached the window.

"Yes, yes, it was. You remember my sisters?" Jane pointed and turned to Lizzy and Mary. They both raised their hands in greeting. One of them fake smiled. The other did not.

"Yes, of course. Hello, ladies." Caroline seemed to purr when her tongue hit the "d" in ladies. She turned her attention back to Jane. "I'm glad I spotted you all walking because my brother is picking up some pizzas now and taking them back to the house. We're going to bend some elbows, play some cards, and treat it like a sleepover. We can swing by your house to get some clothes, or you can just wear something of mine or Lou's. There are plenty of empty rooms, and for some reason, the whole place was furnished when we rented it. Would you all care to join us? We feel so out of place in town and who better to help us than people who've been here for generations?" If she meant for that last part to come out as an insult, she succeeded.

Jane, who never took anything as an insult, responded, "Well, they are not yet 21, although Lizzy shall be soon, so they won't be bending any elbows, but I assume you have some non-alcoholic drinks available. I am open to that if they are." Jane turned to look at her sisters to see how they reacted to the invitation. Her doe eyes were wide and full of hope.

The look on their faces let her know immediately that they were not interested. Mary had used up all of her people time for the day at the movies, and while it is true that most of the time she sat quietly and enjoyed the film squeezed between Lizzy and Kitty, she had to be around people and hear them talking and worry about being touched by strangers, and she needed to go home and have some alone time in her room while Lydia and Kitty were still out. Jane knew this was going to be the case for her, but she wanted her to feel included when she said "they."

Lizzy was not interested for different reasons. The majority of the reasons focused on the fact that Darcy would be there, and she had some feelings to work through before she was around him. She didn't care for the bow, but she also found it endearing and charming. She was hoping to talk it through with Jane once they were alone in their attic space. Without her, she would be forced to either talk to Mary about it, who wouldn't have very insightful advice, or talk to the critters who lived in the eaves, who had as much understanding in affairs of that sort as Mary.

"I'm not really feeling a drunken card party," Lizzy said, but even she was not immune to the doe eyes because she knew that Jane would never use them for nefarious purposes. She just had doe eyes. "You should go." She leaned in and whispered, "Get some alone time with Bingley. If you ride with her, you have to stay the night." She then did a childish sing-song voice, "Jane and Bingley sitting in a tree. K.I.S.S.I.N.G."

Jane felt the blush go all the way through her ears. "Stop." She smacked Lizzy on the shoulder.

"I agree with Lizzy on this. I saw how you looked at him back there. Kissing seems to be the next logical step. You should go. Kissing or no kissing. Drinking or no drinking. There is a zero percent chance I want to go to that, and you know it," Mary added. She turned to Lizzy. "I think you should go too. I'm fine to walk home alone."

"No. No, thank you. I'll walk you home. I'm exhausted," she said to Mary with a tone that made it clear she was not remotely exhausted.

"If you're sure," Jane said. She grabbed Mary's hand with her right hand and Lizzy's with her left.

"Sure," they both said at the same time.

"Have fun," Mary said. While she couldn't imagine it being very fun, she knew Jane would certainly like it, and she loved her sister and did, in fact, wish she would have a good time, even if she thought Caroline Bingley had other motives that she didn't quite understand.

"Not too much fun," Lizzy joked.

Jane nodded at them. "Thank you, girls." She turned and said to Caroline, "I'll come!"

"Fan-tas-tick." Caroline overly enunciated the word and thus almost sounded like she meant it.

Mary and Lizzy watched her climb into the passenger seat of the car that would be quite impractical in the coming months for getting around a small town in that part of the country. Jane waved over the top of the car out the open window as the car peeled away much too quickly for a small town in that part of the country. They waved as people do as cars drive away, even though there is almost no chance that the people in the car can see the gesture.

"Is that going to end well or poorly?" Mary asked as they started walking toward Longbourn.

"I'm not sure. Bingley is clearly into Jane."

"According to Mother, everyone with a pulse finds Jane attractive."

Lizzy nodded. "It's true. You should see her at school. She doesn't even know it, but it's like when we walk through the library, she is on a catwalk. Everyone stops and watches her. She doesn't even notice."

"She is the best of us."

"She really is, which is why I worry about how it will go. Caroline is not to be trusted."

"I had a bad experience with her the one time I met her, and she was loud and obnoxious at The Theater. I've read

so much about her in the paper, and I wanted to chalk it up as gossip, you know?"

Lizzy nodded. "I do. Women hating on each other isn't good."

"Exactly, but so far, she hasn't done anything to dissuade me from believing that she is a shallow, vapid woman. I just get confounded by the reports on her promiscuity. I don't understand how that has anything to do with the other. I can't imagine if you or Jane started having multiple liaisons, and for all I know, you already have, and to be clear, I am not asking for, nor interested in any details, I am just stating the truth here that you've been off to college for several years now, and while you live at home, you don't always come home at night, and neither of you have become vainglorious."

Lizzy laughed. "I promise you that there have not been multiple liaisons for either of us but..."

Mary covered her ears. "No details. I mean it," she shouted.

"Fine, fine." Lizzy mimed zipping her lips. "Still, if you want to avoid getting the details of what is going down up at Netherfield, you are going to want to find something else to do tomorrow because I can't imagine there will be talk of anything else."

Mary nodded and would take it under advisement. Not wanting to talk more about anything of the sort, she asked, "So, feminist or misogynist?"

Lizzy rubbed her hands together and launched into the diatribe she had been constructing in her head as they watched the film. They spoke of nothing else the rest of their walk, and that suited Mary just fine.

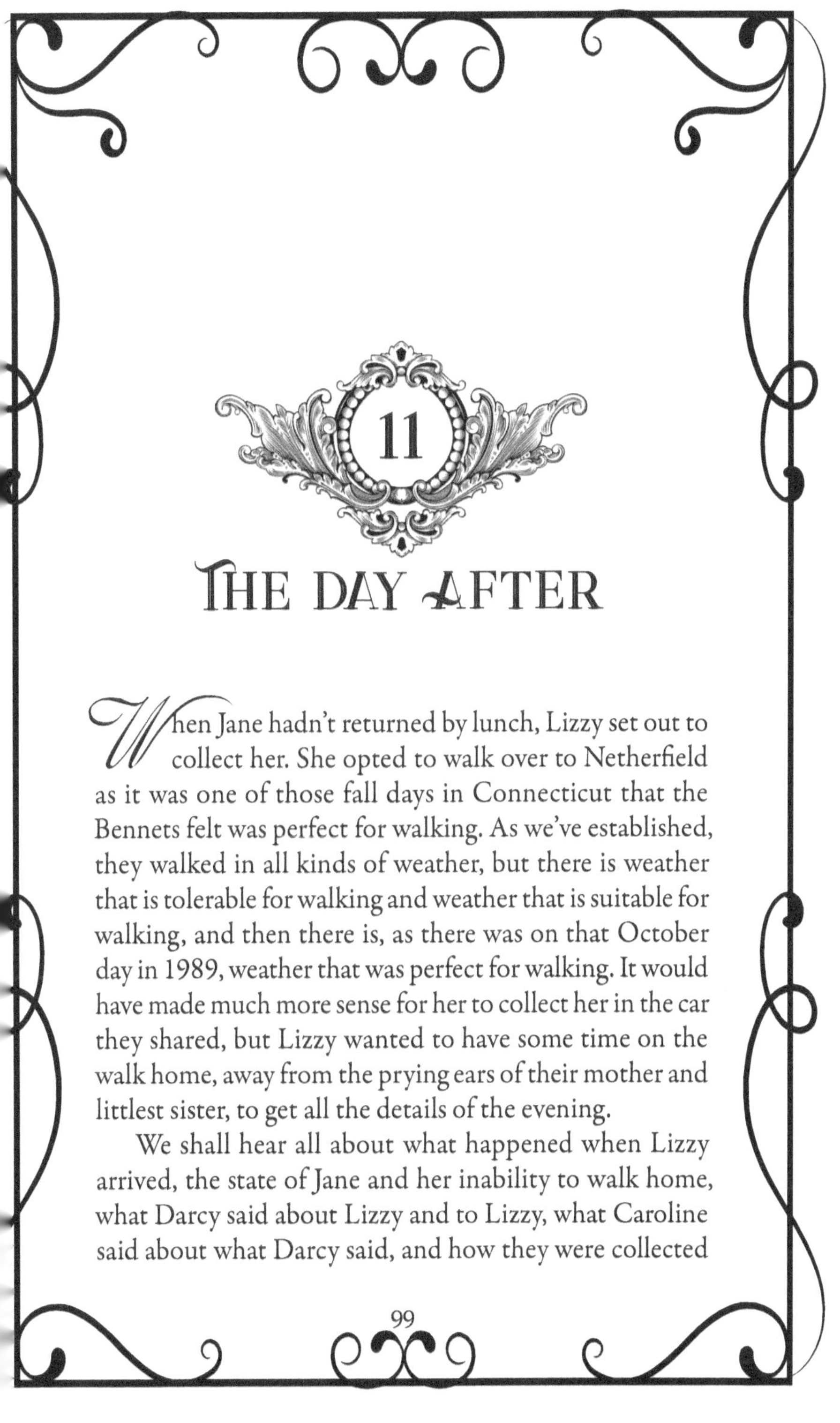

11

THE DAY AFTER

When Jane hadn't returned by lunch, Lizzy set out to collect her. She opted to walk over to Netherfield as it was one of those fall days in Connecticut that the Bennets felt was perfect for walking. As we've established, they walked in all kinds of weather, but there is weather that is tolerable for walking and weather that is suitable for walking, and then there is, as there was on that October day in 1989, weather that was perfect for walking. It would have made much more sense for her to collect her in the car they shared, but Lizzy wanted to have some time on the walk home, away from the prying ears of their mother and littlest sister, to get all the details of the evening.

We shall hear all about what happened when Lizzy arrived, the state of Jane and her inability to walk home, what Darcy said about Lizzy and to Lizzy, what Caroline said about what Darcy said, and how they were collected and finally returned to Longbourn in due course. Everyone in the family, including the patriarch, will be included in the aftermath. However, before any of that could happen, Mary and her father were in the library, having a rousing good discussion about Tan's book. While the book is, as of this writing, decades old, and there was a very good film adaptation made in the early 90s, which caused, as film adaptations often do, renewed interest in the book, and thus, there was a generation of readers who likely know the plot of book and movie and would love to eavesdrop on this conversation. We can't assume that all of you Dear Readers are of that generation or have the faintest idea about *The Joy Luck Club,* so we shall peek into the library after they talk about the major spoilers. Let's join in when they are focused on the theme and how that relates to them.

"I am just not sure that I agree with you on that, Father," Mary said, sitting in the client chair, not her high-backed reading chair. She was much more willing to express her full opinion about almost anything, be it to her father or anyone really, through the lens of a literary or philosophical conversation than she ever would without such a buffer. While she may bare her soul equally, having someone else's ideas open the door allowed her to feel comfortable to walk through. Were she forced to knock on the same door, she wouldn't be sure if she could do it. We shall leave it up to each reader to decide if her father knew this and asked specific questions and made specific claims to get her through the door. She pushed up her wire-framed glasses. "I don't think Tan was disparaging of men at all, but she was telling fraught tales of mothers and daughters, and so what you see as disparaging, I see as agnostic."

"She's agnostic about men? She isn't sure if they exist or not?" He puffed on his pipe and leaned forward.

"No, of course not. You know I don't mean that."

"It is what you said, child."

"Yes, I know. I think she is agnostic about their role in the relationship between mothers and their daughters. She is saying that men have an influence, and sometimes an outsized influence, on the family in general, but..."

"Is that a remark?" he asked while smirking.

"You know it is." She deflected it away and continued, "You are the only man in this family." She held up her hand. "The uncles do not count, and you know it."

He closed his mouth around his pipe and inhaled. His smirk was a smile.

"Even if you were not the sole breadwinner, and thus, financially, we are, for the most part, totally dependent on you, and in a different time, our futures would be even more in your hands than they are now; our futures are already set in motion because we are women without means, and you are a man with means in this country at this time. We pretend we are so far advanced, but women have only had the right to vote for just under 70 years. It will be decades more until we see a woman in a position of real power in this country. The patriarchy is real. You are the patriarch. Even if you don't mean to be part of the problem, you are because it is how it is." She took a beat and gave him time to interject.

He opted for silence and a nod of approval.

She continued, "Hundreds of years ago, I'd be destined to live here forever to care for you and Mother because I have no desire to marry, and I wish to be educated. You being you, patriarchy or not, 1789 or 1989, you wouldn't make me marry. You are not a forceful man, but a man who could make me do things but would choose not to. Staying here would afford me that. You have this library. I would have access to it, and you would, I assume, like you do now, encourage us all to use it and make our own decisions. While people would speak ill of me, and I know they do now for similar reasons, but back then, when I became Mother's sole remaining spinster daughter, they would see me as a saint, even though I wouldn't fundamentally change and would simply be living my best life, considering the situation. I would have just gotten older, but I'd still be a woman who was under the protection and tacit control of you, my father. So, that may be fiction, but in the here and now, your influence on each of us, Mother included, is outsized in comparison to how we each influence each other. You manage to see each of us in a unique light, and we all know that. Some of us know it overtly while other members of the family feel it but don't have the vocabulary for it, be that out of choice or out of ignorance."

"Are you calling members of the Bennet clan ignorant?"

"I am, and they've been called much worse by you. I've heard it. I wouldn't say they are willfully ignorant." She closed her eyes and thought of the best way to say it. "They are more blissfully ignorant."

He nodded. "Well said."

"Thank you, Father." She loved to be complimented by him, and they both knew it. "So, all of that to say, regardless of how you make us feel or your opinions of us, which matter to us all, or how you help us be the people we are, or how you hold us back when you think help is required that way," she paused to see how he reacted to that comment, but he just nodded her to continue, "you can never

ever affect the way we feel about Mother or how she feels about us. You may wish to, but the reality is, you can't."

He took a drag on his pipe, exhaled the smoke, and nodded while squinting his eyes.

"And why can't I?"

"Because you won't lock us in our rooms or send any of us away. You are not a tyrant, and honestly, even if you were, sending us away or locking us in our rooms would only allow the relationship to fester. Your actions can't change how I feel or how any of us feel. You can only, and don't take this the wrong way, Father, get in the way and delay the inevitable. I cannot list all the times I've been outraged at Mother for short, intense bursts at a time. No one can make those feelings better, nor do I think they could make them worse. They just are. I see how she looks at me or doesn't look at me. You telling her to treat me differently would backfire spectacularly for all of us. You tell me not to think badly of her, but you don't tell me to treat her differently. There is a difference."

His pipe had gone out, as pipes often do, so he struck a match and lit it again. He inhaled and pulled the flame into the bowl of the pipe. Once he felt it was going to stay, he shook the match and dropped it in the ashtray. He exhaled and nodded. "So, it is your supposition then that this was Tan's intention?"

"It is. She wasn't denigrating any of the men. She was just making the point that regardless of the power they have in the world, which is, to be fair, still almost absolute, Indira Gandhi, Golda Meir, and Thatcher are obviously the exceptions, not the rules. They were women in power surrounded by men. When all the Parliaments and Legislatures are split 50/50, we will still be getting to where we should have always been. The first female president of the United States will not have a cabinet with one token male on it. That is just a fact, and Tan knows it, and I know it and, let's face it, Father, you know it too.."

"I do?"

She nodded. "You do. You may feel Tan's commentary, or really lack of commentary, as a slap, but she is just acknowledging a universal truth. Men have power and can make women do all kinds of things, but they can't fully understand what it is like to be a woman."

He sat back in his chair and nodded his head. We can't know if it was in agreement or in approval, for a head nod could be either or it could be both, because just as he was opening his mouth to speak, Mary's mother banged the library door open.

"They're back! Poor Jane is hurt. Hurry!" she shouted from the doorway.

By the time they heard her, registered what she said, and looked from each other to the sound of her voice in the doorway, she was gone. "Did you hear it too?" Mr. Bennet joked as he was banging the upside-down bowl of his pipe on the ashtray to make sure it was out.

Mary was already on her feet. While she knew her mother was prone to flights of fancy and hyperbole, if Jane were really injured, she would want to run interference on her mother so that Lizzy or their father could get her to the hospital for urgent medical attention. We shall see her need to make the drive later in this tale, but it will not feel urgent, likely because her mother won't be there. While she had her driver's license, and she occasionally drove one of the many work trucks and tractors, they could all drive tractors by the time they were were double digits;

she didn't feel as though she would be the one chosen to rush Jane anywhere because, on a good day, she drove just below the speed limit.

Mary and her father followed the sound of Mrs. Bennet's voice and discovered that the whole family had gathered in the dining room. Jane appeared to be in one piece, although her foot was propped up on a chair, and Kitty was coming in from the kitchen with a bag of ice. Mr. Bennet walked over to her and pressed his lips to the top of her head as was his way of showing concern. Jane reached up and patted the back of his head while he was bent over as was her way of acknowledging him.

"Give me that, Kitty!" Mrs. Bennet shouted, even though shouting was not required. Kitty's hand was already extended. She wasn't going to put the ice on Jane's foot. Mrs. Bennet swiped the bag and shouted "Lizzy!" She stomped her foot as though that would make her arrive sooner. It was Lydia who came through the door with a throw pillow from the couch. "Thank you, dear," she said to her favorite child. "Put that under her foot and elevate it. Do it gently."

Mary rolled her eyes and resisted the urge to say anything. She pushed her glasses up on her nose and hoped that someone else would take control of the situation. With that, Lizzy appeared at the door with an ace bandage.

"It wasn't where you said it was, Mom," she said with a tone that was equal parts chastisement and annoyance.

"Where was it then?" Mrs. Bennet snarked as she handed the bag of ice to Lizzy.

"Under the sink, not in the mirror. I had to dig for it. You should clean it up in there."

"That is your father's doing." She stamped her foot. "I've told you a thousand times haven't I, Husband?"

"Yes, of course, Mrs. Bennet. My apologies," he said in the tone and voice he used when he wanted to defuse the situation.

Lizzy just shook her head and proceeded to place the ice on Jane's now elevated ankle. "Jane, can you hold your leg up for just a second? Kitty, come help her hold it up while I wrap it. Lydia, go get her something to drink. Mary, I've got some Ibuprofen in my purse. It's hanging by the door."

The Bennet sisters jumped into action, and by the time Lydia and Mary came back into the room, their mother had pulled a chair over and sat next to Jane, facing her. She was holding her hand and patting it in a way that was supposed to be comforting. Jane took the pills and thanked them all profusely, and after she assured them all that she was comfortable, she launched into the story.

Dear Reader, we could tell it *Rime of the Ancient Mariner* style, where Jane launched into a long dialogue that goes on for pages and pages with Lizzy occasionally chiming in to fill in context, but since we are only one-third of the way into our tale, and it is only still October and the next chapter brings another guest and November, we shall do our best to summarize it. Rest assured, we've left nothing of import out. Ready?

Caroline was not kidding about the pizzas and the drinking. Mr. Hurst, whose elbow was permanently bent, was in rare form and the low stakes and friendly game of poker turned into a bit of a mess. Jane, who had no skills at bluffing and would never, ever cheat on anything ever, hit a lucky streak and won several hands in a row. That set him off, and he started making accusations. When both Bingley and Darcy came to her defense, he stormed off, and Lou chased after him. They were not seen for the remainder of the evening. It was a welcome reprieve. The less we see of Mr. Hurst, the better. He is exhausting, isn't he? Can you imagine being married to him? Ugh.

The remaining foursome decided that they would do something less competitive but equally fun. They did what people who were in their 20s in the 1980's did; they played Euchre. For the uninitiated, Euchre is a card game that pits two teams of two against each other and consists of using all the face cards, the Aces, the nines, and the tens. In some instances, Jacks are the best card in one's hand. Each deal can earn a team one, two, or four points, and the winner of a particular match is the first team to ten points. Yes, Dear Reader, there are variations on the theme with two people or three people playing, but there were four of them, so they played it that way. They opted to not play the "stick the dealer" rules as Jane and Bingley disliked that very much as they each thought it too mean, but as a compromise, they did not allow the "Ace, no face" rule to end a hand. There are more rules than that of course, and if one is interested, while the internet didn't exist when this game took place, it does at the time of this writing, so readers who have never played may feel free to investigate further and should round up three acquaintances and play. It is good fun.

They first played in gendered pairs, and after Bingley and Darcy, who'd been Euchre partners for years as they attended the same college and were excellent friends, won three matches in a row, Caroline demanded a switch and insinuated that there was "table talk," which is Euchre-speak for cheating, and so she and Darcy paired up to take on Jane and Bingley. We want to remind readers that there was plenty of regular table talk as in normal conversations about life, but there was absolutely no cheating. It would never have occurred to Bingley to cheat, and Darcy abhorred the practice. Bingley shared a story of a time when they caught a mutual acquaintance cheating during a game and the dressing down he received from Darcy. Bingley smiled brightly while retelling the tale, and Darcy may have smirked. Darcy, who if asked, was enjoying himself very much, said very little, as was his way.

The game came to an abrupt end when Jane, who was tipsier than she would have cared to admit, after a break to use the facilities, tripped over some ornate boot scraper that stood outside the door to the parlor where they were playing their game. We know that it was not just her pride that was hurt. Her ankle was inflamed, and upon Caroline's assistance, she was situated in a guest room with painkillers to sleep off the night.

Bingley brought her breakfast in bed, which was just as sweet and lovely as it sounds, but it was more like brunch in bed as they all slept in late, feeling the effects of the alcohol. To say that Bingley slept is a bit of a misnomer here. He woke up every few hours and peeked in, most assuredly in the least lecherous way possible, to be sure Jane was resting well. He would rap quietly on the door, and if he didn't hear her, he would peek his head around the cracked-open door frame to see how she was. At his insistence, she kept the light in the bathroom on and the door open with the hallway light on so, should she get up at night, she would be able to see and not take another tumble.

One time, around five in the morning, he knocked on the door frame, and Jane replied with a welcoming, "Come in." He poked his head in and found her sitting awake in bed reading one of the books that the owners of Netherfield placed on the bedside tables just in case one of their guests found themselves sequestered in a room and felt the desire to read. This seems like a common practice now, but with no internet, there was no Air BnB, and the home rental game was much different. Most people didn't think about the overall experience of the renter or their guests. Jane found it most fortuitous, and she was deeply immersed in what was likely her fifth reading of *Little Women*, a book she related to in ways that readers of this, who have read that as well, can fully imagine. Jane Bennet and Meg March do bear a striking resemblance to each other in temperament while many a person would mistake Lizzy for Jo and vice-versa. They spoke about all of this for an hour, and it was delightful. Before he left for bed around six in the morning, as the sun had not just risen yet but with the sky turning orange, he'd refilled her water glass and given her some more painkillers.

When they met again, four hours later for brunch in bed, it could be argued that they were already in love. Since it isn't their story and because love at fourth sight over bagels and strawberries may seem like the stuff of childhood tales, we will leave them alone there to eat and talk and be in love or not in love depending on the reader's own sensibilities and beliefs about such things.

As mentioned, just after noon, Lizzy marched from Longbourn to Netherfield. She arrived around 12:30, just as Darcy, who hadn't drunk too much the night before and who had been up since six, having taken a long hike himself along the river, showered, shaved, breakfasted, and read the local Hartford paper, which the landlord had delivered each day as a courtesy, and Caroline, who had way too much to drink the night before, and who'd been up for less time than Lizzy had been walking, were sitting down to have his second meal of the day and her first. Lizzy rang the bell and was greeted by Mr. Darcy, who had been followed by Caroline because she wanted to see who it was.

The eldest Darcy and the second eldest Bennet stood in the foyer making pleasantries while the middle Bingley stood a few feet away with her arms crossed and a sour look on her face. Darcy held out his arm for Lizzy to use as balance as she took off her muddy boots, explaining that she walked in hopes of walking home with her sister only to be informed of Jane's predicament and that she would not be walking home at all.

Darcy gave Lizzy directions to the room where her sister was convalescing and chatting with Bingley. Caroline said something about the frazzled state of Lizzy's hair and muddy boots while Lizzy was still in earshot but walking away. It was intended to be a snarky joke, and it was intended for Lizzy to hear, which she did. However, confoundedly, she heard Darcy's retort about how he thought she glowed from the vigor of the walk and found the concern for her sister to be genuine and heartwarming. He mentioned that, in a million years, he would not describe Ms. Bennet as frazzled.

Caroline took the compliment as a personal attack against her, even though it was no such thing. She was unwilling to admit her own complicated feelings for her brother's best friend, so she sharpened her insult knives and found ways to make the grown-up equivalent of

"Darcy and Lizzy, sitting in a tree, K.I.S.S.I.N.G" over and over, trying to make him uncomfortable. If readers think that doesn't sound very grown up at all, they would find no argument here.

Eventually, after Lizzy was sure Jane could make it home, Mr. Bingley carried her down the stairs and directly into his vehicle. Darcy followed them out and held the door open as Lizzy stood over her sister in the back seat, getting her situated. He closed the door for Jane, walked around to the other side, and opened the passenger door for Lizzy while wishing her sister a speedy recovery. Lizzy, not sure how to take any of it, thanked him for his kindness and well wishes. We shall leave it up to readers to decide if they stared into each other's eyes for as long as possible as the car pulled away.

More will assuredly come from this moment, but we shall leave them both to wallow in their own confusion and consternation. We promised a guest was about to arrive, and the calendar page would turn. The person in question is tangentially connected to Darcy and will accidentally inspire Mary to do something bold. Let's let October fall away. Get a hat and scarf; it is cold in Connecticut this time of year.

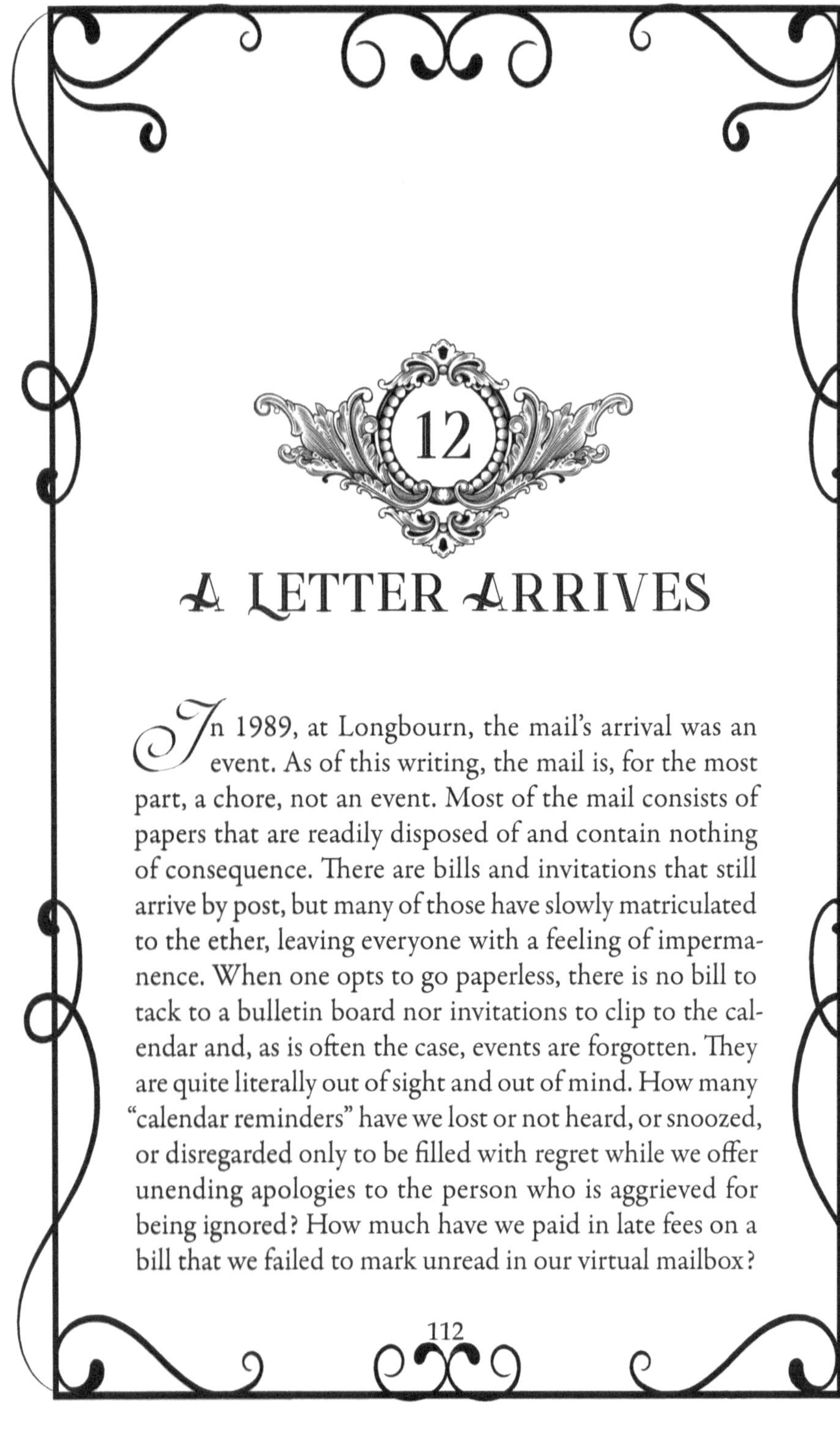

12

A LETTER ARRIVES

In 1989, at Longbourn, the mail's arrival was an event. As of this writing, the mail is, for the most part, a chore, not an event. Most of the mail consists of papers that are readily disposed of and contain nothing of consequence. There are bills and invitations that still arrive by post, but many of those have slowly matriculated to the ether, leaving everyone with a feeling of impermanence. When one opts to go paperless, there is no bill to tack to a bulletin board nor invitations to clip to the calendar and, as is often the case, events are forgotten. They are quite literally out of sight and out of mind. How many "calendar reminders" have we lost or not heard, or snoozed, or disregarded only to be filled with regret while we offer unending apologies to the person who is aggrieved for being ignored? How much have we paid in late fees on a bill that we failed to mark unread in our virtual mailbox?

While, as we have seen, in 1989, phones were readily available, they were not inexpensive. There was no universal plan. There were no fixed prices. A short, three-minute phone call from one town to the other could, depending on the day of the week or the time of day, as evenings and weekends were cheaper, cost around $1.00. In general, in that part of the United States at that time in history, a ten-minute long-distance phone call cost, on average, around $2.50. Long distance is a misnomer here too because sometimes a different town or county could be seen across the street but would be considered long distance while a home that was 15 miles away and in the right township was considered a local call. If it seems capricious now, it was downright infuriating then.

So, back to the mythical ten-minute long-distance call that may or may not be mere yards away. Considering that by the time people got warmed up and asked all the pleasantries about the kids and the grandparents, and the work and nonsense, that $2.50 would be used up long before anyone could get to the point of the call. If one was willing to make phone calls willy-nilly and spend money like it was grown on trees, which yes, technically, paper money is made from trees, there was still a chance that the person who was intended for the call didn't get the message because the receiver of the call failed to remember to pass the message along, or had sloppy hand-writing, or wrote it down incorrectly, or wrote it down correctly, but didn't get the message to the person on time, or a thousand other things that can go wrong on a phone call. Most readers now can't even imagine someone else answering their phone. Phones are individualized. Not so in 1989. How many colds were shared by sick mouths pressed against a communal receiver? More than we can count, that is for sure, Dear Reader.

Let's not even get started about the issues with missed messages and eavesdropping that came with party lines, which, in 1989, still existed as they were not totally eliminated from the United States until 1991. A party line isn't a party at all, but a group of people who share the same phone line because... well, there is really no good reason except that Doris Day and Rock Hudson made *Pillow Talk* with a party line as the premise. That was totally absurd but good fun. So, there is that. Because Longbourn was a home with seven residents and a business with several employees, Mr. Bennet paid extra to have a dedicated private line, and he instructed his children that if they answered the phone during the day, they were to answer it by saying "Longbourn, how may I help you?" instead of "Hello" or the more jaunty "Ahoy!" as Mr. Bell would have preferred upon the invention of the device. We can report that "Ahoy!" was only uttered one time by one of the girls after she learned what she thought was this fun fact. It was her mother calling, and after a long chastisement about foolishness and appearances, no one ever answered the phone at Longbourn by shouting "Ahoy!" ever again. All apologies to Mr. Bell and his ancestors.

In 1989, postage stamps in the United States were only 25 cents, and the cost of a few sheets of paper and an envelope were less than a penny each, making writing letters incredibly cost effective. Physical mail was brought by a government official, who could not tamper with it under penalty of law. The carrier would, in rain or sleet or snow or hail, bring a letter from one side of the country, to the other, including Alaska and Hawai'i. As of this writing, the cost of a postage stamp is 73 cents. We ask readers to imagine giving anyone 73 cents to take a letter from wherever it is they live to any on the other side of town, let alone the other side of the country, and expecting them to do it. We also wonder if readers have 73 cents lying around, or if they would use an app to send the money should they find someone who was not a federal employee to take said letter to its intended destination. For either price, 25 or 73 cents, it was not only a bargain but a miracle.

It may seem like a long digression about the mail in a story that wasn't sold as a brief history of the US Postal Service, but the mail itself will play a factor several times, and so it is worth mentioning here. Hold on; this part is almost done. Inside the letter could be a quick, one-page note with family updates, or snapshots from a party, or a birthday card, or a draft notice, or a copy of a will, or divorce papers, or letters of incorporation, or a check for the aforementioned phone bill, or a wad of cash, or acceptance into a college. All of it delivered for the same 25 cents with the same care and attention six days a week. Postal delivery employees have Sundays and a smattering of Federal Holidays off. If that doesn't seem like a lot of time off, well, it isn't, and all of that for 25 cents per letter, less for a postcard and more for a slightly bigger package, but still. We shall not comment further on the choice of the Christian Sabbath for the day of rest for the postal service. Everyone has opinions; feel free to reflect.

Understandably then, each day, just after those at Longbourn finished their lunch, when the mail finally arrived, was like a surprise party. Those members of the Bennet clan who were home tore directly into the letter or package. Inside the letter or package, the receiver of the epistolary tidings could discover big news, or sad news, or family gossip, which could be both. Different members of the family subscribed to multiple magazines, and they would try to patiently spread the reading of them out over days and weeks as they waited for the next arrival, but they almost always closed the back cover on the same day it arrived, and then they passed it on to a family member who tore through it with equal rapidity. Mary, who did most of her magazine reading secondhand or at the library, received monthly packages from book and music clubs.

So, it was the case on that particular November day at Longbourn, a letter from Maine that would create some chaos in the family Bennet, caused a brief, but not remotely difficult to fix, rift between Lizzy and Charlotte and gave Mary some hope she didn't know she could ever expect. The letter was addressed to "Mr. Bennet of Longbourn." Above the return address read "Rev. W. Collins."

Mr. Bennet was not home on that particular day after that specific lunch. He was at the monthly Friends of the Meryton Library meeting. On those days, he worked for a few hours in the morning and then took the rest of the day off, leaving the farm business to his foreman or one of his daughters. The meeting itself was not held during lunch, but many of the Friends went to the diner afterward and had lunch. It was one of the few social events Mr. Bennet attended. While Mrs. Bennet would have preferred he come straight home so she could find out any of the gossip he may have picked up at the Friends meeting, she understood he enjoyed this monthly foray into town followed by a slow, leisurely stroll home while his food digested, and he puffed on his pipe. Farmers, like postal workers, often find themselves working six days per week, so taking three-quarters of a day off once a month was Mr. Bennet's equivalent of a holiday. We can all agree that one should visit the library at least once a month as it always feels like a holiday.

Mrs. Bennet saw the letter and immediately began to panic. Even though her husband was sanguine about their financial status, Mrs. Bennet was quite gloomy in its regard. While she'd never actually met Mr. Collins the elder, nor the younger newly ordained Reverend William Collins, she often called him "That awful Mr. Collins" or something similar as we've already seen in these pages. She was sure his life's goal was to take Longbourn from them, which would, in turn, cause her husband to have a heart attack and die on the spot, leaving her and her children on the street. It would not be wrong to say that she had many nightmares that consisted of her and Lydia panhandling on the streets of New York. Why not Meryton and why only Lydia? We shall leave it to each reader to decide.

By the time Mr. Bennet came into the house, removed his boots by the door, and walked into his library, his wife was coming through the door behind him. He looked at the high-backed chair in the corner to see Mary sitting there. She was reading Howard Zinn's *A People's History of The United States*. The book was a tome. It had been published at the beginning of the decade, and Mr. Bennet found it remarkable.

He hoped to have all five of his children read it eventually, and he had succeeded in having his eldest three begin the task. He gave each of them their own laminated bookmark designed with a specific color. The rule was that the book was never to leave the library. Any of them could come in and read it if the door was open. They were not to move the bookmark of the other girl. These were easy rules to follow for the eldest three who'd started the task. Jane's purple bookmark was still on the first page of the only chapter in the book that had the word slavery in the title. It wasn't, she knew, the only chapter about the subject, but she cried her way through the first eight chapters, and she never came back to it. It wasn't that she didn't want to know; it was that she just couldn't read about it. Please don't judge her.

Lizzy's red bookmark was placed just before Zinn moved into the 20th century. Lizzy, as a product of the 20th century, wanted to read it, but once she'd gone off to college, she was underwater reading those books. Her general education courses were introductory, but as is often the case, introductory courses cover the most material. Lizzy wanted to learn it all. As she moved into her subjects of study, her reading load only increased. She didn't pick subjects to study that came with thin syllabi.

Lydia's green bookmark sat next to Kitty's yellow bookmark, unmoved and untouched in between the first and second pages. Neither of them had touched the book enough to even read the title page, but keeping them between the cover and the title page only meant they would fall easily.

Mary was, at that moment when her mother chased her father into the library, just beginning a chapter that made reference to a Langston Hughes poem. It was, as she suspected, addressing racial strife in the mid-twentieth century. As she had done with the previous chapter that featured some events that occurred during her father's life, or her aunt's life, she was writing down questions in her notebook. She trusted Zinn, but since his book was a people's history, she thought it wise to ask the people she knew who had lived said history. Robust conversations ensued as we can imagine.

Mary placed her black bookmark in place and jotted down which paragraph she'd finished up in her notebook. She closed the book silently and looked to her father for advice as to what she should do. He motioned his open hand down. She took that to mean he wished her to just sit tight and so she did. She slid her pencil into her hair and rested her hands on the book on her lap. She became part of the furniture.

Mrs. Bennet missed all of this as she was looking down at the letter in her shaking hands and mumbling. She was not the most eloquent speaker on good days, but she rarely failed to get her point across. Just like this book, Mrs. Bennet used 30 words when 10 would do, but hopefully, just like this book, she eventually made her intentions clear. However, when she was frazzled, her nervous tendencies took over, and she struggled to make herself be known with any semblance of clarity.

Mr. Bennet, as we've established, loved his wife very much, and while he liked to tease, he was never mean. He sensed that she would not respond well to a good-hearted teasing. He said in a calm, tender way, "What is it, Dear?"

Her bottom lip trembled, and she looked up at him with tears threatening to spill forth from her big eyes. "Co... Col... Collins," she stuttered. She held out the letter. It was badly wrinkled from her constant handling, but it was not, which may come to the shock of some readers, opened. Mrs. Bennet was a lot of things, and a snoop was certainly one of them, but she was not a violator of her husband's privacy. She may fly into the library regardless if the door was opened or closed, and she may listen attentively next to doors that were open just a crack because if the people in the room didn't want to be heard, they would certainly go somewhere else, but she would never open a drawer or rifle through the piles of papers he had strewn about. The letter was not addressed to her, and so it remained wrinkled and handled with sweaty, nervous hands, but it was sealed. Had Reverend Collins added her name to the envelope following an ampersand, she would have torn it open and dropped the rest of the mail on the floor.

He took it from her shaking hand while smiling brightly at her. "Shall we read it together?" He motioned to his side of the desk, inviting her to come stand next to him.

She shook her head violently. "You read it to me."

"Yes. Excellent idea. Shall we sit?" He started to sit but didn't commit to it until she did the same. Once she plopped down in the chair as though her legs gave out, he pulled out his letter opener and sliced through the envelope. He pulled out one sheet of paper folded in thirds. He opened it and looked down and smiled. "You see, it's just a personal letter. Nothing to worry about." He showed her that it was, in fact, a letter written in a tight script slanted to the left and smeared in several places indicating it was written by Reverend Collins' own hand. It was only a few paragraphs long, and since the advent of the typewriter, letters with bad news are much longer and not written by hand.

"Yes, well..." Mrs. Bennet exhaled. "Read it still." She dropped her head and looked down at her hands as though she was unwilling to see the words coming at her, still sure the news would be bad, and she and Lydia, and possibly the rest of the family, would be out on the street.

"Of course." He cleared his throat and looked up at his middle daughter, who had managed to keep perfectly still and silent as was her way. She was keenly interested in the contents of the letter as well, but she held her countenance as still as the rest of her body. He smiled at her. She smiled and nodded one small, tight nod in return.

"Don't read it first," Mrs. Bennet said. "Read it live." Of course, Dear Reader, all reading done aloud or silently is done live. Mrs. Bennet meant that she wanted him to experience it at the same time as she did without the advantage of a quick pre-read. She mistook his silent look to Mary as said perusal. He understood this in a way that only a person who spent that many years with her could have known. Mary understood it as well.

He cleared his throat again and he read, "Dearest Uncle Bennet." We must apologize and interject here to be clear that Mr. Bennet was not Reverend Collins' uncle in the traditional sense. He is an uncle in the way that close friends feel they are uncles or aunts to the children of other close friends. Mr. Bennet was indeed very close to Reverend Collins' father, but he was not at this point, close to the Reverend at all. However, his father, whenever he spoke of Mr. Bennet to a young William Collins, prefaced it with "Your Uncle Bennet..." Thus, Mary was not his cousin in the way that cousins are normally considered, although she would, as would the rest of the Bennet sisters, think of him as cousin after they finally met him. They shared no blood. Please keep that in mind.

Let's start over, shall we?

Mr. Bennet read, "Dearest Uncle Bennet, I hope this letter finds you well. I wish that you and the delicate creatures in your care are doing well and flourishing. Upon our last communication, you reminded me that lovely Jane and fierce Elizabeth were thriving at college. I hope that they both are comporting themselves well and representing the Bennet name well while out in the world. Attending college is an excellent opportunity for women of a certain age to catch the eye of a suitor. I am sure that they will each find a husband who will respect their intellect as well as their beauty." This is why it is so important to remember they are not related.

Mrs. Bennet looked up and interrupted her husband with a phrase that no one before or after ever uttered about Reverend Collins. "I totally agree with him. He seems quite sensible, doesn't he?"

Mary dug her fingernails into her palms and held her breath. She could forgive Reverend Collins for his small-minded, accidentally sexist remarks because he was an unmarried wealthy man, who was raised by a single man, from a fishing town in Maine who chose to become ordained. All of those experiences came pre-loaded with misogyny. He could learn under the right circumstances, and when we meet him, we shall see he is both malleable and a chameleon. She could not, though, forgive her mother, a woman who had a successful sister and who had five daughters, for being the biggest misogynist she knew. Still, she wanted to hear the rest of the letter, so she remained still and quiet.

Mr. Bennet, who did not agree with the Reverend about his daughters' need to catch the eyes of suitors while at college, nor did he care one way or the other if they married or not so long as they were well educated and, if not happy, not miserable, which was, let's face it, his wish for Mary and Kitty. He didn't expect either of them to ever be happy. However, he knew that saying that to his wife at that moment when her anxiety seemed to be coming down wouldn't help. So he said, "If you say so, Wife."

"I do say so, Husband. Now please continue." She waved her hand at him as though he was the one who stopped the recitation on his own.

He cleared his throat again and continued, "I sincerely hope that your next three girls will follow in their elder sisters' footsteps and become exemplary young women. I know that under the guidance and tutelage of Mrs. Bennet, they are all in excellent and caring hands. Should I ever be granted by God the privilege of having a daughter, I would seek out no wiser counsel than Mrs. Bennet to guide the hands of myself and my wife."

Dear Reader, we must interject again here. Reverend Collins had, at that point, never met any of the Bennet women in real life. He did not attend the Bennet's nuptials, and his only knowledge of any of them was what was relayed in letters from Mr. Bennet. Mr. Bennet, of course, went to Maine for the funeral of his friend and benefactor, and that was the first time he and William Collins ever met in real life. Since then, they each wrote one letter to the other on alternating months, so that 12 communications per year were exchanged. He and Mr. Bennet met once a year on the weekend after Thanksgiving, a time of rest for both men, in Boston, to discuss the financial status of Longbourn and the terms of the land contract and to exchange stories about the man they both loved.

Mrs. Bennet found herself nodding along as she listened, and she imagined all of the wonderful advice she could impart upon future generations of Collinses. Her feelings on the future of the Collins line will change quite violently as this tale progresses. She had a volatile, emotional nature, but those among us who are calm at all times can throw the first stone or become a Buddhist monk.

We now return to Mr. Bennet and shall let him finish up without further interruption. "As you know, Uncle, I've recently taken my orders. While I hoped to find a small parish somewhere to find my voice and help a flock, I have been blessed to have been hired as a spiritual advisor to the Rosings Institute, a non-profit founded by the late British Lord Lewis de Bourgh, situated in Kent County, very near Providence. My employer and benefactor, the regal Lady Catherine de Bourgh, an American who has wedded into the title of Lady, but upon meeting her, I can attest that no person has ever deserved that title more, has bequeathed to me a lovely home as part of the employment. While most of my things have been moved into storage at Hunsford, which is the name of my beautiful home, I've been told that there were a few minor alterations that needed to be done before I could move in properly in the new year.

"So, Uncle, while I can remain here at my father's home comfortably for some time, as I have no intention of selling it and I will eventually let it via a real estate broker to some worthy family, I thought, instead of our yearly meeting in Boston, I would come to Longbourn for an extended stay, at which time I could finally meet your perfect family and get to know them even better than I feel as I already do. I have spent so much time alone with men at seminary that I am desperate to bask in the feminine glow that Longbourn must surely have. As I shall be working for Lady Catherine de Bourgh, it will be her one and only child, a woman of great beauty but infirm constitution, a Lady Ann de Bourgh, with whom I shall be in constant communication and proximity as she heads the spiritual outreach program of Rosings. In order not to feel like an oaf, I feel as though I must learn how to be around and interact with the gentler sex. I could think of no better place to learn than Longbourn.

"I am also keen to see the property as I've only ever envisioned it in my mind. I long to smell the crisp Connecticut air and touch the fertile soil that brings food and sustenance not only to your family but to those around New England. I would also like to see what you have in mind for the long-term health of the property that will finally end our business partnership and leave us with nothing but my favorite kind of ship, friendship.

"I will plan to arrive the Wednesday before the holiday, and I shall leave for my new home shortly after we ring in the new decade together. Sincerely yours, Reverend W. Collins."

Dear Reader, if it sounds as though Reverend Collins invited himself without waiting for permission to come, that is exactly what happened. Unable to say no, due to the precarious position with the good Reverend Collins, Mr. Bennet set the letter down. He pulled out his pipe and lit it.

Mrs. Bennet was up and pacing the room, muttering to herself about what it could all mean. Forgotten was all the praise the reverend heaped up on her and her girls. She only heard a threat. He was coming to look at Longbourn, Mrs. Bennet was sure, and that upon seeing the state of things, he would sell it out from under them. "That blasted Collins" was said no fewer than 35 times in less than five minutes.

Mr. Bennet watched his wife pace and let her talk without interruption. After she said all she could on the

matter, she ran out of the room to do whatever she felt she had to do to prepare for a man, whom she now envisioned as her executioner, to arrive in a few weeks. Mr. Bennet looked up at Mary, who sat stone-still, waiting for her father's reaction to guide her. He smiled and nodded. He wasn't defeated so much as resigned. "Guess we're having company."

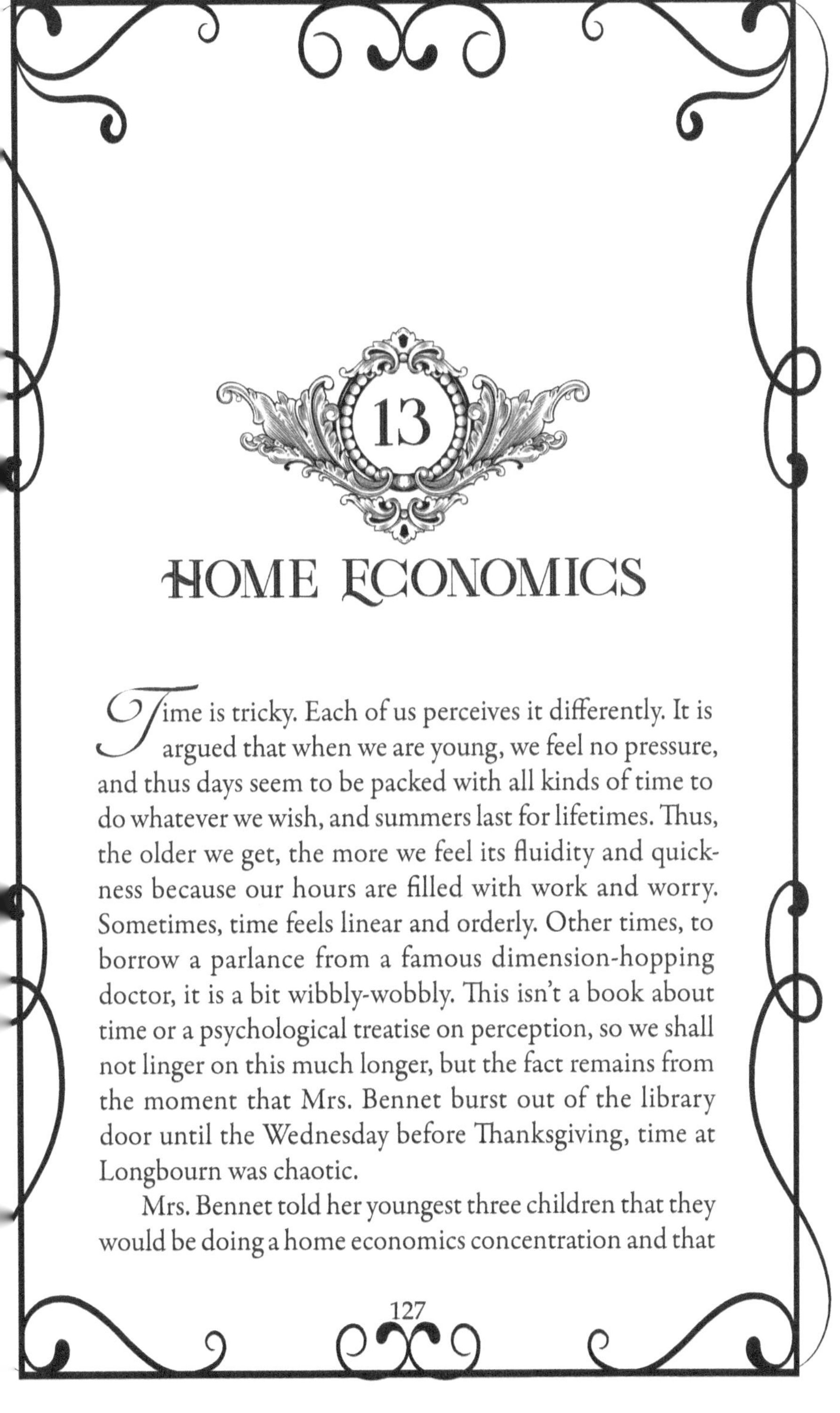

13

HOME ECONOMICS

*T*ime is tricky. Each of us perceives it differently. It is argued that when we are young, we feel no pressure, and thus days seem to be packed with all kinds of time to do whatever we wish, and summers last for lifetimes. Thus, the older we get, the more we feel its fluidity and quickness because our hours are filled with work and worry. Sometimes, time feels linear and orderly. Other times, to borrow a parlance from a famous dimension-hopping doctor, it is a bit wibbly-wobbly. This isn't a book about time or a psychological treatise on perception, so we shall not linger on this much longer, but the fact remains from the moment that Mrs. Bennet burst out of the library door until the Wednesday before Thanksgiving, time at Longbourn was chaotic.

Mrs. Bennet told her youngest three children that they would be doing a home economics concentration and that the rest of school would be canceled until the new year. Lydia was thrilled at this news. Other than music, she cared little for formal education. Kitty said nothing and did what she was told. Mary and her mother had words about this. Loud, passionate words. It was possible that the Lucases might have heard them from their place. Lizzy got involved. Aunt Phillips was consulted. Mr. Bennet closed the library door. Jane made peace.

The resolution was that Mary would continue to do her regular school work as well as work at the law office under the condition that she did what she was asked while in the house. Of course, this meant she had to decide when she did her schoolwork. If she left early in the morning for the library or the law office, that meant she would be up all night Cinderellaing; however, if she prepared to do the housework early in the day, after she and her father finished the paper and their morning conversation, because no matter how much Mrs. Bennet wanted done, she was not waking up at that ungodly hour, then Mary worried that she wouldn't get out of the house to do the other work she needed to do.

Ultimately, she decided to split it up. On days she had to work at the law office, which as part of the Jane Bennet accords was a valid reason to stop what she was doing in the house and leave, she would stay home until she was required to shower and head to town. She would stay behind and work on school in the closed office, or if the library was open late, she would go there. On days she didn't have to work at the law office, she would skip out right after her morning chat and head to the law office where she would work until they opened and then go to the library until dinnertime. She would then put in several hours of labor after that. Those nights often ended with Mary getting an earful from Lydia, after she woke her up when she finally climbed into bed in their shared bedroom, long after Lydia and Kitty, who had put in full days of just manual labor, passed out. Eventually, she took to sleeping on a couch in the living room with the cat to keep the peace.

The home economics concentration curriculum had three parts: cleaning, cooking, and creation. While she would later sign off on this time as actual school work for graduation, and to be fair, it was mostly skills that high school students learned in home economics courses, it was obviously self-serving and a way for Mrs. Bennet to keep herself from crawling out of her skin. As Mr. Bennet can attest, during the chaotic time leading up to Reverend Collin's arrival, Mrs. Bennet ground her teeth every single night. Her nerves and he were, as he said, well acquainted. He insisted she see the dentist to be fitted for some kind of protective device as he was both worried that she would crack a molar and that he would never sleep again. Sometimes caring for others can be selfish and that is OK.

As part of the cleaning lesson, she demanded that every single piece of furniture be moved, every speck of dirt be picked up, and every dust bunny captured and exterminated. The living space at Longbourn was never a dusty, dirty place. However, it was a house on a farm in the country. Dust happens. Dirt is tracked in regardless of when people remove boots, which at Longbourn was always at the door. There was a lot to do and to be done again and again. The process happened every three days until the guest's arrival. Lydia tried to explain that really, the deep clean only needed to happen once, the day before he arrived, but Mrs. Bennet would have none of it.

Additionally, every scrape on a floorboard or stain on a carpet needed tending. This was a much bigger task. Most of this fell to Mary as her irregular hours afforded her the chance to apply stain or carpet cleaner while the rest of the house was relatively quiet, and her blockade of a walking path wasn't as cumbersome to the rest of the daily activities. By the time Reverend Collins arrived, Longbourn shone. While he was there, the cleaning curriculum was severely truncated with a weekly flurry of brooms and dusters every Saturday morning, which was an all-hands-on-deck situation, including Jane and Lizzy, that took place while Mr. Bennet took the Reverend on a walking tour of the property.

The cooking portion of the curriculum was a crash course in how to make it seem as though the Bennets had big family dinners every day that rivaled what would be the big Thanksgiving dinner. In reality, while the Bennets did try to have meals together most nights, it wasn't always possible, and so dinners were generally big pasta dishes with salads and bread or some kind of giant crockpot dish that could cook and simmer all day. Quick and easy meals to make in bulk that would last for an hour or five as people made their way home and through the kitchen. Feeding seven people is no joke.

So, for the several weeks leading up to the arrival, Mrs. Bennet and her three youngest daughters learned how to make bread from scratch, and how to cook all kinds of fauna while dressing it with all kinds of flora. Mr. Bennet would comment shortly after Reverend Collins' departure that he couldn't tell if the tense muscles between his shoulder blades, the pounding headache in his temples, or his waistline were more pleased to see him go. Obviously, the cooking portion was a huge success. Mary found a lot of pleasure in making bread. It was something she could do either early in the morning or late at night. She slipped on her headphones and played her Walkman while pounding dough into submission. Because she found so much joy there, the Bennets enjoyed freshly made bread from their own kitchen until Mary moved out.

The creation aspect of the curriculum had two subsections. Subsection one involved the creation of new coverings for anything that couldn't be saved with a good buff and clean. The piece of furniture in most need of a covering was the formal dining room table. The formal dining room table, which, as we know, had been the main desk for the Bennet girl's schooling was, as one would expect, a mess. It had seen art projects and penmanship practice, back when people learned how to write longhand, in script, and were graded not just on the ability to write the letters and words correctly but neatly and legibly.

Thus, it was stained with paint and markers, and the scratches went deep. Rings from glasses left unattended were everywhere. Aesthetically, it was unappealing. Structurally, it was sound. It was made of oak. It was heavy. It took several Bennets to move. No one ever bumped the table and saw it slide across the floor. This was good because had that happened, there would have been a lot of fights when one of them was writing an essay at one end of the table while another was drumming on the other end or nervously bouncing a knee and occasionally hitting the underside of the table. Instead, the writing went on smoothly, the drumming continued, the knee was bruised, and no cross words were exchanged. Well, none about that anyway. In a room full of sisters and an overbearing mother, cross words were exchanged freely and frequently.

Lydia was best suited for the creation of the new table and furniture coverings because her nimble fingers and long arms afforded her the ability to handle yards and yards of material and work it through the sewing machine. She handed the completed coverings to Kitty, who was tasked with hand-sewing flair on the ruffles. Mrs. Bennet decided she was best suited for the task because she offered no objections.

Part two of the creation lesson involved making the house look less "lived in." Readers may assume all the above-mentioned things would do just that, and readers would be correct, but Mrs. Bennet would disagree and not just out of spite. She didn't like to disagree all the time, just most of the time. No, she felt that the house looked like a home where seven people who barely tolerated each other lived, which was, of course, accurate on most days, but she wanted to create an image of what she thought of as a "Storybook Family."

Mary was keen to point out those families don't exist in storybooks. That phrase "families that only exist in storybooks" is, on its face, a lie. Storybooks are filled with matricide and infanticide and gaslighting, and some very troubling racist and sexist stereotypes. Mrs. Bennet was nonplussed by this commentary. Yes, Dear Reader, we are aware that nonplussed means both shaken and untroubled, and thus, using it to describe someone thusly without extra commentary seems rancorous. Rest assured, there is no spite involved here. Mrs. Bennet was shaken by her middle child's commentary as she hadn't ever spent that kind of time thinking deeply about how mothers were depicted in those stories. She'd always seen herself as the princess. However, after a quick shake of her head, she brushed off the commentary of her middle child who was, well, Mary, and thus, she was untroubled and set Mary on her task of sorting through the boxes of photos to start framing their family history and hanging them up on the recently cleaned and barren walls.

To make the illusion really sing, she insisted that Mary go thrift shopping to find "old looking but not ratty" frames. She insisted that each girl have an equal number of photos hanging on the wall and that there be at least four full-family photos and at least three of just Mr. and Mrs. Bennet in addition to their wedding photo. Since Mrs. Bennet wasn't going to actually put the new furniture coverings on until the morning of Reverend Collin's arrival, Mary was able to set up shop on the big table. She began by touching every single picture and making piles. She made seven. One was for any photo that featured more than one member of the family, and the others were for each of the Bennet women individually. There were, unsurprisingly, no photos of Mr. Bennet by himself. Candid snapshots of the bookish, land-loving family outcast were not plentiful during his childhood in Maine, and he didn't bring any of his official school pictures with him when he moved down. We can report that there was a leak in the attic of his family home shortly after he left. His family didn't hang pictures on the walls either, and those pictures were stored in the same fashion. They were thrown haphazardly in a cardboard box, and they didn't survive. The first known, non-governmental issued picture of record that anyone can remember still hangs in the Meryton Library depicting the day he met a young Miss Connecticut for the first time.

Unsurprisingly, to Mary, or to the readers who've made it this far and met the Bennet family, the biggest pile was the photos of more than one of them. There were, after all, a lot of bodies and little space. Someone was always entering into someone else's orbit. We can't confirm that the Bennets of Longbourn invented the concept of photobombing, but even photos that were supposed to be of just one of them often ended with a hand or foot or a receding head in the corner of the picture.

For readers of a certain age, we shall add a brief explanation here which will be a jog down memory lane for those of a different age. All the Bennet family pictures were taken before digital photography, the ubiquity of phones with cameras, and online photo alterations at little to no cost. Now, when someone has a photo taken, that really means somewhere between 10 and 500 pictures are taken with a quick push of a pixilated image of a button on a smartphone screen, thus allowing the photographer the opportunity to riffle through all the images and cut, edit, and find the perfect shot where everyone's face is glowing, and no one is blinking, and that annoying truck resting in the background can be erased. It is a rusty mess after all. We are sure we told someone to move it. The boxes through which Mary sorted were full of pictures that would be deleted without a second glance. Mary found hundreds of photos that featured a blinking Bennet, the profile of a sister passing through the open door, or their father walking by the window outside at the moment the shutter closed. Thus, the pile was large as it featured all these accidental group shots as well as the planned and candid photos taken of more than one of them.

The next largest pile was of Mrs. Bennet; she *was* a local celebrity after all. She couldn't help it if people used to take her picture all the time. The next largest pile, which was almost the same size as their mother's, was filled with pictures of Lydia. Generally, the youngest child is forgotten, and photos are lost, but Mrs. Bennet liked Lydia best, so there you have it. Jane and Lizzy were nearly equal, but the edge did go to Jane, who was, as we all know, extremely photogenic. Shockingly, the smallest pile was not reserved for Mary as readers would have expected. It was what Mary was expecting. Kitty featured the most in all pictures total, but there were fewer than 20 total pictures of just Kitty and the majority of those were while she was in a crib or on the pitch.

In an effort to make all things equal, Mary made each of her sisters get a shot of themselves in the reading chair in the library. She had Kitty take hers. Even Mary thought it turned out pretty good because she wasn't looking at the camera but at her book. She opted to put those in new frames that she bought with her own money. She asked Charlotte to come over and take a new family photo as well. It took the whole roll of 24 to get one where all 7 of them were looking in the same direction and where all of them were almost smiling and none of them were scowling. So, it was then, that by the time the Reverend arrived, the Bennet girls earned straight A's in Home Economics until the end of time.

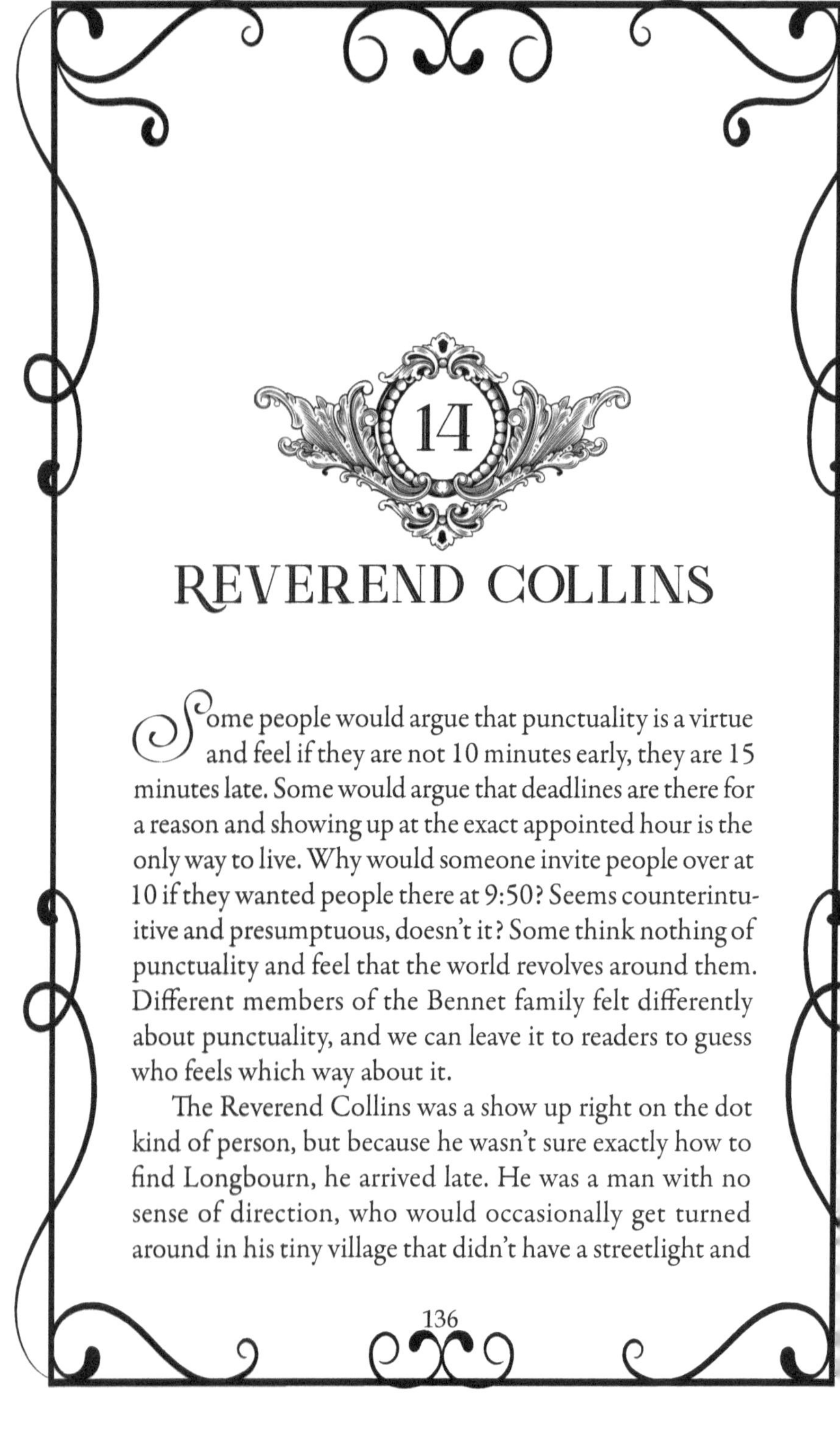

14

REVEREND COLLINS

Some people would argue that punctuality is a virtue and feel if they are not 10 minutes early, they are 15 minutes late. Some would argue that deadlines are there for a reason and showing up at the exact appointed hour is the only way to live. Why would someone invite people over at 10 if they wanted people there at 9:50? Seems counterintuitive and presumptuous, doesn't it? Some think nothing of punctuality and feel that the world revolves around them. Different members of the Bennet family felt differently about punctuality, and we can leave it to readers to guess who feels which way about it.

The Reverend Collins was a show up right on the dot kind of person, but because he wasn't sure exactly how to find Longbourn, he arrived late. He was a man with no sense of direction, who would occasionally get turned around in his tiny village that didn't have a streetlight and children as young as five walked themselves to and from school every single day. He was also pretty worthless when it came to reading maps. While maps always are written with north at the top and south at the bottom, if one can't find north in the world, the map is just art.

The only reason he could make it to his yearly meeting with Mr. Bennet was that he paid a driver to take him to the Portland Airport in Maine where he boarded a bus that dropped him off in Boston where Mr. Bennet waited for him to arrive. Readers of a certain age may be surprised to know that this story takes place in the year when the first commercially available Global Positioning System was on the market, but the Reverend didn't know what that was, nor did anyone, really. It was actively being used by the military, but the public version was heavy, volatile, had a short battery life, was less accurate than asking a drunk guy at a bar for directions at closing time, and cost $3,000. So, while he could have afforded that gadget, he didn't know of its existence. At the time of this writing, we can confirm that Reverend Collins always has his location on his phone, and he has it shared with his wife because sometimes, she has to call him and talk him through the directions because he finds her voice "infinitely more pleasing than the robot that lives inside the phone."

Why didn't he just take public transportation? Didn't we learn that Meryton was easily accessible for commuters? We did, Dear Reader, and he did. The problem is that Longbourn is, for the uninitiated, a bit of what Mary Bennet called, after hearing an R.E.M song of the same name, a "Can't Get There From Here" situation. In fact, we will let readers in on a little secret here. Mary Bennet, in one of the many notebooks she wrote in furiously throughout her life and that she still owns, has her own lyrics to that very song. She changed it up to "Can't Get Away From Here" for reasons that should, at this point in our tale, seem obvious.

We know that the Bennets and the Lucases walked pretty much everywhere, but they followed the walking path along the river. The walking path had a bridge that was excellent for fishing, wishing, or playing Pooh Sticks. Many a young resident of Meryton had, upon a dare or because that person was a daredevil, jumped from the bridge into the river, which was, depending on the time of year, deep enough for such shenanigans as long as the person didn't dive. It was a feet-first situation. The walking path and the bridge made the trek from Longbourn to town safe and easy. It was such an easy path that one needed not even look where one was going. Both Lizzy and Mary often traversed the path while their noses were firmly placed in books.

However, if one were to be dropped at a train station at the edge of Meryton, was bad with maps and directions, and didn't know about the walking path, one would wander around for several hours trying to find the road that had the bridge. To go south to Meryton, one had to drive north a mile or so out of town to cross the bridge and then west a few miles to the country lane that went back south for several more miles until one turned east into the long, unpaved, and bumpy drive that ended at Longbourn proper.

So it was, three hours after his appointed time to arrive, with dinner almost ready to be served on the Wednesday before Thanksgiving, that a totally frazzled and nearly soused Mrs. Bennet answered the door to find Charlotte

Lucas standing shoulder to shoulder with Reverend William Collins. Shocked to see her, frustrated that he was late, even though we can imagine that Mrs. Bennet was one of the people who believed punctuality was for other people, and with a tongue loosened from her third Tom Collins, Mrs. Bennet shouted, "Charlotte, what have you done?" Charlotte had been verbally abused by her best friend's mother before, and she shall be again.

Charlotte Lucas was always adaptable and pleasant in all circumstances, and while she was not as familiar with Mrs. Bennet's nerves as Mr. Bennet or the Bennet girls, she and they were well acquainted. Due to this, instead of responding the way most normal people would respond when delivering a lost clergyman to the tipsy mother of her best friend, Charlotte ignored the question and said with that cherubic smile of hers, "Look who I found! I believe you've been expecting him."

Reverend Collins removed his stocking cap and bowed his head. "Mrs. Bennet, please forgive my tardiness. I became discombobulated upon exiting the train station in Meryton, and after walking from one end of the town to the other several times, the lovely Miss Lucas here overheard me asking for directions from the librarian. I feel that I owe her a debt that can never be repaid now that she has delivered me to your humble abode unscathed and intact."

"Yes, well." Before she could say more, Lizzy appeared behind her mother in the door and saved the day.

"Reverend Collins. Good to finally meet you. Lizzy Bennet." She placed her hand out to the good reverend, who took it in both hands and kissed it.

"It is I who am honored," he said as though he was participating in a different conversation where Lizzy said something about the honor being hers. She did not say that, nor did she feel that way, but as we shall see while we spend time with Reverend Collins, what is being said and what he hears, or thinks is being said, or maybe, more likely, wishes was being said, are rarely the same thing.

Lizzy extracted her hand from his damp palms and surreptitiously wiped it on her pant leg. She turned to her best friend and said in a pleading voice, "Charlotte! Can you please join us for dinner as a thank you for bringing us our long-awaited guest?"

Charlotte, who had nothing pressing as her family was not having guests the following day, as Thanksgiving for the Lucases was a small, intimate family affair that ultimately ended with the four of them walking to Longbourn for dessert, agreed readily. She was always willing to spend time with the Bennets as they were the people whom she loved most outside of her sister and her parents. Acting as spectator as the sisters bickered made her feel like she was living inside an anthropological documentary made just for her. She and Lizzy would often decompress afterward by breaking down all the outrageous things Mrs. Bennet would say or do. Fun was always had at Longbourn, but a slightly drunk and unhinged Mrs. Bennet added a layer of joy she didn't know she needed until she saw it.

In the short time that all of that happened, Mrs. Bennet left the small group huddled around her door and burst into the library to let Mr. Bennet know that "that awful Collins man" had arrived, which, of course, Mr. Bennet already knew, but he stood and kissed her gently on the cheek and thanked her for letting him know. He asked her to please go let the girls know that they could set the table, and he reminded her that he was lucky to call her his wife. He may or may not have patted her on the backside as she exited the library. We shall leave it for each reader to decide if, all things considered, that was a good idea.

Back in the entryway, Lizzy offered to take the Reverend's jacket and shouted for Mary to come and take his bags to the guest room. Yes, that very guest room whose necessity was questioned in the early pages of this very book looks like a good move now. No one wanted to wake up one morning to find the good Reverend splayed out on a couch in public, and there was no way that Mrs. Bennet would want him to sleep on the couch in the office because she would be sure he would rifle through the business documents only to discover … something, she couldn't say for sure, but something he shouldn't know anything about.

Mary appeared and came face-to-face for the first time with Reverend Collins. Considering he was such a larger-than-life presence in their lives, she assumed he would have some sort of physical presence. While he was not as short as she, he was the exact same height as Charlotte, who was marginally taller than Mary. The top of his head stopped at Lizzy's shoulder. Reverend Collins was a wisp of a man. His shoulders were not as broad as Mary's, and while she was short, she was not dainty. He was the first grown man she'd ever met whom she thought she could take in a fight. He would not be the last. Fear not, Dear Reader. Mary Bennet has never, as of this writing, ever been in a fist-fight with anyone, of any gender, regardless of size. His clothes, which already looked like they were purchased in the boys' section, were ill-fitting. The neck of his shirt, which was buttoned up to the top, had room for several fingers to fit between the fabric and his skin. The tie, which was not a clip-on, thank you very much, just happened to be crooked because the shirt was too big.

Other men of Reverend Collins' size, shape, and stature often allow those characteristics to work against them. Not so with Reverend Collins. It is true that some people who are short in stature take up physical space in other ways because they have audacity and confidence. His ratio of stature to confidence has never been rivaled in the history of the world, and that is only because Napoleon wasn't as short as people presume. He allowed his verbosity to fill the space that his body did not. There wasn't any topic about which he wouldn't freely share his opinion. It didn't matter if he had any in-depth knowledge of the subject, as he did with theology in general and Christianity in particular, or if he had a cursory knowledge of the subject, for instance, The Boston Red Sox, or if he had almost no knowledge, for instance, farming, women's studies, directions, the weather, the history of Connecticut, how the United States Army Reserves worked, or a plethora of other things relevant to the residents of Longbourn, he freely shared his opinion and talked, and talked, and talked.

When Mary arrived, Reverend Collins was in the middle of explaining why the librarian was wrong to not give him the exact directions to Longbourn. It was quite a wind-up, and poor Charlotte had already heard it once before, so we will just join when Mary did. To say it was the midway point would assume that there would be an end point or a point at all.

"...and so I explained to her that Mr. Bennet was one of the original patrons of the library, not patron in the sense of a person who uses the library, you see, but a patron in the sense that he gave financially to the library, it's glorious that the word means both things, as one rarely has the chance to use both words in the same sentence, as I've been able to just now, and so I told her that since Mr. Bennet's money actually came from a business relationship with my father, and that I am now the sole heir and legacy holder of my father's vast enterprise, that I was essentially one of the founding patrons of the library, and thus, she should have no reservations about giving me the specific directions to Longbourn as I had the address already, and I knew that the Bennets live there, but she refused to share that information and just kept saying that she could not ethically divulge anything about any patron. I tell you that I was just getting ready to disabuse her of her wrong definition of ethics while also being willing to doff my cap to her, metaphorically obviously, one doesn't doff a stocking cap, at her staunch defense of her own *brand* of ethics when Miss Lucas arrived and introduced herself and said she would be gracious enough to walk me to Longbourn as she knew that the Bennets, who were technically patrons of my family, the Collinses, were expecting me. Of course, she didn't say that part about the patronage; that was a fun aside I wanted to add for context. Context is everything, don't you think, Miss Lizzy?"

Mary coughed as she approached. We will leave it up to each reader to decide if it was to announce her presence or if she was choking on the expelled carbon dioxide or on his actual words. Mary and Harriet were, if not friends, friendly, and no one respected the ethical stances of librarians more than the members of the Bennet family, well, most of the Bennet family, those who thought about such things. "Hello, Reverend, I'm..."

He interrupted, "No, no, no." He waved his hand at her. "Let me guess." He pulled on his non-existent beard in a way that was supposed to mime that he was thinking. "Hmmm. Glasses. Ponytail with pencil. Crease between the eyes. The early signs of crow's feet. Studious, stern, and sturdy. You must be Mary."

Of course, eagle-eyed readers will notice that Lizzy called out for Mary just a few moments before. It could be that Reverend Collins didn't hear it, or it could be that he did, and he was just looking at Mary, describing her, and making it seem as though he knew all about her from her father's letters. Mary, who was not vain then or now, felt no feelings any particular way about his description of her. She appreciated his willingness to use alliteration. She would have gone with something different than stern. She didn't think of herself as stern. There is a difference, she thought, between being excitable and being stern. Still, she gave him points for effort.

"Yes, Mary Bennet. Hello, Reverend. Welcome. Our father has told us much about you." She extended her hand to shake before Lizzy could get her attention and tell her not to do it.

He grasped her hand in both of his damp, sweaty hands and, just as he did with Lizzy, and we can assume with Charlotte Lucas before, planted a too wet for her liking kiss on the back of her hand. "I, too, am delighted."

Mary looked at Lizzy, who was at that point laughing into her hands and over to Charlotte, who was smiling serenely. She unsurreptitiously wiped her hand on her jeans. "Yes, well, may I take your bag and show you to the guest room? Would you like to freshen up before dinner?"

"Freshen up?" He laughed, thinking it was a funny joke. "Men don't freshen up."

"Don't they?" Lizzy asked. The laughing stopped. If this were a movie and the composer had written a silly circus-like score that accompanied Reverend Collins wherever he went, the director would have called for a record scratch here. She wasn't really asking but offering a challenge that he missed. He did hear the question though, and as was his way, he set about answering it.

"Men are rough and unpolished. Women are rubies. They must be..."

Lizzy cut him off. "Rubies? Rubies? Fordyce didn't..."

"Oh, good, you've read him." He cut her off right back. "I brought a copy with me just in case." He patted his messenger bag. "I thought it wise as I would be spending time with young women to have the preeminent scholar on the subject."

Lizzy's hands curled into fists. She set her jaw. She was ready to do battle, but before she could throw the first punch (of course, it would have been a verbal blow; like Mary, Lizzy Bennet wouldn't strike anyone, even when they deserved it, for if she did, Lydia Bennet would have plenty of bruises), Charlotte, who was well acquainted with Lizzy Bennet's nerves as well, was ready to step in and be the diplomat, but she need not bother. It was Mary Bennet who saved the day. She said, "Well then, I look forward to having a robust conversation with you on the text. Do you have an early edition? It is still in the two volumes, or do you have the combined printing? We needn't speak of it today, but I would very much like to discuss it before you leave for Rhode Island. Please, follow me to the guest room. I will show you where you are staying." She turned and walked, expecting him to follow and carry his own bags, which he did.

Mary, who also read Fordyce at Lizzy's insistence, found him less problematic than Lizzy did. She saw it for what it was: a work written by an old man who didn't know anything about women, which was, to be fair, in the late 18th century, not uncommon at all, nor was it uncommon at the time this tale takes place, nor at the time this tale is written. Much to the chagrin of many a person, lots of men who've never spoken to a woman, but *at* a woman, write books, and laws, and all kinds of things also that affect women. It's a whole thing. Not a good thing but a thing nonetheless. Still, Mary thought he did have some interesting ideas about women's education. She thought it was a bit ahead of its time while also very *of* its time. She didn't love the phrase "masculine women" at all, but she was always searching for the truth in anything she read. She thought there was merit in reading things about which she disagreed.

Honestly, the fact that Reverend Collins had a copy with him excited Mary. She genuinely hoped to have a conversation with him about it. It may have been a quick and easy way to get him to stop talking to Lizzy about it at that moment, but she was also truthful about wishing to speak to him. At that point in her life, she only had discussed it with Lizzy and her father. Her sister had very passionate opinions about it and wanted to do nothing but share them with Mary, and her father wanted to know Mary's but refused to give his. While she suspected that Reverend Collins would be more like Lizzy than Father when it came to a conversation about it, she was, despite what people thought of her, hopeful. Pragmatists have hope. They are not pessimists.

Reverend Collins spoke non-stop on the short walk from the front door to the guest room and back to the dining room. He was a man who rarely had anything to say but never let that stop him from using all the words he knew. To that end, we need not spend time listening in. It was a lot of sound and fury signifying nothing. While we wouldn't necessarily call Reverend Collins a fool, he was often foolish. Was he full of good intentions or malicious? Dear Reader, you must decide on your own as this tale unfolds.

However, as we shall soon see, the good Reverend would have plenty to say that was of vital importance to our heroine during the following day's Thanksgiving festivities. So, instead of lingering on too much about the first meeting and what was said or not said, we think it best to give a brief synopsis and get to the main event the following day.

Regardless of what he called it, Reverend Collins did stop off in the bathroom. No need to go into detail, but to an objective observer, he freshened up. Mary waited for him outside the door and then gave him a brief tour of the Longbourn residence. Most people, when given a tour of someone else's home, stand in the open door of the living spaces and peek in without entering. If invited into the room, most people would not sit on anything. They may stand still and look about. Maybe, most people would peer out the window to see the view. That seems reasonable. Most people would absolutely not open books or touch any personal effects. Reverend Collins was not, and to this day, is not, most people.

Eventually, Mary was able to invoke her father's name to get him steered into the dining room before he started opening the dresser. His anxiety to see Mr. Bennet beat his curiosity, and off he went to join the rest of the Bennet family in the dining room. Mary led the introductions which consisted of more wet, sloppy kisses on the back of hands followed by lingering damp hand-holding with Jane, Lydia, and Kitty, whom he called Catherine even though Mary introduced her as Kitty. She didn't correct him, and thus, for the rest of his life, he called her Catherine as he assumed silence was tacit approval. It is something he and a lot of the men previously mentioned thought. For the record, silence is not approval. Silence is silence.

Mr. Bennet, accustomed to the damp handshakes, prepared himself the best he could. He clamped his teeth down on the stem of his pipe and took the shake with the same disdain his daughters felt. We regret to inform readers that no matter how much his manners improved over the years, which were, vast compared to where he began, the damp hands never went away. Some people are cursed to have damp hands, and some people are cursed to shake hands with those people. You know which one is worse, don't you, Dear Reader?

After hands were wiped and compliments were paid on the beautiful look of Longbourn in general and the tablecloth in particular, which made both Mrs. Bennet and Lydia stand a bit straighter, as compliments are compliments regardless of who gives them, the group sat down. Mr. Bennet was at one short end of the table, as was his custom, and Reverend Collins was placed at the other. Lydia, Kitty, and Mrs. Bennet with Mrs. Bennet sitting nearest her guest, while Mary sat across from her followed by Charlotte, Jane, and Lizzy, sitting as closely to her father as possible as they often did so they could whisper to each other under the cover of the din that a room full of people eating often made.

As to not outshine the big meal on the following day, dinner that evening was a simple affair designed to put people at ease and to just get used to spending time with each other. Mr. Bennet conducted the meal conversation as he often did when speaking with Reverend Collins, and so he and Lizzy didn't have the chance to snark with each other, but they would later. The table was big enough that all the prepared food sat on the table in the center. As is the case with large gatherings of the sort, the food was passed around, and each person was responsible for serving him or herself. In other homes around town or in other stories, there may be people who did the serving, but this is not that home, nor that story. It was pasta, salad, and home-made breadsticks. The meal was something Mary wanted to try, and if we judge success by how many times the guest interrupted himself, and others, as they made small talk and tried to get to know each other, by exclaiming how good everything tasted with a mouthful of food, then it was a smash hit.

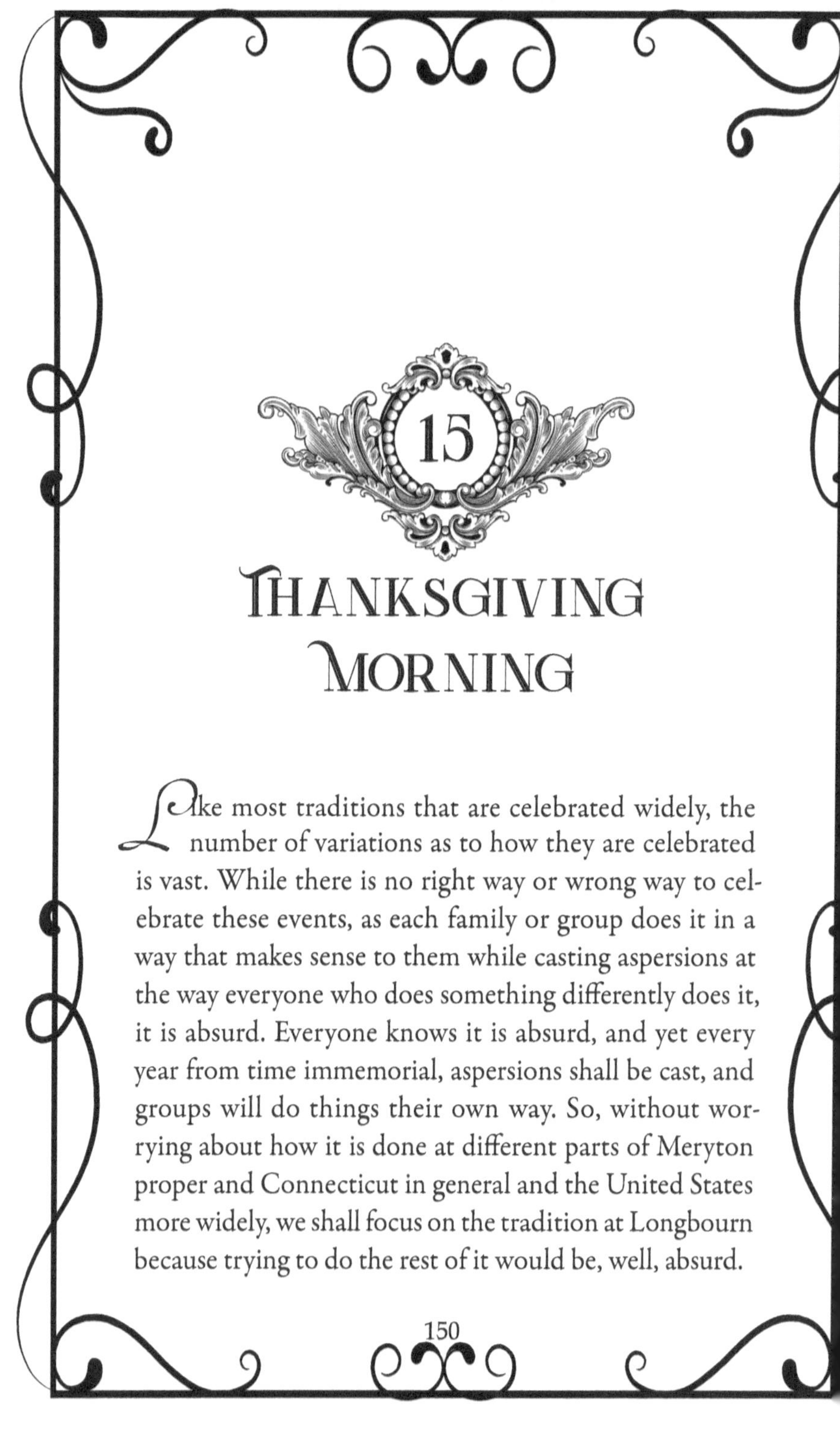

15

Thanksgiving Morning

Like most traditions that are celebrated widely, the number of variations as to how they are celebrated is vast. While there is no right way or wrong way to celebrate these events, as each family or group does it in a way that makes sense to them while casting aspersions at the way everyone who does something differently does it, it is absurd. Everyone knows it is absurd, and yet every year from time immemorial, aspersions shall be cast, and groups will do things their own way. So, without worrying about how it is done at different parts of Meryton proper and Connecticut in general and the United States more widely, we shall focus on the tradition at Longbourn because trying to do the rest of it would be, well, absurd.

Normally, as the tradition went, the Bennets began the day by watching the Macy's Thanksgiving Day Parade on TV while eating pre-packaged donuts, breakfast pastries, and coffee cake off paper plates or napkins or just over a cupped hand, depending on which member of the family it was and what the food was. Does a store-bought chocolate frosted donut need a plate? The answer varies. Arguments were made on both sides. We submit that it all depends on who is eating it and the care they take to eat it, how many bites they take, and how still they hold while eating it. Mary Bennet would not need a plate, but her mother most certainly would. After the parade ended, Mr. Bennet would heat the oven to 350. While it was heating, he situated the turkey, which had been thawing in the refrigerator for four days in the turkey pan. Once it was in the oven, he would retire to his library, only to emerge once an hour to check the turkey and do whatever was required to keep it edible.

The rest of the family busied themselves finishing up the leftover pastries and scattering far away from each other for several hours. They would emerge at 4, just around the time when the Phillipses arrived. Their uncle Gardiner used to come in from the city as well, but ever since he married his wife, who would become Jane and Lizzy's new favorite aunt, and they had children, he started celebrating with her family in the Hudson Valley. One of his sisters had plenty to say about this choice, and the other just wanted him to be happy and was glad he finally found someone to love.

Once hands were shaken and hugs were given, Mr. Bennet would do the final turkey check. After that, he and his brother-in-law would go into the library while the Gardiner sisters and the Bennet sisters made the side dishes and set the table while listening to The Beatles. It was always The Beatles, and it had been for their whole lives because they were Aunt Phillips' favorite band, and she had started the tradition when they were teenagers helping their mother in the kitchen on Thanksgiving. The tradition would continue far into the future for those members of the Bennet family who went on to have children of their own. The irony of a family in New England, quite obviously not Old England, listening to a band that led the British Invasion of America to celebrate the exodus from the old world to the new was not lost on Mary, but she kept it to herself.

Promptly at 5, with the table set and the whole family situated at their places at the table, Mr. Bennet would get the turkey out of the oven and bring it into the dining room. He carved it, they talked amongst themselves, and by 5:15, without prayer or preamble, the family was eating and talking, and for an hour or so, there were rarely cross words. They would clear the table, and at 7, fully satiated and unable to eat another bite, the Lucases arrived with the desserts, and they all found room for more food, cocktails, and coffee. At 10, the elder Lucases would head home, leaving their daughters behind for a late-night gossip session which always led to a late-morning layabout.

Early the next morning, during the said layabout by the young people, Mrs. Bennet, Aunt Phillips, and First Lady Lucas snuck away at the crack of dawn for Hartford to spend a day of Black Friday shopping. While each family was in a different situation regarding their financial security, none of them were spendthrifts, and Black Friday was an excellent way to save a lot of money. They were willing to maneuver through the warrenous aisles inside the stores of Westfarms Mall in West Hartford. They enjoyed the day away. They would generally return to Meryton around 3 when they would have a late lunch or early dinner, depending on how one wishes to categorize it, at the diner, and then they would wander through the Meryton shops to get boxes, wrapping paper, ribbon, and other tree decorating accoutrements.

They would all return to their respective homes to eat leftovers with their respective families and put up their respective Christmas trees. Two of them had real trees, and one of them had a plastic tree from a box. One of them thought it made perfect sense as there were only two people in the small house, and they had no children; the other thought her sister was a scrooge and ruining everything just like their brother who refused to come around anymore.

It seems idyllic, doesn't it? While not everyone loves holidays for a variety of reasons, some valid and some capricious in nature, it was during this time of the year that the Bennets of Longbourn came together in a way that reminded them why they all loved each other so much. They didn't always like each other, that is to be sure, and that dislike would justifiably keep some of them apart for years and years, but they did really love each other.

Sometimes, there would be a fly in the ointment. One could expect minor variations when something new is thrown into the mix. For instance, when Teddy got married and decided to quit coming to Connecticut for Thanksgiving, there was one fewer set of hands in the kitchen doing the prep in the final hour. The truth was, there were often more people than tasks anyway, so it wasn't that big of a deal, but the responsibilities had to be changed up. One year, Kitty broke her foot doing a totally legal, absolutely ball-first, game-saving slide tackle that ensured her team made it to the U-14 championship game, which they lost without their best center back, the most underrated position on the pitch. Keepers and strikers get all the press, but the sweeper cleans up messes. That year, Kitty rolled the silverware into napkins on top of a TV tray while sitting on the couch watching *Miracle on 34th Street* in the living room.

Of course, on November 23rd of 1989, things were vastly different. No one expected Reverend Collins to help in any way, nor did they expect to change anything about their routine. He was a guest. Extra pastries were purchased to be sure, and it was expected that he would likely spend time with Mr. Bennet in the library while the turkey baked. Shortly after he rose and discovered the house was not full of noise and bustle as he expected, he wandered into the dining room where he found Mr. Bennet and Mary drinking coffee and reading the paper. While they withheld their normal breakfast ritual to eat with the family in the living room, the paper still arrived bright and early, even on a holiday. After he was offered coffee, which he accepted but not until he had enough cream and sugar to create frosting in the bottom of his cup, did he finally sit down at the table.

After taking a sip and declaring it to be "perfection," he started making assumptions about how the day would go based on the Collins' family traditions, which involved the Thanksgiving meal being served at noon. "I was so sure I'd be roused to the sound of feminine voices diligently working in the kitchen, so imagine my surprise to hear the quiet murmurs of the two of you, not that your voice isn't feminine, Mary, although it is a much lower register than Lady Ann de Bourgh, who is, just, like your eldest sister Jane, the paragon of femininity."

Mary opened her mouth to speak, but Mr. Bennet was already talking. He explained the Longbourn tradition. No need to repeat it; you just read it. The good Reverend launched into a graphic detail of his family tradition and why he thought it was the best tradition. He said, "While I would never speak ill of my dear friends at Longbourn, I would love for both of you to just consider why the Collins' way is much more efficient. We have our tree up by the end of the day on Thanksgiving. What could be more thankful than that? Nothing, I dare say. There is nothing more thankful than a tree on Thanksgiving night. Going to sleep with an erect tree, lit up to honor the lord is just the most thankful thing ever. I am certainly always thankful when I say my nightly prayers when there is a dressed tree and a full stomach."

They sat in silence for a few seconds as he looked back and forth between Mary and Mr. Bennet. Mr. Bennet knew this was the way to get Reverend Collins to talk himself into a new topic, for he never talked himself out. His quiver was always full of words, and he never tired of shooting. However, Mary Bennet didn't know this trick yet. She would quite soon, but some lessons must be learned the hard way, and so, she foolishly thought she could address one aspect of his claim.

"As you know, Reverend, we..."

He cut her off, "You may call me William if you'd like, Mary."

Mary would never call him William, nor would any member of the Bennet family. Many years in the future when she would, for a short time, be his boss, she did not call him William. She continued, "As you know," she just left a space where the name would go, "We live on a working farm. We three youngest girls are homeschooled by our mother. My elder sisters have jobs as well as school. I have a job working for my aunt. We are all very busy, and we do our best on every day of the year to be as efficient as we can." She paused here to give him the chance to say whatever he was thinking as she could see his lips vibrating as they fought to hold in whatever it was he was bursting to say.

"Yes, of course. You are a tightly wound clock. I can see that for myself." He smiled brightly.

Not knowing what that meant or how to respond to it, she pressed on with her point. "Yes, well, the Thanksgiving holiday is a time when we Bennets enjoy throwing off the yokes of our schedules and just letting things happen at a more leisurely pace. We find it gives us time to enjoy the time we spend with each other. None of us are getting any younger, and who knows how many more of these holidays we have to spend like this? While I understand why the Collinses do what they do, I hope you can appreciate why the Bennets do what we do."

They stared at each other for a moment. She smiled a closed-mouth smile. She didn't want to show teeth and frighten him. He looked from her to her father and back. He did it again. He looked either perplexed, or upset, or both. Most readers likely read the explanation that Mary gave and nodded along in understanding. Even if one's family has a different tradition, which is likely, or if one lives in a country that does not have a Thanksgiving celebration, or if one chooses just to ignore it completely, or if one's employer doesn't give the day off because some places must be open on Thanksgiving, it would seem that Mary's thoughtful and heartfelt explanation would calm the most ardent naysayer.

"I understand how you feel about your time, Mary, and while that may be a valid reason, if you would just consider that if you started sooner and put your tree up at the end of the day, you would have more time on Friday to do whatever you so chose instead of being forced to be home at a specific time to erect the tree. The Collins' way actually gives you more time, and you wouldn't have to worry about breaking any eggs or having any yolks spilled on you as problematic as that must be for young women of your age."

Mary, stunned into silence, with her mouth agape, looked to her father, who stood and folded the paper. He handed it to Mary while speaking to Reverend Collins. "Why don't I give you a quick tour of the property? It is really something to see when it is at peace during this time of day. With the staff off for the day, I could use a hand with the morning feeding. We have plenty of time before the rest of the family rises and watches the parade."

Reverend Collins tried to jump from his seat but banged his knees on the underside of the table. In any other home in Meryton, his sickly-sweet coffee would have spilled everywhere, but in Longbourn, nary a drop was spilled. He just had bruises on his knees for the days following. "Of course, Sir, it would be my honor to roll up my sleeves and join you in the labor of keeping New England full of nutrients. I brought work clothes for just this occasion." He bowed to Mary and ran out of the dining room.

They watched him run out and waited until they heard the guest room door close. They looked back at each other. "Eggs?" Mary asked.

"How do you think he'll take it when he discovers the feeding is done by machine, and he changed his clothes for nothing?" her father asked back.

"I suspect he will find a way to get dirty anyway, and it is cold, windy, and it has started to snow, so it was likely a good idea."

He nodded. "Yes. Yes, that's true." He reached into his vest pocket and pulled out his pipe. He put it in his mouth and bit down on the stem. He pulled it back out. "I'm proud of you, Mary."

While there were fewer words in the English language that Mary liked to hear more than her father saying he was proud of her, she wanted to earn the pride. Thus, she asked, "For?"

"Jane would have patronized him very nicely. Lydia wouldn't have given him the time of day. Your mother would have encouraged him. Kitty would have not even been invited to the conversation. Lizzy would have eviscerated him at best and laughed in his face at worst. You said nothing. Sometimes, child, regardless of who is speaking, silence is golden and incredibly difficult. It is almost always true when it comes to the good Reverend. He and I have engaged in some good rousing conversations for sure, but mostly, he repeats things he's heard without context, and as you saw, he didn't know you meant yoke with an 'e' and not an 'l.' Context is his problem. He has a shockingly good memory. If you say something to him once, he will not forget you said it. If he heard someone liked going to the Whalers game, he would buy that person hockey-based paraphernalia in perpetuity. He often has no idea what he is saying, but if he ever managed to get on *Jeopardy*, he would be an unstoppable force." Dear Reader, the Whalers were a professional hockey team in Hartford at the time this story takes place, but not at the time of this writing, yet there is always a chance by the time this book finds hands, there is a team there again. It has been bandied about.

Mary nodded. She looked to the empty door to be sure he wasn't on his way back. "I've always said there is a difference between information and knowledge." Mary was only 18 at the time, and so, some readers may scoff at her using the term "always" there. How long is "always" to a teenager? It is true that Mary Bennet didn't utter that concept when she could first speak, but we've already heard her thoughts on standardized tests, knowledge, and information, thus she'd thought for over half her young life, and she would continue to think it forever and ever. That should be good enough to vouch for the veracity of the claim. "There isn't anything wrong with having a bunch of facts, and it can be helpful to have a good memory, but the problem comes when one employs those facts. Knowledge is using facts to find truth. Truth is the key."

Mr. Bennet nodded at his middlest daughter, and the pride he felt just moments before paled in comparison to the pride he felt in that exact moment. He was nodding and not crying, thank you very much, it was just morning allergies, when Reverend Collins arrived dressed in clearly brand new, creased from the factory, bright orange, full-body coveralls which he had zipped right up to the underside of his chin. Thankfully, he wasn't a jowly man, for if he were, there would be some rubbing.

Thankfully, on that, the most thankful of all days, for Mary and her father, Reverend Collins was not a man who ever once asked, "How do I look?" Instead, he entered the room like he knew that he was dressed perfectly for the task at hand and that if anyone were to see him walking the grounds of Longbourn, that person would assume he was a regular employee who had been there for years. As we shall soon see, no one thought that. He exclaimed, "I'm ready!" He rubbed his hands together in anticipation.

Mr. Bennet stood up, put his pipe in his mouth, and bit hard on the stem. He nodded at Reverend Collins. He looked at Mary who was sipping her coffee and looking into her cup while she did it. She was a quick study. Silence echoed through the dining room. He removed his pipe and said, "Wonderful. Let me just pack my pipe and get my matches. Please, follow me to the library, and we shall leave Mary in peace to finish the paper."

She looked up from her cup after taking the longest drink of coffee ever and smiled at her father. "Yes, thank you, Father." She turned to Reverend Collins. "Enjoy yourself." She gave him what she hoped was a tight-lipped smile that showed him that she really did want him to enjoy himself and that she didn't want to talk about his potential enjoyment level.

"Thank you for the well wishes, Mary. I will certainly do just that as I already have had the most glorious morning just conversing with you. It can only get better." He bowed and exited.

Mary, under normal circumstances, would have refilled her coffee and finished reading the paper just as her father suggested. However, she wanted to get some more ideas down about information, knowledge, and truth. So, she topped off her coffee and grabbed the portable radio from the kitchen. She had left her Walkman next to her bed. Because she planned on her morning chat with her father, she didn't need to bring it, and there was no chance she was going back in there to get it and risk waking Lydia.

She brought the radio back in with her to the dining room and turned it on low; the oldies station was playing "The Way You Do the Things You Do" by The Temptations. She smiled. She liked the song and felt it was appropriate, considering all the thoughts running through her head. She pulled the pencil out of her hair and the notebook out of her pocket. She sat down and started writing. Readers of a certain age may remember the English reggae band UB40 would, just a few days after the events of that particular Thanksgiving, release an album of covers that would contain that very song, and it would feature in the film *Black Rain* that Mary and Lizzy would later go see. Some things just happen that way.

Mary put herself into a writing trance, and while she tapped her foot along to some Motown classics by Martha and the Vandellas and Stevie Wonder, and she bobbed her head along to some Dave Clark Five and The Beach Boys, it wasn't until the absurdly infectious, can't help but dance along song, "ABC" by the Jackson 5 came on that Mary pulled herself out of it. Of course, it could be that it was the music that suddenly seemed louder, which it actually was as Lizzy had come by and turned it up several songs prior, or it could have been the sound of Lizzy and Jane in the kitchen dancing and singing one of the many Bennet sisters choreographed numbers. Either way, powerless to resist, Mary scooted into the kitchen in time to get in step next to Lizzy to sing the line about education not being complete. The three of them danced, sang, and spun. Kitty joined just before for the rocking cymbal solo as Lydia walked in during the infamous "come on girl" line that would, occasionally during live shows, feature Janet, the youngest of the Jacksons, walking on stage. Was Lydia waiting just outside the door for just that moment? Of course.

As the song ended and an advertisement for the Westfarms Mall began to play, the sisters, noting that it was almost time for the parade to begin, moved into preparation mode. Kitty and Lydia went into the living room to get the TV warmed up and to make sure the antenna was turned and the station was clear. Mary and Jane started getting the food out of the boxes and onto the serving trays. Lizzy went to get the glasses down and happened to look out the window at that moment.

She gasped. "What is Father doing outside in the snow with an Oompa Loompa?"

Mary, having already seen the very person in the dining room that morning, snickered guiltily, but felt no need to go look. She didn't like to pile on. He was just a person who couldn't help being who he was.

Jane came over to see her father, walking with his long stride, across the grounds with the orange-clad Reverend Collins seeming to skip and jog while trying to keep up with him. Some things are funny, and while Jane would never wish to laugh at the expense of another person, she could not help it. A trumpeted burst of laughter forced its way out of her mouth, which she promptly covered with one hand and smacked Lizzy on the shoulder with the other. "Stop," she said, and she covered her mouth with both hands to hold in the giggles.

Jane Bennet was, and still is as of this writing, unsurprisingly, a giggler. One laugh often set off an avalanche of giggles that could, if left unchecked, last for hours. She could get them under control in a few minutes, but eventually, someone would look a certain way, and she would once again fall into a fit of belly-hurting, muscle-screaming giggles. The person who did, and still does, know her best, her closest sister, could not help herself, and so, Lizzy began singing the "Oompa Loompa" song from the 1971 classic film. She made up a dance and her own lyrics that rhymed "dee" with "misogyny" and "daa" with "drama." Considering she was making it up on the spot and the original rhymed "daa" with "far," it wasn't bad at all. Mary, who was unsurprisingly not a giggler, did laugh.

Only when Lydia finally shouted "IT'S STARTING" from the other room did Jane start to get herself together, and the three eldest Bennet sisters made their way to the living room with breakfast.

"It's about time. We're starving," their mother said from her chair.

The three eldest all said something different in response.

Jane said, "Sorry."

Lizzy said, "It's only just started."

Mary said, "Good morning to you too, Mother."

To which their mother replied, "It's fine, Jane, dear."

"Where's Dad?" Lydia asked as the show started in earnest. "He never misses the parade."

"He and the..." Lizzy started.

Jane cut her off, "The Reverend..." Jane held in a giggle and cut herself off.

Mary finished, "He took Reverend Collins out to show him the farm and to do the feedings."

"They're automatic?" Lydia said it as a question as though she knew, which she absolutely did know, but was second guessing herself as often happens when people take things for granted as fact but are then confronted with new information.

"Yes, well…" Mary started but was cut off by the sound of a ringing phone.

"Who would that be?" Mrs. Bennet asked Mary directly as she was looking at her because she was speaking, but it was to the room in general. Dear Reader, it may seem shocking to learn that for decades, people asked this very question when a hard-wired landline rang. While Caller-ID had just been released to the public in 1989, it didn't make its way to Longbourn until the turn of the century. Not because it wasn't available at no extra cost by then, but because Mrs. Bennet, who was the person who asked about who might be calling more times than not when the phone rang, did not feel it was "necessary." Some people just like to complain. Solutions only offer cold comfort because they must find something else about which to complain.

The Bennet girls knew better than to actually offer any guesses as to who might be calling because that would lead to a discussion about why or why not that particular person could or would be calling at that particular time, and by the time it was or likely was not resolved, the phone would stop ringing. Mary spun on her heel and went to find out the answer to her mother's quandary.

She went to the kitchen and picked up the receiver from the wall-mounted, dingy yellow, rotary phone. Even though it was a holiday and the call would not likely be a business-related call, muscle memory took over, and she answered the way she was instructed to answer during the day. "Longbourn, how may I help you?"

"Happy Thanksgiving, Mary," Charlotte said. Charlotte Lucas was one of the eight people in the world who could differentiate which Bennet sister was speaking by her voice. To a trained ear, they didn't sound alike at all, but to an untrained ear, five young women all born within the same decade who grew up in the same house might as well be the same person.

"Happy Thanksgiving, Charlotte."

"How are things over there?"

Unable to really assess the overall feeling of Longbourn on a regular day, Mary was unable to answer the question directly. Instead, she just explained what was happening. "Father is showing the Reverend around. We are eating and watching the parade. I would say it is normal adjacent. Odd that Father is outside in the snow with our guest and his chair is empty in the living room."

"Yes, well, that's why I'm calling."

"Because Father is outside?"

"No, the snow. Sorry. The snow."

Mary pulled the long pigtail cord across the kitchen and looked out the window. The wind had picked up. "Yeah, it's getting pretty bad. The weather page in the paper said we should get a few inches before it is all done."

"Right. The radio says it is going to maybe get up to five, and well, we were wondering if maybe it would be best for us to either come over now while it is just blowing and starting to drift or not come at all as it will be really bad for dessert."

Dear Reader, it might seem strange that a teenager and a young woman in her 20s were having this conversation instead of the parents. It was common for information to pass through children all the time. The game isn't called Telephone on accident. Mary knew that everyone in the family looked forward to having the Lucases over and would be disappointed both emotionally for not having the pleasure of their company but would be gastronomically distraught as the only desserts they had on hand were being consumed for breakfast.

"Yeah. I vote for now, not later," Mary said.

"Me too, but Mom wanted me to check."

"Be right back." Mary placed the receiver crossways on the top of the phone and went into the living room. She walked in and said, "The Lucases wonder if we want them to come now so they can beat the snow or if they shouldn't come at all."

Mrs. Bennet looked up from the TV and at Mary, seemingly forgetting who this young person was and what she could be talking about. "What?" It took much longer to read the full report of the conversation than it did in real life, so Mrs. Bennet could not have possibly forgotten anything of the sort.

Mary refused to repeat herself. She just looked away from her mother while exhaling a short but huffy breath. She turned her attention to Lizzy and Jane who were sitting shoulder to shoulder on a loveseat. Oftentimes, if one of them, well, OK, if Jane said something was a good idea, it happened. She opened her eyes big, hoping to send a mental sister-telepathy link to Jane.

"I think they should come now. We always have plenty of food. We can make room for four more at the table or set up a second table for Kitty, Lydia, and Maria. They just whisper to each other anyway, and I'd hate to miss dessert. We should phone up Aunt Phillips and tell her to come over now too. What do you think, Mom?" Jane turned her doe eyes on her mother, who was, like all other humans in history who'd ever met Jane Bennet, powerless to resist her.

So it was that Mary went back to the kitchen and passed the good news on to Charlotte. She called her aunt, who admitted to being the one to call the Lucases and get the whole thing in motion. They were already dressed and would be out the door in less than five minutes. Traditions are important, but sometimes, it snows.

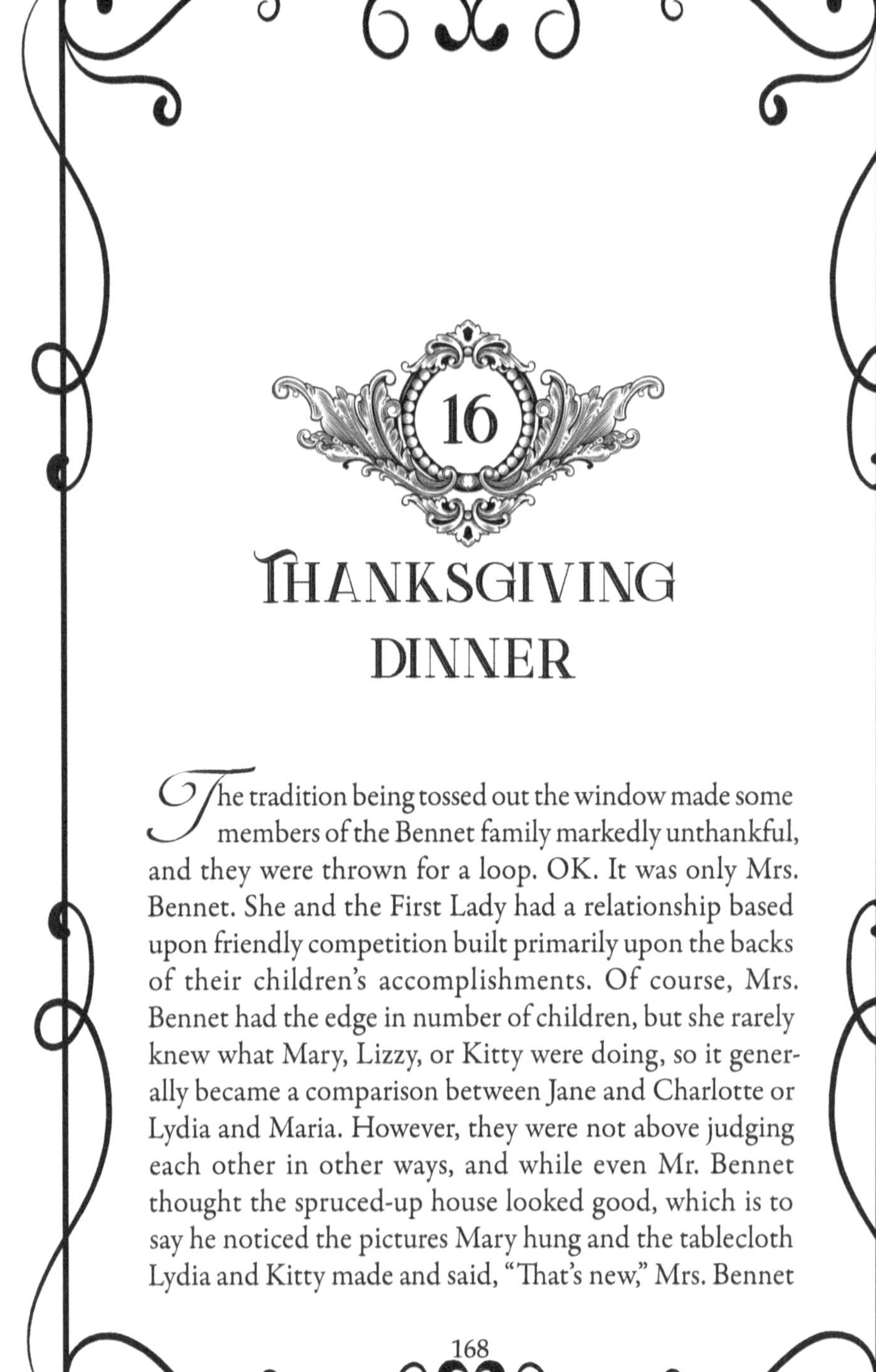

16

Thanksgiving Dinner

The tradition being tossed out the window made some members of the Bennet family markedly unthankful, and they were thrown for a loop. OK. It was only Mrs. Bennet. She and the First Lady had a relationship based upon friendly competition built primarily upon the backs of their children's accomplishments. Of course, Mrs. Bennet had the edge in number of children, but she rarely knew what Mary, Lizzy, or Kitty were doing, so it generally became a comparison between Jane and Charlotte or Lydia and Maria. However, they were not above judging each other in other ways, and while even Mr. Bennet thought the spruced-up house looked good, which is to say he noticed the pictures Mary hung and the tablecloth Lydia and Kitty made and said, "That's new," Mrs. Bennet was nervous to show off the new look to First Lady Lucas. She hoped to get a full assessment from her sister early in the day so that if any changes needed to happen, she could make them before the arrival of the Lucases. Additionally, the Lucases never came for dinner, so the only food that could be criticized as a group was the desserts they brought. The thought of having her family's meal open to critical inspection made her angry at Mary for her decision to answer the phone that morning and because of the snow, as though that too could be Mary's fault.

Everyone else at Longbourn was quite thankful indeed. Lizzy and Jane were always thankful to spend more time with Charlotte. Even though they were adults, they were all still living at home and off for a holiday break, so they acted like silly teenagers. Lydia and Kitty were thankful to spend time with Maria. Even though they were all silly teenagers, having all their older sisters and parents around, coupled with the fact that they would have an actual kiddie table, afforded them the chance to act like wild children. Mr. Bennet was thankful to have his brother-in-law and Mayor Lucas over so that he didn't have to bear the brunt of entertaining Reverend Collins all day by himself. While Mr. Bennet still took care of the turkey at the appointed hour, he and the three men spent time behind the closed door of the library. Mary was thankful that her favorite aunt and best friend was going to be around for a few extra hours. It is true that she either saw her at the office or spoke to her about work most days, and they always found time to talk about other things; there was something particularly joyous about getting to see her without worrying about any agenda.

This tale has already gone on for some time, and we are not quite at the halfway point, so we shall not spend a lot of time with all the factions around the house. Each conversation could easily be a chapter. Revelations were made and stories were shared. The younger girls locked themselves away in one bedroom, and the other older girls, whom we know are women but have already said were acting like girls, locked themselves away in the other. Mary and her aunt had the living room to themselves where they discussed a wide range of topics about Mary's future and what the law office might look like if she were not there. Suffice it to say that all the Bennets save one had a great day. Dinner was served on time despite having more people "in the way" while dinner was being prepared, and it is there where we shall spend our focus, as the title of the chapter indicates.

The piano was thankfully on wheels, so it was pushed into the living room, and the kiddie table was arranged in the dining room. The three youngest were pleased with the arrangement. Mr. Bennet sat at one end of the table, and Mayor Lucas was at the other. The spot was offered to Reverend Collins who said he couldn't possibly, which is what everyone thought he should say and were surprised when he said it. A broken clock is right twice a day and all of that. On one side of the table, Lizzy sat closest to her father as was the tradition, followed by Charlotte, Jane, Mary, and Reverend Collins. On the other side, there was an empty seat across from Lizzy where the turkey was placed on the table. Mr. Phillips sat across from Jane, followed by Mrs. Bennet, First Lady Lucas, and Aunt Phillips. The food was out, and the meal was ready. Mr. Bennet stood to begin the carving, and as usual, the conversations continued as they waited for the official time to start eating.

Reverend Collins clanged a knife against the side of his cup, and as always happens when that sound is made in any circumstance, everyone quieted down and looked at the sound. Even Mr. Bennet, who was in mid-carve, stopped and looked up. "I was hoping to have the honor of leading this collection of amazing people in the saying of grace." He bowed his head. "Dear Lord," he began without waiting to hear approval as he wrongly made the assumption that Mr. Bennet at best or Mayor Lucas at worst would lead the family prayer, "it is with a humble heart and mindful mind that I ask you to bless this feast of glorious magnificence as I am blessed to spend this day with friends new and old as we celebrate this day of thanks. I am thankful to be here, invited into this beatific home full of angelic faces and warm hearts. Amen." He kept his head bowed, waiting for the response he was expecting.

The rest of the congregants sat in shocked silence. In years to come, this event would be referred to as the Reverend Collins guerrilla prayer attack in full, but anytime anyone launched into an unwanted diatribe, they were shouted down or called out afterward for "pulling a Collins" for short. In that moment though, they had no words. Some of them were not even breathing. Some of them were stifling laughter. Thankfully, on the most thankful day of the year, Mary Bennet kept her head, as she was wont to do, and said, "Amen."

Her response prompted the rest of the family to follow suit which freed Reverend Collins from his bowed posture. "Since I've shared my thankfulness in my prayer, I don't feel the need to participate in the part where we all say what we're thankful for, but just know, I'm now and forever grateful." He turned and looked at Mary.

Mary Bennet had been called a lot of things in her life up to that point, and she would go on to be called many things that were much, much worse. These names and accusations were often uttered out of spite by her mother, her youngest sister, peers in college who thought they were in competition with her, without knowing she only ever competed against herself, or subordinates who simply didn't take the time to get to know her or ask why she was doing the thing she was doing. Most of them were untrue. One thing no one ever called Mary Bennet was flappable. In fact, it was her calm demeanor that often bothered others the most. On that Thanksgiving in 1989, her cucumber-ness saved the family again in back-to-back moments.

She stood and looked at their guest and said, "Thank you, Reverend." She began, "I would like to say that, this year, I am thankful for the fact that the snow came early so we could spend extra time with our family and friends..."

"I was going to say that. She took mine," her mother interrupted huffily. We will leave it to each reader to decide if she meant to say that aloud or not.

"...and," Mary continued, ignoring her mother's outburst, "I am incredibly thankful that this is my final year of homeschooling and that I will be able to begin my educational journey outside these walls. While the library here in Longbourn is exceptional and the library in Meryton is a home away from home, I am thankful that I will be able to sit in a classroom of my peers with college professors so I can learn and grow." She sat down and looked to Charlotte, indicating it was her turn.

We shall not share the rest of the speeches but know that Mrs. Bennet once again had some choice words to say about Mary before she launched into a long list of disparate things, mostly about Lydia. By the time they were done, they were quite a bit behind their normal schedule, but considering everything had gone the way it had gone that day, no one was incredibly upset. The food was still excellent, and the company was, all things considered, good. The conversation was even better, and while we could fill another book documenting all the words that were uttered during the meal, we shall however spend some time with Mary, her aunt, Mayor Lucas, and most importantly, Reverend Collins. Seems shocking, but it is true. It went thusly.

"Your Magnificence, I've heard tale that you have some outsiders staying at Netherfield Park. Quite famous people if I hear correctly," Reverend Collins said through a mouthful of mashed potatoes.

Mayor Lucas, who had never before nor ever again been called "your magnificence" finished chewing and nodded his head. "It's true; we have some famous temporary residents in town, but I don't ever like to think of anyone as outsiders. We have the reserve base here, and so, our town population waxes and wanes periodically, and we like to think of them as guests, not outsiders."

"Yes, of course, Your Highness. I meant no disrespect. I've felt very welcomed. In fact, before I was saved from my wandering by your lovely daughter yesterday, the residents of Meryton were quite welcoming."

"How did you happen to hear about the Bingleys, Reverend?" Aunt Phillips asked. "Were they a topic of conversation around town? Did people think you were looking for them? One new visitor coming to visit the other visitors would make sense."

"It would indeed, madam, but in fact, I was aware of their presence before I even arrived. You may know that my employer and benefactor is one Lady Catherine de Bourgh; she is a well-known philanthropist. Her nephew," he made finger quotes when he said those words, "Mr. Fitzwilliam Darcy, is staying there as well." When no one inquired about the finger quotes, he pushed on. "I say nephew because he is not actually related to Lady Catherine de Bourgh by blood. You see, Mr. Darcy's mother and she were roommates at boarding school, and they treated each other as siblings and considered each other's children as niece and nephew. When Mrs. Darcy passed shortly after the birth of young Georgiana, it was Lady Catherine de Bourgh who stepped in to offer the maternal advice for both Darcy children. It was always understood that the two sisters," again with the finger quotes, "hoped very much that their eldest children would marry and join the families formally as they were not actually related. It is very much like I consider Mr. Bennet my uncle and the Bennet girls my cousins although we share no blood, and nothing would be untoward should we decide to merge families to make the union permanent."

He paused here to see how people reacted. When no one asked about his intentions in that quarter, he moved on. "They both even went to the same first-class middle-western college, and so it seemed all but assured that as they blossomed into adulthood, their romance would bud as well. While it seems they both had a glorious time at their alma mater, it was where Mr. Darcy and Mr. Bingley met, in fact, but alas it seems that if there was any spark, it has been snuffed out by conflicting ambition. Lady Catherine de Bourgh fears that the match shall not be made as Lady Anne de Bourgh seems intent on staying in Rhode Island and running the spiritual outreach division, and while Mr. Darcy has an ancestral home in Rhode Island, he seems to have no plans in working in philanthropy in general or spiritualism in particular. That is not to say that he is a Scrooge," he chuckled at his own quip, "in that his purse strings are knitted closed. He gives to many charities, and he supports his," finger quotes, "cousin in her pursuits, but he has bigger plans for the Darcy publishing fortune than just giving it all away."

Dear Reader, if different members of the dinner party had been present, different questions would have most assuredly been asked. We can all guess what those questions would have been. Because Aunt Phillips was chewing on one of Mary's buttered handmade dinner rolls, her third, and because Mayor Lucas was pouring out the contents of the bottle of wine that had been passed his way and was focusing on not spilling it on Lydia's newly made tablecloth, he did not; he wasn't really paying attention. Our heroine, who was not old enough to drink and who had nary a bit of food in her mouth, was allowed to ask the follow-up question. She cared very little for the ins and outs of the Darcy/de Bourgh romance possibilities. She cared very little about anyone's romantic possibilities. She heard "first-class middle-western college," and that was all she cared to hear more about.

"So, they all went to the same college? Did Lou go there as well? What's it called?" Mary resisted the urge to pull the pencil from her hair and the notebook from her pocket. Should she feel the need, she could excuse herself for a trip to the bathroom where she would sit and write everything down. It was a trick she used all the time. Mr. Bennet, Jane, and Lizzy all knew she did it. Mrs. Bennet and Lydia didn't think about it at all. How Kitty felt about it was anyone's guess as no one bothered to ask. It was just assumed she felt the same way that Lydia did. Did she? Excellent question.

"Excellent questions all," Reverend Collins replied. "They did, in fact, all go to the same college. It was intentional for Mr. Darcy and Lady Anne de Bourgh, as was the wishes of Lady Catherine de Bourgh, and I would think that Georgiana would attend as well. Mr. Darcy's entire paternal family line has gone there back to its founding. The Darcy family donated money to build the presidential residence there. You'd think they would call it Darcy Mansion or some such name."

By this point, even Mayor Lucas was listening, and he, Aunt Phillips, and Mary nodded that it was just what they were thinking. "It's not?" Mayor Lucas asked.

"It is not, in fact. The Darcy family, as I said, do many charitable acts, but unlike the de Bourghs, they do it, not necessarily in secret, but quietly. Thus, only those who know would know that the name of the presidential residence is named for the Darcy estate. Thus, it is called Pemberley, the name of the aforementioned ancestral home in Rhode Island. They don't even call it Pemberley House or Pemberley Mansion although I've been told that it could easily qualify as such. However, the presidents use it for much more than living. It is more like a White House in that there are office spaces, dining rooms, and the like. There is even a small theatre as the home was built before the actual campus theatre was built, and the dramatists would perform there. I don't know what they use it for now, as Lady Anne de Bourgh didn't share that information with me, but I am sure we could find out when we next meet Mr. Darcy, or that is to say, when you next meet him and I meet him for the first time, for you see, while I am intimately acquainted with his," finger quotes, "cousin and aunt, I have heard great things about him and his family. Lady Catherine de Bourgh has a nephew," no finger quotes, "Colonel Fitzwilliam, which was Lady Catherine de Bourgh's maiden name, and Mr. Darcy's first name, which was given as a tribute from one friend to the other. He is many years older than Mr. Darcy and Lady Anne de Bourgh, but much like Charlotte and the Bennet sisters, age has been no restriction to an incredibly bonded friendship. He is old enough to be their father, but military life kept him single and kept him young at heart. He is not a full Colonel but a Lieutenant Colonel, but people of that rank are called Colonel. It is confusing, I know, but that is the vernacular as was described to me. In fact, the Colonel is listed as Georgiana's guardian should anything happen to Mr. Darcy. He is a man of that kind of reputation that he would be trusted to oversee her emotional and financial well-being."

Reverend Collins nodded and took a sip of his wine. He picked up a dinner roll, thinking that he'd answered all of the questions Mary asked. Readers who were not worn down by the Reverend's meandering storytelling style will remember Mary asked two more questions. Of course, eagle-eyed readers will realize she really only wanted the answer to the final question.

So it was that she skipped over the second question and resubmitted the final question. "What is the name of this college, Reverend?" She wasn't fast enough, and the dinner roll was missing a chunk. We've already learned that a mouthful of food couldn't stop him from talking, but it did sometimes make him more difficult to understand. Instead of giving him a chance to quite literally make a show of his masticated dinner roll, Mary pressed on with a comment instead of a question. "I've been pouring over *Barron's Guide*, but I do know that not every college is in there. Harriet, that is Ms. Harrington, the librarian whose acquaintance I believe you made, has been helping me. Aunt Phillips has been helping as well to fill in the gaps," Mary nodded to her aunt, "but we know that there are going to be some things that slip through the cracks, so I'd love to know the name so I could cross-reference it, and if I've never heard of it, I can learn more about it and maybe send away for information." She spoke long enough for him to finish his bite, and she said enough to pique his interest that he resisted the urge to take another.

"That is an excellent use of your time, Mary. While I know the Nutmeg State has plenty of glorious institutions of higher learning, one of the best in the country, it is important to consider your options. I'm sure you don't mean to disparage your home state's reputation by looking elsewhere. Of course, while I did my seminary studies in my home state of Maine, I did look across state lines just to be sure. Sometimes looking elsewhere reminds us what we have right at home, and other times, it shows us what we think we've been missing."

"The name of the college, Reverend," Aunt Phillips said, trying to hide her annoyance. She failed to hide it from her niece who opened her eyes wide at her aunt's outburst. Mary didn't inherit her unflappable nature from the Gardiner side of the family. Aunt Phillips took a breath and calmed herself. "Could you please say the name and tell us more about the college that Mr. Darcy attended? While we would love to hear more about your seminary, Mary won't be attending one, so maybe you could share more about your experience over dessert."

Reverend Collins was terrible at picking up on such things that he mistook her angst for enthusiasm. "Yes, of course. I shall regale you with all kinds of tales over pie. Excellent. I can't wait. I have many stories as you can imagine. My first roommate..."

"The college name," Mayor Lucas interrupted. "Please, sir, the name of the college about which you've spoken so highly but didn't attend yourself."

"Ahh, yes, quite right. Thank you, Your Excellency." He wiped his mouth although there was no food. "Mr. Darcy, Mr. Bingley, and Lady Anne de Bourgh went to Mansfield College."

Finally.

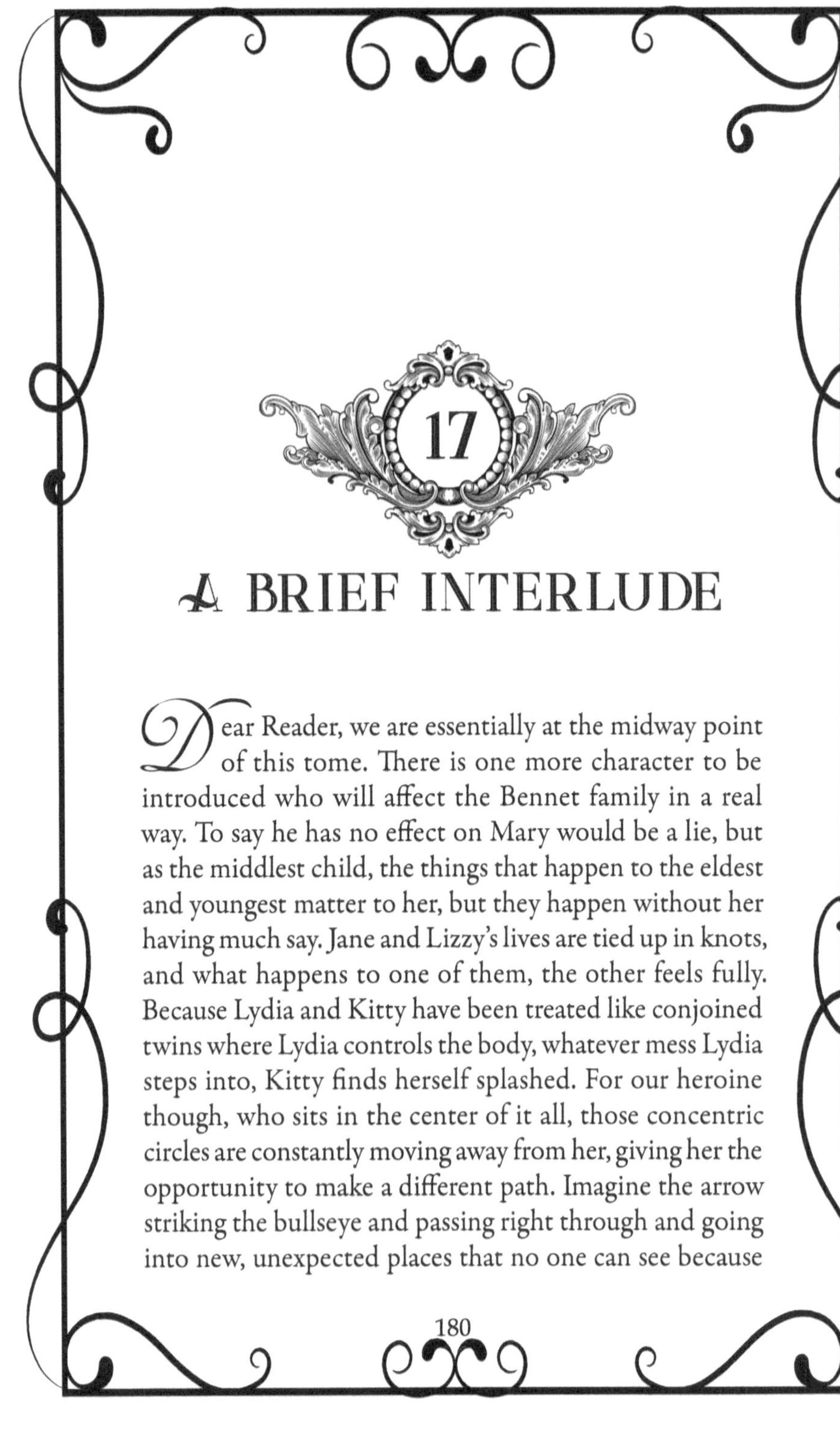

17

A BRIEF INTERLUDE

Dear Reader, we are essentially at the midway point of this tome. There is one more character to be introduced who will affect the Bennet family in a real way. To say he has no effect on Mary would be a lie, but as the middlest child, the things that happen to the eldest and youngest matter to her, but they happen without her having much say. Jane and Lizzy's lives are tied up in knots, and what happens to one of them, the other feels fully. Because Lydia and Kitty have been treated like conjoined twins where Lydia controls the body, whatever mess Lydia steps into, Kitty finds herself splashed. For our heroine though, who sits in the center of it all, those concentric circles are constantly moving away from her, giving her the opportunity to make a different path. Imagine the arrow striking the bullseye and passing right through and going into new, unexpected places that no one can see because the hole through which the arrow has slipped is small, and no one was expecting that to happen. Mary's life was forever altered when Reverend Collins showed up and finally got around to saying the two words we've all been waiting for him to say.

Mary peppered Reverend Collins with several follow-up questions about Mansfield College as it was not a college that appeared in the *Barron's Guide*. It didn't need to advertise itself. There had never been a time since its inception that it had an enrollment problem. That is not to say there wasn't an admissions office that worked with the marketing department to make up brochures and informational material. At the time of this writing, if a student from Connecticut heard about a small, private, prestigious college in the Mid-West, that person would simply look it up on the supercomputer that lived in that person's pocket, and with a few taps on a glass screen, for it is not really a click of a button any longer, that person could have all the virtual information, could take a virtual tour, and chat with an admissions representative either on the phone or over text. All of it would take a matter of minutes.

In 1989, it was not so. There was no information to be gleaned that wasn't provided by Reverend Collins which was often convoluted because he liked to diverge from the point so much that some readers may think it is he who is the narrator of this work. That is a fair point. However, unlike the good Reverend, this book always ends up back on track without being nudged. Because Mary wasn't going to see Bingley or Darcy anytime soon, nor did she feel close enough to them to ask, nor did she ask her sisters to ask them, which Jane most assuredly would have done, Mary had to wait until the following Monday when the Meryton Library finally opened back up so that she could get help from Harriet in finding the address so she could write to them and request any and all information she could have. It took a while to arrive. Here is what happened while Mary waited.

Jane and Lizzy prepared for the push into their finals. Thanksgiving break always falls at such a bad time in the semester. Schools would be smarter to just start school earlier and end the week before or go to 12-week semesters where the classes met longer, but traditions are what they are, and there are a lot of other logistical reasons for this change not happening as well. So like college students all around the country, they carried on.

Lydia and Kitty, having earned their home economics credit, took their mother at her word that they would not be required to return to their studies until January, and so they spent several weeks being generally underfoot and becoming even more acquainted with their mother's nerves. They spent a lot of time being shooed away to spend time in town when the weather was fair enough. Fair enough in Connecticut in late November and early December is relative. In the case of the youngest Bennets, it just meant that it wasn't snowing sideways or sleeting.

Having Reverend Collins in the house was irksome for Mrs. Bennet, and thus her judgment, which was not crystal clear on a normal day, was abnormally clouded. The fog had rolled in and settled upon her judgment. She hatched a scheme to get Lizzy and the Reverend romantically linked. Yes. She'd met Lizzy, but she tried anyway. Desperate times and all of that. In the few times she was alone with him, she would make comments about how she was so sure Jane and Bingley would be married soon that it would be lovely to have a joint ceremony if only there was some "godly man with a steady income around." He was easily led and had, let's say, antiquated views of how women would express themselves. He thought that adult women were a mixture of 12-year-old girls who asked their friends to ask someone else if they wanted to "go out" and characters in regency films where women couldn't be alone in a room with a man or directly speak their own feelings for fear of being untoward. Thus, when he heard this from Mrs. Bennet, he assumed, and we all know about assuming, she was speaking on behalf of her daughter. His heart, which was actually pulled in the direction of another member of our cast, was easily swayed by proximity and small-mindedness. All he needed to confirm it was a note that read "Do you like me?" with a box for yes and a box for no.

Once she had him hooked, he started following Lizzy around like a lost puppy when he wasn't following Mr. Bennet around like a newborn duckling. Lizzy, as readers can imagine, didn't care for it at all. The ruder she was to him, the more he thought she was playing hard to get. It was as exhausting as it sounds.

It was only when she complained to her father one day in the library while her mother was in there "dusting," which consisted of her standing with a duster and complaining about how lazy Mary and Kitty were for not doing the dusting, that the scheme finally was revealed. Mrs. Bennet explained her reasoning. She argued that if Lizzy married him, there was no way he would ever kick the family off the land. She explained that after a year or two, they could divorce, and Lizzy would demand ownership of Longbourn in the settlement which she would then sign over to her parents. On paper, to Mrs. Bennet, it made a lot of sense. In practice, to Lizzy and everyone else, it sounded like human trafficking and real estate fraud. When this was pointed out to Mrs. Bennet, she waved her hands and said that everyone was always "so sensitive" and "at least *she* was trying to come up with a solution to the problem."

Mr. Bennet explained to Lizzy that she had a decision to make. She could either have her mother mad at her for not marrying the Reverend or have him mad at her if she did. Lizzy laughed. Mrs. Bennet screamed about her nerves and ran out to find someone who would comfort her. Even her dear sister was no help. Eventually, Mr. Bennet straightened Reverend Collins out, and he was left to follow his heart which was best for everyone involved. More on that to come.

Meanwhile, Jane and Bingley were getting very close indeed, which meant that Lizzy and Darcy were spending more time together as well. It was contentious but not totally unpleasant. Lizzy liked how smart he was. He liked how smart she was. They liked to disagree. They didn't agree to disagree per se. They just debated. It wasn't bickering, nor was it arguing. It was something else. Caroline and Lou were always there as well. Lizzy and Caroline were like oil and fire, but Jane was like a row of sandbags that kept them apart.

Mary returned to her studies and her job at the law office. She and her aunt spent time during breaks and lulls to work on her other college applications. She applied early to the local, inexpensive state college and already had her early acceptance. She'd also been accepted in two other state schools, so she wasn't worried about going to college. She knew she could go, but she really wanted to *go* to college. The big state schools would have class sizes of several hundred, and while she was convinced she could learn in any environment, she didn't want to be a number but an actual student. She'd spent her whole life being overlooked by many members of her family and most members of the community; the last thing she wanted was to be overlooked in the world. She applied to schools in New Haven. Yale was a long shot for a home-schooled kid whose only extracurriculars were working on a farm for no pay and working in a law office, so she applied to the small Dominican liberal arts school, Albertus Magnus, as well. Aunt Phillips was sanguine on her chances to get in there. They had the word "Veritas" right in their mission, and Mary found that appealing. Any school that's mission was the truth was a place that she could get behind.

Both of those came with hefty price tags, and while she would certainly be eligible for financial aid, those dollars went much farther when one lives at home and commutes than they do when one goes to live on campus. Both of those schools were within commuting distance as one could drive on I-91 from the north end of the state to the south end in an hour, without traffic. Getting into one of those schools would be academically outstanding, but it would mean sharing that room with her sisters for four more years. Would that be worth it? She wasn't sure.

They poured over the *Barron's Guide* and made note of which out-of-state schools didn't charge out-of-state fees or application fees. They leaned into schools that weighed test scores and essays over extracurriculars. It was, for several weeks, a full-time job on top of the class load and the part-time job. It was a great way for Mary to pass time and stay out of the fray of the drama that swirled with her sisters. She loved having a task. However, as is often the case, things don't happen until we quit thinking about them, and so, on Saturday, December 16, 1989, when Mary finally decided to begin her holiday break, two things arrived in Meryton. The first was the package from Mansfield College. The second was a young 19-year-old member of the Army reserves. One enters in the next chapter, and the other, in the following.

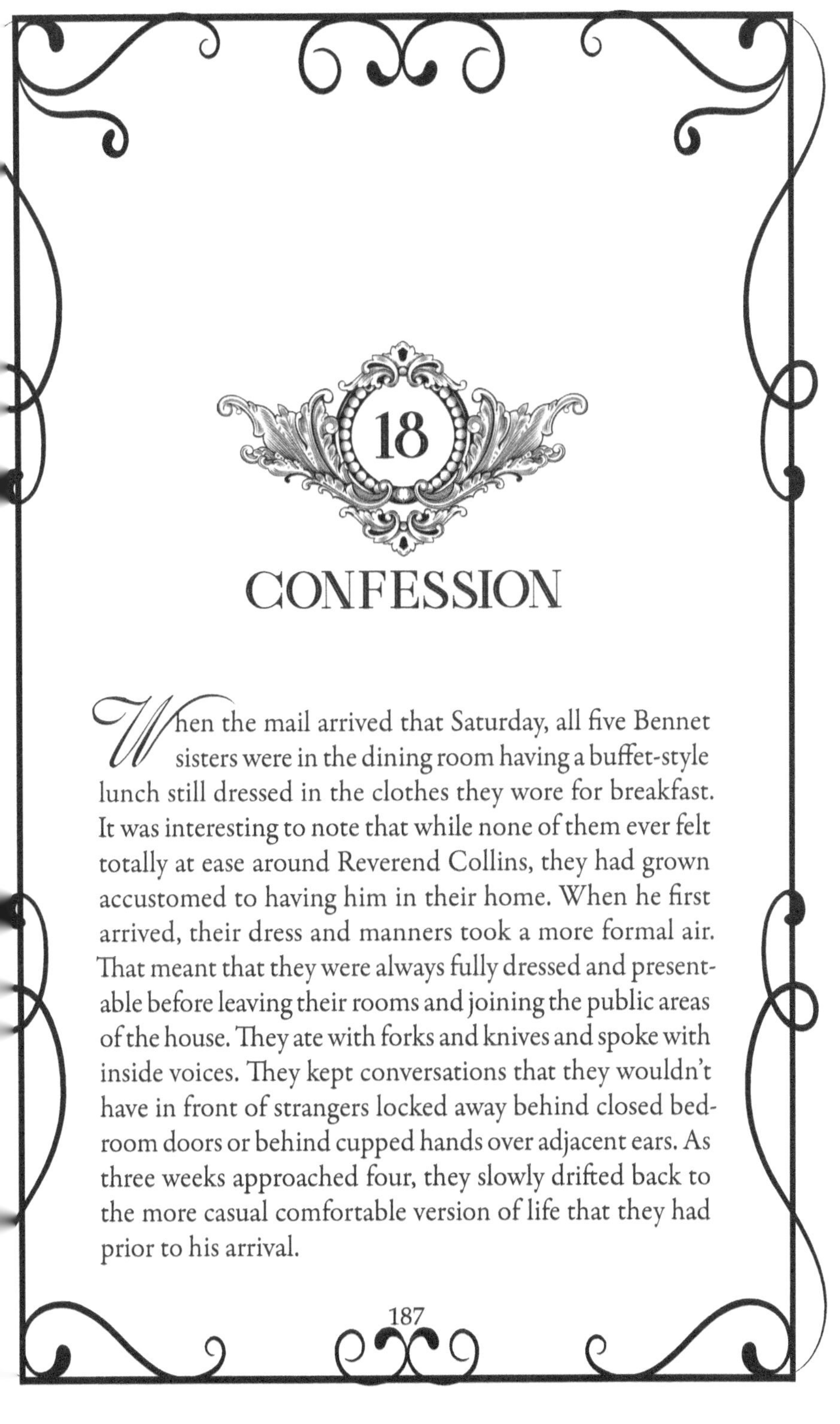

18

CONFESSION

When the mail arrived that Saturday, all five Bennet sisters were in the dining room having a buffet-style lunch still dressed in the clothes they wore for breakfast. It was interesting to note that while none of them ever felt totally at ease around Reverend Collins, they had grown accustomed to having him in their home. When he first arrived, their dress and manners took a more formal air. That meant that they were always fully dressed and presentable before leaving their rooms and joining the public areas of the house. They ate with forks and knives and spoke with inside voices. They kept conversations that they wouldn't have in front of strangers locked away behind closed bedroom doors or behind cupped hands over adjacent ears. As three weeks approached four, they slowly drifted back to the more casual comfortable version of life that they had prior to his arrival.

Once the whole mishegoss about Lizzy marrying him was resolved, which was honestly absurd, he truly became part of the family, more than just a cousin in name only regardless of the blood they didn't share. Thus, the sisters arrived in public areas of the house in mismatched socks and unbrushed hair. Before, only Mary wandered around without makeup as she never wore any, but eventually, the sisters reverted to showing their natural faces and talking about whatever came to mind, even if it was "feminine" in nature as the Reverend referred to any topic he didn't understand, ranging from actual feminine hygiene products to feminist studies. Besides, he was going to be living with women soon enough when he took his station at Rosings. They assumed that no matter how magnificent he thought the Ladies de Bourgh were, they were still women who needed tampons and had opinions about the world. It was better for him to learn how to handle it in a safe environment. The sisters also became comfortable wearing pajama pants, or shorts in Lydia's case as she ran hot unsurprisingly, all day with unshaven legs and armpits in tank tops while gnawing on a Danish and shouting at a sister to pass the sugar for the coffee. It was, after all, regardless of what their mother believed, still their house.

It was Reverend Collins who came in with the mail as he and Mr. Bennet had been out on the farm. Each day since his arrival, Mr. Bennet would share another one of his ideas to make Longbourn more profitable and how they could make some advancements that were sustainable and allow them to resist the urge to sell off tracts of land to developers who had their eyes on Meryton. Mr. Bennet knew that he needed to give the Reverend information in drips and drabs because while he could remember everything, he could not process it all. What may seem like drinking from a garden hose to some was like drinking from a fire hose to Reverend Collins. Things were progressing nicely, and Mr. Bennet was confident everything would be alright in the end; until there was something in writing, Mrs. Bennet didn't believe it.

When he came in dressed in his no longer new and absolutely permanently stained orange coveralls, he shouted over the din of five women talking, "Morning, cousins!" Three of them looked up at him. Two of them smiled genuinely. One of them still had to stifle a laugh at the sight of his outfit, so it looked like a painful, fake smile, but he didn't know the difference. "I've been tasked with the great honor of delivering your mail today." He was holding a paper bag. "Your father asked me to get it, and when I looked in the box, I saw it was quite a lot, so I got this bag from the farm." He pointed his head back at the door. They knew he meant he got it from the farm office and that they had not started growing paper bags out there. "I trust that you can trust that I've not read any of it or done anything untoward in any way."

"Yes, of course, Reverend," Jane said. She held out her hand. "I'll take it from here. Why don't you get out of that," she waved her other hand at his outfit, "and come join us for lunch? We've a bit of everything. Leftover buffet, we call it."

"That sounds excellent, Jane. Thank you." He handed her the bag, bowed awkwardly, and went back to the entryway to get out of his get-up. It always took him longer than it should.

Had it been Lizzy who'd been given the task, the mail bag would have been upended on the table, and people

189

could scramble for their goodies. If it had been Lydia, she would have searched through for her items and left the rest in the bag without a word. If it had been Kitty, she would have handed the bag to Lydia. If it had been Mary, she would have just pulled the items out one at a time and made piles. Because it was Jane who had the mail bag, it was turned into a game.

She turned her back on her sisters and reached into the bag. She read aloud the return address, and each of them had to guess for whom the mail was intended. It was more fun than it sounds. She was going to be an elementary teacher after all, and they can make the most mundane tasks, like tying shoes or matching words with images, sound like the most amazingly fun thing in the world. While her sisters were not in elementary school, she was Jane and their big sister who loved them all so much, who taught them dance moves, and got them to bond and get along even when they didn't want to, so it was easy to feel that way around her.

They were halfway through the bag, having guessed correctly 50 percent of the time when Reverend Collins returned. Miracles happen, and so it was that he sat quietly and watched the game be played without hazarding to shout out guesses. Even as the Bennet sisters shouted out answers with mouths full or when they reached to clamp their hands over the mouth of a sister who had been getting the answers right first each time and was on a hot streak or when they laughed and threw playful elbows into ribs, he said nothing. He was certainly tempted to say something about sisterly love and solicitude, but he ate his leftover buffet and drank his iced tea. Only when the final piece of mail was pulled out, a glossy brochure with a picture of a college campus on the front of it, did he shout out. Of course, he immediately jerked his head in the direction of Mary as soon as Jane read the return address. While none of the sisters actually knew anything about Mansfield College nor Mary's interest, they all knew it must have been for her as there were two other college brochures and one early acceptance letter in the bag.

With the bag empty, the two older sisters and the two younger sisters disappeared to get dressed for a walk into Meryton to meet up with their mother who had gone to town to have lunch with her sister. After which, they would all buy some final gifts and do some final window shopping. Thus, Mary and Reverend Collins were left to clean up.

It was then and only then that he finally said anything. "I wasn't trying to be intrusive, but I couldn't help but notice that you got your brochure from Mansfield College today."

Mary looked at the pile of her mail sitting on the table in front of her seat as she picked up the plates and stacked the silverware on top of the pile. "You brought in the mail, and you saw it come out during the game. You are not being intrusive at all." She pointed at the pitcher of iced tea and the two-liter of generic diet cola with her chin. "Can you bring those in?" she asked, but as is the way with people in big families, questions are really not questions. He couldn't say no. It wasn't an option.

Still, as is the way when people ask questions that are demands, he replied with, "Of course," which should have been enough, but nothing was ever enough for him, "I'd be delighted to assist you. That is what family does."

Not wanting to go down that rabbit hole, she just went back to responding to his first comments as they walked into the kitchen. She pointed again with her chin at the fridge, indicating she wanted him to put the drinks in there while she set the dirty dishes down on one side of the sink. She put in the plug on the other side, turned on the hot water, and squirted in some soap. "I saw the Mansfield brochure. I'm sure it is out of my price range if the Darcys and Bingleys and de Bourghs can go there, but I want to dream big. Aunt Phillips and I have been filling out a lot of financial aid forms and..."

He interrupted, "I'm sorry to say that Mansfield College doesn't take financial aid money."

Mary cocked her head to one side the way people do when they hear something but don't quite understand it. "How's that possible?"

"Yes, it's odd but true. It is likely one of the many reasons why it wasn't in the *Barron's Guide* either. Something in their history from their founder. They are accredited and highly regarded. Maybe one of the best private colleges in region, possibly even the whole country, they fill up quickly, and they always meet enrollment, every bed is full on campus, but they don't take federal money. I do suppose people could take out a personal loan and use that money. Most people don't, of course, but considering the quality, it might be a good investment. Although the interest rate on a private loan is different, and I'm not totally sure if private loans allow one to hold off until graduation until you must repay it. I could look into it if you'd like. I'm sure..."

Mary tried to hide her disappointment. "Well, that is disconcerting." She didn't try hard. Unflappable doesn't mean unfeeling.

"Yes, well, there are plenty of amazing colleges and universities out there. Hardly anyone has ever heard of my school outside of Maine, and even many a Mainer have not heard of it. In fact, I'd never heard of it when I was growing up. It was only through a friend of an acquaintance that St. Josephs came up in conversation. If I didn't mention it, I would imagine you would not have heard of it, and from what I understand, you are neck deep in the college application and investigation process, and yet I managed to gain the attention of the de Bourghs. It isn't the degree that makes the person, Mary; it is the person that makes the degree." Just because a person says a lot of absurd things doesn't mean that person *only* says absurd things.

It was a salve that she needed. It was true. She recognized it as the truth. Mary nodded. She shut the water off and moved the stack of dishes from one side of the sink into the other. She turned and looked at him. He had his ever-present nervous half-smile plastered on his face. "You are right. I know you are. Honestly, if you'd not arrived, I shouldn't have ever heard of Mansfield, and I'm not even sure if it is the right fit for me. It is just, well..." She paused to consider if she could trust him, and likely because he was a man of faith, she took a leap of faith and said to him something she'd not even said to her aunt, although she need not bother saying to her aunt because Aunt Phillips already knew it all. "I am not sure how supportive my parents are going to be about me going out of state for college. It hasn't ever come up. They've never asked or offered any suggestions. They talk about me staying here like Jane and Lizzy as though it is a done deal. That is really lovely of them. Really. We are not cheap. You've seen us eat. I know that would save me so much money, but there is so much more to this choice than just money. Money matters. Of course, it does. I'm not a fool, but sometimes, money needs to be only part of the decision, not the only reason. I thought if they knew someone who went to Mansfield, and if you said such good things about it, they would be open to supporting me. It might seem a bit safer, even though one place isn't more or less safe than another."

He had been remarkably silent for much of the day, and so we can't expect him to keep quiet forever. "I can't speak for your mother, as I've only gotten to know her a little in my time here at Longbourn, but I feel that I've known Uncle Bennet very well for many years through our correspondences and yearly outings in Boston. I can tell you that he has the upmost," yes, Dear Reader, he said upmost, not utmost; please forgive him as his intentions were always good, "faith in you and your sisters' abilities. I can plainly say that I've never met a person who was prouder of his children."

"I do think he is proud of us. Of that, I have no doubt. Thank you for saying it. However, I think they think that we are meant for smaller things. They expect Jane to teach locally at best and in Hartford at worst. Even that would be a huge culture shift for her. For all of Lizzy's speechifying and big ideas, they expect her to sit in that attic room of theirs and write books and manifestos. She may change the world, but she will be changing it from Meryton. Father is pragmatic. Mother is terrified. We are home-schooled girls who've never left our hometown for much of anything, and so going to CCSU and living at home is all we can handle."

She paused here and pushed up her glasses, which had not slipped down at all. "Frankly, I understand why

they think that. On paper, it is the safe route. We really have been sheltered here. It's not been a bad life at all. Our personal library is unrivaled in the whole state, and our public library has almost everything we need. Three of us have worked in a law office. We can all change tires, milk cows, do the most basic math in our heads, read complex material, and carry on thoughtful conversations about that material. Lydia included. She plays dumb because she thinks it is appealing to boys, which is the dumbest thing about her. She isn't dumb. Plus, she plays music beautifully. She could study it. She could compose it. She could be the next great maestro. Will she?"

It was rhetorical, of course. Reverend Collins rarely heard a rhetorical question he didn't try to answer. Thankfully, Mary didn't give him a chance. She plowed on. Except for her father and her aunt, she rarely had a captive audience and space to speak unfettered.

"Kitty is an athletic wonder on the pitch. No one plays defense like she does. It is spectacular really. We are all okay. We all played, but we all stopped by the time we were around 16. The U18 leagues are brutal and for the elite. They came to her and asked her to play. I've seen college scouts at her matches.

"On top of that, I wager we all are more educated than our peers who've gone to public schools. We all score higher on the tests than the average Meryton high schooler, but those tests don't mean much in the grand scheme of things, do they?"

Reverend Collins opened his mouth to answer this rhetorical question as well, and because Mary took a breath that lasted just a bit too long, he managed to answer it. "I suppose it depends on what the grand scheme is."

It turns out some rhetorical questions need answers, for it was a good prompt. Mary continued, "For me, the grand scheme begins with college. The fact that I've already been accepted to several means that those numbers are very important. I just want to be more than those numbers. The truth isn't in there, though. They are just numbers. The truth is out there." She pointed out the window. Her voice clicked up an octave as she let it all out. "Sure, I can find it here in my books, and here," she pointed to her head, "and here," she patted herself on the chest, "but I won't know for sure if I don't get out there. I know if I stay here, I'll be safe. I'll be successful. I can get a degree or three and never move out of Longbourn. I could take over the farm, or the law firm, or both. I could buy the bookstore or become a teacher. By rights, all those things are great aspirations, and maybe I'll do all those things, but doing those things here, in Meryton, is all just safe, and maybe the truth is I don't want to play it safe. I want to have the chance to fail spectacularly. I just need the chance, and while until a few weeks ago, I hadn't heard of Mansfield College, the reality is something swelled inside me when you talked about it. Just saying the name feels right. It feels like I'm supposed to go there. I did the math on the student loans. I thought I could make it work. It was my path. Because you spoke so highly of it, and because we knew someone who went there, I thought I could get Father to go for it. It feels like all roads lead there. Now that you've told me what you have, I feel a bit foolish, like I've been having some delusions of grandeur."

Before he could say whatever it was he would have said, which would likely not have been much comfort, Lydia and Kitty came into the kitchen, fully kitted up to go for a walk to town. "You're not done cleaning yet?" Lydia huffed at Mary. It really hadn't been that long since they vacated the dining room to get ready, but they were used to Mary being left alone with her thoughts and the radio and working quickly and efficiently. Lydia never thought about the fact that Mary was often alone, cleaning up after them as though it were her place in the family hierarchy. However, if the shoe had been on the other foot, Lydia would have been on the lookout for a glass slipper, thinking she'd been wronged so badly.

"You're welcome, Lydia." Mary's voice returned to its normal, flat affectation, all the passion and emotion from the moment prior gone.

Lydia opened her mouth to retort when Jane, also fully dressed for an outdoor winter excursion, came into the kitchen with her arms piled high with the leftover containers stacked on top of each other. "Get the fridge, someone, please?" she asked the room. Her mere presence didn't always stop Lydia from being "bad Lydia" as Lizzy called her, but she was more successful than anyone else. Upon hearing her sister's voice, Lydia closed her mouth and settled for a glare as Mary, who had never taken the bait in Lydia's whole life, remained still. Other people may have wished to return the glare with a smirk, or mouth something obscene, or use a particular finger to push up her glasses, but Mary Bennet rode the high road.

Reverend Collins, who was still standing in front of it, obliged and did a strange bow while he did it as he tried to be out of the way and gallant at the same time. It was as awkward as it sounds.

"Thank you, kind sir," Jane said, acknowledging the bow but not the awkwardness. She looked to her younger

sisters. "Ready then?" They both nodded. "Sure, you don't want to come, Mary? Reverend? Nothing like a brisk walk with family."

"That is a lovely offer. I would certainly take you up on it on another day, but I did promise your father that I would join him in the library to discuss some business. May I take a raincheck?"

"No need. It is a standing offer. Where one of us goes, we can all go," Jane said to him while she looked at Mary, who shook her head slightly.

"LET'S GO!" Lizzy shouted from the other room.

With that, the sisters Bennet skittered out of the kitchen and out the door, passing their father as he was coming in. They gave him hugs or kisses on the cheek as they passed by. Hearing that Mr. Bennet was back in the house, Reverend Collins bowed his head to Mary and left the kitchen.

Mary took in the empty room and a deep breath. She held it for a count of three and let it out. She turned on the radio and, as Lydia would have expected her to, had the whole place back in order in less time than it took for three songs to play.

She got her stack of mail from the dining room table and took advantage of the time she could have alone in their shared bedroom. Habit forced her to grab her Walkman instead of playing the music on their shared second-hand boombox with a working tape deck and a hanger where the antenna ought to be. She pulled her tape case out from under her bed and found The Smiths' *Louder Than Bombs* album. It was set to play on side B, which was just fine with her. It didn't really matter which side played as almost all the songs were a bit upsetting. It was her go-to for when she felt maudlin. She felt that no matter how bad she felt, Morrissey felt worse even if he was a rich, beloved rock star.

Instead of doing the things that would make her feel better right away, like opening her early acceptance offer from Trinity College, back then thick packages meant acceptance and single letters meant rejection or wait-list, she decided to wallow a bit in what could have been by going through the Mansfield College brochure. The first half was filled with images of each building and the surrounding town. There were all things that could be expected from a college brochure. She lingered on the images of Pemberley. It was a mansion worthy of a college president. She touched the page, trying to get as close to it as she could.

The back half wasn't like other brochures full of clearly staged pictures of students who never really met but who were thrown together for the photoshoot. There were candid shots of students eating in the cafeteria. There were shots of students performing what she assumed was a Shakespearian play. There were some shots of the women's field hockey team in action. Each image was accompanied by a corresponding explanation of who the student or students were when they graduated and gave a bit of information about the activity.

When she got to the final page of the brochure, the short, but hopeful song, "Please, Please, Please, Let Me Get What I Want," which Mary first heard in the John Hughes classic *Pretty in Pink*, played. She laughed a bit at the song as it was a bit of a confession. It was in the movie to explain how Duckie felt about Andie while sitting alone on his bed feeling miserable for himself. While Mary didn't think twice about the romantic need that Duckie felt, she did understand longing. She had confessed it all to Reverend Collins over a sink of dirty dishes. She knew he wouldn't know what to do with the confession nor would he repeat it. Still, she surprised herself by saying it all. She hadn't meant to; it just seemed to happen.

Sometimes, there is a glorious confluence of events. As Morrissey wailed, she saw a picture of a young Pakistani man, who according to the caption was called Rayan, who had been a recipient of something called The Mansfield Gift. There was a full explanation of what it was as well as directions about how to apply and where to send the materials. She had not missed the deadline. She sat bolt upright. Hope blossomed.

19

This Charming Man

Mary was unable to run to the phone to call Aunt Phillips to share the big news because she knew that her mother and sisters were with her shopping in town and unable to talk to her father about it as he was closed up in the library with Reverend Collins, and unlike her mother, she would never barge into the library when the door was closed. While she knew if she knocked, she would be admitted and likely included in the conversation while being treated like an equal, she didn't really feel as though she wanted to share this with her father just yet. She wasn't keeping a secret. She planned on discussing it with him when the brochure arrived. Now that there was more complicated information regarding Mansfield College, she wanted to wait to talk to him when she could explain completely.

So it was that she found herself in her Buddy Holly glasses, which were the preferred eyewear when the weather was bad, just in case she took a tumble, hooded sweatshirt with the front hand pouch filled with the rolled-up brochure, hood up, winter jacket on, headphones on, Walkman clipped to her waistband with the cord running inside her jacket, headed to town. She swapped out The Smiths in favor of INXS' 1987 album *Kick*. The tones could not be more different, and both records fit her moods as they happened. She did love the radio in the way the members of Generation X loved the radio, but sometimes she needed to control the message. Some people liked to pair socks with shoes or accessories with makeup; Mary Bennet liked to pair art with her mood. Some cold winter days simply called for Chekov, and other sweltering summer nights begged for Kate Chopin.

The album *Kick* was appropriately named. It starts out with a kickdrum on "Guns in the Sky," and it doesn't allow listeners to take a breath until the first side ends. The big breakout hit, "New Sensation," dares listeners to sit still whilst listening. Feeling buoyed, she rode the wave as she walked to town to find her family. If anyone were to watch, it would seem as though Mary was the main star in a one-woman musical performance of her life. She walked in 2/4 time and found herself in town before the first side ended. While Lydia could, while walking alone and unencumbered by her sister's short legs, make it in that time with ease, and Lizzy doing an angry purposeful walk could as well, it was a record for Mary.

While the auto-reverse option existed at that time, a feature that played the tape's side until the reel ran out, paused, then played it back the other way, in reverse, while playing the music on the other side, thus eliminating the need to open the front and flipping the tape over, it was admittedly revolutionary and likely invented while Sony was in cahoots with the battery industry as the tape would play over and over and over until the user stopped it or until the batteries died. Knowing that she would be a victim of such battery waste, as she often laid in bed listening to music to block out the sounds of her sisters until she fell asleep, Mary opted not to buy one with that feature. Her player shut itself off when the tape wound down or was stopped by the user.

So it was that she was standing outside The Theater flipping her cassette over, her head down, making sure she didn't drop it in the snow piled up in that transom of space between sidewalk and road as often happens in small towns where the shop owners shovel and care for their own storefronts while the city cares for the roads. Since she had her hood up, her vision was blocked, and those who would walk by wouldn't have necessarily known it was her.

The side door that led upstairs to the bookstore/video rental/record store opened, and the unmistakable sound of her mother and youngest sister speaking simultaneously bombarded her senses. For those uninitiated with the sound, it was a bit like the sound of several waterfowl squawking at each other. It sounded noisy and chaotic, but it was clear that those animals knew exactly what they were saying to each other. For the initiated, that is to say the rest of the Bennet family, Aunt Phillips, Aunt Gardiner, and Charlotte Lucas, but not Maria Lucas, could not only discern the two voices but follow the conversation. Like the immersion model of language learning, which Mary Bennet read quite a bit about and the research bore it was the best way to learn, and if she was ever able to live any-where besides Meryton, she would try, people just sort of became fluent in the language due to proximity.

Dear Reader, it will be impossible to replicate it here, so we shall run the conversation back and forth, begin-ning with Mrs. Bennet. Consider these blank verse cou-plets the two lines were said at the same time, and the responses were then said at the same time and on and on until Mary put a stop to it. Also, bear in mind only one of them involved in the below "conversation" was a teenager at the time.

"Well, he was certainly something. Charming. Handsome. Clearly smart."

"Do you think he liked Lizzy? Why does everyone like her?"

"He is a grown man, after all, honey. Lizzy is a woman. You are a girl."

"He's beyond handsome. He's dreamy."

"Yes, sometimes the uniform makes the man."

"If it were like 1813, I'd be considered a woman. I'm fully grown anyway. I'm the tallest. I have the best curves. I look more like a woman than she does. From the back, people think she's a boy half the time. I mean, if he likes waifs, I suppose."

"Yes, you do have my figure, but some men like more than just that. Your Uncle Teddy, for instance."

"I'd love to see what's under that uniform. It's a shame he's here to train in the winter. I so love to watch the sol-diers run in the heat."

"Yes, well, we can invite him over to dinner and turn up the furnace."

"Aunt Gardiner is at least a C. Lizzy is at best a B. At best. I'm still not convinced she isn't padding her bra."

Mrs. Bennet giggled.

Mary had heard more than enough. She spun to face them. She shoved back her hood, pulled her headphones down to rest behind her neck, and pushed her glasses up on her nose. "Hello, Mother," Mary deadpanned. "Lydia." She flicked her eyes to her youngest sister, who didn't remotely look chastened but who did seem annoyed at being interrupted.

"Ahhh." Mrs. Bennet's giggle became a squeal. She clutched her heart. "Mary, what are you doing lurking there?"

"Lurking? Here in the broad daylight?"

"Well, I didn't see you, and you were standing there all quiet with your back turned."

Yes, Dear Reader, Mary caught the lie too. "My fault then."

Mrs. Bennet waved her hands in the air. "Yes, well… you're forgiven."

Mary sighed. She shook her head.

"What are you doing here? I thought you were going to stay home and study Gödel's Proof," Lydia said.

If that doesn't sound like a good putdown, that is because it wasn't one. Mary didn't take it as one. She wouldn't have been opposed to doing just that. She had spent many hours in the high-backed chair in the library reading Douglas Hofstadter's *Gödel, Escher, Bach: An Eternal Golden Braid* and hours more dissecting it with her father while listening to Bach and looking at Esher prints in his oversized coffee table book that featured 29 of the artist's prints. On more than one occasion, one of the other sisters, Lydia included, joined in. To be fair, it was before Lydia went through puberty.

Also, the fact that Lydia knew who Gödel was and that there was a proof named after him only proved the point Mary made earlier in the day. While she may have chosen to skip the academic fun in the library once she aged and her hormones ran her brain, the knowledge was in there whether she liked it or not. A dumb person would have just made some snarky remark about her nose being in a book and made a degrading comment about her glasses. She would have emphasized the word *glasses* as well to make it sound as though she was saying "dork."

So, feeling that she proved something herself that day, Mary stood stone-faced and, for the billionth time in her life, didn't take Lydia's bait. However, Mrs. Bennet, who imagined Lydia made up the word Gödel and that it was some fictional thing that only dorks who believed in the fictional world would prove, thought her youngest was indeed putting Mary down. She believed it was funny enough that her giggle returned, even though she swatted Lydia on the arm as she laughed.

Mary centered herself and decided to answer the question Lydia asked. "I'm looking for Aunt Phillips."

Mrs. Bennet's giggles slowly petered, and she caught her breath. She held up her finger asking Mary. No one could wait like Mary Bennet. She waited 18 years for the chance to get out of Meryton on her own terms; she could wait three minutes for her mother to laugh at her. Every time she thought she was calm enough to start giving an answer, she would start giggling again and muttering "Gödel" under her breath. However, because she didn't actually know that Gödel was a person and that was his last name, it morphed into "Good All" by the time she was ready to stop.

The door opened behind them, and Kitty and Aunt Phillips walked out. Mary looked to Lydia, who obviously knew that she was up there and could have answered her at any time. She shook her head at the closed-mouthed, smarmy smirk on her little sister's face. Her father always said that Lydia wasn't mean; she was misguided. Mary never responded by pointing out that he was right there and could easily be a guide. They all understood that her mother had claimed Lydia as hers and hers alone when she was very young. It happens sometimes that one parental figure has more sway than the other. It is rarely discussed. It just sort of happens. Mrs. Bennet clearly felt that her oldest three children were a lost cause, which really only upset her when it came to Jane because she was so absurdly good-looking. She and Kitty had never really clicked. It wasn't that there was anything "wrong" with Kitty. She was, and this pun is entirely intended, her own kind of animal. Because Kitty was just a smaller, quieter version of whomever she was with, her mother couldn't see her as her own person. Perhaps her nickname should have been chameleon.

Unaware of the immediate tension among Mary, her sister, and her youngest niece, but aware of the overall tension among them, Aunt Phillips smiled at seeing Mary standing there. "Hello, dear. To what do we owe the pleasure?"

Mary heard the "we" and knew it was performative. Still, she liked it. It was likely that Kitty was glad to see her too. If Jane came out of the door next, she knew she would most certainly be happy to see her as she really did want her to join them in the first place. "I wished to speak to you about something, Aunt."

"Well, Kitty and I were just going to the diner for some hot chocolate. Would you care to join us? I'm sure Kitty won't mind, will you, dear?"

"Hot chocolate sounds delightful," Mary responded.

"I'm too full. We couldn't find room for all those empty calories, could we, Lydia?" Mrs. Bennet said at the same time while patting her mid-section, which admittedly was the mid-section of a woman half her age with five fewer daughters.

"That's too bad," Aunt Phillips said in a way that made it clear that it was not too bad at all. She hadn't invited her after all. "More for us." Yes. It makes no sense. Aunt Phillips knew it when she said it. Mary heard it as did you, Dear Reader. It was a diner after all. It wasn't as though there was a limit on hot chocolate there. While the resources were not infinite, had Lydia and Mrs. Bennet joined them, each of them could have had the same amount of desired hot beverage. Be there three or five at the table, there would be no risk of a sudden hot chocolate shortage. Sometimes, frustration makes the brain short circuit, and oftentimes a younger sister is, no matter how old, still a source of frustration.

"Yes, well..." Mrs. Bennet said, having not heard the faux pas at all. "Lydia and I have much to discuss as well, don't we, darling? Let's go home." She locked arms with Lydia and pulled her toward Longbourn.

"Thank you for the lovely day, girls!" Aunt Phillips shouted after. It was a parting gift to her frustrating little sister, who loved to be included with the "girls."

While neither of them turned, they each lifted an arm and did a backward wave as they leaned into each other to start talking at the same time about the rest of the women in their family and overeating and who knows what else. While it would be quite easy to follow them back to Longbourn and find out, no one wants that.

Once they were out of earshot so as not to draw attention to her aunt's weak retort about the hot chocolate, Mary asked, "Are Lizzy and Jane upstairs? Shall I fetch them?"

"They are not." She pointed toward the diner with her head, indicating they should start walking. She had already locked one arm with Kitty, so she locked the other with Mary and the three of them walked down the sidewalk. "We met a charming young man at the five-and-dime who joined our party for a short time. He is going to be doing his two weeks in January." The phrase "doing his two weeks" was a Meryton shorthand for the reservists who came and went from town like clockwork. "Apparently, he has no family, so he just came to town to get acclimated to the weather. He said he'd been traveling around South America for some time. He certainly looked sun-worn, didn't he, Kitty?" She didn't wait for Kitty to answer as she continued, "He said he was staying at Long's. They have those small cabins out back by the pool that have kitchenettes. He is staying with another reservist called Denny. We met him as well, and he was, well, less charming. He is a lieutenant, and he made sure everyone knew it. He had that weekend warrior vibe that so many of the reservists have. Grown men playing war. George seemed to be interested in the actual work the reservists do."

They reached the diner, and Mary opened the door and let Kitty and their aunt go in ahead of her. The place was small enough that it was a seat-yourself situation as the staff always noticed when a table or booth filled up. It was about half full, which was odd for the time of day, but due to the fact it was a Saturday and because it was near a holiday, there were plenty of other locals and quite a few tourists who were doing their last-minute shopping as well and needed a break. The three of them took a booth that was in the window. They took their coats and gloves off and put them on one side of the booth against the window. Aunt Phillips sat next to them. Kitty slid in on the other side against the window opposite the coats, and Mary sat opposite their aunt.

The server brought them water. They ordered the afore-mentioned hot chocolate, and with very little convincing from Aunt Phillips, they each ordered a slice of pie. They made small talk about the gifts Aunt Phillips bought for her husband and how she had been trying to convince him to eventually give up on the whole gift thing and start spending the money on trips and adventures. They really did have everything they needed and could do anything they wanted anytime they wanted. Law offices hardly ever lose money if the person who runs it, that would be Aunt Phillips and her nieces, pay attention and do a good job collecting fees. They lived above the law office in property they owned free and clear as it was paid in full by her father when it was his firm. When her father owned the office, the apartment was given to Mr. Phillips as part of his salary, and after they married, she moved in. They always thought if they had chil-dren, they would move, but when that proved to be not in the cards, they settled in for the long haul. So it was that the place was small, and they were "rich enough," and there was no reason for them to keep filling it up with "garbage." Uncle Phillips was happy enough to try the experience idea instead of gifts, but he wasn't really that adventurous. To try it out, she bought him tickets to see the Rockettes. They could go to New York, see the show, have dinner with her brother, and be back on the same day. If that went well, she thought that she would get him to actually spend the night in the city for the next time.

Mary thought that was an excellent idea, and she told her aunt so. Kitty seemed to agree. The hot chocolate and pie were delivered, and then, after they were settled in, Aunt Phillips went back to the story from before about the "charming man" they met that day. "His name is George Wickham. He is 19 and in the reserves. We met him in the back fabric room of all places. The girls were getting ribbons to wrap up the gifts with real bows. The home economics lessons really took root and spread out as both Jane and Lizzy were excited about it as well. I suspect that he saw a collection of pretty girls and followed them in. Regardless, Lizzy's scarf fell, and he picked it up."

We shall cut in here to point out that Mary didn't care about any of this. She wasn't interested in reservists or weekend warriors or ribbons. She wanted to talk to her aunt about The Mansfield Gift, but she loved her aunt, and her aunt wanted to tell this story. She lived vicariously through her nieces. It was why Mary was so hopeful for the coming adventures of her aunt and uncle Phillips. She wanted them to have their own experiences outside of Meryton. She wanted everyone to have them, but of course, she wanted that for herself most of all. She wanted more than anything to pull out the brochure and talk to her aunt about her future, but first, her aunt had to tell this story. So, she waited and listened.

This story goes on for some time. There will be more hot chocolate for Aunt Phillips and Kitty while Mary will switch over to coffee. By the time it finally ends, they will have been in the diner so long, with several bathroom breaks, that a guilty Aunt Phillips, who really did lose track of time, felt terrible for taking up so much space in the diner for so long and for taking up so much of her nieces' time, one of whom was actually with her the whole day and experienced the event in real-time, will have bought the girls dinner.

The short version of the story was that George Wickham and Denny joined the party and did some shopping. Denny leered at Jane while George flirted unabashedly with Lizzy, who was not resistant to his charms. Lydia was infuriated that no one was paying attention to her and tried desperately to make a spectacle of herself. It was only when they were about to enter The Theater that the party came across the group from Netherfield Park. Jane and Bingley were elated to see each other but were not yet sure what their relationship was, and so, they didn't embrace or even touch, but snow around them may have melted. Caroline whispered to Lou. Mr. Hurst sighed loudly for having to stop. Darcy, who seemed genuinely pleased to see Lizzy, was genuinely displeased to see her with George Wickham, whom he apparently knew. Darcy stormed off without a word. Caroline followed him. Hurst suggested they get a drink. Jane accepted and went with them. Denny suggested that drinks were a good idea, so he invited Lizzy back to Long's for drinks in their cabin. She went with them. The rest of them went to The Theater, and then Mary arrived. Whew.

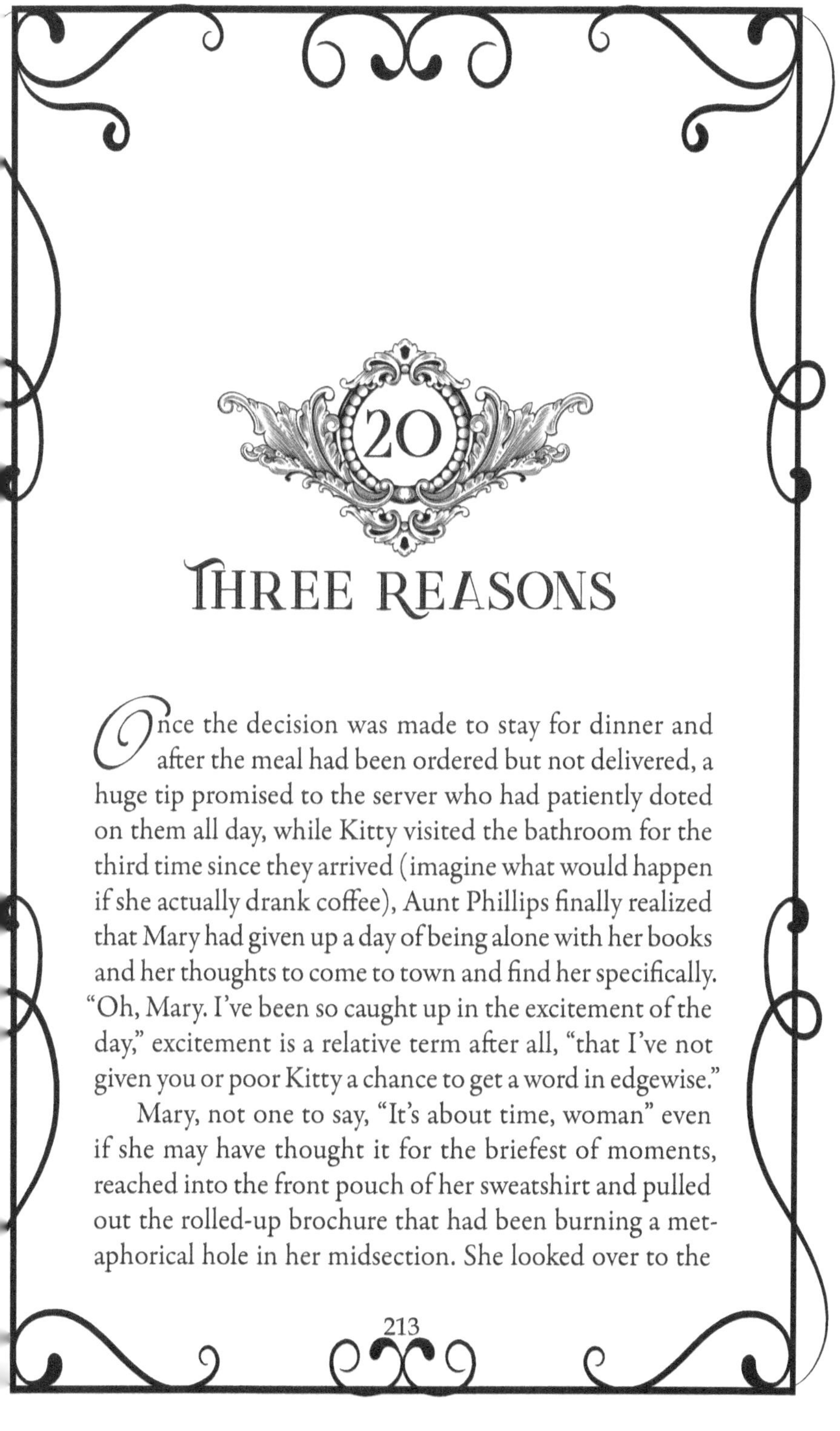

20

THREE REASONS

Once the decision was made to stay for dinner and after the meal had been ordered but not delivered, a huge tip promised to the server who had patiently doted on them all day, while Kitty visited the bathroom for the third time since they arrived (imagine what would happen if she actually drank coffee), Aunt Phillips finally realized that Mary had given up a day of being alone with her books and her thoughts to come to town and find her specifically. "Oh, Mary. I've been so caught up in the excitement of the day," excitement is a relative term after all, "that I've not given you or poor Kitty a chance to get a word in edgewise."

Mary, not one to say, "It's about time, woman" even if she may have thought it for the briefest of moments, reached into the front pouch of her sweatshirt and pulled out the rolled-up brochure that had been burning a metaphorical hole in her midsection. She looked over to the restroom and debated on whether or not she wanted to continue the conversation in front of her sister because she still hadn't discussed it with her father. Ultimately, she knew she would tell him about it as soon as she had a moment alone with him, so she set the rolled-up brochure down. As she flattened it out on the table, she explained what Reverend Collins told her about the financial aid situation. Aunt Phillips listened with empathetic silence. Her face showed all of her emotions, but she dared not interrupt. She said all the words possible in the few hours they spent together, and she felt a pang of guilt for not allowing Mary the chance to go first. Mary, feeling the brochure was going to be as flat as it could be, flipped it open to the page with the picture of Rayan. She slid it across the table and let her aunt read the page. At that moment, Kitty returned.

Since Mary had to stand anyway to let Kitty back into the booth, and because she noticed consternation on her aunt's face while she was telling her much more succinct and direct story, it took only slightly longer to say than it did to read these words, she decided to go to the restroom to let her aunt read the information about The Mansfield Gift. While few people withstood indignity like Mary Bennet, she wasn't a glutton for punishment.

When she returned, the food was sitting on the table. Kitty saw her coming and smiled. It was a genuine smile. Had Lydia been there, Mary wasn't sure if Kitty would have looked at her at all, let alone smiled. She took it as a sign that the rest of the conversation would go well because Aunt Phillips had told Kitty all about it. As we shall soon see, it wasn't that at all, as Aunt Phillips, having noticed the glance at the bathroom when Kitty was gone, had not mentioned it. She wanted to give Mary the opportunity to share what she was willing to share. It turns out that Kitty was just genuinely pleased to have spent all this time with Mary and their aunt, and seeing Mary actually made her smile. Stranger things have happened.

Mary returned the smile at her sister and slid into the booth. The server arrived and set down some barbecue sauce in a small bowl. Mary looked at her aunt, who shook her head. It was Kitty who remembered that Mary liked to dunk her onion rings in barbecue sauce and must have noticed that Mary failed to order it. "Thank you, Kitty. That was very kind," Mary said as she picked up one onion ring and dunked it in.

Aunt Phillips tapped the now-closed brochure and said, "So?" OK. She asked it more than said it.

Mary nodded and swallowed. She took a sip of her water and relayed the whole story about what Mansfield College was, the Darcys, the Bingleys, the de Bourghs, and on and on. When Kitty was officially caught up to where you've been this whole time, Dear Reader, Mary turned her attention to the real reason she made the trek into town: The Mansfield Gift. "So," she flipped to the back page, "it says here that every year, five students from all around the world win a chance to go to Mansfield College without paying tuition. Tuition is... let's just say exorbitant. Even if I could get the money, I couldn't go in the fall. They fill up fast. There are no seats for me the regular way. I know that other schools give students until spring to make choices. They don't have to do that." She took another drink. "However, they don't make the decision on The Mansfield Gift until May, and I haven't missed the deadline. So, while it is a long shot, it is the only shot."

Aunt Phillips chewed on a French fry and nodded. She was thinking. She nodded when she worked things out in her head. Mary had seen it enough times to know the drill. "OK. I think you should apply for this, but you are going to need to convince your parents. I know you are an adult and your own woman, but I also know that you would rather not leave with any bad blood, so we need to have some compelling reasons."

Mary nodded. "Yes. Of course."

Aunt Phillips lowered her voice to mimic that of her brother-in-law. "Well, Mary, this is a big decision. Tell me why. Give me, say, three reasons why this place instead of, say, Albertus Magnus, Yale, UConn, or CCSU. I know you well enough to know that you don't think that you will be better educated at one than the other. You know that the student sets the educational tone as much as anything."

Mary didn't need to think about that. She had way more than three reasons. "The first one is the class size and the school size. I think it is because of me, as a learner, that I shouldn't go to UConn regardless of how many scholarships they offer me. I could earn a graduate degree there, but I don't think the big research university is for me. I don't think I could go from being alone in the library to a 400-person lecture hall. If it were my only choice, I would do it. I don't want to disparage those educators or the students who graduated from there. I only applied because it is something everyone in Connecticut does. Jane and Lizzy did too. I don't really want to go there. I would rather take out loans and learn than go for free and fail out."

"You wouldn't fail out. You could easily adapt. You are capable of all kinds of things. I will concede that point, but CCSU and Albertus Magnus have small classes."

Mary nodded. She held up two fingers, indicating her second point. "They do, but they are both commuter schools for me. I could live on campus at Albertus Magnus, but would I? Would I really? None of the Connecticut options give me the chance to live somewhere else."

Aunt Phillips switched to her sister's voice, which she did remarkably well. "What's wrong with here? Meryton was good enough for me to become Miss Connecticut, don't forget. People from *New York City* come here to vacation. One place is no better than the other. This Mansfield looks like another small town in the middle of nowhere. The nearest big city is hours away by car. The trains they have are not commuter trains. You'd be cut off. Why go there when you have the whole world right here?"

"Well, Mother," Mary smirked as she said it, "it is true that I can access all those things here, but you are not going anywhere. Longbourn isn't going anywhere. I can always come back having experienced something. If I stay here, I won't actually know what it is like out there. If I stay here, I will have my plan mapped out. I will go to CCSU and then what? Get a teaching degree like Jane? Law School at UConn like Uncle Phillips? Library School at Southern Connecticut? Maybe. Those are good choices, but wouldn't those be my only choices? If I stay in Meryton, those are really the only things that suit me. Who knows? Maybe I will be one of those things or all of those things, but I need to have some choice."

While she was trying to stay in character, Aunt Phillips found herself nodding along. These were good points, and she could help her niece's cause should it come to that, which she expected it would. It wasn't that her brother-in-law meant anything by being the way he was, but his homebody nature had rubbed off on Jane and Lizzy, and if he wasn't careful, it would rub off on all of them. She would certainly miss Mary when she was gone, but she also knew that Mary needed more. She couldn't find the truth she was desperate to find within the borders of Meryton.

Mary, seeing the nod, felt empowered to plow on. "Which," she held up three fingers, "leads me to the final point. If I win The Mansfield Gift," she tapped the brochure with her other hand, "I have to enter college undecided. For two years, I have to take everything. Math, science, sociology, art, music, and... well, *everything*." She leaned into the word and let it hang there. "I won't be able to declare a major without trying out all my options. I will have to spend two years investigating everything. We all know I'm going to get more degrees. There is no way I am stopping with a BA, but I need that first. I need to start somewhere."

Aunt Phillips switched back to her brother-in-law's voice. "What stops you from doing that here? You have the discipline to approach things however you want. Why not just start here and then leave?"

Mary nodded. "That is true, but would I? Would that be practical? Really and truly? If I go here," again she tapped the brochure, "I have to take all four years. If I go to CCSU, I would go year-round and be done in two and a half or three like Lizzy. CCSU does have a lot of options, but it doesn't have everything. At Mansfield, people can build their own majors if they want. I could get a Multidisciplinary Studies degree there if I wanted."

As her sister, Aunt Phillips said, "What's that? That sounds made up. That sounds like a degree in nothing. Why bother at all?"

"Because, *Mother,* a Multidisciplinary Studies degree isn't a degree in nothing; it is a degree in everything. It's like taking four minors, one in Humanities, Business, Math and Science, and Social Science, and smashing them together into one major. With my electives, I could essentially get a quadruple major. Can you imagine? With a degree like that, I could go to law school, *or* library school, *or* medical school, *or* all three. I don't have to do that degree, but I could. It is an option there, and if I do end up getting an education degree or a pre-law degree or majoring in English, all things I could do here, I know, it would be my choice because I would have the choice. I could maybe become a journalist and travel the world and never come home again. I don't know. I just need the chance. I just..."

She cut herself off as she realized she hadn't taken a breath because until she heard herself say it, she didn't really know how badly she wanted it. The more she talked about it, the more desperate she was. She took a deep breath and another drink of her water. She placed both of her hands on the table. She took another breath. "Look, we all know that this is my only chance to go out of state. I'm going to get into some of those other out-of-state schools, but the out-of-state fees make the whole thing out of reach. Everything is triple or even more with out-of-state fees. I know that this scholarship doesn't cover room and board, and it is currently around four thousand a year. I have around ten thousand in the bank. It's only December. I can easily save another two before I go to school in the fall.

"I can finish school early. I mean, I think I already have all the credits I need to graduate now. I could work full-time at the law office or get another part-time job. I can come back and work in the law office in the summer if they'll have me, and I can get a job there and save up more money. It might be tight by my fourth year as I know I will need to spend some of the money on living expenses that are not covered in room and board, and I know the cost will go up a bit each year, but I can cancel the book club and record club. I will have a full huge academic library at my disposal for four years. I can get by. There will always be radio, and that is free. If I had to take out a small loan by then, I would, but if I am frugal, I can pay for it. We don't even know if I am going to win this. Thousands of people apply each year. Please, just let me try."

Aunt Phillips' small nod morphed into an emphatic one. "Sold!" She pounded her hand on the table like she was an auctioneer. She held up her hand to finally collect the check. "Let's get you home. You have a conversation to have with your father and work to do."

Mary smiled a broad genuine smile. She looked at Kitty who may or may not have been crying. Were they tears of joy? Were they tears of sorrow? Did she accidentally poke herself in the eye with her straw? Everyone has done it. You can decide on your own, Dear Reader.

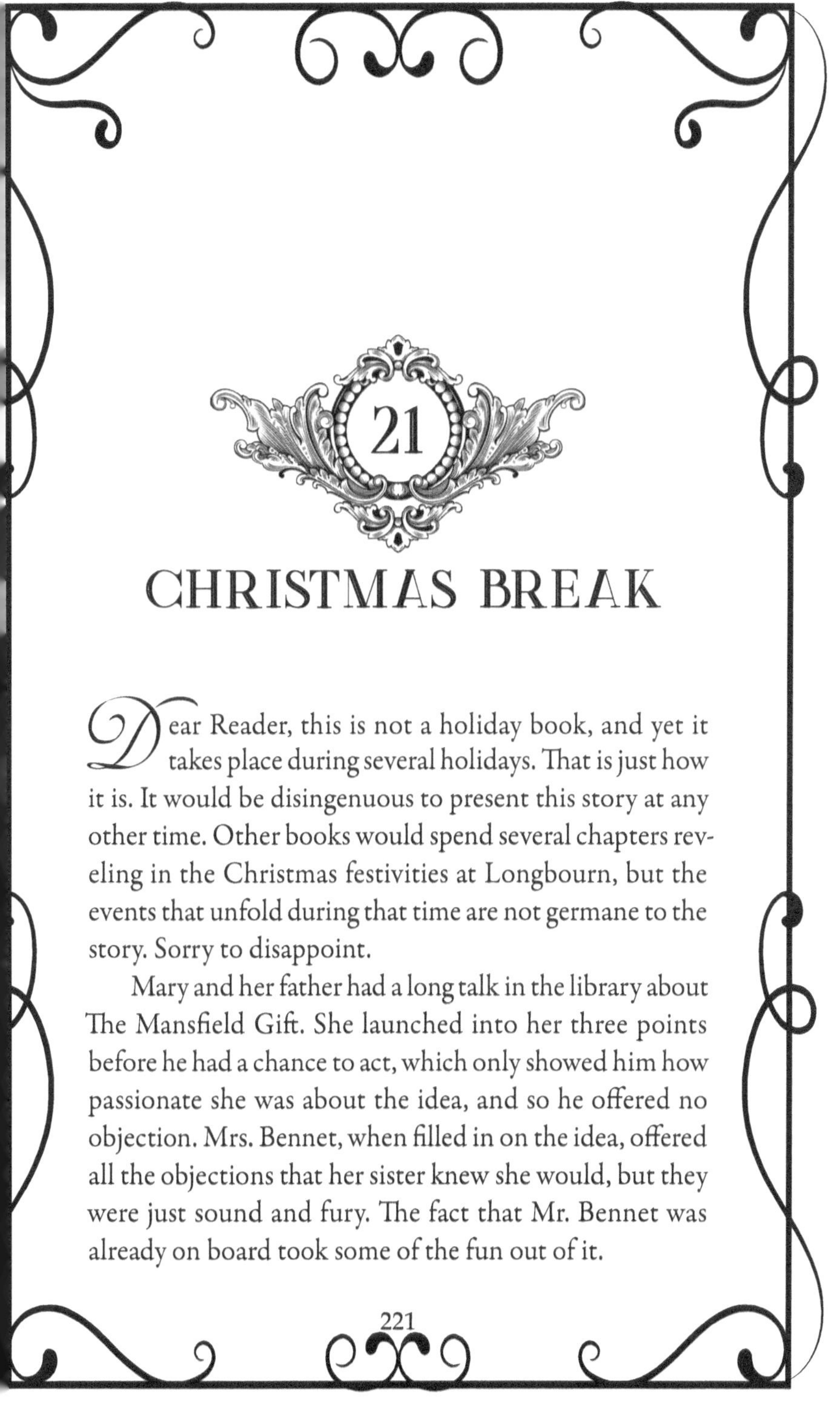

21

CHRISTMAS BREAK

Dear Reader, this is not a holiday book, and yet it takes place during several holidays. That is just how it is. It would be disingenuous to present this story at any other time. Other books would spend several chapters reveling in the Christmas festivities at Longbourn, but the events that unfold during that time are not germane to the story. Sorry to disappoint.

Mary and her father had a long talk in the library about The Mansfield Gift. She launched into her three points before he had a chance to act, which only showed him how passionate she was about the idea, and so he offered no objection. Mrs. Bennet, when filled in on the idea, offered all the objections that her sister knew she would, but they were just sound and fury. The fact that Mr. Bennet was already on board took some of the fun out of it.

Additionally, the simple truth was that she didn't really think she would miss Mary if she were gone. She rarely talked with Mary as it was. At that point, 18 years into her life, Mrs. Bennet couldn't think of one actual conversation she had with her middle child. She spoke *at* Mary, and sometimes, although very infrequently, about Mary, but she wasn't interested in what Mary was doing because she didn't understand Mary at all. With Lydia there to keep her busy, she didn't need to try. Did Mary and Lydia know this? All signs point to yes. How did they feel about it? That is more complicated, isn't it? We all wouldn't be friends with our family if we met them on the street, would we?

With that decided, that Mary would have the support of her father and the tacit approval of her mother, she began work on her application. After one quick long-distance phone call, which she promised to pay for, she discovered that she could have taken the Graduate Education Development test at any time after she turned 18. She couldn't muster up the energy to be annoyed because if she had done so, she would have been on a different path that didn't involve applying for The Mansfield Gift. She signed up to take it in early January and officially declared herself done with high school. To be honest, she had been reading college-level material and doing college-level work since she was 14.

She felt that the essay was the most important part, so to prepare, she did what Mary did best. She studied. The public library was only closed for a few days, so she managed to ransack its collection on educational theory while putting in several requests for books via interlibrary loan. Harriet managed to request several documents from the Educational Resources Information Center, which was commonly called ERIC, resources as well, so she had piles of faxed and photocopied journal articles. She scoured her father's bookshelves for anything she might find useful. She asked Lizzy to take her to the CCSU campus when the new year began so she could go through their journals. So, while she was technically out of school, she studied even more, took more notes, filled up notebooks at a seemingly inhumane rate, and was, let's face it, in her element.

The youngest Bennet girls did what most teenagers did during holiday breaks. They ate, they slept, and they spent time with friends. They repeated. They did their best to have adventures, but Kitty wasn't very adventurous, and Lydia was too constrained while in the confines of Meryton. When she finally does get out of town, which happens shortly in this tale, there is fallout even for our heroine, who had nothing to do with it. It is frustrating to be sure. More on that in 1990.

The eldest Bennet sister spent a lot of time at Netherfield. Jane and Bingley, two of the most painfully shy and romantically inept people in the world, were trying to figure out how to make a relationship work, but due to the aforementioned ineptitude, they never found themselves alone. Thus, in a grand gesture, Bingley decided to have a party to ring in the new decade. The Bingleys were and still are obscenely wealthy, so there is no telling how much money was spent on the party. It was a lot. Was it more than the entire town spent on the Founder's Ball? Possibly. Bingley had pint glasses made special for the event. They read "Netherfield Park's New Year Celebration." For the very special members of the guests, he had them individualized. The special guests were the Bennets and Lucases. He thought it was a nice touch. To be fair, it really was nice, and it was really too much.

He wanted to make a memory that he and Jane would never forget, but honestly, if the two of them had just sat alone and watched Dick Clark and had champagne and kissed at midnight, they would have been happier. Still, socially awkward people with conniving sisters struggle to know what to do. He literally invited all of Meryton, and while not everyone came, the entire Bennet family, yes, shockingly enough, even Mary and her parents ended up going. Oh, the things people were willing to do to make Jane happy, which was silly because Jane Bennet was and is, almost always, happy. To be fair, there will be a few moments of despair that happen in these pages, but it is short-lived. You'll see.

Lizzy split her time between going with her sister to Netherfield and wandering about town with George Wickham. There was a lot of bad blood between Darcy and George, and because George wouldn't stop talking about it and because Darcy refused to speak on it, Lizzy was influenced one way on the matter. Things will come to a head soon between all of them. Mary will try not to care, but her actions will be tangentially part of why things come to a head. She won't even know about it until later. By then, things will be chaos. Families seem to breed it.

So, let's just sum up here by saying Christmas was joyous. Gifts were given. Food was eaten. Awkward statements were made by Reverend Collins. Mrs. Bennet said several things to offend everyone, except Lydia and Jane, although Jane was upset on behalf of everyone and did pull her mother aside to "have a word" about it. That went as poorly as you might imagine. It resulted in Jane in tears and

Mrs. Bennet on the phone with anyone with a local number who would listen. Not surprisingly, almost no one took Mrs. Bennet's side, so she apologized. To the bystanders who heard it, that is to say, Aunt Phillips and Lizzy, it was half-hearted and shallow, but to Jane, it sounded heartfelt and sincere. They hugged. Merry Christmas to all and to all a good night and all of that.

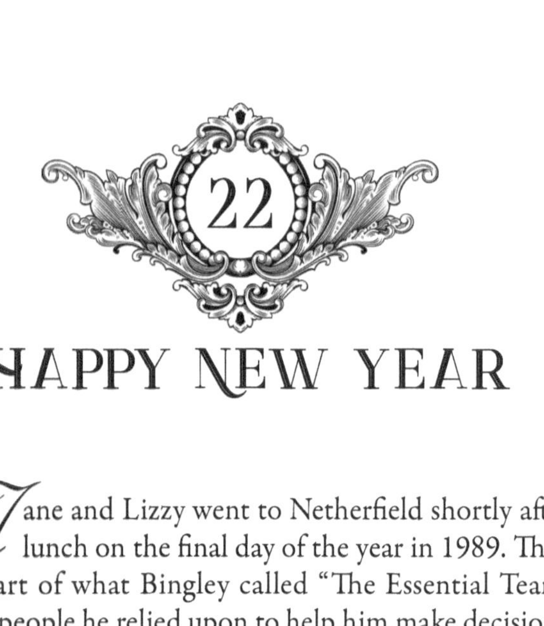

22

HAPPY NEW YEAR

Jane and Lizzy went to Netherfield shortly after lunch on the final day of the year in 1989. They were part of what Bingley called "The Essential Team," that is, people he relied upon to help him make decisions. Bingley's strong suit was being led, not leading. Not all people are leaders. Some follow. Some get out of the way. All are valid options. Some people make themselves great, and others are born rich and male. The patriarchy is real, and so it was that people expected tall, rich, handsome men to be leaders. That isn't to say that men like that can't be leaders, but having certain genetic markers and being born to the right people at the right time does not make for greatness or for being good at deciding how to throw a party after inviting several thousand people.

Lydia and Kitty invited Maria Lucas over to Longbourn to "get ready." Maria would normally have walked over, but she had with her a garment bag full of clothes, and so she had Charlotte bring her. The three of them went into their room where they tried on every item of clothing in different combinations. They would occasionally open the door and call for Mrs. Bennet to join them. She was all too pleased to be included. She was very much just a grown-up girl in many ways. If this book was about them, or if there were a film version of what went on behind closed doors, Van Morrison's "Wild Night" would play over the montage. Feel free to imagine that now. Mary did. All the girls did, in fact, get dressed up for each other.

Charlotte came in and found Mary hunched over her notebook with copies of articles strewn all over the table and books piled up. She was wearing her house cardigan. It was several sizes too big, but it was warm, gray, and had two oversized pockets. This afforded her to carry about multiple notebooks for multiple purposes. Mary Bennet wasn't the kind of person who wanted to mix her research notebooks with her reflection notebooks. She would in a pinch if she only had one with her, but around the house where she spent most of her time and had most of her ideas, the more the better. If she had been allowed to be in her own room, she wouldn't have needed to keep them all with her, but since she couldn't be sure what would happen if she went into her room to fetch anything, she loaded them into her cardigan that morning and stacked them up on the table next to her piles of research. There was a cold cup of coffee next to her as she often lost track of time and space when she was in truth-digging mode. Countless times, she would take a drink of the cold coffee, make a face at the bitterness, shrug her shoulders, and chug the rest down anyway.

"Knock," Charlotte said aloud. She wasn't sure if actually knocking on the table would have made Mary jump or not, and as Charlotte was not a monster, she opted not to do it.

Mary looked up and smiled her genuine but closed-mouth smile. Mary was not a grin-from-ear-to-ear kind of woman. Still, she and Charlotte had always gotten along even though there were nine full years between them. Charlotte's kindhearted optimism and Mary's old soul shaved at least five to six years off that age gap. "Hi. You're still here?" She looked at her watch. It was after 3, and she knew that Maria arrived just after lunch. "I had no idea. How rude of me. What have you been doing? Do you want some coffee?" She slid her pen back into her hair next to the pencil that was already there. The work she was doing was serious enough that she wanted it to be permanent.

"I'd love some coffee actually. Is the pot fresh, do you think?"

Mary looked at her watch and shook her head. "I'll go make us some."

"I'll join you."

The two of them walked into the kitchen. "Cookies?" Mary asked as she poured out the coffee that had indeed started to burn into the sink. Research proves that using a lot of brain power burns up to 150 calories an hour. Mary wasn't playing chess or high-stakes poker, so she didn't go that far, but to be sure, she was in a calorie deficit since lunch.

"Yes, please."

"Up there?" She pointed with her chin to the cupboard over the refrigerator.

Charlotte pulled the foldable step ladder out from its spot next to the fridge while Mary poured fresh water into the coffee pot. "So," Mary began, "are you back to get Maria or did you stay the whole time?"

"Thin Mints or Do-si-dos?"

"Can it be both?"

Charlotte laughed. "It most certainly can be." She opened up the boxes and pulled out one sleeve of each. If they were going to drink coffee and eat cookies, they might as well eat cookies. "Thin Mints are much better out of the freezer, I find," she said as she climbed down from the ladder. She folded it up and put it back, something that not all of the Bennet girls would have done.

Mary, having poured the water in the back of the maker, was filling the filter with coffee. "Agreed. Mother can reach the freezer. She can't reach up there. It is a terrible place for cookies in general. She is not tall enough to reach the cupboard without a ladder, but she insisted that they be left there. Her desire for a cookie is not stronger than her disdain for heights. If the Thin Mints were in the freezer, she would eat the whole box. We know this because Father used to hide a box in the back behind the chicken, and she found them once and complained that he ruined her dinner by leaving the cookies out." She flipped the switch, starting the coffee maker up. It made the air-sucking sound it made, announcing to the world it was doing its job.

"That sounds like her," Charlotte said. There are some unwritten rules about comments like this of course. Mary could complain about and/or make fun of her mother all she wanted, but strangers could not. Mary had, on more than one occasion, to respond sternly to a person or two in Meryton for having the gall to say something snarky about the "former Miss Connecticut" as she was known around town. Even if the criticisms were valid, Mary couldn't allow it, and after a few curt words, generally about glass houses followed by a reminder of some bone or two that stuck out of their closets, the chastened people never again forgot that the studious, serious, short, plainly dressed, bespectacled girl who haunted the public library belonged to Mrs. Bennet. Charlotte, who like Maria, was an unofficial Bennet sister could say it because, as Mary knew, she was only being honest, and should the need arise for her to defend Mrs. Bennet's honor in public, she most certainly would. She rarely needed to say much to defend her own family in public because everyone knew that she was the daughter of the first family, and they were universally loved, even by Mrs. Bennet, regardless of how heated their friendly rivalry got.

"Father apologized, of course, in the way that she took as an apology, and the rest of us heard as a comment on her being an adult woman who ran a small business and had five children who could make her own choices about spoiling her dinner. Only Lizzy laughed aloud." Mary got down a plate and an extra mug. She handed the plate to Charlotte. She grabbed some napkins and put them in the pocket of her cardigan.

"That sounds like her," Charlotte repeated about her closest and dearest friend. "She can't help herself. Your mother pushes every single button she has. If I didn't know, I wouldn't think they were related at all."

The coffee pot, which had the automatic pause feature, had filled up enough that Mary was able to pull it out and fill up her cup and one for Charlotte. "Shall we?" She pointed with her elbow back to the dining room.

They went back to the other room. Charlotte moved two seats down from the area Mary was working and sat down. She didn't want to disrupt whatever was happening there. She took a sip of her coffee and set the cup down. She picked up a Do-si-do and twisted it in half. "Yes! Clean break." She held up the insides of what was now two cookies to Mary to show her that the peanut butter was on one side and the other was clean. She put the whole clean side in her mouth and chewed it up. Not wanting to be rude, she pointed at the piles on the table and then shrugged her shoulders and raised her arms out to each side, indicating that she was asking what it was all about.

"I'm writing an essay for a scholarship. It is likely over-kill, but there are not really any specific guidelines for the essay, but it seems to be the most important part. I know everyone who is going to apply is going to have good test scores and has done all the stuff outside of school, work, or sports, or volunteering, or whatever. It seems that the essay is the key to getting the interview. I want to get there. It's a longshot. There are only five, but I want to try."

Having finished the second half of her cookie and sipped more coffee while Mary was talking, Charlotte said, "Well, no one tries harder than you. If there were an Olympic medal for effort, you would win the gold every time."

Mary was genuinely moved. She wasn't sure how to take a compliment like that. Much like when Jane told her that Lizzy paid attention to her, she was taken aback. When one wears house cardigans and haunts libraries and isn't invited to a dress-up day in her own bedroom and wouldn't go if she were invited, one doesn't really think too much about being seen by anyone.

"Thank you." She reached out and placed her hand on Charlotte's. Mary was not, uninspiringly, a hugger.

"Tell me about it?" Charlotte asked.

So, Mary did. They spent the next two hours talking. Mary gave her the full history of things. Charlotte had been there when Reverend Collins first mentioned Mansfield, so she started there and explained the rest. Charlotte asked questions, posed arguments, and volunteered to be a mock interviewer when, not if, Mary made it to that round. When the conversation was over, and the cookies were gone, and the coffee had been refilled several times, Charlotte left to go home to get ready for the party without taking Maria with her or ever answering Mary's question about what she had been doing at Longbourn all day. Mary was so elated by the conversation and support that she didn't even notice. Did you notice, Dear Reader? It is OK if you didn't. Cookies, friendship, and scholarships are very distracting.

The party at Netherfield was due to start at 6, and Mary hoped to eat one more time before she walked up with her parents, Reverend Collins, her sisters, and apparently Maria Lucas, who wished to be there exactly on time as she didn't want to miss one second of the fun. It turns out Thin Mints can ruin one's dinner. Mary knew there would be plenty of snacks and finger food to eat at the party, so she collected her research into an orderly pile that she put at the far end of the table, put her notebooks in her pocket, and sat with her family as they ate and while the women of the house commented on what she was wearing.

She assured them that she was not going to wear her house cardigan to the party. She decided that she would wear jeans, a turtleneck, and a suit jacket. This was several years before Steve Jobs would make the jeans and turtle-neck thing look, if not cool, normal. Had he been famous in 1989, it would be possible that the ribbing she took from her youngest sister and mother would have been less severe. They did like to follow trends.

Mr. Bennet said that he thought it was a practical choice because then she could keep her notebooks in the jacket pockets instead of her back pocket, plus unlike everyone else, she wouldn't need to worry about finding her jacket at the end of the evening. He decided that he would follow Mary's lead and wear a suit jacket himself. He had a wool one that he thought would just do the trick. This then spurred Reverend Collins to launch into a story about Lady Catherine de Bourgh and her varied pant-suit collection that was featured in *The Providence Journal's* Lifestyle section. It was as riveting as it sounds. Mary went off to get changed.

Dear Reader, we want to assure you that there will not be a detailed description of everything that happened at the party. It began at 6 and wouldn't end until daybreak. All told, over a thousand people came through the doors of Netherfield. It would take more words to detail each moment in that twelve hours than there have been in this book already. Some of the people in Meryton wouldn't be pleased if something like that came out. It would be scandalous and funny and sad and hopeful. That really does sound like it would make for an interesting book though. It would be great fodder for a docudrama series. It just isn't this book. So, let's leave that speculation behind and leave that book for someone else to write and catch up with the Bennets in general and Mary in particular.

Lydia, Maria, and Kitty found their way to the dance floor and didn't leave it except to occasionally eat, drink, or when nature called. They moved and jumped and swayed and burned the number of calories that is only possible when one is a teenager. Most adults would have passed out long before midnight. They most certainly caught the attention of many, and while they were not the belles of the ball, when "Dancing Queen" played, the three of them broke into a dance they learned from Jane, who of course joined them along with Lizzy, Charlotte, and yes, even Mary, who was pulled along by Jane's magnetism as no one can say no to Jane, and so for a brief moment they felt like they were queens, and that is all that mattered.

Lizzy was disappointed to discover that George Wickham didn't arrive. He'd made a whole speech about Darcy needing to be the one to leave and how he couldn't be bullied, but at the last minute, he and Denny had "some pressing matters" that needed their attention. It was more disappointing that the information didn't come from the charming man himself, but via Charlotte who heard it from her father, who ran into the men at the gas station as they were fueling up. Fortunately, or unfortunately for Lizzy, it meant she found herself itching to dance with someone and complaining thusly to Charlotte, and so when Darcy shockingly asked her to dance to The Bangles "Eternal Flame," she heard herself say yes.

She looked over her shoulder at her best friend as Darcy led her to the dance floor. They started with the typical "room for Jesus" space between them that could be seen at a middle school dance, her arms on his shoulders, his on her waist, but as they circled and slowly moved, she found her left hand in his right, and he slipped his hand farther behind her back. When the DJ blended one love song for another, and Cyndi Lauper's timeless classic, "Time After Time" started up, they just kept dancing, and much to Lizzy's surprise, they were talking amiably and not just arguing. She'd been meaning to ask him about some of the things George told her about the causes of the strain on the friendship that he and Darcy once had, but slow dancing with a racing heart didn't seem like the right moment.

When the DJ said, "And now for something completely different," and faded into Adam Ant's "Goody Two Shoes," Lizzy was sure that they would part, but as the swing beat on the drums gave way to the guitars, which gave way to the horns, Darcy spun Lizzy around, twirled her out, back in, and began to swing dance with her. Of course, she wasn't classically trained in the dance form, but as evidenced in this book, she and her sisters could dance to pretty much anything. If the sight of the Bennets and Lucases doing a 7-woman choreographed dance to ABBA stopped the show, Lizzy Bennet and Fitzwilliam Darcy swing dancing to a new wave rock-a-billy song brought the house down. When the song came to its crashing end with two guitar licks and two drum beats, Darcy dipped her and held her there long enough for the gathering crowd to burst into applause. DJs know how to read rooms, and so he didn't start up another song until the applause died down. Darcy mumbled a thank you to Lizzy and said something about a dance class when he was in college, and he was away without another word, leaving Lizzy and the crowd of onlookers with more questions than answers.

Meanwhile, unable to have a quiet moment to talk, Jane and Bingley circled each other all night. They too were locked in an embrace during the abovementioned back-to-back, 80s love songs and were part of the crowd who applauded and guffawed at Lizzy and Darcy's two-person dance party. They shouted over the music and said a lot of "huh?" and "what?" at each other's ears. When the ball dropped at midnight, they were not together as Jane hoped they would be for she had been asked to "console" poor Caroline Bingley, locked in one of the many bathrooms, as she was distraught about something or other regarding Darcy, something about which Jane cared very little, but Jane, being Jane, couldn't say no to a person in need, even if this need seemed to come out of the blue and was poorly timed. Thus, as though it was planned, actions were placed into motion that would in fact cause Jane some heartbreak. Poor Jane. If there was ever a person who didn't deserve heartbreak, it was her, but sometimes, a little heartbreak leads to greater happiness. It will for Jane. Sorry. Spoiler alert. Jane is destined for happiness and joy. She is the best of them. It only makes sense.

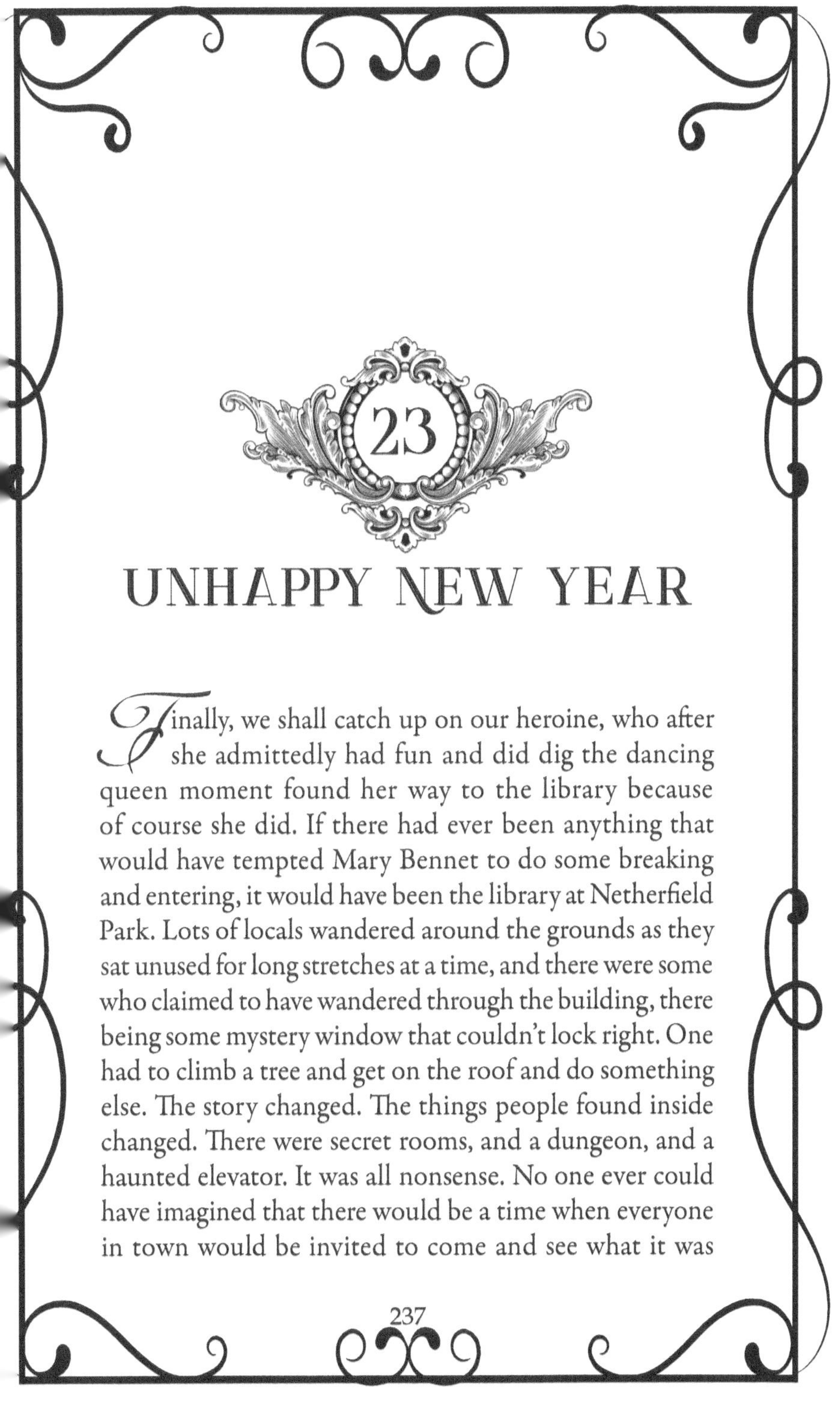

23

UNHAPPY NEW YEAR

$\mathcal{F}$inally, we shall catch up on our heroine, who after she admittedly had fun and did dig the dancing queen moment found her way to the library because of course she did. If there had ever been anything that would have tempted Mary Bennet to do some breaking and entering, it would have been the library at Netherfield Park. Lots of locals wandered around the grounds as they sat unused for long stretches at a time, and there were some who claimed to have wandered through the building, there being some mystery window that couldn't lock right. One had to climb a tree and get on the roof and do something else. The story changed. The things people found inside changed. There were secret rooms, and a dungeon, and a haunted elevator. It was all nonsense. No one ever could have imagined that there would be a time when everyone in town would be invited to come and see what it was really like. What would happen to those legends? Would they change? Would they fade away? Would they lead to new and more bizarre stories? It was likely that. Now that people saw the inside, they would all have to come up with something else. Maybe it would be haunted and become Wuthering Heights.

Of course, Mary would never break nor enter, but Bingley said, as he greeted them when they arrived at 6:05 pm, that the whole house was open to them and to feel free to explore. Of course, she wanted to head straight to the library, but decorum and her mother's scornful eye precluded her from coming straight there. She ate a bit, although not really enough to fill up. She hadn't had a full meal since lunch, and even then, it was just a sandwich. She danced the one dance and did her best to mingle. For her, that mostly meant standing on the edge of a group where she knew one or two people and nodding and smiling, sipping from a pint glass that literally had her name on it, the sparkling ginger ale concoction that was sickly sweet but very good. Jane told her, Lydia, Kitty, and Maria that the drinks in the punchbowls were safe to drink, but that they shouldn't drink any of the stuff in the decanters, as that was the hard stuff. Because the younger three danced up a storm and one of them was a world-class athlete, they stuck to water all night. Unfortunately for Mary, not all of the hired wait staff got the memo, and thus, about half of the punch bowls that had been scattered around the grounds had champagne in them while the other half had non-alcoholic sparkling cider.

Mary Bennet, who to that point had never tried a sip of alcohol in her life was, by the time she arrived in the library, slightly tipsy. She wasn't drunk at that point, but she was a bit light-headed. She could tell something was wrong with her, but she assumed it was the fact that she was up well past her bedtime, she was tired and stressed about the essay, and she was hungry. While the Bennets didn't have a lot, they always had food.

Mrs. Bennet wasn't the most observant parent in the world, but she knew when it was time to get her girls some food. Each of them handled hunger differently. Jane was weepy. Lizzy was angry, well angrier than normal. Lydia was mouthy, the normal amount of mouthy, but she gave sass to her mother, which she only did when she was hungry. Kitty was borderline narcoleptic. One time, when Kitty was forced to choose between eating after a game and staying home from a trip to Hartford to see a new release movie or showering and jumping in the car in 10 minutes, she chose the latter, and she slept through the entire film. Mary became light-headed and unfocused. Thus, it was easy for her to misconstrue her symptoms although the fact that she hadn't had a good, real, rib-sticking meal all day surely contributed to what happened next.

The library was everything she hoped it would be. It was built in a room with 30-foot-tall, vaulted ceilings. Save for the windows, the side door that led to a small covered outdoor patio that went out into the massive lawn, and the double doors that opened into the room, every inch of wall space had a 12-foot-tall bookshelf, and each shelf was full. Across the front of each wall of books was a rail with a rolling ladder. The center of the room had two couches across from each other with a coffee table in the middle. Two men sat on each couch. She recognized one of them as Mr. Richard, the Meryton High School English teacher. He'd worked for her uncle before Jane came of age to do so. He went to CCSU, earned his education degree, and began work at the high school right away. He was a bright and kind man. She'd sought him out on several occasions at her father's suggestion. Mr. Bennet knew that he and Mary agreed on so many things that he thought she should get new perspectives. He was under no obligation to help any home-schooled children, but one becomes a teacher for a reason, and when a 15-year-old girl shows up to your office and asks if you would be willing to discuss the lack of women or people of color in the American canon, you say yes.

Currently, there sat a bowl of the ginger ale punch on the coffee table. It had a ladle sticking out of it and appeared to have recently been refilled. Mary assumed it normally had coffee table books, as it should. There were also two love seats and four high-backed brown leather chairs situated around the room that would allow people to sit and converse or read or both. There were no overhead lights, just reading lamps on the end tables next to each place to sit. To the right of the doors sat a 5-foot-by-5-foot card catalog. The drawers went almost all the way down to the floor.

Just above those shelves, with just enough room for the sliding ladders to move without causing a problem, hung a second floor. It was a 6-foot-wide walking track suspended from the ceiling by steel cables. The floor seemed to be made of glass with steel beams every few feet, but Mary wouldn't know for sure until she got up there. The edge of the walking track had a 4-foot-high railing around it. Each of the four walls had 6-foot tall, totally filled bookshelves save for three of the four corners which featured two high-backed chairs with a reading table and lamp between them.

The fourth corner had a wrought iron spiral staircase. The rumors were true. She was in awe.

"Mary!" Mr. Richard waved at her. "Why doesn't it surprise me that you'd end up here?"

Mary smiled her closed-mouth smile. She had hoped the place would be empty so she could spend the evening touching everything without humans there to comment on her behavior. Still, she figured, if she had to share the room with someone who wasn't her father or Aunt Phillips, Mr. Richard was fine. "Hello, Mr. Richard." She waved. "It is good to see you. Happy New Year." She approached the two couches.

"Mary, please meet my colleagues. Mr. Jonas, he teaches Math." He pointed to the man sitting directly opposite of him. "Mr. Rhodes, music." He pointed to the man next to Mr. Jonas. "And this," he reached out and touched the man's shoulder next to him, "is Mr. Tucker. History." They nodded and smiled politely at her. "Gentlemen, this is Mary Bennet. One of Meryton's brightest, although we can't take credit for her."

"Bennet?" Mr. Rhodes asked. "Is your sister Lydia?"

"She is."

"Does she still play piano?"

"Quite often, sir."

"Good. That's good. You know I tried to get her to join the band? I've called once a year for several years now, and she flatly refuses."

"Ahh. Yes. I'm aware. I appreciate your dedication, sir, but Lydia is quite stubborn. Being homeschooled, as we have been, means..."

Mr. Tucker interrupted, "You and your sister were homeschooled? That's what he meant when he said we couldn't take credit for you?" He was sitting with his back against the couch, but he slid forward.

"Yes, sir." Mary walked forward and stood closer to the group, just at the end of the coffee table. "There are five of us. We were all homeschooled. The two eldest are in college now. I've been accepted to several colleges already. The younger two have several more years."

"How is it that you know Richard here if you were too good to attend Meryton High?" There was a bit of edge to his voice.

"Tuck," Mr. Richard said, "be nice."

"Oh. I'm nice. I'm nice. Come sit. Slide down, Rhodie. You've got room over there. I," he patted his sizeable belly, "don't think there's room over here."

Mary just wanted to be alone with the books, but she heard the tone in Mr. Tucker's voice as well, and well, she was a bit tipsy, stuffed with pages and pages of educational theory, and as Mr. Richard said, one of Meryton's finest. While she never laid eyes on him, she heard plenty of tales. She knew from both Charlotte and Maria that Mr. Tucker was a blowhard, old-school, white, male sexist who believed that Black History Month was race-baiting and that the more recently launched Women's History Month was a "joke," and he refused to acknowledge it in class. He felt that if women were "important enough," they would make it into the books without a "step stool." Charlotte was particularly annoyed that he called the male students "men" and the female students "girls." To be fair, they were, for the most part, girls, but "ladies" was right there as an acceptable word for teenagers. He knew the word, of course; he was a history teacher.

Mr. Rhodes did as he was instructed and slid down, leaving plenty of room for Mary. She sat down on the edge of the cushion and set her glass down. She used the ladle to fill up her glass. Yes, of course, Dear Reader, the punch bowl in the library was one of the spiked bowls. There is no reason to speculate. The Latin phrase "in vino veritas" means "in wine, truth." The saying has been used to mean that under the influence of any kind of alcohol, one is more inclined to speak the truth, and one's true personality comes through. We are not going to debate the finer points of that argument, but in Mary, there was always truth, and that night, in Mary there was champagne, which is, a sparkling wine after all.

While The Beastie Boys, "(You Gotta) Fight for Your Right (to Party)" played in the other room, Mary was willing to remain calm and not make this a fight. She wasn't a fighter. She was a reasonable, highly educated woman who could debate without causing a scene. She decided to answer both of his questions with poise and grace. "Well, sir, I've no disdain for Meryton Public Schools. As you can imagine, when the choice was made to homeschool us, I was a small child. My sisters and I were not consulted, as I suspect most parents do not consult their children on most legal decisions." Mr. Richard snickered. He had drunk plenty of the spiked punch. Mary heard it but didn't react. "Mr. Richard is an old friend of the family. He used to work for my uncle, but he was kind enough to meet with me a few times a month over the past few years to discuss literature."

"Did you pay him for his time to tutor you? Since you don't go there, why should you get to benefit from his expertise? That is part of the social contract."

"Tuck..." Mr. Richard started.

Mary spoke at the same time. She could defend herself, but she appreciated it. "Of course not. My family pays plenty of property and income tax. We employ people who have children who go to the public school. We own the biggest farm in town. My aunt and uncle own property on Main Street and have no children. Being homeschooled and being childless doesn't preclude anyone from participating in the system. My aunt and uncle place ads in the yearbook and are band boosters. The band, as you heard, Mr. Rhodes wants my sister to join. If the school chose to field a women's soccer team, my sister Kitty would certainly be a starter. Unfortunately, they don't, so she, and many of the other female athletes, have to pay extra to play sports that the boys get to play for free." She smiled, picked up her drink, and took a sip. "Mr. Richard is not tutoring me; he talks to me."

"Yes, well..." He faltered and looked up. Did he think there would be an answer up there? Maybe he did. Maybe the answer was in one of the thousands of tomes.

Mary gave him no quarter and took the pause as an invitation to keep going. "As for Mr. Richard's expertise, we met after school. Yes, we met on school property, but that was just because it was more convenient. The school is open for hours at the end of each day. We didn't use up any electricity or resources that wouldn't have been used if we were not there. I believe we both likened it to having a robust conversation about a shared passion. Wouldn't you say that is what it was, Mr. Richard?"

They all turned to look at Mr. Richard, who nodded emphatically while clamping his mouth shut with every single facial muscle he had. He did not trust himself to speak as he was trying desperately not to burst into laughter at the turn of events. Like many of his colleagues, he was not a big fan of Mr. Tucker who, about 10 years prior, had been removed from his position as elementary school principal because his approach was too harsh and placed back in the high school as a history teacher. He had tenure, and since he didn't really do anything "wrong," he couldn't be fired. He also didn't have any shame, so he took the demotion without complaint and taught the same old tired lessons he taught in the years prior to his promotion to principal.

Mary nodded and smiled. She took another sip and pushed on. "See there? As he said, he wasn't surprised to run into me here. I love books. Do you request payment from people when in the course of a conversation you educate them on some historical event? I would hope you would correct someone who thought Hannibal was Turkish because he died there instead of from modern-day Tunisia, where he was born, without sending them a bill afterward for services rendered. If I were to ask Mr. Rhodes if he thinks Jimi Hendrix was the greatest rock guitarist of all time as Eric Clapton claims or would he think Slowhand himself is the best, would I need to give him some money before he could give me his answer? If Mr. Jonas and I had a discussion about Julia Robinson's solution to Hilbert's Tenth Problem, would he require payment before he replied to me?" She knew she was showing off a bit with the last reference and likely Robinson's accomplishments would never be covered in a high school math class or even a college math course considering she passed away shortly after the discovery, but she was rolling. She took a drink and smiled.

Mr. Tucker hadn't expected anything like this from the short bespectacled "girl." He huffed, "The two things are not the same. If it were a regular conversation, I wouldn't be on school property utilizing school resources. It is true that the building would be open after hours, but you were seeing Richard in his professional capacity. There is no room for that. What you and he were doing was essentially private tutoring. You can say it isn't, but it is. Since Meryton has a policy against teachers tutoring for money, he couldn't help you. If you wanted his help, then you should have enrolled in the class."

She made a serious face, which most people would just call her face, and nodded. He assumed he scored a point. There were no points being tallied, of course, but he was the kind of man who felt like life was a competition that he needed to win. Instead of responding, she asked a question, "So, would you argue that this conversation is acceptable? Here we are, engaged in an intellectual conversation. You, a professional educator, and me, a student. Are we allowed to have this conversation without fear of reprisal or worry that I am stealing your time from the great city of Meryton?"

"Yes. Yes of course. This is a holiday party. This is my time. This is your time. We are in a private residence. The school grounds are for school business." He took a big swallow of his drink. He was smirking and imagining himself marking another tally on the scoreboard in his mind. Old powerful man: one billion; small mouthy girl: zero.

"Right. Sure. Totally makes sense. We wouldn't want to steal those tax dollars. We wouldn't want to cheat the system. I'm sure you've never engaged in any personal conversations while on school property. You've never participated in a NCAA bracket or a Superbowl pool on school grounds." Readers may have noticed that she didn't push up her glasses. She will not during the whole exchange. Take from that what you will.

"Well, of course, but we conduct those things in the teacher's lounge during our breaks. It isn't the same..."

She cut him off. It wasn't like her, but the champagne was coursing through her veins, and let's face it: he was being awful. "And do you think that you are, what was the phrase you used about our conversations, 'helping me' right now with this conversation? I could cite at least four different educational theories that could make your point for you, and of course, I could use those same theories to back my point. Do you think I will be a better person for hearing what your thoughts are on the matter? This is the first time we've met, and two of your colleagues had kind things to say about my family, and yet you felt the need to make unfounded claims and weak arguments based on, what, geography? Are you tutoring me, or are you talking *at me?*"

It is a truth universally acknowledged that whenever a fight breaks out at a party, it draws a crowd. It could be the raised voices. It could be the pheromones. It could be that there is a source of heat that draws people to it like moths to a flame. It is true that most fights begin with a step on the toe or an elbow to the ribs or a snide comment about one's date and end with two people engaged in a physical altercation while onlookers standby in shock or awe or both until one person "wins" the fight, or someone breaks out of the mob mentality and physically pulls the people apart. In some movies, someone fires a gun at the sky to scare everyone back to reality.

So it was that for most of the night, people wandered the grounds and peeked into the library. Some were unimpressed. Not everyone is a book person. Those people won't be reading this, so it is safe to think bad thoughts about those people. Really? A library with a second-floor wraparound balcony doesn't impress? What is not to love about that? Others rightly "oohed and aahed." At some point, they all moved on. They were at the party of the century, after all. Of course, some people came in and touched the books or said hello to a former or current teacher, as the four men had essentially set up camp in the library early in the evening in the way the people who work together do at social events.

However, shortly after our heroine walked into the library and was goaded into a battle of wits with Mr. Tucker, as people walked by or peeked in, hearing the heated voices and sensing the tension, they stuck around. Those people were at the party with someone or another and that person or those people noticed someone was missing and went to find them. The people they were with found them eventually, and they too stuck around. One or two people told one or two people, and soon enough, the room had dozens of people in it, standing around the sides, some up on the upper level, unsure of what to do or say as an old history teacher and a young woman did battle.

Mr. Tucker decided to test Mary's claim about educational theory. Sadly, for him, he only knew two. He thought she was bluffing about being able to name four. She could name way more than four. She was still trying to reel back in the grandstanding comment she made about math. She might have been tipsy, and her tongue might have been loosened a bit, but Mary Bennet was not, is not, nor ever shall be, a bluffer. He couldn't know that. If he chose to be less of an overbearing, thin-skinned jerk, he could have discovered all her positive attributes, but he was an overbearing, thin-skinned jerk; so, his loss.

As is the case of most teachers of his generation, he started with Watson and Skinner. Of course, he actually lobbied at the State House against the removal of corporal punishment. Yes, Dear Reader, Connecticut didn't outlaw the beating of children in schools as a form of negative reinforcement until 1989, the year in which our tale takes place. So... yeah, of course, he was a behaviorist. Hitting one kid with a paddle will really get the rest of them to straighten up and fly right. So it was, he argued that behaviorism can only work in large groups. The rest of the students needed to see the negative consequences of the actions modeled. One student needed to take the punishment, but the rest would follow suit.

She countered with the fact that he was being myopic because behaviorism works beyond the social learning aspect of it. He also failed to mention the idea of positive reinforcement, which had, historically always worked better. It was Pavlov who first cracked the positive reinforcement code, and while dogs are social animals, they reacted to the bell, not to each other. The experiment would work on one dog, just as positive reinforcement worked on one child. Only children respond to behaviorism, even if it is negative reinforcement, as some parents were spankers long before they got to school.

Mary suspected he would try to pivot to constructivism as it was generally considered to be an acceptable foundational theory. She wasn't against it, but she was in a debate, and because she didn't bluff, she said she could use each theory to argue either side of the point, so she took the wind out of his sails by saying that Piaget was all about children's individual development, and what could be better than homeschool to create individualized education? The foundation of invitational education was rooted in constructivism, and homeschooled kids had more choices and could be guided as they learned, whereas state standards and arbitrary grade levels worked against the practice.

As the educational theory debate portion of this story is coming to an end soon, we shall let it play out without summation. For a point of reference, you must be wondering, Dear Reader, Mary did finish her entire pint glass of punch, but she didn't refill it. Good news for Mary, bad news for Mr. Tucker. If she had, she might not have been able to do what she did next. They were both sitting on the edge of their respective couches, leaning forward over the coffee table, red-faced and heated. It had gone on for some time.

Mr. Tucker was losing. He knew it. When people are desperate, they often rely upon insults. "Montessorism is just some sort of religious fanaticism. No wonder you brought that up. You religious nuts are all the same."

"Did you really just hurl an ad hominem attack at me?" Yes, more Latin. Mary wasn't fluent, but she dabbled. "Dr. Montessori was Catholic; she accepted children of all faiths into her schools just as she treated people of all faiths in her medical practice. That is just a wild claim to make. Like most of the things you've said tonight, sir, they are unsubstantiated. Yes, it is true, my parents are Christians. They believe in God. We have a Reverend staying with us right now, in fact, but they are hardly fanatics. That is like saying all people who served in the Army at times of war are jingoist xenophobes." She was up on her feet now. "Besides, I didn't say Montessorism, I said Invitational Education. Purkey invented it in this century, you..." She was interrupted by a hand on her shoulder. It was a good thing too because as you can tell, Dear Reader, she was about to go full ad hominem herself. That is likely why the interruption happened just when it did.

She heard her father's voice, close, quiet, and in her ear. "That's enough now, Mary. He's had enough. You've won. Let someone else have a turn."

Mary looked up at her father's kind understanding eyes. She hadn't known he was there. She looked around the room and saw the whole crowd. She hadn't known they were there either. The argument. The alcohol. The pursuit of truth. Terrier Mary took over, and she lost all track of time and space.

Reality crashed down on her. She covered her mouth with her hand. "Oh. Father. I'm so..." She trailed off, fled from the room, and ran right out of the building. She didn't stop until she got home. Between the blood rushing in her ears followed by the counting from the ballroom as 1989 had only ten seconds left and the gathered Merytonites were counting it down loudly and with fervor, she didn't hear the round of applause that erupted behind her.

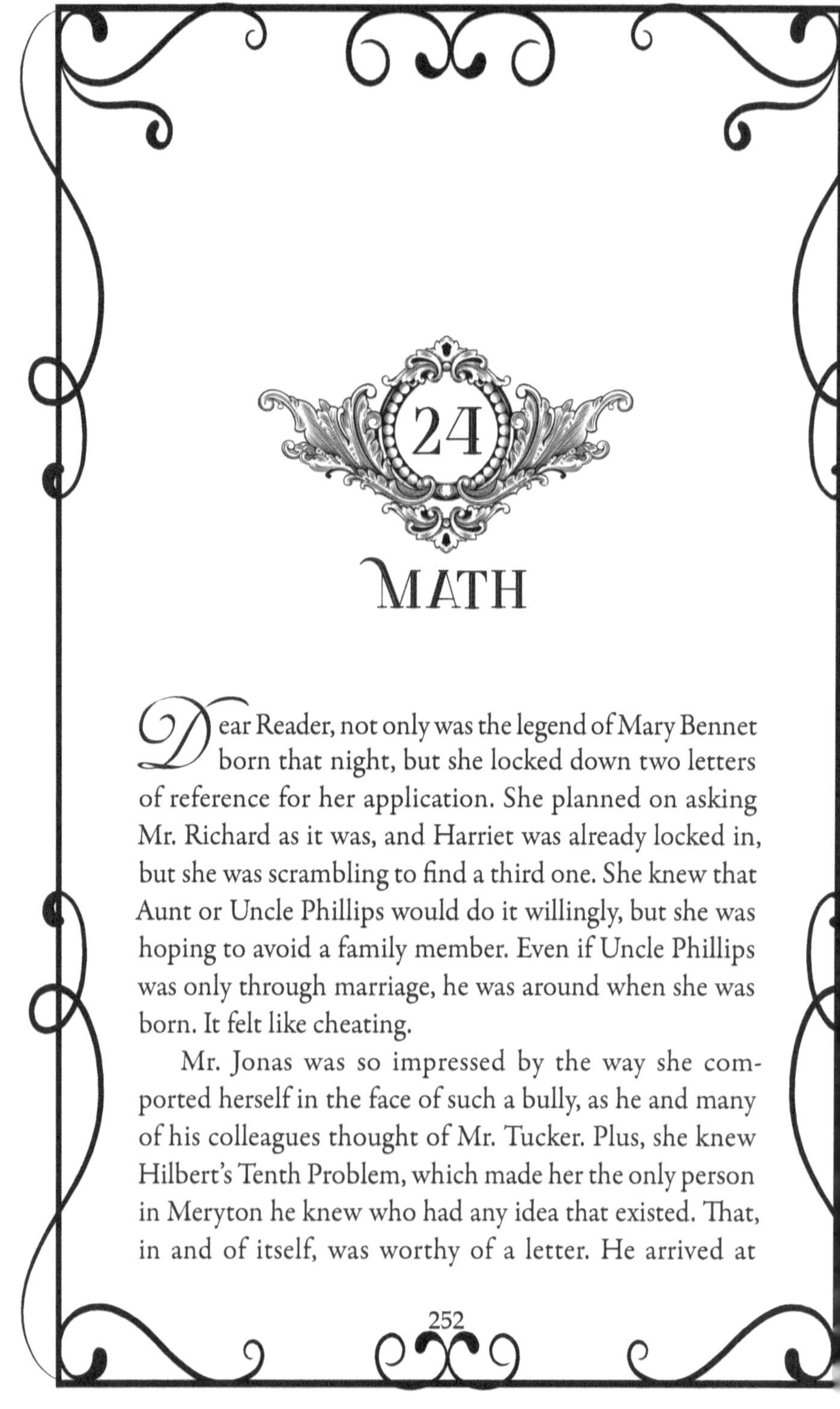

24

MATH

Dear Reader, not only was the legend of Mary Bennet born that night, but she locked down two letters of reference for her application. She planned on asking Mr. Richard as it was, and Harriet was already locked in, but she was scrambling to find a third one. She knew that Aunt or Uncle Phillips would do it willingly, but she was hoping to avoid a family member. Even if Uncle Phillips was only through marriage, he was around when she was born. It felt like cheating.

Mr. Jonas was so impressed by the way she comported herself in the face of such a bully, as he and many of his colleagues thought of Mr. Tucker. Plus, she knew Hilbert's Tenth Problem, which made her the only person in Meryton he knew who had any idea that existed. That, in and of itself, was worthy of a letter. He arrived at

Longbourn on January 2nd quite unannounced as was the fashion of the time.

Drop-ins were common. Centuries before, showing up unannounced was a perfectly fine form of communication. People "called" on one another and dropped off calling cards that had pertinent information about the uninvited interloper. He could have called using the phone, but he was not only essentially a stranger, he was a grown man, and she was 18. He thought it best to show up when he assumed her whole family would be home.

It was Mr. Bennet who answered the door when he knocked, and when he explained that he wanted to speak to Mary about math, Mr. Bennet said, "Of course, you do." He led Mr. Jonas into the library, where Mary sat in her house cardigan, open book on her lap with a notebook on the pages of the book. She was hunched over writing. Her father had been sure to pick up each book in the Radcliffe Biography Series, a collection of books that highlighted brilliant women throughout history. He didn't buy them because he only had daughters. He bought them because they were well-researched and interesting. He wasn't one of those men who said, "I have daughters so..." fill-in-the-blank thing a man does to "accommodate" his female offspring. While he wouldn't ever say it himself, he was more of a feminist than was his wife. Mary's argument with Mr. Tucker got her to think about some of the aspects of Montessorism that could be useful in her essay. While she had read the Radcliffe series, she didn't have it memorized.

Mr. Bennet cleared his throat loudly and knocked on the door jamb. "Mary. You have a guest." He knew he would have to speak to her, or she wouldn't have looked up when he walked back in, as she didn't flinch when there was a knock at the door, nor did she hear her father when he got up from his desk and said in a joking way, "No, I'll get it, Mary, dear." He raised his voice, not to a shout necessarily, but he certainly used his diaphragm.

She held up one finger without looking up to finish writing her idea. Her father pointed to one of the chairs in front of his desk, and Mr. Jonas sat in it. Mary wrote. Mr. Bennet lit his pipe. He asked Mr. Jonas if he wanted anything to drink. He declined. Mary wrote. She flipped to the next page. Mr. Bennet smiled. Mr. Jonas looked over his shoulder at her. He shook his head in awe. Mr. Bennet shrugged his shoulders. Mary stopped and looked up.

"What, Father?" she asked. She just heard his voice and knew it must be important if he knocked and spoke loudly. She saw Mr. Jonas. "Oh, my." She stood abruptly. She slipped her notebook in her pocket and her pen into her hair. She looked down at the page to make note of where she was in the text and closed it. She set it down on the table next to the chair. "Mr. Jonas. What brings you here?"

"I was wondering if you wanted to talk about math. I'm the only advanced math teacher at the school, and my wife, who is a pastry chef in Hartford, likes math just fine, she uses it every day, but she doesn't really want to talk about it in the way I talked about it when I was in college. I spoke to Mr. Richard at some length at the party after your," he paused to think of the kindest way to say it, "abrupt exit, and he told me that your..." He paused again not wanting to say the wrong thing and offend her.

She filled in a word for him. "My performance?" She pushed up her glasses.

He nodded. "Sure. Yes." He shook his head. "No. That's just it. He said it wasn't a performance. He said that was how you are. He said you are absolutely committed to learning and that you hadn't likely just read some random fact about Robinson, but that you actually likely studied Hilbert's problems in detail, and so I wondered if maybe you would like to come and meet me after school some time and talk about math the same way you talk to him about literature." He turned back to look at Mr. Bennet, who sat still as a statue save for the occasional toke on his pipe. "That is, if it is okay with you, sir."

Mr. Bennet pulled his pipe out of his mouth by the bowl. "It has nothing to do with me, sir." He pointed at Mary with the stem of his pipe. "As you can imagine, she is perfectly capable of making up her own mind on the subject."

Mary made her way over to the other desk chair and sat down in it. "I would like that very much, Mr. Jonas. In fact..." She launched into an idea she had about the 19th problem's solution and the philosophic use of the word "analysis" in the problem itself. We shall not linger, but suffice to say, by the time she submitted her application, Mr. Jonas' recommendation was effusive. They never spoke of the events of that fateful New Year's Eve. Unfortunately, Lizzy will hear about it, but it will likely all be fine in the end. Right? Who could hold a slightly tipsy genius for defending herself against a person who should have known better and not started the argument in the first place? We shall see soon enough.

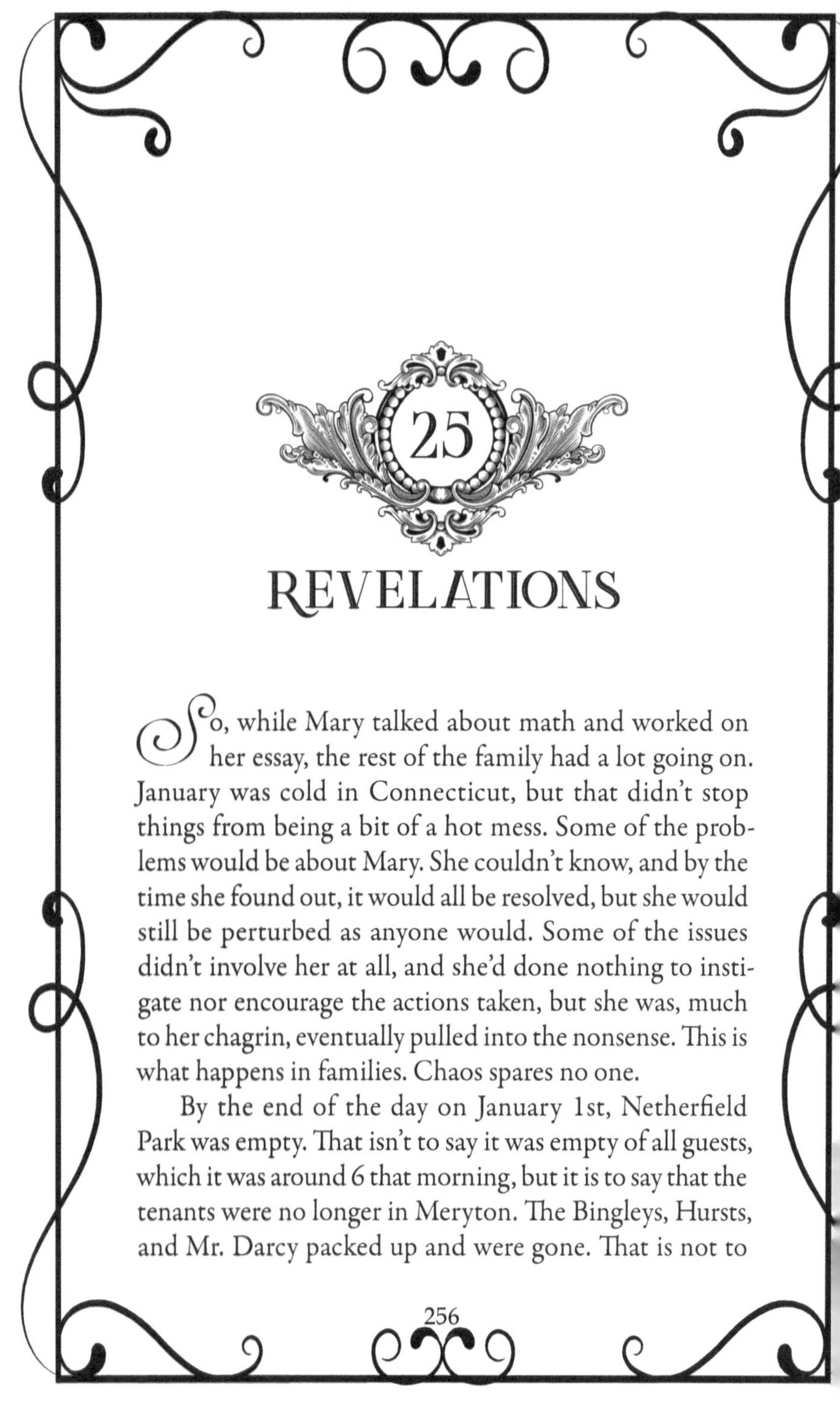

25

REVELATIONS

So, while Mary talked about math and worked on her essay, the rest of the family had a lot going on. January was cold in Connecticut, but that didn't stop things from being a bit of a hot mess. Some of the problems would be about Mary. She couldn't know, and by the time she found out, it would all be resolved, but she would still be perturbed as anyone would. Some of the issues didn't involve her at all, and she'd done nothing to instigate nor encourage the actions taken, but she was, much to her chagrin, eventually pulled into the nonsense. This is what happens in families. Chaos spares no one.

By the end of the day on January 1st, Netherfield Park was empty. That isn't to say it was empty of all guests, which it was around 6 that morning, but it is to say that the tenants were no longer in Meryton. The Bingleys, Hursts, and Mr. Darcy packed up and were gone. That is not to say that Charles Bingley was not still the legal tenant as he signed a lease with the Morris Agency that would run until May, but he and his group vacated the premises. The Meryton gossip train was in the station for the holiday, and none of the Bennets bothered to go into town on the 1st, and no one thought to call with the big news, so, although several people in town knew what was happening, they remained in the dark about all of it.

They spent the morning preparing for the departure of Reverend Collins. He rose early to share coffee and the paper with Mary and Mr. Bennet. After saying more platitudes than we would care to share here, he packed his bags and took one final turn around the property with Mr. Bennet, where he agreed in principle to the new plan of action. He granted Mr. Bennet a ten-year, interest-free, payment-free extension on the land contract in exchange for a five-percent stake in Mr. Bennet's new venture once the loan was paid in full.

Mr. Bennet wanted to keep Longbourn as a farm but knew that it couldn't just be a farm. He had been resisting the offers from many developers for years who wanted to buy up the property, install prefabricated homes, and build up a little private community for rich city dwellers who wished to "summer" or "winter" in the country. It was a lot of money to turn down, but he worried that if he cracked, the rest of the town would crack, and Meryton wouldn't be the town that they loved. So, instead, he thought he would develop his own property. He would build a farm-to-table restaurant as well as some "rustic" cabins that could accommodate those who wished to visit for the season. Longbourn would become a resort but not a community. Teddy obtained the financing. It was a risk, but he thought a good one. He knew at least fifty people who would be interested in renting a cabin for a season or two.

It would take at least two years to get the permits and build and maybe another five for it to become profitable. It was a terrible deal for Reverend Collins. Mr. Bennet even told him so, but he said something about family and quoted some scripture and that was that.

He agreed to let Mr. Bennet break the news to the family in private, and so he spent his final lunch at Longbourn heaping praise upon each member of the Bennet family. It was actually kind of sweet, but like everything he did, he took it too far and made several of them uncomfortable. Not everyone takes kindly to compliments. He insisted on leaving the way he came, and so Charlotte arrived just after lunch and walked him to the train station. The family spent the rest of the day in relative silence, which was not something they were able to experience in all the time that Reverend Collins was there.

We know that Mr. Jonas arrived on the 2nd and he and Mary talked about math. Other than that, nothing much happened. No one went to town. The phone didn't ring. There wasn't even any bickering if you can believe it. Miracles never cease.

However, on January 3rd, the mail arrived at noon with a letter from Caroline Bingley addressed to Jane with a local postmark on it "explaining" everything. She claimed her brother had some business in New York that needed his attention. Even though the company was based in Hartford, one of their father's original partners, something, something… It went on and on and was clearly fabricated. It read like it was written by a person who knew nothing about her family business and was trying to make it sound as though she did. Jane and Bingley spoke quite intimately about the business. He never mentioned an original partner. It is true that they did have an apartment in New York, so it is possible that part was true. She ended by mentioning that Darcy needed to see his sister Georgiana as well and that she would be in New York for an audition for a summer music program. That was, in fact, true as it had been mentioned on several occasions in Jane and Lizzy's presence. Still, his attending his sister's audition had no bearing on the rest of them. He was a guest, not a tenant.

Jane was distraught, as one might imagine. She really did think that she and Bingley were falling in love. She hadn't said the word aloud to him, or to anyone, even Lizzy, but she thought it. She asked herself if she loved him, or if she could love him, or what loving him and being with him would mean. Would he understand that no matter how much money he had, she was going to be a teacher? Would she be glamorous enough for the tabloids? Would she want to be in the tabloids? Then, upon reading the letter, she felt foolish. If he felt remotely for her the way she felt for him, he wouldn't skulk away in a holiday, hungover haze. Lizzy tried to assure her that this was all Caroline's doing, which was a good guess but shockingly wrong. It wasn't *all* her doing. She had help.

However, it was Mrs. Bennet who took it the hardest. She was banking, literally and figuratively, on Jane marrying Mr. Bingley. She was banking on his money to buy out the land contract from Reverend Collins; she'd stopped always adding the qualifier "that awful" in front of his name. That would change soon enough. Figuratively, she was banking on Jane being married before Charlotte so she could rub that in the next time she spent time with the Lucases. Why it mattered whose children were married first, or second, or at all to either of them was shrouded in mystery. It shall never be explained either. Some things just are.

While this information wasn't totally brand new to Lizzy, the full story of the George Wickham versus Fitzwilliam Darcy drama finally came to light after the former arrived back in Meryton to serve his two weeks only after the latter departed for New York. According to George, his father worked for the Darcys as the groundskeeper, maintenance man, and Jack-of-all-trades at Pemberley. As part of his compensation package, they lived at the back end of the property in a house made for just that purpose. Darcy's father took a shine to young George and felt that he was a comfort to Fitzwilliam when his mother died shortly after Georgiana's birth. While he was younger than Darcy, he was a good friend and companion to him, and while some would argue Darcy never got over the loss of his mother, having a constant companion during that hard time was a salve.

Mr. Darcy agreed to pay for George's education if he went to Mansfield. Thus, George matriculated to Mansfield College the previous fall. However, once he arrived there, he discovered people seemed to like him more than they liked Darcy, who was in his fourth and final year. Enraged with jealousy, Darcy took the money back, and George, now broke and homeless, joined the Army Reserves, got some training, and signed up as a private military contractor to put his training to good use.

There was a lot more money in the private sector than in the public one. He made quadruple going private. His time in South America was part of several assignments that he wasn't at liberty to disclose. While he found the work to be exhilarating, he would have much preferred being at Mansfield studying geography so he could teach high school social studies than he would have been traveling around the world in armored vehicles.

In fact, he was so "important" to his commander that the reason he was called away earlier was to pick up his pager. If you don't know what this is, Dear Reader, you can simply pull out your phone and look it up online. That was not remotely an option then. By the standards of the time that this story is being written, this device seems as useful as sending carrier pigeon, but in 1990, it was the most cutting-edge technology there could be, and believe it or not, having one at that time did mean the person was considered important. By the middle of the decade, so many people had them that movie theaters had to remind people to silence them before the movie started.

Jane wasn't sure if she was ever going to share that story with anyone, but since they were gone and Lizzy was mad, she decided to spill the beans. George hadn't told her not to share. He'd talked about it openly in front of Denny and really anyone who would listen over drinks at the bar. While Jane was shocked to hear it, she did think that maybe there were some circumstances that Lizzy didn't know about and maybe there was more to the story. Typical Jane. Finding the good in everyone. Wonder if that will pay off for her in the end.

Lydia and Kitty returned to their formal education. They might have slacked off if not for the fact that they were still accompanied by Mary to the public library several days per week. While Mary was officially done, she had taken her test and unsurprisingly scored what would be the highest score of any of her sisters, she still was focused on her studies. She knew she couldn't put all of her eggs in the Mansfield basket, so she spent time applying to other colleges and universities while doing research, with Harriet's help, on other scholarships and grants both public and private. It wouldn't be for some time that she took a moment to reflect on why she hadn't thought about those things regarding her educational prospects. Sometimes, one is so focused on swimming that one fails to think about the size of the ocean. It is only when one sits on the beach and looks out at the endless horizon, that one can process it all.

The biggest revelation came a few days later, not from a formal member of the Bennet family but someone who was, for the most part, treated like one. Remember when Charlotte was cagey about why she was still around on New Year's Eve? Well, she finally came over to come clean. She came over for dinner and heard all the above-mentioned shocking news, and so she almost didn't tell, but time was, as we shall see, of the essence, and so after dinner, she and Lizzy took a walk. It was Connecticut in January, and so it was cold and the sun had already set, but Charlotte wanted to be alone with Lizzy, and they were New Englanders, so what was a bit of cold to them anyway?

In case you haven't guessed it, Dear Reader, which there was no way for Lizzy to have guessed, but you could have for sure, it turned out that Charlotte and Reverend Collins had been spending time together. He fell in love with her almost instantly when she saved him that first day, and while he was willing to consider Lizzy for half a minute because he thought it was the right thing to do, he was relieved when things went the way they did. While it seems that he was always around and underfoot, the fact is, the Bennets lost track of him for hours at a time, and when he was suddenly there again, having returned from spending time with the Lucases, they just assumed they had been tuning him out, and he didn't notice that they were not listening.

Charlotte didn't reciprocate immediately as she was practical and not subject to love at first sight, but she didn't find the prospect of a relationship with him out of the question. She was in her mid-twenties and lived with and worked for her parents. She, like so many residents of Meryton, set her sights on staying in Meryton. It was comfortable and safe, and while not everyone liked everyone, and not everyone was nice, as we saw in the case of Mr. Tucker, it was a good place to live. They were close to everything they could ever want, even though, for the most part, no one ever left. It was as though the borders of town had an invisible film that could, if pushed hard, be stretched to the edge of Hartford County but not much farther. She assumed that she would stay put and transition to being the permanent caretaker for her parents as they aged while playing aunt to Jane and Lizzy's potential children. She told herself it wouldn't be so terrible. Honestly, that phrase says it all. It implies that there is a degree of terribleness involved with her choice, which of course, there would be.

When Reverend Collins proposed on New Year's Eve, she wasn't surprised. He'd made long, rambling speeches about being married and setting a good example for the people at Rosings and how Lady Catherine de Bourgh felt about marriage, and on and on and on. What surprised her was how quickly she said yes. She didn't even think about it. He asked. It took longer than it should have, but once his knee hit the ground, she was nodding, and she said yes by the time he finally stopped talking. While he was objectively ridiculous, he was kind-hearted; Charlotte could overlook one thing for the other. Marrying him gave her the chance to get out of Meryton and see more of the world. Providence wasn't San Francisco or London, but those things seemed more in reach as Mrs. Collins than they ever did as Ms. Lucas. They were to be wed before the end of January. Charlotte wanted to get on with her new life, and she didn't want to wait, but she did need to tell her best friend before the gossip mill got the news out.

Lizzy laughed when she first heard the news, and this hurt Charlotte's feelings immensely. She gave Lizzy a speech about always thinking she was better than everyone, and she turned on her heel and started for home. Lizzy started walking back to Longbourn but, chastened and crying, ran after her and apologized profusely. She too fell to her knees, begging Charlotte to forgive her. They returned to Longbourn arm in arm, as was the way the people of Meryton liked to walk, frozen-faced but warm of heart, the crisis averted quickly, just as promised. They couldn't really ever stay mad at each other. Told you they wouldn't fight for long.

There were degrees of congratulations from the Bennets that ranged from shocked admiration from Mr. Bennet to concerned optimism from Jane. Mary realized then that she was just in the other room when the actual proposal took place. They whispered some things to each other when they hugged. Mary was not, as we know, a hugger, but if there was ever a time that called for one, this was it. She loved Charlotte and knew that a hug was the best way to show it.

Mrs. Bennet feigned happiness for as long as she was able but made it about her before the door was even closed upon the soon-to-be Mrs. Collins' exit. She was sure that First Lady Lucas was laughing at her and was mentally measuring the windows for new drapes as Longbourn would most certainly fall into their hands when that "awful Reverend Collins," as she started calling him again, gave it to them as payment for taking Charlotte off their hands. It was a horribly sexist thing to say, and Lizzy and Mary most certainly told her so. She screamed at them about her nerves, stormed off, and slammed the bedroom door. Through all the hullaballoo with Jane's emotional shunning, Mr. Bennet hadn't been able to get a word in edgewise to tell his wife about the deal that would keep Longbourn in the hands of the Bennets for the rest of time. He shook his head and laughed to himself. He told his daughters he would make it better and followed her into their private space to tell her the good news.

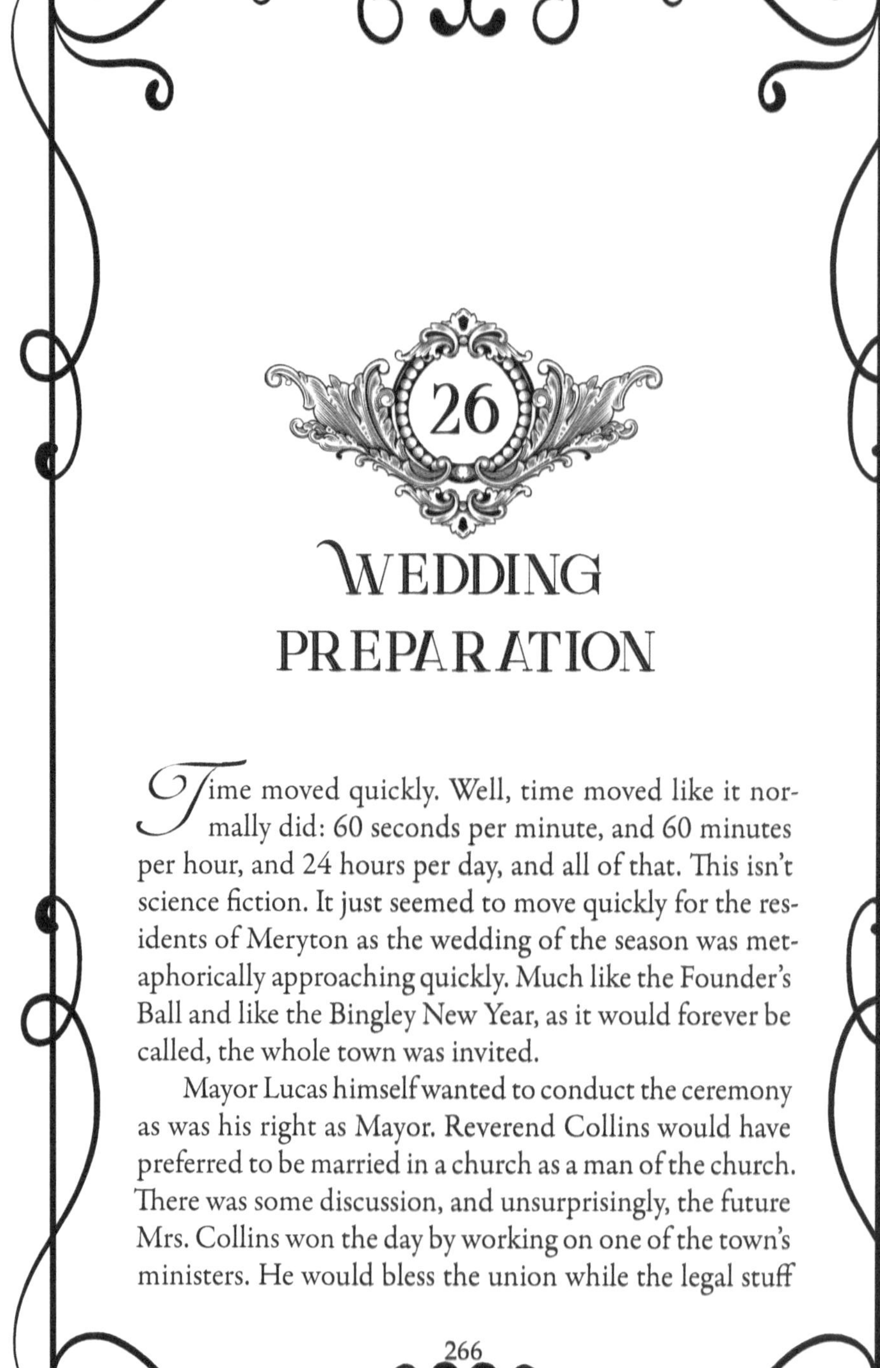

26

WEDDING PREPARATION

$\mathcal{T}$ ime moved quickly. Well, time moved like it normally did: 60 seconds per minute, and 60 minutes per hour, and 24 hours per day, and all of that. This isn't science fiction. It just seemed to move quickly for the residents of Meryton as the wedding of the season was metaphorically approaching quickly. Much like the Founder's Ball and like the Bingley New Year, as it would forever be called, the whole town was invited.

Mayor Lucas himself wanted to conduct the ceremony as was his right as Mayor. Reverend Collins would have preferred to be married in a church as a man of the church. There was some discussion, and unsurprisingly, the future Mrs. Collins won the day by working on one of the town's ministers. He would bless the union while the legal stuff would be handled by her father, and it would all be done in the church itself.

Lizzy was appointed as Maid of Honor and her father as best man. One request took a matter of seconds, and the other took several long-distance phone calls from Rhode Island and two letters. Mr. Bennet would have said yes immediately, just as Lizzy did, but he hadn't been given the chance as Reverend Collins never officially asked. It was only when Charlotte arrived one day and explained the situation that Mr. Bennet willingly accepted the duties and, at the request of Charlotte, wrote a letter expressing his honor at being asked. She gave him a kiss on the cheek and said this was the only gift she needed for the wedding.

Lydia was asked to play the wedding march and the rest of the music during the ceremony much to the chagrin of the normal organist. Kitty was asked to help Maria make centerpieces for the reception which was to be held in the Meryton High gymnasium. Not the most romantic of venues, but it was the only place that was indoors and could fit the residents of town. Jane was asked to hire the DJ and arrange the caterers. She was fully engaged with her student teaching, but her school day ended at 3 each afternoon, and so she had ample time to make phone calls and make arrangements. Mrs. Bennet was asked to help First Lady Lucas with her clothing choices. She wanted to wear one dress to the wedding and a different dress to the reception. It sounds strange because it was.

One may assume that Mary Bennet was left out of the workforce when it came to the wedding. She was busy with her essay and other applications; plus, she had never shown any interest in the institution of marriage except for one particularly philosophical debate she once had with Uncle

Teddy about the use of the word "institution" as a way to describe something that was supposed to be blissful when for all intents and purposes the word had negative connotations regarding being incarcerated. The occasion was his wedding anniversary party. She was just 12 at the time. He had no real answer for his niece. Numbers made much more sense to him than words, and so, he laughed and tousled her hair, which she disliked very much and told him so. Jane saved the day when she decided it was time to serve the cake. Cake has a 93 percent success rate when it comes to changing the topic. The story became legend, but it was true. Mary liked it when words were used correctly, and so if being married was like being locked up, she had no interest in that, thank you very much.

With that story in mind, Charlotte tasked Mary with the most important job of all. She needed help writing their vows. Mary cared about words. Charlotte didn't want to use the word "obey" at all, and while she was OK with "love and honor," she thought that "cherish" seemed too infantile. She wasn't a doll or a plate, nor was he. Her first thought was to write her own from her heart, but she knew that if she wrote her own, her fiancé would want to write his vows as well. There was a 100 percent chance that he would let his "passion" get the best of him, as he was wont to do. Wedding vows needed to come with a roadmap. Charlotte believed that Mary could do research and help her find some poetry, lyrics, and passages from literature, be it fiction or memoir about marriage being a partnership, and then they would read the same vows to each other that captured the essence of what Charlotte wanted from her marriage.

Mary agreed for several reasons. First, she loved Charlotte, and this was a reasonable request that fit her skill set. Secondly, she needed a serious break from her essay, which was slowly becoming a novella that would need some serious revision. Finally, it was a worthy project. What was the real story behind a marriage? What was the truth? How could she distill that in a way that did what Charlotte wanted while giving herself a distraction that also used her time well?

She attacked the task with fervor almost as soon as she accepted. She got out a brand-new notebook and wrote the word "Marriage" on the front page. Shakespeare ends his comedies with a wedding, but the heart of his tragedies also involve some kind of marriage. She knew that she couldn't only rely on Shakespeare, but it was a good place as any to start. She went into her father's library and pulled down the collected plays. She took it to the dining room and flopped the massive tome down with a thud that made her heart glow. Nothing quite like the sound of a heavy book dropping on a sturdy table. She set her notebook down and went into the kitchen to make coffee and get the radio.

She spent the next few days and weeks digging through books and the card catalog and the music collection at the library. Her marriage notebook was filling up. She tried to organize some of her ideas into coherent thoughts. She was asked to help with the vows to ensure they flowed and to keep them from becoming a fever dream. She spoke to Aunt and Uncle Phillips, to Mayor and First Lady Lucas, and she laid down ten dollars of her own money to call Uncle Teddy. He, of course, remembered that conversation all those years ago, and he finally felt ready to offer his niece, whom he once thought of as precocious but whom he came to understand much better as she wasn't playing around, she was deadly serious. They had a long conversation about what marriage meant to him and his thoughts on why it was that all members of the family married someone who was 10 years older or younger than them and what that said about the "institution" according to the Gardiners. She took a lot of notes. It was helpful, and she told him so.

He ended the call by telling her about his realization about her being precocious, which led to a much longer conversation about the power of words in general, and her thoughts on that word in particular, and how she felt that not only was it often misused, it was more often gendered and that girls were labeled precocious and boys were called clever. He agreed and would have continued to talk if not for the fact that his eldest, whom he would never call clever nor precocious again, needed his attention. He promised to continue the conversation with her at the wedding. He was looking forward to getting back to Meryton. They wanted to be there for New Year's Eve, but the youngest was sick, and so they didn't want to leave her with a sitter overnight. It cost her ten more dollars to continue the conversation as she did and had nothing to do with her task at hand, but she felt it was worth it.

With one week to go, Jane had everything settled. Kitty and Maria made all the centerpieces. Lydia could play "Here Comes the Bride" and "The Wedding March" in her sleep. Mrs. Bennet and First Lady Lucas settled on clothes that were "tasteful, but not distracting." Mr. Bennet had his best suit drycleaned. He owned only two, so "best" is relative. Charlotte and Lizzy had final fittings for their dresses.

Lizzy arranged a bachelorette party, which, at Charlotte's insistence, was just a Friday night sleepover at Longbourn with all seven of them like it used to be in the old days. They moved all the furniture to one side in the living room and pulled mattresses down. They ate junk food, watched sappy movies, and danced, and the eldest three drank wine and fended off the youngest three who begged for some. They made quite a racket, but it was so joyous that even Mrs. Bennet didn't complain. It is likely because she was invited to participate in several of the group dances, and they even let her "take lead" on "Respect." She witnessed the dances thousands of times over her life, and so it should not surprise anyone that she knew all the moves.

The afternoon after the sleepover, after they ate breakfast for lunch, as only one of them was awake and functioning before 11 am, Mary and Charlotte sat down with the notebook and worked through everything. Mary envisioned a collection of the ideas strung together as a bit of a found poem. Charlotte loved this idea and, with Mary's permission, gathered Lizzy and Jane to help finalize the wording. Lydia, Maria, and Kitty returned to the living room and were sleeping soundly.

Mary appreciated the request for permission. She wasn't remotely offended. She was coming at the task from a purely academic perspective, and she knew that her older sisters, who had an emotional interest in love and affection, were better suited to come up with the final product. They worked for another few hours. They wrote out different couplets and passages on pieces of paper and spread them out on the table. They moved them around and had Charlotte read them over and over in seemingly thousands of combinations.

They felt as though they were getting no closer to a solution when Mr. Bennet came in with boxes of pizza and demanded that they clear the table and clear their minds. He was sure that if they just took a break, they would come back to it with a new sense of focus and that would help. He found that when he was particularly vexed, a walk around Longbourn or having a conversation about something totally different helped him regain focus. They were hungry and the pizza did smell amazing. They still had seven days until the wedding. What was an hour or two of thinking about something else?

After dinner, the younger sisters were tasked with clearing everything up and getting the living room back in order. After that was done, Lydia and Kitty packed an overnight bag, and the three of them headed to the Lucases to keep the party going for one more night. Since only Maria had weekends in the traditional sense, as she attended public school, she thoroughly enjoyed spending every waking moment of hers doing something fun. Mrs. Bennet walked with them to see if there was anything she could do for First Lady Lucas. The word frenemy wasn't invented to describe them, yet it might as well have been invented for the often fraught, contentious, and somehow loving relationship between the two matriarchs.

Mr. Bennet retired to his library, giving the four remaining women in his dining room final words of encouragement. He even kissed all four of them on the top of their heads, which three of them willingly accepted and one didn't totally hate. They thanked him for the pizza and the perspective and promptly forgot all about him.

They spread the pages back out and started moving them around. Mary was convinced that Shakespeare needed to go first, and Lizzy heartily agreed. They had a lot to choose from there, and they ultimately ended up with something from *The Tempest* of all things. The lines, "I would not wish any companion in the world but you: Nor can imagination form a shape, Besides yourself to like of," from Act 3, Scene 1, just really seemed to be the best way to start. While the play is, objectively, the least funny of the comedies, it could be that maybe marriage should be fun, but not funny so that is why it worked so well. Jane wanted the vows to end with a line from Queen Elizabeth II's 25th anniversary speech. It needed a bit of editing to fit the mood, as this was a wedding, not an anniversary, but it was literally on the table, and so, it was on the table. She wrote it so that it went, "As for being married to you, I can answer with equal simplicity and conviction, I am for it."

From there, they moved song lyrics from The Beach Boys, Bob Dylan, The Carpenters, Bryan Adams, The Platters, Stevie Wonder, and the Dixie Cups. They sprinkled in some poetry from Kahil Gibran and a line from Matthew 19 in the New Testament. They hemmed and hawed a bit about this one because they wanted to alter it just a bit, and considering one of the participants was a reverend, would that be acceptable?

They changed Gibran's line a bit to accommodate the voice from second to first person. It just sounded better if they said, "We shall be together even in the silent memory of God" instead of starting with "you" as was the line in the original poem. It would fit perfectly then if they followed that up with, "So we are no longer two but one flesh. What therefore God has joined together, let not man separate." Ultimately, they decided it was OK because the pronoun swap was done out of love, so said Jane, and for proper context and grammar, so said Mary. They couldn't find any flaws. They laid it out from end to end on the big table, and Charlotte read it aloud. Even Mary cried a little while the rest of them cried a lot.

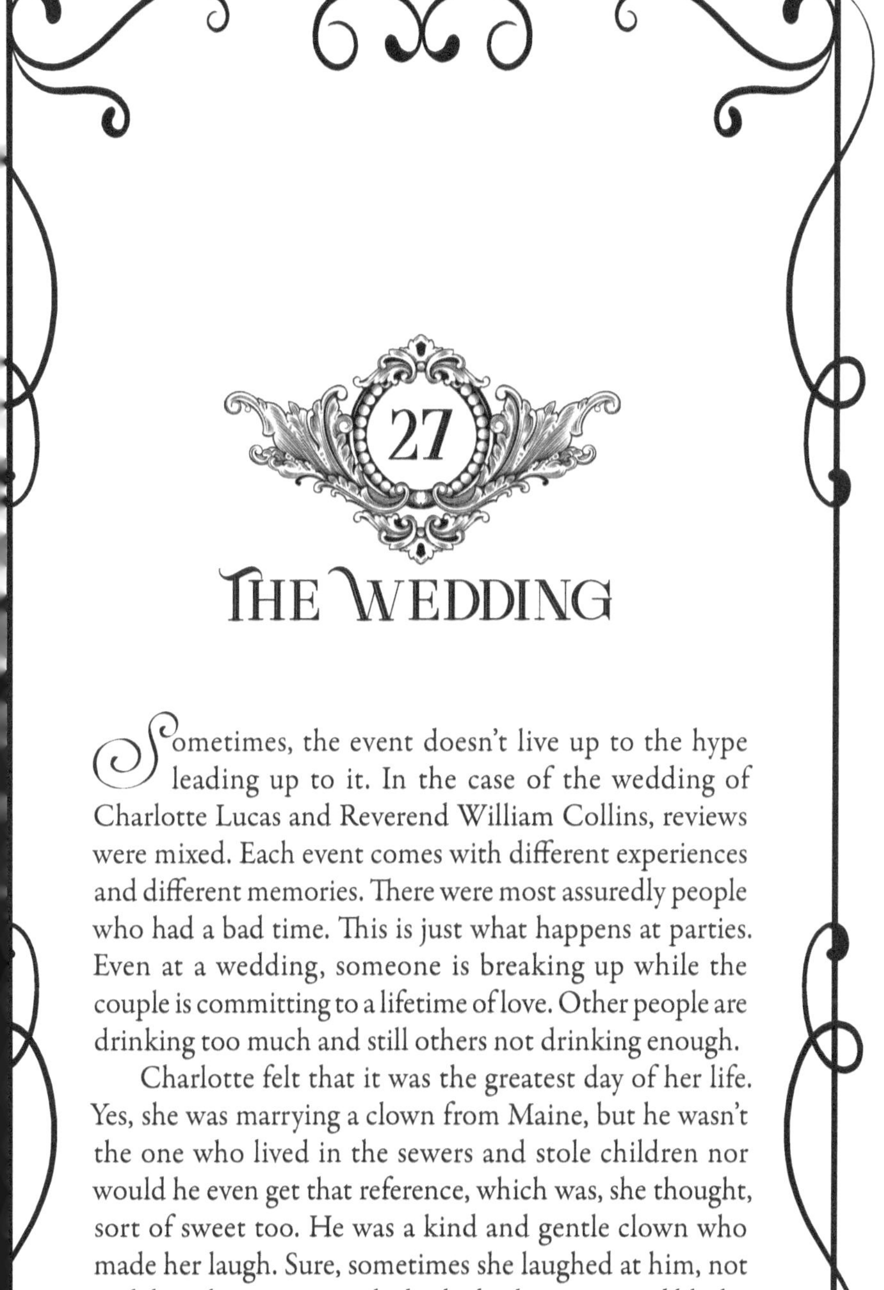

27

THE WEDDING

Sometimes, the event doesn't live up to the hype leading up to it. In the case of the wedding of Charlotte Lucas and Reverend William Collins, reviews were mixed. Each event comes with different experiences and different memories. There were most assuredly people who had a bad time. This is just what happens at parties. Even at a wedding, someone is breaking up while the couple is committing to a lifetime of love. Other people are drinking too much and still others not drinking enough.

Charlotte felt that it was the greatest day of her life. Yes, she was marrying a clown from Maine, but he wasn't the one who lived in the sewers and stole children nor would he even get that reference, which was, she thought, sort of sweet too. He was a kind and gentle clown who made her laugh. Sure, sometimes she laughed at him, not with him, but every time he looked at her, it seemed like he was watching the sunrise. He, too, would forever mark that cold January day at the dawn of the decade as the greatest day in the history of the world. While he was never really able to articulate his feelings, he definitely knew how to say words, and he said all the words to everyone for the remainder of the day and long into the evening.

The most coherent he was all day was during the recitation of the vows, which she made him practice over and over. She utilized his excellent memory and read them aloud to him several times a day for six days in a row. By the time the big day arrived, he had them fully committed to memory. It was a rousing success, and there was nary a dry eye. He didn't know the context of the words, and except for the line from Matthew, which he agreed the good Lord would forgive them for changing one pronoun, he didn't know any of the other material. Surely, you say, Dear Reader, that he must have read *The Tempest* at least once or at least seen *Forbidden Planet,* but alas, he had not. Still, he loved everything about it and thought it was beautiful. They opted to read them in turn, but since he memorized the whole thing, he had to mouth her parts along with her. For years to come, he would be able to quote those lines to her, which would never fail to melt her heart.

Because the wedding party was so small, the decision was made to have Mrs. Bennet and First Lady Lucas at the main table with the rest of the bridal party. There was a straight, long table up on a riser so everyone could see the happy couple at all times and have an unrestricted view when the speeches were given. There was a brief issue about where the matriarchs were seated. They expected to sit next to each other, but *someone* placed them at opposite ends of the table. Since the someone was Jane, it was easily fixed, and the crisis was averted.

Mr. Bennet's speech was more about Charlotte than it was about the Reverend as he actually knew her better, but he directed it at Reverend Collins by telling him that he was a lucky man who was going to have the honor and privilege of spending the rest of his life with a woman that Mr. Bennet loved like another daughter. Mr. Bennet was not much into public displays of affection, but he was coached by Jane, and he spoke from the heart. It was actually very good.

The few people who thought that Maria Lucas should have been named maid of honor instead of Elizabeth Bennet forgot all about that by the time Lizzy completed her speech. First of all, why do those people even have an opinion on the matter? It wasn't their wedding, was it? Some people really need to get hobbies. Seriously.

Lizzy raised a glass and said, "I am blessed to have the four sisters I have. I truly love them all even when they are prettier, smarter, more athletic, and more talented than I am. Each of them has made me the person I am in her own way, but they were stuck with me. They didn't have a choice. They didn't choose me. They had to wake up in the same house with me for all these years because where else were they going to go?

"It might seem strange to you all that Charlotte and I are best friends. We seem to have so little in common. I am the second born of a pack of wild girls, and Charlotte is the eldest daughter of Meryton royalty. She is neat and kind, and I am sloppy and rude. She has empathy, and I have rage. She sees the best in every person, and I look through them to find fault. She has been the yin to my yang for most of my life. She has found a way to balance me out, and she did the same for all of us. Charlotte Lucas arrived at my house because my mother thought we needed a tutor. It turns out that we didn't need a tutor, but we needed Charlotte. Each one of us has been touched by her, changed by her, nurtured by her in ways we didn't even think we needed, but in hindsight, it was exactly what was required.

"So, now, Cousin Collins, it is your turn to find out all of the amazing things that Charlotte Lucas can do for you. Your life has been good so far, but it is going to get exponentially better. We wouldn't give her to just anyone whom we didn't think was worthy." She raised her glass. "To the happy couple."

The crowd replied, "To the happy couple." Charlotte stood up and wrapped her best friend in a huge hug. They rocked back and forth and whispered into each other's ears. Jane gathered up the rest of the sisters, and they engulfed the two of them in a bigger hug. It took some time and a nudge from the DJ to get people to calm down and stop crying.

Lizzy was pleased to find that George Wickham was still in town. He finished up his two weeks the day before the wedding, but since he and Denny paid for the cottage through the end of the month, he opted to stick around. He decided to wear his dress uniform, which was a bit of an extravagance, but it made him stand out, and while Lizzy did find something appealing about him, with his charm and his stories and his good looks, he was a bit of a peacock, and for that, she cared very little. She hadn't moved beyond serious flirting with him, and she wasn't sure if she ever would. He was essentially a soldier of fortune, and there were a lot of questionable politics that came with that, in addition to the fact that he would be unreachable for many months of the year. Was he relationship material? She wasn't sure, and she only had a few days left to decide.

He didn't make it easy on her to sit down and chat about everything as he made sure to dance with everyone who asked. When he wasn't cutting a rug to an upbeat number or slow dancing without room for Jesus with all manner of females of all ages, he would have to "take care of business," as his pager was going off all night. To be fair, he had it on vibrate, so no one actually heard it go off, but he would occasionally grab his waist, remove the device, push some buttons, and then disappear with a wink or a touch of the face, or whatever was just appropriate enough for his dance partner at that time. While everyone agrees that the wedding is always about the bride, as it should be, the reception rarely is. There will always be one person who shines like a star, and on that cold, January evening, George Wickham was the Beau of the Ball.

Lydia, Maria, and Kitty each had a turn or two dancing with George, as well as anyone else who would have them. Their performance at the Bingley New Year preceded them, and the people who didn't make it to that, but who did make it to the Lucas/Collins wedding, were anticipating a good show. They were not let down. Unfortunately for them, wedding receptions come with breaks for food, speeches, bridal dances, and the like, so there were plenty of times when the attention was not on them, and they were left to their own devices. For two of them, that meant eating and gossiping. For one of them, it meant eating, gossiping, and sneaking out undetected now and again.

Jane and Mary sat with Uncle Teddy's family and had a lovely time. Jane and her Aunt Gardiner were very good friends in the way that an aunt or uncle by marriage sometimes can be. She always thought of Uncle Phillips as her uncle with all the rights and responsibilities of that job, whereas she thought of her Aunt Gardiner as her slightly older equal. Had she not had four children in quick succession, there is a very good chance that she would have been invited into the sleepover circle. They made plans for Jane to spend some time with them in New York during spring break. Jane managed to keep her spirits up regarding the Bingley situation by focusing on her student teaching. She would be fooling herself to say that she was "better" and that she didn't think of him often. Having the chance to go to New York and "run into" him was appealing, if not fatalistic.

Mary and Uncle Teddy talked about the free market. It bored his children and his wife, but it was the basis upon which his fortune was built. Mary had complicated feelings on the subject. She understood that the stock market was essentially a casino and that there were a lot of risks. She did think that the market should dictate if a business was successful or not, she didn't want the government to prop up a bad idea, but she did think that regulation had value. He made a point about private businesses doing whatever they wanted, and people didn't have to support them, and she made a point about private businesses using public services like roads and the fire department. He was in favor of repealing the Glass-Steagall Act. She thought that was a terrible idea. They each gave five reasons for their reasoning. Neither of them moved from their position, but Uncle Teddy left for home with a new favorite niece. Years later, when she turned out to be right about deregulation, she didn't even call to gloat, thus cementing his reasons for naming her his favorite.

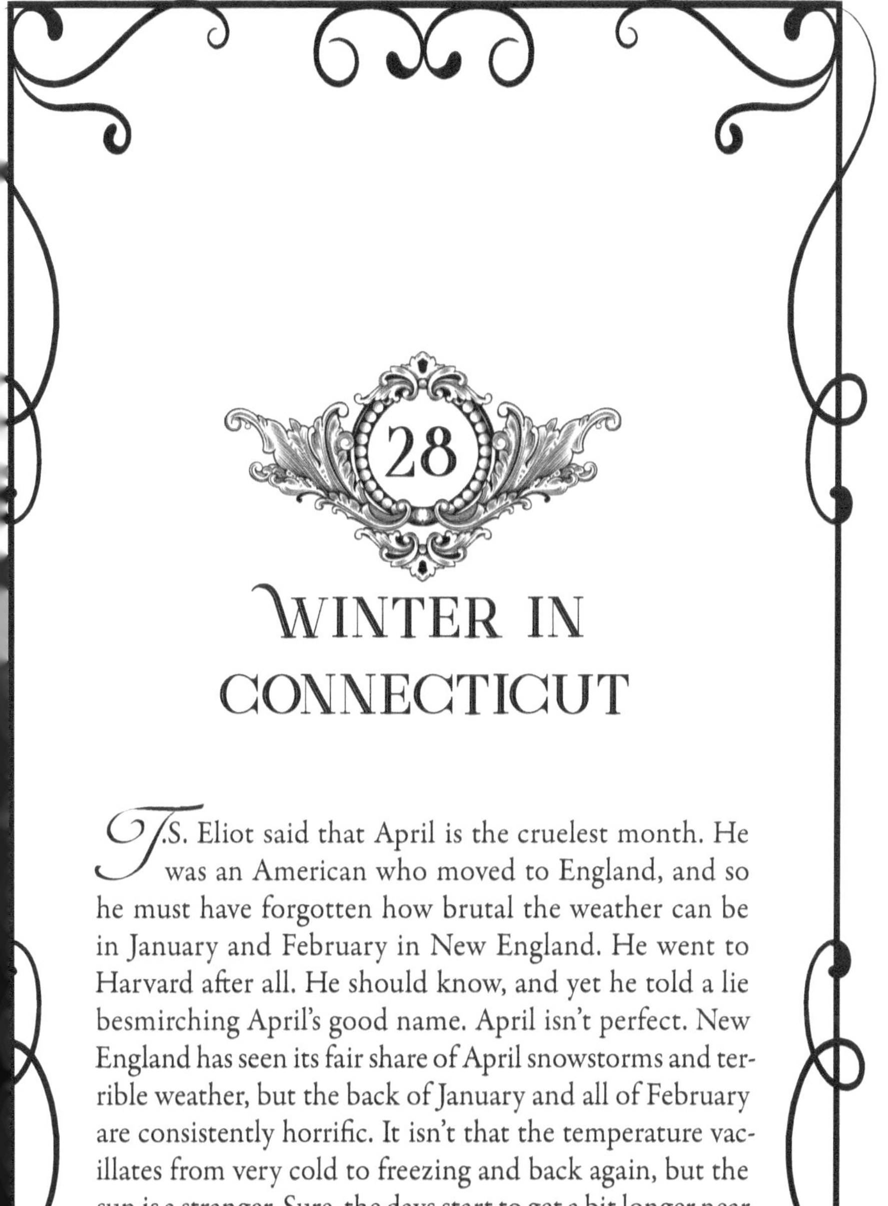

28

WINTER IN CONNECTICUT

T.S. Eliot said that April is the cruelest month. He was an American who moved to England, and so he must have forgotten how brutal the weather can be in January and February in New England. He went to Harvard after all. He should know, and yet he told a lie besmirching April's good name. April isn't perfect. New England has seen its fair share of April snowstorms and terrible weather, but the back of January and all of February are consistently horrific. It isn't that the temperature vacillates from very cold to freezing and back again, but the sun is a stranger. Sure, the days start to get a bit longer near the end of February, but would anyone know? Granted, he was making a comment on Chaucer, so maybe we shouldn't take the word of a poet so literally.

The Bennets of Longbourn felt the weight of the season. They needed a break. The winter blahs were on full display. For each of them, this meant something different. It made some people more irritable and some more maudlin. Lydia took to banging the keys extra loudly while playing angry, jangly, experimental classical music that was written to unnerve the listener. Kitty took to kicking the ball against the wall with a bit more force, which on more than one occasion knocked a picture or two off the wall. Lizzy took to arguing with her mother more frequently about things that she would normally ignore. Mrs. Bennet ended most of the arguments by calling Lizzy an ingrate while claiming she was "just like her father." Lizzy took this as a compliment, and then Mrs. Bennet would storm off and slam her bedroom door. She would emerge hours later acting as though nothing happened, which infuriated Lizzy even more. No one loves to be gaslit in general, and being treated that way by one's mother is difficult to take.

Jane managed to keep her happy, smiling demeanor every day at school as she was genuinely happy to be student teaching. She'd only been at it for a short time, but her classroom teacher was already working on her to take a permanent position as there were at least three teachers who were in their final year before retirement. It was nice to hear, and she was happy to feel needed, but she was a bit gun-shy regarding commitment. Besides, she promised her Aunt Gardiner that she would take a tour of some of the schools in New York as there was a desperate need for teachers there, and while Jane could not afford to live there on a teacher's salary, she could live with them for a few years while she gained some valuable experience outside of Meryton. However, when she returned to Longbourn each night, she was weepy and forlorn. She couldn't even be bothered to intervene between her mother and Lizzy, nor did she try to stop Bad Lydia from rearing her snarky, adolescent, hormonal head. She would later blame herself for what was about to happen to Lydia. She would say that if she only paid closer attention during February, maybe she would have seen the future in Lydia's actions. Oh, Jane. It wasn't your fault. The damage had been done. Even Kitty didn't know. All shall be revealed soon.

Mr. Bennet even found the mid-winter of 1990 to be confounding. Farm life was, for the most part, on hold during most of the season. The livestock had to be kept alive. They had some partnerships with family-owned butcher shops around Hartford County and the bordering Litchfield County. He kept those places well stocked, and it was good enough business to essentially pay for itself, so for the most part, they broke even. The price for the live-stock couldn't skyrocket during the winter even though it actually should. Heating a barn is notoriously expensive. People don't want to think about what it took to keep the cow, pig, or sheep alive before it became dinner. They try to only think of it as beef, pork, or mutton as they com-plain about how cold it is and how much it costs to heat themselves inside a well-insulated house. He was hard at work on his big plans. They seemed good on paper, but the paper stage was over. Teddy had the loans procured, and so he had to work on the rest. He wanted to serve as the project manager himself, but he was second-guessing that decision in the cloudy, bleak February chill.

It was only Mary who shrugged off the winter blues by remaining laser-focused on her tasks. She was working as much as her aunt and uncle would allow so she could save up even more money. Since she was technically an adult and out of high school, she could work more hours for them, and because they were busy helping with the legal aspect of the expansion and transformation of Longbourn, they were busy. Of course, Aunt and Uncle Phillips would have done the work pro bono, but Mr. Bennet wouldn't hear of it. He wanted to do it the "right way" just in case things went belly up; at least he wouldn't ruin his in-laws as well. She put in three 10-hour days at the law firm.

She always suspected that she and her sisters knew more about the business than did their mother, but for the first time, she knew it to be true. She actually thought for the first time ever that she knew more about it than did her father. Personal finances tell no lies and keep no secrets. She was, of course, silent on the matter around the house, but she didn't like knowing what she knew. However, she believed that the new venture would be successful. It was just the right change of pace at just the right time. She would be lying to say if she didn't worry that the plan got moving several years too late. She just hoped to see Longbourn thrive while her parents still owned the property and that they were not setting up some vulture who picked off family farms at auction which had become more and more common after President Reagan's, let's just say, myopic farm policies. There shall not be a lot of talk about the politics of those choices, but history is what it is, and some people noticed while it was happening. John Mellencamp didn't write that whole album about the death of the family farm in the middle of the Reagan administration as a lark.

Most people would clear their minds from doing extensive work in a law firm reading tens of thousands of words of legal jargon every day by watching bad action movies or terrible comedies with inappropriate jokes about flatulence. Not Mary Bennet. She spent Tuesdays at the local library and Thursdays riding into CCSU so she could dig through their library archives. She was still in the early draft writing and information-gathering phase of her essay; yes, it was as long as a novella, and it was good enough for most people, but most people are not Mary Bennet. It seems like a lot of work for something like a scholarship essay, but Mary Bennet has never been called lazy.

She knew it was getting out of hand, but she couldn't help it. Every new discovery led her down another road and started a new notebook of ideas and pathways. She wanted to have her essay to Mansfield College done, proof-read, and read again by Aunt Phillips and her father, with some final insight from Lizzy and Jane before she felt it would be finalized and sent by mid-March. That seems like a long time, but asking your family to read over 20,000 words about the value of the liberal arts and offer up ideas for revision means you need to give them some time. Some children may ask their parents to drop everything they are doing to look something over the night before it is due, but Mary Bennet was never one of those children, and thus, she was not that kind of adult. Anathema, thy name is procrastination.

Lizzy found the drives to and from school with Mary to be the best parts of her week. While the two were never overtly antagonistic with each other, they were not objectively friends. They certainly loved and respected each other, but Lizzy had Jane and Charlotte in whom she could confide all her fears. She didn't really think of her younger sisters as people. It sounds worse than it is. That is to say, she objectively knew they were humans, and she would get into a fight with anyone who so much said a bad word about them, even if the word was the exact same word she said about them seven minutes prior, but she didn't consider them as having a future or plans outside of being little sisters. Sure, Mary was technically 18 but had always been 40 with a mortgage and a rental property with bad tenants, and Lizzy sort of knew that about her, but it wasn't until she had to spend an hour or so in the car along with hour-long lunches for seven weeks in a row that she finally saw Mary for who she was. She wasn't just the "smart" Bennet. Sure, she was the smart one on paper, but as Mary pointed out, they were all very smart on paper.

Mary, though, was so much more than that paper girl that everyone, including Lizzy, saw. She wasn't just scores. She wasn't just pencils in ponytails and crazy scribbling in notebooks. The work she was doing had meaning. She had a plan. She was a passionate, serious, brilliant woman who, as far as Lizzy could tell, was going to be the first Bennet to leave Connecticut. It was shocking, terrifying, and inspirational at the same time.

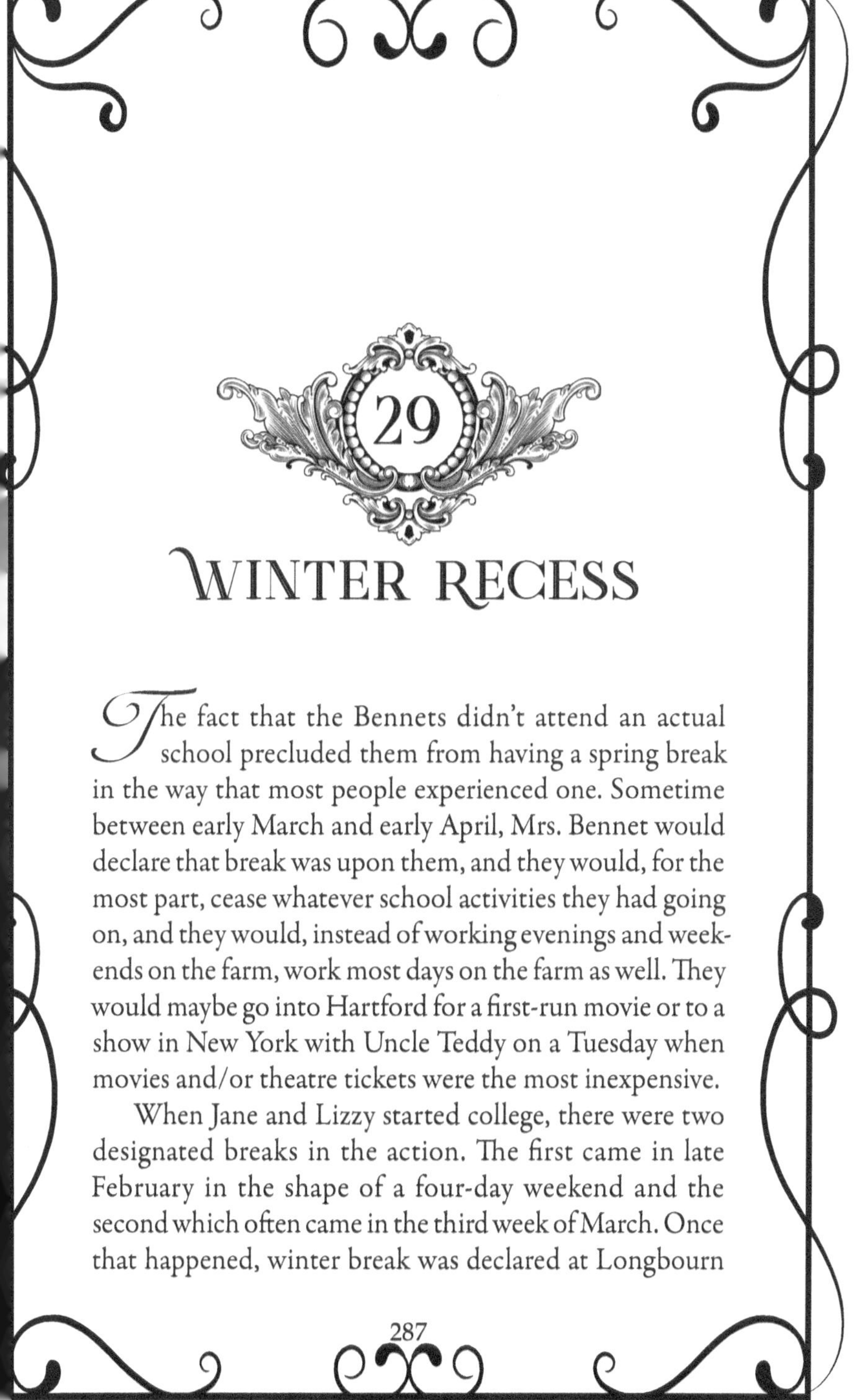

29

WINTER RECESS

The fact that the Bennets didn't attend an actual school precluded them from having a spring break in the way that most people experienced one. Sometime between early March and early April, Mrs. Bennet would declare that break was upon them, and they would, for the most part, cease whatever school activities they had going on, and they would, instead of working evenings and weekends on the farm, work most days on the farm as well. They would maybe go into Hartford for a first-run movie or to a show in New York with Uncle Teddy on a Tuesday when movies and/or theatre tickets were the most inexpensive.

When Jane and Lizzy started college, there were two designated breaks in the action. The first came in late February in the shape of a four-day weekend and the second which often came in the third week of March. Once that happened, winter break was declared at Longbourn as well. However, in the spring of 1990, with Mary done with school and Jane doing her student teaching, for the first and only time, there would be even more breaks at the Longbourn home school. Meryton Public Schools offered the same winter recess as CCSU, around Presidents' Day, which thankfully had the same Friday and Monday off for the four-day weekend. They also offered a traditional spring break in early April. This means that there were, at any given time, one to three of the eldest Bennet sisters who were "off the educational clock." Of course, Mary was technically in limbo, but she had, as we saw, kept up a pretty busy schedule nonetheless.

With the younger sisters not being particularly interested in doing things if the older sisters were not doing something, they requested a break of their own. Winter had been particularly cruel and all of that. Mrs. Bennet relented and essentially any learning that might have been happening for the youngest two Bennets was put on hold for roughly six weeks. Mary wondered if there had been any learning going on at all for the six weeks prior, but she kept that to herself.

On Thursday night, right after Meryton Public Schools shut down for Winter Recess, Jane jumped on the commuter train and went into New York over the long holiday weekend. Lizzy took their car and went off to Rhode Island to spend time with Charlotte and Reverend Collins. The older sisters gave Mary permission to use their room while they were gone as she was most certainly not on break and would need the space to sleep at a reasonable hour. It was unprecedented and caused consternation. The younger three had rarely stepped foot into the elder sisters' room, even when they were home.

For Mary to get to spend four nights alone in there reeked of favoritism. Well, it did to Lydia. She felt that she and Kitty should get to use the room as it was big enough for two people, and why would Mary need all that space anyway? She would just be sleeping and reading. She could do that in her own bed, and the two of them could have all that space to invite Maria over and do all kinds of fun things. Mrs. Bennet was inclined to agree with Lydia, which came as a huge shock to absolutely no one. However, Lizzy anticipated this and had a document written up with terms that she and Jane both signed and had witnessed by their Uncle Phillips, thus making it legal and binding, that under no circumstances were Lydia nor Kitty to cross the threshold of their room. It was silly and childish, but siblings can bring out the worst in us.

Mary, who never had any space to herself ever in her life, was as nervous and as excited as she ever got to be alone with her thoughts for four whole days. Shortly after dinner on Thursday, the first night of her epic journey into solitude, she took her books and her notebooks, her house cardigan, and several changes of clothes into her elder sisters' room. They gave her free reign to do whatever she wished, which included playing their records on their stereo. Together, they had amassed quite a collection. Mary would occasionally buy a blank tape and ask one of them to record something for her, but she rarely listened to the originals. She played the music just loud enough to not disturb anyone in the house, but loud enough that she could hear it clearly. She was used to hearing everything either through one speaker in the old radio that moved from kitchen to dining room and back again or in her headphones through her Walkman or at an ear-splitting, brain-splattering volume when Lydia was in control of the second-hand boom box that she, Lydia, and Kitty shared.

By the time she flipped over her first record of the night, Duran Duran's *Big Thing,* she found that her thoughts were quite orderly. By the time she started her second record, Madonna's *Like a Prayer,* she found that her notebooks were organized in some kind of coherent order. By the time she flipped that record over she saw a full narrative coming into shape. She dropped the needle on 'til Tuesday's criminally underrated second album, *Welcome Home*, and by the time she was through with both sides, she had written an entirely new draft of her essay, and it was only 5000 words.

She put on Tears for Fears *Songs from the Big Chair* and laid, fully clothed, on top of Jane's bed with her hands behind her head and a smile on her face. The album seemed perfect for the occasion. The song titles alone made it seem right. Did she want to shout? Did she believe? Was she head over heels for her new essay? Did she want to rule the world? We shall never know as she fell asleep before she could even finish one song on the album. Did she find herself totally refreshed, having slept more soundly than she ever had in her whole life and discussing Virginia Woolf's *A Room of One's Own* at breakfast with her father? Absolutely.

She spent the next day, a Saturday, holed up in her sisters' room, only coming out for food as she wasn't the kind of person who would leave crumbs in someone else's space. Plus, she knew if she didn't force herself out of the space for meals, she would lose focus, and she wasn't going to waste such an excellent opportunity. Her father came by to check on her but found her hunched over writing furiously, so he just backed away and left her to it. He knew that when she was ready to share, she would. By the time she went to sleep on Saturday night, she had a draft she felt comfortable showing to people.

On Sunday morning, after breakfast, she wrote out a copy on lined notebook paper, making sure to leave a space between each line for comments, and presented it to her father in his library. She didn't want to sit and watch him read it, nor did he want her to sit and watch him do it. Feeling ready for advice from all quarters, she took her notebook to town and had lunch with Aunt Phillips at the diner. She explained her process and shared the rundown on how she spent the past two days during the meal portion of the visit. She felt a minor thrill when her aunt made a remark about Virginia Woolf as well. Great minds and all of that, after all. She slid her notebook over to her aunt just as the dishes were cleared and the coffee had been topped off. She pulled the pen, not the pencil, out of her ponytail and handed it to her aunt, then excused herself. She used the bathroom and walked around the block a few times. Aunt Phillips had only a few notes regarding the organization. She didn't think Mary should cut a thing and overall found the whole thing to be exceptional. They celebrated by sharing a banana split. Winter Recess was going very well indeed.

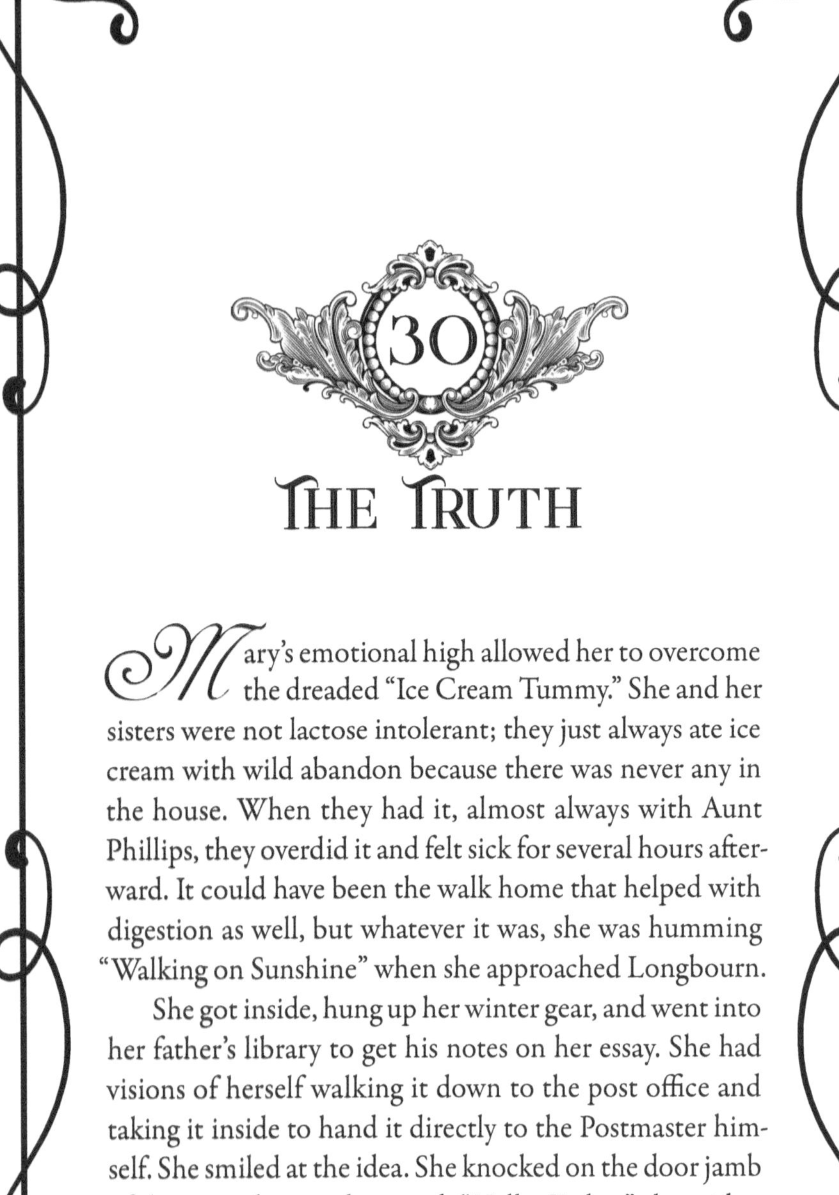

30

The Truth

Mary's emotional high allowed her to overcome the dreaded "Ice Cream Tummy." She and her sisters were not lactose intolerant; they just always ate ice cream with wild abandon because there was never any in the house. When they had it, almost always with Aunt Phillips, they overdid it and felt sick for several hours afterward. It could have been the walk home that helped with digestion as well, but whatever it was, she was humming "Walking on Sunshine" when she approached Longbourn.

She got inside, hung up her winter gear, and went into her father's library to get his notes on her essay. She had visions of herself walking it down to the post office and taking it inside to hand it directly to the Postmaster himself. She smiled at the idea. She knocked on the door jamb of the open door and entered. "Hello, Father," she said as she came in. "Is this a good time?" She saw her essay turned over on his desk.

He had his pipe in his mouth, but it wasn't lit. He had half a glass of iced tea sitting next to him. While it was cold outside, he only liked to drink hot beverages in the morning. Everyone has a quirk. He seemed to be engrossed in Tim O'Brien's *Going After Cacciato.* She knew he was early anticipating the author's forthcoming collection *The Things They Carried,* and so, he was rereading everything in preparation. He looked at the bottom of the page to note where he was in the book and closed it. He smiled up at her. "It is a perfect time. Your mother and sisters have decided to go to Hartford for something or other. I'm not sure what exactly."

Mary sat down. "Kitty needs new cleats. Practice starts up next week."

"That's it." He nodded. "Soccer cleats. She's quite good, isn't she?" It was rhetorical. He knew she was. "Something for Lydia as well?"

"Sheet music. Well, a song book actually," she corrected herself and then offered even more context. "Carole King. Should be excellent to hear her play it."

They both chose not to comment on the fact that Mary, who had been keeping herself to herself for three straight days and who went unacknowledged by her younger siblings on most days unless she was "in the way," knew exactly where the rest of the family was, and he, who had been around for the holiday weekend and slept in the same room with his wife, who must have mentioned this at some point, had no idea.

He nodded. He packed his pipe. "Anything for you?"

"No, Father. I have everything I need." She pointed to the library walls.

He lit his pipe, and they sat in silence for a moment as he got it going. Mary looked at the overturned pages, eager to see the other side.

"Do you?"

"Have everything I need?"

"Hmmm." He nodded. He pulled the pipe out of his mouth and used the stem to point at Mary's overturned essay. "Because it doesn't seem that you do." He tapped the stack of papers.

Mary worried that he might feel this way. The essay was supposed to be about why she was worthy of this precious gift over the thousands of other applicants from all around the world. To do that, she had to show what her life was like, warts and all. She didn't mean for him to take offense, and she ultimately decided that he would understand. She was certainly not ashamed of the life they had, and even though she knew the full extent of the debt and troubles that could be facing Longbourn, she still wasn't embarrassed. She was, if nothing else, even more proud of her parents. Yes, her mother too. For all of her mother's issues and inability to fully communicate, Mary did have love and respect for Mrs. Bennet. "Well, of course, I have everything I need. You and Mother have provided everything. Food, clothing, shelter, and love. I hope you know that has never been in question."

He opened his mouth to reply, but Mary held up one finger. He put his pipe in his mouth and took a puff. He nodded his head, indicating she should proceed.

"However, I may not necessarily have everything I want. I know that sounds selfish, Father. I know it does, but I have asked for almost nothing in my whole life, and even with this," she gestured to the stack of papers, "I am not asking for anything from you. I am trying to get something that I want, something that is entirely selfish, something that only benefits me, on my own."

"When you first brought up this scholarship, I assumed it was just that. It was for the academically worthy, which you most certainly are. When we talked about it, you gave your three reasons why you needed to do this, and while I didn't agree with all of them, I gave you my full support. It was impassioned, which was something I know you have, but I have rarely seen in you, so I was elated. However, now that I've read this," he pointed again, "it seems that there is more to it than you let on."

It felt like a slap. She physically recoiled from the allegation by blinking and shaking her head. While it was true that she spoke to Aunt Phillips before she spoke to him about The Mansfield Gift, it was only by a few hours, but that had been the case several times throughout her life. She knew that the relationship she and her sisters had with their parents wasn't the same as other people of their generation had with their parents; they were still her parents. There were still some universal truths when it came to talking to one's parents. She might have kept some of her thoughts to herself, as he expected her to when it came to her feelings about her mother for instance, but she never lied to him. Never once in her life. She worked on the essay for months, and it evolved over time. That is what happens when one writes and revises. The final draft is never the first draft and is even further from the outline.

He interpreted her silence as admission and moved forward. "While this essay is certainly well written, everything you do is, and you've done a lot of research about the value of a liberal arts education, and a variety of educational theories are sprinkled throughout this, some overtly and some covertly, which, I will admit, are expertly represented. If I were an adjudicator of this contest, I would sense the skill here and find myself nodding along without actually knowing why. It doesn't read like someone who faked her way through this. It isn't an essay written by someone copying from sources but written by someone who integrated and synthesized information she fully grasped."

She wanted to say thank you, as it was heavy praise, and it was exactly what she intended when she wrote it. She was still stinging from the accusation that she had lied and, if she admitted it to herself, was disappointed in his decision to call it a contest. She nodded, thus acknowledging she heard him, which served as his cue to keep going.

"This isn't just an essay written by a brilliant woman who *wants* to see the world. This isn't just an essay written by a person that any institution of higher learning would be honored to have as an alumnus. It isn't just an essay written by a person, who, if given the chance, will apply all of those educational theories to whatever her field of study is. It is those things, of course. The body of the text is all about that. I found myself nodding along on more than one occasion, and when I disagreed, I could not find fault in your reasoning."

Again, she nodded. It was all she wanted to hear. She worked hard on all of that. She spent literal weeks of time to make it be just that very thing. She knew there was more to it though. She knew what he was going to say next, and while she could cut him off again and get out in front of it, she just nodded and let him continue. She would have her say when he was done.

"Still, I am not an adjudicator. I am your father, and while I know you asked me to read it objectively, I have to admit that I simply cannot. Layered in here, again, just covertly enough to pull on the heartstrings of the reader, specifically in the introduction, and less so, but it is there if one squints in the conclusion, is an essay written by a poor girl who *needs*," he emphasized the word on purpose just as he emphasized *wants* previously, "to get out of her untenable situation. If she stays where she is, she will suffer. Suffering is, and you know this, Mary, a result of not having what you need, and yet you made it very clear just now that you are not suffering. So, what is it? What is the truth?"

Mary licked her lips. She was suddenly very thirsty. She had, on more than one occasion in her life, excused herself in the middle of a deep debate with her father to get something to eat or drink. Sometimes, they would speak for hours, and they needed to take "nature breaks" as they called them. She could have, she knew, done that right then, but everything felt wrong and so she second-guessed herself. He had most certainly challenged her before. She was expecting him to find some faults in her reasoning. She wanted him to. They didn't have to agree. His counterpoints had always made her main points stronger.

She licked her lips again and felt her tongue go thick inside her mouth. She reached forward, took his iced tea off the desk, and gulped it down. She smacked her lips and made an "ahhh" sound. She wiped her mouth on her sleeve. She set the glass back on the coaster and took a deep breath. "Right." She looked directly at him and found her resolve. "The truth is, as you know, Father, complicated. It is true that I need nothing. I can live here forever and be comfortable. Let's face it: everyone expects it of me."

"Now, that isn't..." He drifted off and started over, "I don't... That is, to say..."

She cut in. "I'm not mad about it, Father. If I was like everyone else, and I met me, I would think so as well. From the outside looking in, I was born to be a spinster. I know that Mother thinks that Aunt Phillips only got married because Uncle was there and that had Grandfather hired a different junior partner, Aunt would have married that person instead. It also looks like that from the outside, but I know how much they love and respect each other. It may not be the romance of the ages. No one is going to make a movie about them, and by now, it looks like a marriage of convenience, but whose doesn't at a certain point? Even your marriage makes people wonder."

"Your mother and I..."

"I didn't say it was one, Father. I said, whose doesn't look like it? From the outside looking in, you have to admit that you and Mother are a strange match."

"Yes, well, she has many qualities that didn't help her win Miss Connecticut. She may not be the smartest person I've ever met, but she has a big heart. She loves you all. Even you. Even when she is giving you grief. She does it out of love. She just doesn't understand you."

"I know, Father. That is my point. Perception isn't the truth. The perception of your marriage is not the reality of it just as the perception of what I am and what I can do isn't the truth. We are a decade away from the 21st century, and the general public doesn't understand people like me. It took me a long time to accept that because I am nothing like my sisters. For a long time, I thought something was wrong with me. They are hormonal, boy-crazy, stereotypical girls. I'm not like them. I never wanted to be like them, but I would be lying if I said that when I was younger, I wished I could be more like Lizzy. She seems to be in both worlds. Everyone respects her for being a woman in the world and an intellectual. But when I thought about it and wrote about it and did deep contemplation, I didn't want that. Not really. I don't want to be with anyone in that way. I don't feel disgusted at the thought of being romantic. I just don't feel anything about it. There is no thrill there. Sure, I recognize if someone is pretty or handsome, but I feel more moved by hearing a song for the first time or reading the ending of a book like that." She pointed at *Going After Cacciato.* "Do you remember when we talked about it? I thought about it for days and days after. I still think about it sometimes. That moves me."

He nodded. It was his turn to sit quietly, unsure how to react or what to say. He knew she wasn't really talking about O'Brien's book, and yet she absolutely was. He thought they were talking about her essay, but suddenly, he was having a conversation about her sexuality. It was something he was tangentially aware of but never really addressed with her. Mr. Bennet never had "the talk" with any of his children. He was aware that he lived in a house with women. He bought tampons and paid for birth control. He saw them go out on dates. He knew that some nights his eldest didn't come home at night. He wasn't a fool, but he never really was forced to think about how to talk about it. That was one of the agreements he and his bride made when she was first pregnant with Jane. She would handle the situation if the baby was a girl, and he would if the baby was a boy.

"I've done the research. I've read Kinsey. I've read Myra Johnson. I've read Paula Nurius. I'm not acting like anything. People, out there," she pointed at the always stuck window, "think they understand me. They think that I am stuck up or that I am a closeted lesbian or both. I know that isn't true. This is me. People on the *outside* think I'm broken or strange or an abomination or whatever they want to call it, but this is just who I am. I know that they are wrong. I didn't always know it, but I do now. Not being interested in sex in general makes me different, and I am okay with that." As if she could hear her father's thoughts, she continued, "I know this isn't what you thought we would talk about right now or maybe ever. None of you have ever asked me, and I've never volunteered the information. I suppose that makes me equally part of the problem, but Father, you know the other girls fit the default, and I am not the default."

He shook his head in agreement, which isn't an easy thing to do. He was, of course, agreeing with the last thing she said but not agreeing with her shouldering the blame. She was the child. He was the adult. It wasn't her fault. There are few times when one can silently shake one's head but mean yes and no and all of the things at once. This was one of those times. Mary knew. He knew. You, Dear Reader, likely knew as well.

She wanted to get back to his original point lest he thought she was trying to distract him, and so she drove the conversation back there. "My point here, Father, is that what my sisters and I need are the same. We have what we need. You've provided it. We are all thankful. Even Lydia. Even if she doesn't know it."

He laughed at that and felt his shoulders sink a bit. He hadn't realized he was so tense. He and Mary had often disagreed, but they never argued. He was prepared for an argument. He set her up with the question about needs. It was petty and foolish, but she had never hurt his feelings before. The rest of them most certainly did, and they would all do it again. He absorbed each blow without a problem because it was what he expected. It was the job of being a parent. He knew he would hurt their feelings again, and they would be mad and forgive him as was the way of children. Families can take more than they give, but they often give way more. He took a drag on his pipe and inhaled, letting the nicotine do its magic and relax him even more.

Mary continued, "There is a perception that we are all the same. The world thinks, and unfortunately, you and Mother agree, that we all want the same thing. We are all Bennets. We are raised by the same parents in the same house and less than a decade separates us in age. On paper, we all want the same thing. Sure, they all want different careers than each other, and they all want different things that will make them successful, but on the same base level, they all four have the same desire, and it is different than mine. What I want and what they want are different. They all plan on marrying a man at some point and having a family of their own with their own children, and they will have a life similar to that of yours. Mother wants that for them as well. She actually thinks it is her duty to make us wives and mothers. I understand why she thinks that. I really do. What Mother wants for them and what she wants for me are the same. What you want for them and what you want for me is also the same."

He was inhaling his pipe when she said that, and he made a face indicating that he disagreed. He shook his head and held up one finger.

Mary saved him the trouble. "What you want is not the same as her, of course. What I mean is that Mother wants us to be like her. You want us to be well educated, to be smart, to be kind, to be worthy of the last name Bennet."

He nodded. "You are all worthy. I am proud of you all. Even Lydia." He winked.

She laughed. She appreciated the levity. Maybe he didn't want to continue with the conversation. Maybe he was overreacting. He was emotional and frustrated with the big risks he was taking regarding the farm, the business, and his life. He gave her an off-ramp, but she didn't take it. She was totally sober, but she felt the same sense of freedom as she felt on New Year's Eve. Her tongue was loosened and was driving the car without brakes. Her glasses remained untouched. The only thing that could stop her now was to run out of gas. "I know that you are, but the thing is, Father, you want us all to do all those things, but you want us to do them here. You want to keep us at Longbourn for as long as possible. If I said to you right now that it was my wish to live here forever, you would make sure that it would be so. You would have no problems making one of those new cabins for just me. You could justify it as a business expense as I would be working here full time, and it would be part of my salary."

He nodded. "I will admit the thought crossed my mind. I thought it would be Kitty though who would ultimately stay and work the farm, but you could then have Jane and

Lizzy's room as your own, and you could do whatever you wanted. The law firm. The library. CCSU as a professor? All options and you could have your own room very soon. I don't imagine Jane and Lizzy staying for much longer, and I see you've taken to having space to yourself."

Mary made what she thought was a thankful but grim face. It just looked like her argument face to him. She nodded and continued, "I appreciate that. I do. Maybe Kitty would want to work the farm. She is the strongest and most physical of us. I don't know though, and I am not sure she would even know. If she wants that, I want that for her, but what if she gets a scholarship? You know the scouts are coming already. Not just from the small schools. Not just from UConn and Providence, although they are most certainly in the picture. She's remarkable."

"She is indeed."

"So, what would happen if her soccer prowess took her across the country or out of the country? There is going to be a Women's World Cup next year. The Americans are very good from what I understand. That means more opportunities for her to play at other levels. Will there be a professional league? Is she good enough? Let's say she is. What then? Would you think that she would want to come back and live in Meryton? Maybe. It is certainly possible. There is nothing inherently wrong with Meryton, but it is all we know, and more importantly, it is the only way you know us. This is your view of us. We are small-town girls to you, and we all love you for it. Really. We will always be small-town girls, but maybe, just maybe, we are not small-town women."

He tried to take a drag on his pipe, and it was empty. He held up one finger and set about rectifying the

situation. He banged his pipe out and made a bit of a show of repacking it. It was a stalling technique Mary had seen him use countless times. He would rather say nothing than say something and regret it. It was a noisy and attention-specific affair. She suspected it was why he smoked a pipe and not cigars or cigarettes. She also thought those things smelled like death, whereas a pipe, while clearly not healthy, had a lovely, homey smell. It really is all about what one knows and accepts after all. He struck a match and got it going. He finally looked up at his middle child and realized he didn't really have anything to say just then. Apparently, he just needed a time-out. He nodded.

She continued without missing a stride, "You don't want to leave, and Mother doesn't want to leave. That is okay. It is okay for you. This is the home you've built, and you want to keep us in Meryton at best and in Hartford County at worst. It is my supposition that because you left home and you set out on your own with a big debt to the Collinses, you worry about us being put in the same situation. You had big dreams, and they haven't come true in the way that you expected they would, but that doesn't mean they are not true at all. It doesn't mean that you have failed. You have made it so easy that you are offended by the idea that I would see all the work you've done on my behalf as anything other than the gift. It may feel that way for you. You may not want that for us, but the reality is, we need to try. We need to reject your gifts, and this is the part with which you are taking umbrage. You read my essay as my father, not as my teacher. You saw it as a caregiver, not as a cheerleader. I didn't preface it when I gave it to you because I never do that. The rest of them," she waved her hands at the door to signify the rest of her sisters and her mother, "do it. They all set you up. They say things like 'Now Father, keep in mind...' or Mother will say, 'Now, dear Mr. Bennet, remember that...' and then they launch into whatever it is they are trying to convince you to do."

"I'm well aware they are all doing it, though." He chuckled while he said it.

"Yes, of course you are. They are, for the most part, aware of it too. It is a game to them, to you, to everyone but me. That isn't a fun game for me. Chess is a game. Trivia is a game. Gin Rummy is a game. While I was not good at it, soccer was just a game for me. I want to earn your respect and support, not play for it. Yes, I know you think there is an element of chance with The Mansfield Gift, as there will be thousands of people entering, but I worked for months on this, and I wanted you to see that."

"Of course I see it. I have seen how hard you've worked."

Mary shook her head. "No, Father. You don't see it. You allowed your feelings to get involved today. You called it a contest when you know full well that it isn't a contest. That was, quite frankly, hurtful, and it felt intentional. You were belittling my work by calling it that. It may be called The Gift, but it is antiquated and traditional. It isn't a gift. Everyone can randomly receive a gift. This isn't random. There is a long arduous process. This is just the first part but is crucial to me moving on to the next part. Maybe I'm wrong, but it felt like you were being willfully ignorant of the situation. There are no adjudicators. I am not trying to earn full marks at a music festival nor am I trying to earn a 50-dollar gift card to a bookstore. I am trying to earn, not win, but earn, my place at Mansfield College."

"I've spoken to some people, and from what I understand, you are more than qualified to go there. Your acceptance wouldn't be in question."

She nodded. "Yes, of course. Everyone who meets the minimum requirements is accepted. I supersede the minimum requirements by quite a lot."

He pulled his pipe out of his mouth and pointed at her. "There you go."

She resisted the urge to shake her head. She wanted to remain respectful. "I have already been accepted into many excellent schools. My academic prowess has never been doubted by anyone. I know what my scores are. I know who I am. I work very hard, and I will continue to work hard if I go to Mansfield or Albertus Magnus or CCSU. I will continue to learn anywhere I go. Any person who wishes to become educated can and will be. Professors everywhere are qualified and excellent. There are terrible professors everywhere as well. The environment matters as well, as you know. I don't want to attend a large school where I have to sit in a room with 300 people for an introductory Trig course. I would hate that. I wouldn't be successful."

"Exactly. So why not stay here and go to CCSU or to Albertus Magnus? Small classes. Excellent professors and, most importantly, you will be there. You will elevate any place you attend. You've made all your sisters better students. You've made your uncle a better lawyer. You've made Mr. Richard a better teacher, and he isn't even your teacher."

"Of course, I agree with you, Father, on many points. There is a sense that a degree from one place is better than another, of course. If I get into Yale, it would mean," she did finger quotes, "more than a degree from UConn or

CCSU to the world at large. A degree from Yale would most likely mean more than a degree from Mansfield College, but it wouldn't mean more to me, and that really isn't the point of this conversation, and I am afraid that this part of the conversation is obfuscation."

He sat back hard against his chair. "Well, I guess I've lost the point then." He seemed genuinely perturbed. He obviously recognized the tone of voice that she took with her mother all the time and, for the first time, understood what it was like to be spoken to that way. None of them ever tried it before. Sure, Lydia smashed things and said hateful things, and Lizzy said "You're wrong" on many occasions in the middle of a heated argument about something political about which they disagreed, but they never, ever, spoke "down" to him before.

She didn't mean for it to happen. She never spoke to him that way. Her mother was at the receiving end of it all the time. She didn't want to speak to her mother that way, but she just brought it out in her. Mary saw Aunt Phillips and Uncle Teddy do it all the time, and so she learned it from watching them. None of them thought they were better than Mrs. Bennet, and they didn't mean to speak down to her or "at" her in that way, but she just wore them down, and they were human after all. Everyone had a limit, and Mary, for the first time ever, reached her limit with her father. She never made him angry before. She frustrated him from time to time when they debated, and she upset him with her opinion of her mother, but even then, he could remain somewhat objective and see her point.

He could not see her point at all. Like you, Dear Reader, he thought this conversation had gone on long enough. It is coming to a conclusion shortly. Promise. He leaned forward and pointed his pipe stem at her. "Enlighten me, Mary. Tell me what this is really all about."

The moment arrived. She nodded, took a deep breath, and slid forward to the end of her seat. She placed both hands on his desk and looked directly at him. "With every college acceptance letter that arrives, you shine a bit. It proves that homeschooling us was the right choice. It silences the naysayers in town. It makes Mother look good, which you love because you love her. It proves to us in general, and to me in particular, that we are wrong about her. She can't be a fool if we are so brilliant. If I get into Yale, you will see that as a feather in your cap. An Ivy League Bennet would be something special.

"Plus, if I get into Yale, I can live at home. Best of both worlds. Keep me safe, show me off, and," she was coming to it now, there was no way for her to get out of it once she said it, and even though she knew she was right, it was going to hurt them both, "it keeps your cover. No one would blink if I commuted and stayed home. It would only make sense. It is what we do. We are those eccentric Bennets. The patriarch is a founding donor for the library. They own the biggest tract of land in town but turn down offers to sell all the time. Big offers. Life-changing offers. They must be doing really well. Who would turn down that money? They must really love each other. They all live on top of each other in that house. Eccentric indeed.

"However, if I *earn* The Mansfield Gift, everyone will find out that all of the things we do are not just choices. Rich people get to be eccentric, and poor people are strange. Rich people turn down money because they don't need it. Poor people turn it down on principle. It is honorable, and I think you did the right thing, Father. I do, but your honor has kept us poor. We are poor. This feels like it was written by a poor girl. That is because it was."

She checked in with herself to see if she was okay, and remarkably, she felt only slightly shaky. "None of this has anything to do with me. I am not ashamed of being poor. I don't need anything. I agreed with you as soon as I walked in here. I may want more, but of course I do. You should want me to want more. You should want us all to want more. Us wanting more isn't an indictment of you as a parent. Look at us. Look at me! We are good. We are great. Poor but exceptional. I would rather be poor and exceptional than rich and boring. That is fine with me. It is better than fine. I am proud of it. The truth is, if this essay gets me The Gift, your secret will be out, and your pride will be hurt. I'm not the one suffering, you are, and this essay, which you admit to being well-written and effective, proves it."

For the first and only time in the history of ever, on that cold winter day, it was Mr. Bennet, and not one of his daughters who stormed out of the library, went to his bedroom, and slammed the door. He had, after all, learned from the very best.

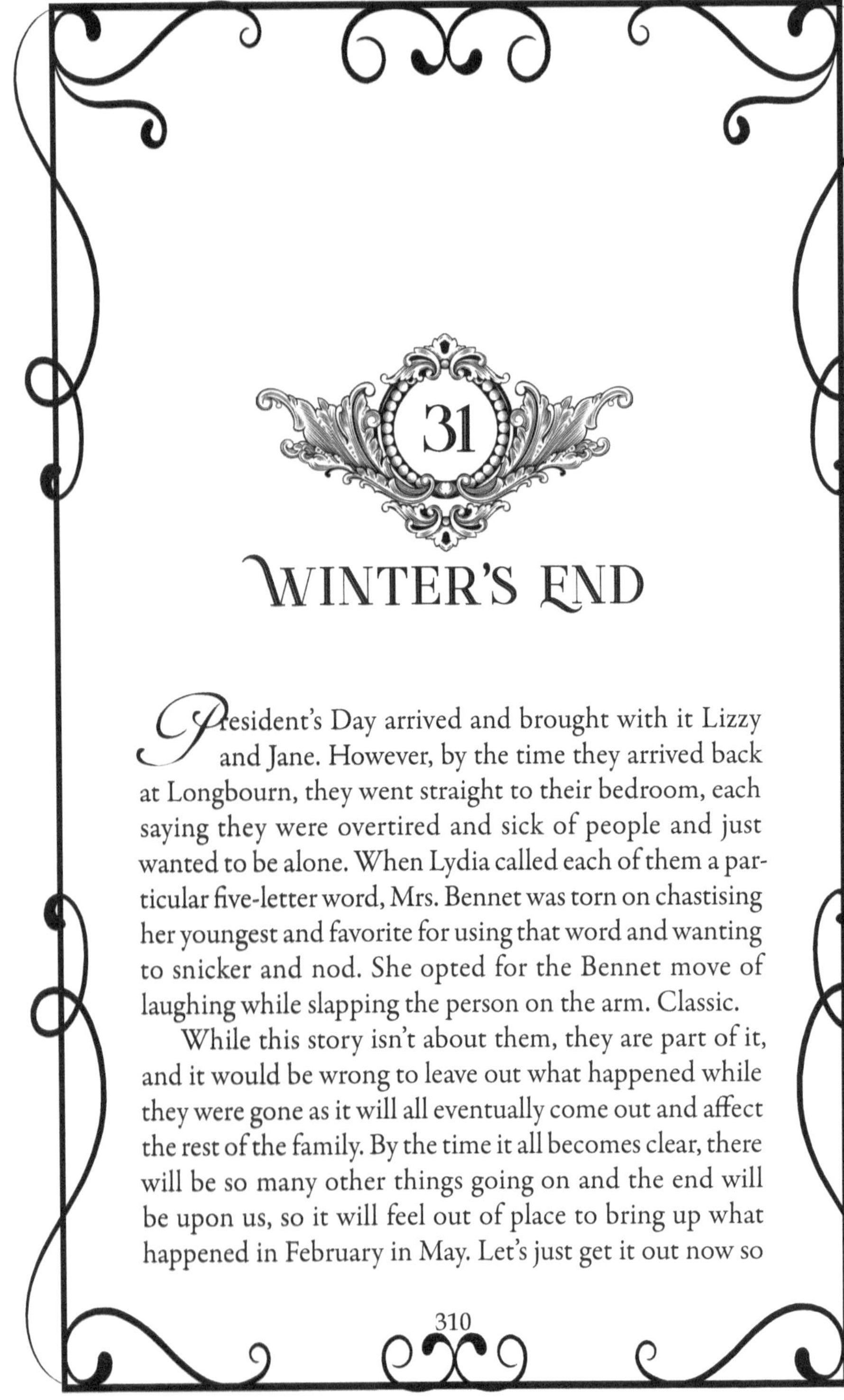

31

WINTER'S END

President's Day arrived and brought with it Lizzy and Jane. However, by the time they arrived back at Longbourn, they went straight to their bedroom, each saying they were overtired and sick of people and just wanted to be alone. When Lydia called each of them a particular five-letter word, Mrs. Bennet was torn on chastising her youngest and favorite for using that word and wanting to snicker and nod. She opted for the Bennet move of laughing while slapping the person on the arm. Classic.

While this story isn't about them, they are part of it, and it would be wrong to leave out what happened while they were gone as it will all eventually come out and affect the rest of the family. By the time it all becomes clear, there will be so many other things going on and the end will be upon us, so it will feel out of place to bring up what happened in February in May. Let's just get it out now so you have the full context of everything lest you agree with Lydia's assessment of her eldest two sisters.

Lizzy reported to Jane that Charlotte was in good health and happy. Reverend Collins adapted to married life incredibly well. He was a lonely man who was lonely no more. It hadn't curbed his incessant need to fill every silence with a running commentary and interesting facts about everything, but since he liked to talk about Charlotte, Lizzy didn't mind so much as she, too, could talk about Charlotte forever.

She met the mythic Lady Catherine de Bourgh and found her to be rude and overbearing. Had she not been a guest in her home, she would have returned the actions in kind. She also met Lady Anne de Bourgh, who was a lovely woman, but who was clearly terrified of her mother. Lizzy may have, on more than one occasion whilst alone in Charlotte's "private room," made a remark about the potential of poor Anne being forced into eternal spinsterhood. Charlotte laughed while smacking Lizzy on the arm.

The big news though was that Colonel Fitzwilliam was on leave and was visiting his aunt. Lizzy explained that he was everything Reverend Collins said about him: a perfect gentleman who seemed much younger than he was. Because he was there, so was Darcy. That isn't the big news. People visiting each other isn't big news. The big news was actually what Lizzy discovered both the night before in conversations with the colonel and Darcy and then in a letter given to her from Darcy, via Charlotte, just that morning.

It turns out that Darcy was in love with Lizzy, and he hoped that the colonel, whom everyone took an immediate shine to, could maybe act as a rasp and remove some of his rough edges in Lizzy's eyes. If that sounds like some middle-school drama, well, that's because it is. Just like all plans made by 12-year-old boys, it backfired spectacularly as the colonel, who was trying to show what a good guy Darcy was let it out that Darcy had recently "saved a friend from a bad match" because of the woman's "apparent disinterest" and her scandalous family.

So, while Lizzy was trying to process the information, Darcy arrived and told her that he loved her, and he wished to be with her if she would have him. Okay, this part is not really middle school. It is pretty bold, but to be fair, he thought his friend's kind words cleared the way for him and that Lizzy was ready to fall into his arms. That is some magical thinking right there. She told him in no uncertain terms that would never happen. She was so mad about the Jane and Bingley thing, which she certainly screamed at him about, that she ended up bringing up Wickham as well and the whole situation with his money and schooling.

It was both a non-sequitur and an ad hominem attack, but Mary wasn't there to point that out, and she was quite angry and would not have been open to the comment anyway. She said some words to him that are not appropriate here. He had the gall to apologize for insulting her with his declaration of love and walked away. Some people really can take the steam out of an argument. They had fought about all kinds of things in the past six months. How dare he?!

Wanting to clear things up as best he could, he wrote a long letter and gave it to Charlotte to give to Lizzy, who was too angry to read right then, so she drove home like a crazy person and read it in the parking lot at the train station while she was waiting to pick up Jane, who was planning on walking home to Longbourn, as the Bennets do, but Lizzy wanted to catch her first and tell her everything about Darcy and Bingley and the middle-school nonsense.

His letter explained that yes, he told Bingley to get away from Jane because she was so reserved, and he apologized for mistaking her shyness for indifference, but he couldn't overlook her mother telling everyone who had ears that Jane was going to marry Bingley and become a kept woman. That didn't sound like indifference or shyness to him; it sounded like cold calculation.

Also, he and many of the guests at the New Year's Eve party were shocked by the fact that the youngest two sisters danced and gyrated for six hours on any person who happened upon them. They are minors, and it could be seen as scandalous. Granted, they were not drinking all night, but it seemed that way, and perception can be everything. Also, Mary got drunk and got into a shouting match with a respected member of the community and had to be taken away by her father, who, he must admit, comported himself well.

Did Bingley want to deal with that? He already had a sister who was a scandal machine. Did he want sisters-in-law in the paper? Was it fair to him? Was it fair to them? Were they ready for that kind of scrutiny? Wouldn't it just be better to cut ties and leave everyone out of it? He admitted that it wasn't really fair of him to nudge Bingley to make that decision for the Bennets, but he couldn't bear it if their lives were upended. It wouldn't be their fault. If Jane was really indifferent, why bother letting it get into the press? Why let a fling ruin lives? Truth be told, he thought he was doing the right thing for Lizzy as well. Did she want to be wrapped up in all of that? Seemed like a lot to ask, so why bother asking? Did he say they were scandalous? No. He said they could be fodder for scandals, which could easily be misinterpreted by the colonel. Was he wrong? Maybe. Would he do it again? Maybe. Not great, but still, an apology.

He ended his missive by explaining that Wickham wasn't the man he claimed to be and that his version of events was false. He was a layabout, lush, and letch. He was asked to leave Mansfield College after one semester because he failed to attend classes, and when he requested that Darcy give him the cash equivalent of the tuition for the rest of the three years, Darcy refused and sent him on his way with ten thousand dollars, which he felt was more than adequate to get himself on his feet. Unsatisfied and angry, Wickham tried to seduce Georgiana, who was just 14 at the time so he could worm his way into the family fortune that way. It was the colonel who happened to be visiting at the time who found him out and who sent him packing. Darcy included Colonel Fitzwilliam's military address and phone number as well as Georgiana's contact information in the letter should Lizzy wish to corroborate his story.

Obviously, Lizzy was awash with all kinds of angry emotions when Jane got off the train. How dare he make a decision like that for Jane and her family? How dare he take away their choice? However, it was sort of sweet too, but they still deserved the right to choose these things, or at least Jane had the right to discuss it.

Jane was feeling forlorn as well as she never managed to see Bingley while she was in New York, but Caroline did make an appearance at the Gardiners only to disparage where they lived, and the fact that Aunt Gardiner used to be a bartender. It was so upsetting that even Jane couldn't find a way to say something nice about what happened. It was likely the attack on her aunt that did it, but it could also have been the realization that Caroline Bingley might actually be exactly who people thought she was. Jane didn't like that. She didn't believe in the caricature version of anyone. She knew Lydia wasn't so vain, and that Lizzy wasn't so angry, and that Kitty wasn't so passive, and that Mary wasn't so remote, and Darcy wasn't so stoic, and that Bingley wasn't just a stupid rich boy. Sometimes, when someone wears red in a novel, it signifies passion, and sometimes, the person just happens to like wearing red. This is one of those times. Caroline was a vapid, mean, rich person. Full stop.

The two sisters consoled each other as best they could and ended up taking a short but restorative nap curled up together with Lizzy as big spoon, like they did when they were younger. When they finally came out of their room for dinner, they apologized for their previous behavior and shared only the happy parts of their stories with the family. Charlotte was in good spirits. The Gardiners were a delight. They, in fact, invited Lizzy to spend her official spring break with them in New York. It was something Jane failed to mention when they were alone, so it was a genuine delight. Lizzy wrote a letter letting them know she would attend, and Mary promised to drop it in the mail the following day.

Mary didn't let her father's outburst stop her from moving forward with her plan, nor did she stop her morning routine of eating with him and reading the paper. They were civil to one another, but the ease they felt had gone away. He felt that she was being selfish and only thinking of herself. She knew that it was true, but since it was the first time in her life she had ever been selfish while only thinking of herself, she agreed with him, which only infuriated him more. She didn't feel that she needed to apologize, and so, she didn't.

She was not pleased to be, for the first time, at the center of his ire, but she wasn't going to hold herself back. She understood that if she went to Mansfield, people would ask about it, and he wasn't a man who could lie. He could omit. He could walk away. He could change the subject, but he would never lie. Gossip often rips through a small town like wildfire during a drought. Like a wildfire, it adapts and changes as it goes, depending on what is in its path. Gossip begins as one thing, but fueled by pettiness and rumors, by the time it peters out and everyone in town has heard the news, the real story is much different. It was likely that the residents of Meryton could decide that Longbourn was bankrupt or that the surveyors who were coming and going from the property were government agents who were measuring up the property for auction or that the Lucases were moving in at any moment now that their daughter technically owned the property or a myriad of other equally absurd notions.

Of course, Mr. Bennet would do nothing to dissuade the rumors and gossip and so, until his farm-to-table, residential, sustainable farm vacation idea took root and showed everyone the reality of the situation, the whispers would happen, and they would lead to shouts from her mother inside the walls of Longbourn as it would, no doubt, be all her fault. On paper, if one squinted, one might see that it was Mary's fault that the town found out about the situation at Longbourn, but even through squinted eyes, no one, not even Mrs. Bennet, could blame Mary for the fact that the farm had suffered, as many family farms did at the time, and that they were woefully behind on payments and that without Reverend Collins' magnanimity, many of the rumors would be true.

Dear Reader, at that point in 1990, none of that had come to pass, but Mary knew, as one knows how to breathe without trying, that it most certainly would happen in some shape or form. If things went the way she would like them to go, she would be in the Midwest, in her dorm at Mansfield, and out of the spill zone by the time it would all come to pass. She was not a braggart and not the star of her own story, and thus, no one would really realize she was gone until she was. Someone, maybe one of the servers at the diner would ask of the Gardiner sisters as they met up for a Saturday lunch where Mary was, and Aunt Phillips, who was instrumental in her success, would crow a bit about it. Someone would overhear, and someone would ask someone who would say something, and it would eventually get out that Mary got into the same school where Charles Bingley went but only because she was poor. Someone would say it in front of Harriet, who would straighten them out because she knew the truth, but by then, it would have been out of control. Residents of Meryton wouldn't know that The Mansfield Gift was an academic competition given to the brightest and best who just so happened to be from families who were not from the upper crust. Instead, they would think it was charity for the destitute Bennets, and who were they to have fooled us all these years? No wonder they homeschooled those girls and on and on and on.

Because her mother was unwilling to spend money on long-distance calls, even to air grievances, and she was not much of a letter writer as she found that she didn't have the patience to sit still long enough to write a thank you card, let alone a long missive, Mary knew she would miss out on all the abuse. Sure, when she returned to Longbourn for holidays and the summer, she would suffer quite a bit of it, but she would be willing to endure it. Besides, she knew that it was just how her mother was. Her nerves were what they were, and there was nothing any of them could do about it.

So it was that on Tuesday, as Monday was a holiday, Mary stopped at the post office before she went to the law office. Just as she imagined, she handed the Postmaster her packet as well as Lizzy's letter for the Gardiners. This wasn't part of the way she envisioned it, but it didn't really take anything away from it either. She paid extra for Priority Mail and did her best to not think about it anymore. She knew she wouldn't hear from anyone for a month or so if she made it to the second round of interviews, so she went about her life. She continued to apply for other private scholarships and grants.

She realized that even if she didn't win The Gift, she would do her best to live on campus. Yale released their final decisions by April 1st which also happened to be the cut-off for reserving a room at CCSU. She didn't want to waste the money, but she also wanted to prove that she was serious and as pragmatic as everyone claimed she was, so on Thursday, she went with Lizzy to the CCSU campus and paid the 90-dollar non-refundable binder fee that said she would matriculate in the fall as well as the non-refundable housing deposit. Nothing else was due until August, and so, if she chose not to come, she would be 190 dollars less wealthy, but she could make that up in no time at the law office. On that day, she made a statement. She was going to CCSU or Mansfield. Even if Yale accepted her, which they would, because of course they would, but she couldn't know that yet, she would not go there.

Also, she realized something that many people much older than her don't realize until they are much, much older; there is no price too high for one's peace of mind. She spent the rest of that day listening to music on her Walkman and giving herself a tour of the six residence halls where she might find herself placed. There were two female-only residences and four co-ed halls. She imagined herself living there, sharing a room with just one other person, or being part of a suite of women, which was something to which she could obviously relate. While it wasn't her dream, it wasn't a nightmare either. That was something at least.

She returned to Longbourn content that she had done everything she could have done to shape her own future. It was with that new sense of confidence that she spent the rest of the winter sifting through all the notebooks and past drafts of her essay without consulting her father, her aunt, or anyone. This was her work, and she was proud of herself. If she was selected or not, she managed to do some college-level research and writing. She began to shape her castoffs into the beginning of a collection of essays that she would, years and years later, shape into a dissertation that she would successfully defend on the day she became a doctor.

32

SPRING THAW

r. Bennet had never held a grudge before. When he left Maine, he left the hurt feelings of his childhood behind and with it his family. He wasn't mad at them for not understanding him; he just chose not to dwell on it. When each new daughter was born, he didn't bother to send notice. They didn't get holiday cards. They were essentially some friendly strangers with whom he shared genes. When people cast aspersions about his choice to homeschool his children, he let them roll off his back, and he would be seen sharing a meal with those people during his library board days in town. He was a human non-stick pan. Thus, it was surprising how long it took for him to quit being angry at Mary, who, even Mrs. Bennet had to admit, didn't do anything ... yet. Applying for a grant isn't the same as winning the grant or, gasp, accepting the grant. Until it happened, which she was sure Mary would come to her senses and not do, she chose not to discuss it at all, even with her husband behind closed doors.

Still, as February turned to March, Mr. Bennet remained steadfastly distant from his middlest daughter. While Mary asked for no support from her siblings, it was obvious to Lizzy that something needed to be done, and she tried to get her father to warm up and get over it. She knew he was hurt and did her best to "see his side," but ultimately, Mary was leaving in the fall be it for CCSU or Mansfield, so he should, she said it that way without giving him the option, make up with her. They didn't have to agree, but they needed to get along and get back to normal. Mary was, Lizzy argued, the most like him, and he must miss his talks with her. He conceded that he did miss them, but he wasn't sure he was ready to move on. He felt betrayed. Lizzy rolled her eyes at him and made a remark about him acting like Lydia. He didn't care for it and said, "Et tu, Elizabeth?" She laughed. He didn't. Fortunately, Mrs. Bennet barged in to say something untoward about someone in town, and Lizzy slipped out.

It could be argued that Lizzy's motives were selfish because without her father to talk to about antiquated things and arcane passages, Lizzy was the person to whom all of these ideas were directed during their weekly trips to New Britain. Mary didn't really need to keep going, but she did find that spending a day alone in the University library to be relaxing and exhilarating. She would tell Lizzy all of the things she wished to look up on her way to campus and then share everything she learned on the way home.

Lizzy, who was quite academically minded, found herself worn down by it. It wasn't that she didn't have some interest; it just wasn't her only interest. She had other things on her mind regarding Darcy and the Wickham news and poor Jane's broken heart, and while Mary was an excellent listener, she didn't actually care all that much. That is not to say Mary wished her sisters to be lonely or miserable or heartbroken or that she thought Wickham was a hero instead of a villain, but she just didn't think it was a great use of time to worry about any of it, and so she didn't. She could offer no real advice on the matter. Mary's insights were all pragmatic, and while Lizzy wasn't run by her outrage like her mother or her hormones like Lydia or her empathy like Jane or her adrenaline like Kitty, she occasionally wanted to feel all of those things either at once or in part, and she needed a sounding board who would reflect the proper emotion back to her. It was in moments like that when she missed Charlotte the most. She considered ponying up the money for the long-distance call to Rhode Island, but she was saving her money for the upcoming trip to New York. While her aunt and uncle would provide the basics, she wanted to see a show and get out and about in the city.

So it was that the great Bennet frost continued on for several more weeks. It wasn't as bad as it could be. Mr. Bennet didn't say, "Jane, tell your sister…" and Mary didn't say, "Mother, can you please tell Father…" They just shared space. The only noise that came from their mornings was the rustling of the paper, the striking of his matches, the slurping of coffee, and most frustratingly for Mr. Bennet, the mad scribbling of Mary in her notebooks. Breakfast was, for years, a scribbling-free zone because she felt that she could say whatever she was thinking to him and work through it only to reflect on it in writing later.

With her father fully immersed in his musings and grudge, Jane fully immersed in her student teaching, Kitty fully immersed in her conditioning drills, Lydia fully immersed in her whatever-it-was she was doing, and Mary fully immersed in her work, Lizzy took off to New York without much fanfare. She considered asking Mary to drive her to the train station, but the weather was fine enough for a walk. It had been one of those Marchs where they saw temperature highs nearing 80 and lows in the single digits all within a week, which is to say, late winter in New England, so a fine day with the temperature being a crisp 55 just after the vernal equinox seemed like a perfect day for walking. She hopped the train for New York having failed in her scheme for familial reconciliation. Unbeknownst to her, by the time she made it back to Longbourn in a mere week, Mary and her father would be just fine.

Dear Reader, you will be shocked to learn that the person responsible for the ultimate reconciliation was inadvertently Lydia. Seems unlikely, doesn't it? She didn't mean to do it. She wasn't thinking about her father or her sister. She wasn't thinking at all actually, as we shall soon see. She hadn't really noticed the tension between her sister and father because it wasn't about her. Kitty had started soccer practice, and so Lydia had taken to spending time with Mrs. Forster, who was Mary's age, but already married after she recently found herself in the family way after her dalliance with a visiting reservist. He married her but left her behind in Meryton as he "figured some things out" back at home.

During this time of familial distraction, she and Mary so rarely spoke. Lydia's time in the library with her father had been slowly dwindling as she cared less and less about her studies. She had other things on her mind, and because she was the one child over whom he had hardly any say, he didn't push the issue. He mentioned it in passing to his wife one night, and she assured him that Lydia was keeping up with her studies at the public library and that Mrs. Forster was an excellent influence on her, and most importantly, she was on track to graduate on time. It was good enough for him, and so he quit thinking about it as best he could and went back to worrying about the upcoming construction project and the future of the farm. He thought it would be his biggest concern for the coming months and years, but little did he know that his perspective was about to change forever.

33

LYDIA

*L*ydia Bennet would be outraged to discover that this book is near its conclusion, and this is the first chapter with her name in the title. Of course, if it were up to her, this whole thing would be about her. Yes, she is that person who heard Otis Redding's classic "Hard to Handle" and thought of it as an instruction manual. She would say she was the "woman on the scene" and all of that. In fact, in February of 1990 when the Black Crowes released what is a top-ten cover of all time of that very song, Lydia and her mother were overjoyed. Lydia was so inspired that she learned to play the song on the piano, and her rendition was a rollicking good time.

While she was, as Mary has constantly reminded us, more than the sum of her parts and was an exquisite musician who was, like the rest of her sisters, incredibly intelligent, she was also silly, vapid, and didn't always use the good sense her parents gave her, and so it was that we finally discover why it is that this chapter is named after her. Although, Dear Reader, the irony here is, as you shall soon discover, that while this chapter is all about her, she isn't in it at all.

Because Lizzy was on her break and planning a trip to New York, Mrs. Bennet thought it fine for Lydia and Kitty to take a break as well. Lydia accompanied Mrs. Forster to the Brighton neighborhood of Boston where Mr. Forster was said to be living and where everyone assumed Mrs. Forster would be living soon. Lizzy thought this was a mistake to let her go and to give her more time off from school. While Lydia and Kitty were only a few years younger than she and Jane, they acted much more immaturely than either of them ever did. Could it be because this is what happens when the eldest children are relatively good? Could it be that by the time Lydia was born, the parents were exhausted and had lowered the bar for success? Could it be that Lydia was just born a certain way and genetics play a bigger part in personality than people want to admit? Would Mary Bennet write several papers about the nature vs. nurture theory to try to crack this exact question? The answers are three maybes and a resounding yes.

Outside observers are big fans of the nurture side of that coin. Anyone who has ever sat at a family event and pondered how it was that you and those people came from the same place, understands how only looking at families through that nature lens is absurd. Still, it weighed on Lizzy a bit, and so she expressed her concerns to her father who waved it off. Had they not just discussed the rigor of the girls' education, Mr. Bennet might have mentioned this as concerning as they were seemingly just on a break, but he was distracted and not going to pick a fight with his wife over this, so he made no comment.

Having stated her case and "done her part" to save Lydia from embarrassment, Lizzy went to New York for a week with the Gardiners. Unbeknownst to her, if she really wanted to change the trajectory of Lydia's life, she would have needed to take action sooner. It might not have mattered at all although the guilt of it all sat with her for many years. It wasn't until years in the future, after a long weekend and multiple conversations with Mary where they walked, talked, and drank many bottles of wine, that she would come to agree with her middlest sister, that Lydia was going to be Lydia, and if it hadn't been this, it would have been something else.

Spoiler alert for where Mary came down on the whole nature vs nurture thing. Sorry to anyone hoping to dig up the Mary Bennet archives and do some reading. Obviously, her first bad experience with drinking that night at the Bingley New Year didn't swear her off of alcohol for the rest of her life. During that same weekend, she admitted to Lizzy that while she wished she hadn't been tipsy when she gave Mr. Tucker that verbal thrashing, she learned to be proud of herself for doing it. Lizzy admitted she was proud of her too. It was quite lovely.

Long before any of that happened, in late March of 1990, Mary Bennet found herself at the dining room table with her notebooks spread out all around her. She bought several hardbound journals at the five and dime and was compiling all of her ideas from pencil to pen into something that had more object permanence than floppy, cardboard-covered pocket notebooks. As we know, these would be the foundation for her doctoral thesis later, but she didn't know that at the time. She just wanted to make sure she could read her own writing in later years, and she wanted to make sure the writing didn't fade.

If you wonder, Dear Reader, why she didn't type these things up instead, you need to remember that it was 1990, and the Bennets were, as we know, not well-to-do. Personal computers were not cheap, nor did they, at the time, seem like a necessity. Remember, all research and writing Mary Bennet did in the pages of this tome was done on paper. 1990 had more in common with 1890 than the time this was written and when you are reading it. For the residents of Meryton, the technological revolution was slow to develop. To be fair, it wasn't so much a revolution as tacit acceptance with much gnashing of teeth and con-sternation about the way things "used to be." In fact, the first personal computer wouldn't make an appearance in Longbourn until the turn of the century.

While she was an excellent typist from her time at the law office and there was a portable, manual typewriter on the premises, and the ribbon for it would have cost her the same or possibly less than the hardbound journals, two things kept her from doing this. The first is that she actu-ally liked the feeling of writing. Writing longhand con-nected the ideas to her brain. She felt as though with each stroke of her pen, she was etching the information inside her, forever creating knowledge, which we know was, and is, important to Mary.

The second reason was that the sound of banging keys and the ping of the bell at the end of each line followed by the sliding of the bar to move the keys back to the left every few seconds for hours in a row would have, to be fair, driven anyone crazy, and as everyone in the family was well acquainted with Mrs. Bennet's nerves, there was no way she would dare do that to herself or the rest of her family. It may not have mattered that she and her father were barely talking, but she loved him nonetheless and knew he would defend her right to type, and it would all be very dramatic.

She was, of course, listening to the radio playing while she was working and the phone rang, ironically, just as the song switched over to The Beatles' "Do You Want to Know a Secret?" It rang a second time, and Mary looked up, wondering if anyone else was going to get it. On the third ring, she realized either she was the only one home, which was entirely possible, or she and her mother were playing a game of patience chicken.

She walked into the kitchen and picked up as the fourth ring ended. "Longbourn, how may I help you?"

"Mary! Get Father!" Lizzy's voice was panicked. She was crying and was so stuffy that Mary thought she must have been crying for some time, which she had been.

Many people would have followed up on this demand while hearing the tone of Lizzy's voice with questions or concerns about her well-being. Others would have done the thing that so many people do when they hear disconcerting news, ask "What?" even though they heard the request just fine. It is just something brains do to help the mouth. Mary did neither of these things because Lizzy rarely called their father "Father," and it was obvious that there was no time to delay.

She said, "Yes," nodded, and let the receiver drop to the floor. She was shouting "FATHER!" over and over as she was running toward his library.

Mr. Bennet had never, in 18 years, ever heard that tone of voice from his middle child, and in a moment, without knowing what was the matter, he felt his pulse pound in his ears. His blood pressure spiked. His mouth went dry. Anyone who thinks fear is a construct has likely never felt love. By the time the first of her many shouts reached his ears, his grudge was over. How could he ever have been upset with a person who could make that sound? What was he thinking? How dare he? He was a foolish, prideful man. No wonder his youngest child was so silly. She learned it from watching him. This wasn't even a trifle. Mary hadn't betrayed him or been evil or said hurtful things or lied or stolen or tried to use his good name for nefarious means or committed a crime and implicated him or manipulated him physically or emotionally.

Grudges should be reserved for people who did those things. Those things can, and maybe should be, grudge-worthy. This, whatever it was, was absurd. Mary was being who she was. She was being the woman, frankly, he wished she would be. She was being the person she was always destined to be, and he'd wasted months of what could and would likely be the final few months of his life that his daughter would live under his roof. Of course, he didn't actually articulate any of those thoughts, but he certainly felt them all in a splash of guilt and misery and, of course, fear. He was on his feet moving his long legs toward the library door while he interrobanged "MARY?!"

In a different book, they would smash into each other in the open doorway and fall hilariously to the floor. This is not that kind of book, nor is this the time for jokes. Thank you very much. He was in the dining room before she could cross it.

"Lizzy!" she shouted and pointed back toward the kitchen as she slid out of his path.

He raced past her. She continued her slide into the wall, bounced off, and headed back to the kitchen after him. While Lizzy didn't ask for her or tell her what was going on, she wanted to know what she needed to do as a voice like that surely demanded that everyone in Longbourn *do something.*

She came into the kitchen as her father was placing the receiver against his ear. "I'm here." He held his hand to his chest and looked at Mary. He didn't smile, as this wasn't a smiling moment, but he nodded and said all the things he wanted to say in that look, hoping she understood.

She nodded back, having heard it all. She walked over and took his hand which wasn't holding the phone to his ear. She squeezed.

"Yes. Are you sure? What time?" He too didn't waste time with a random "What?" All business, that Mr. Bennet. Cool under pressure. He looked up at the clock above the sink. "Yes." Well, maybe not so cool that he could actually remember what time it was although he had looked only seconds prior. "Okay. Yes. Of course. Call Teddy and tell him I'm on my way. I'll meet him there," he looked back up at the clock, "at noon." He squeezed back. It wasn't a kind, reassuring squeeze; it was more of a hold-on-for-dear-life kind of squeeze. "Yes, outside the hotel."

Mary didn't like the sound of that. Her father loathed going anywhere that wasn't the farm or Meryton, and even then, he tried to limit his trips to town to once a week. When he did need to travel, for his yearly visit with Reverend Collins, for example, he prepared for weeks ahead of time making sure things could run smoothly without him for way longer than he planned on being gone.

The fact that he would be wherever he needed to be in two hours without planning didn't bode well.

"Good. Do that, and Lizzy, you did the right thing." He hung up and looked at Mary. There were tears in his eyes. "Lydia's run off with George Wickham!"

"What?!"

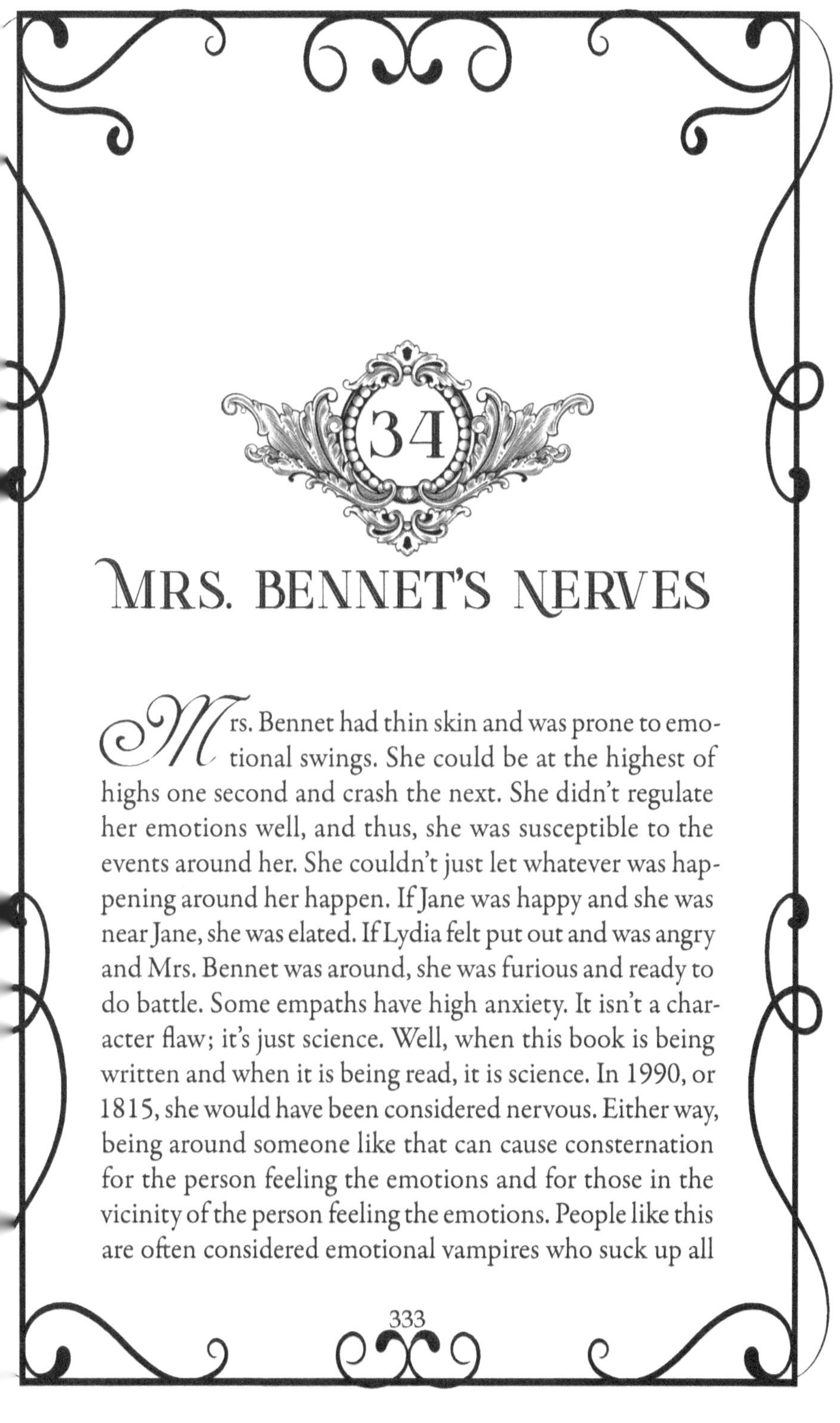

34

MRS. BENNET'S NERVES

Mrs. Bennet had thin skin and was prone to emotional swings. She could be at the highest of highs one second and crash the next. She didn't regulate her emotions well, and thus, she was susceptible to the events around her. She couldn't just let whatever was happening around her happen. If Jane was happy and she was near Jane, she was elated. If Lydia felt put out and was angry and Mrs. Bennet was around, she was furious and ready to do battle. Some empaths have high anxiety. It isn't a character flaw; it's just science. Well, when this book is being written and when it is being read, it is science. In 1990, or 1815, she would have been considered nervous. Either way, being around someone like that can cause consternation for the person feeling the emotions and for those in the vicinity of the person feeling the emotions. People like this are often considered emotional vampires who suck up all the attention in every room, and because the patriarchy is real, when those people are women, they are called hysterical, even by other, well-meaning women. Sigh.

"She's being hysterical," Aunt Phillips said to her three nieces who were standing in the hallway as she came out of her sister's bedroom.

"Oh, Aunt..." Mary started because well-meaning or not, some things need to be corrected.

However, Jane started speaking at the same time, and as younger sisters often do, she deferred to Jane and cut herself off. "What do you recommend we do to ease her pain?" Jane asked. Sweet, sweet Jane.

"I'm afraid the only thing that will do any good is to get some word from someone that Lydia is alive and well or that your father hasn't," she held up finger quotes, "challenged that horrible Wickham man to a duel and been killed or both."

Mary shook her head. Her mother made it so hard to defend her sometimes. She looked at Jane, who was nodding along as though that seemed like a totally reasonable possibility. She looked at Kitty, who was looking down, her hair hanging around her face. Her head was bobbing up and down. Laughing or crying? Could it be both?

"Until we know more, I am going to prescribe our mother's favorite relaxing tincture: whiskey with soda. One for me and a double for her." She walked past them and headed for the kitchen.

They followed her in age order as often happens in big families. Mary, of course, still in the middle. They got to the kitchen, and with nothing to do and no new information, they each set about doing something useful. Kitty got out the step stool, climbed up, and got the cookies. She wasn't interested in her grandmother's tincture even if her aunt was the kind of woman who thought it was fine for minors to drink under the supervision of an adult, which she was most assuredly not. Still, sugar always made her feel better. Plus, she was in the midst of training for the new season and could essentially eat anything she wanted and still be in a calorie deficit.

Jane got out the glasses, including one for herself, and once Kitty was safely off the stool, opened the freezer and filled them with ice. She set all three glasses in front of her aunt, who would be in charge of the pouring and mixing. Mary, who was not in training, but who agreed that cookies were the right drug of choice, started making hot chocolate. She got the milk and candy bars from the fridge. She figured if they were going to go into a sugar coma, they might as well go all the way.

The phone rang. They all froze. Logically, they should wait for Mrs. Bennet to come out and answer it. There was not a phone in the bedroom. Mr. Bennet was adamant about that, and most of the time, Mrs. Bennet agreed with his choice on the matter, but whenever she was bedridden and miserable, she cursed his name for making such a stupid choice. The phone rang a second time, and they didn't hear her coming, shouting, or making any noise at all. Had they been able to see through the walls, they would have seen her, knees pulled up to her chest, arms wrapped around her legs, holding her breath, waiting for someone to take action.

On the third ring, it was Mary who broke the spell. She shut the stove off, always practical, that one, no reason to have scalded milk stinking up the house on top of everything else. "Longbourn, how may I help you?" At one point in time, each of the Bennet girls would, in their adulthood, answer their own phone in that exact way. Habits and addictions are first cousins after all.

"We found her. She's alive and seemingly quite pleased with herself," her father said.

Mary felt her back muscles relax. She hadn't quite realized she was so tense as one doesn't until the stress leaves. She covered the mouthpiece and said to the room, "They found her." Before she could get back to the phone, they all started speaking at once. Mary plugged her left finger in her left ear to block them out and put the receiver back up to her right ear. "What do you need me to do?"

"Go get your mother. She should be the first to hear the rest."

"Yes, Father." She handed the phone to Jane, who started asking a thousand questions at once. Mary walked to her parents' bedroom door, knocked twice, and opened the door a crack just so her mother could hear her voice clearly. "They found her. Father wants to speak to you."

Mary left the door open a crack and stepped back. This wasn't the first time she was the one who had to retrieve her mother from her self-imposed isolation.

The door flew open, and her mother, face streaked with tears, hair disheveled, one slipper on, and shirt misbuttoned, streaked past her toward the kitchen, muttering about having a phone extension installed in the bedroom just as soon as he returned.

She ran into the kitchen with Mary trailing behind her. Jane heard her coming and had the receiver extended ready for her mother. There was no reason to be chastised for making it take microseconds longer. Jane would always have the most experience with her mother's nerves of the five of them as she was the eldest and most willing to make peace.

"Oh Husband, tell me everything!" she shouted into the receiver. She caught her breath while she listened. Her sister handed her a glass. She took a sip, realized what it was, looked at her sister, nodded a thank you, and took a big pull. She smacked her lips and released a long "Ahhh." Mrs. Bennet thankfully finished her drink and didn't have a mouthful of tincture when she shouted. "What?!... No!... OH?... Well... That seems like... Oh... I see... Are you sure? Yes! That is wonderful! We'll celebrate when you get back, Grandpa!"

"What!?" Jane and Aunt Phillips asked at the same time.

Kitty's mouth was full.

Mary shook her head, not remotely surprised.

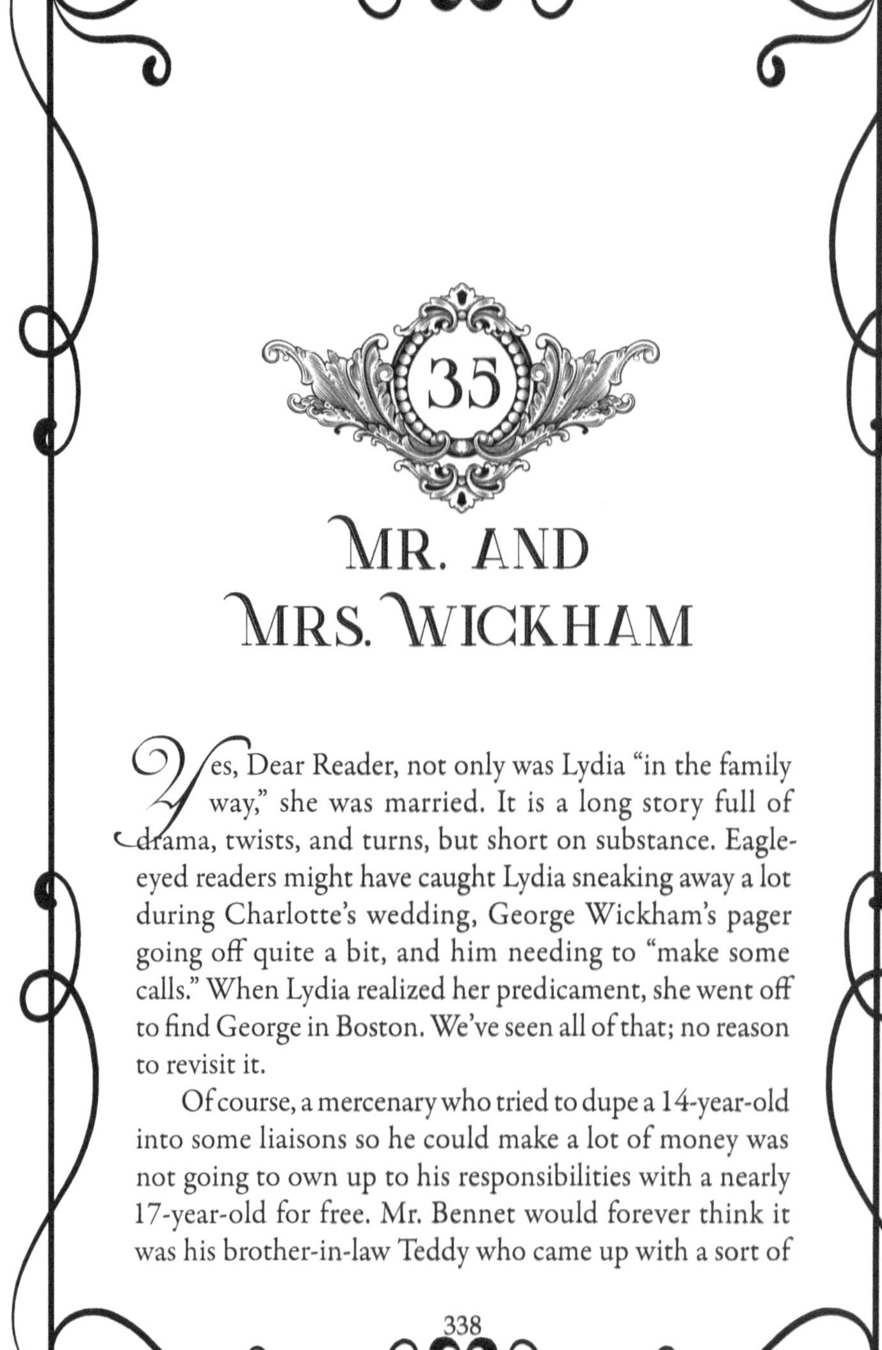

35

MR. AND MRS. WICKHAM

*Y*es, Dear Reader, not only was Lydia "in the family way," she was married. It is a long story full of drama, twists, and turns, but short on substance. Eagle-eyed readers might have caught Lydia sneaking away a lot during Charlotte's wedding, George Wickham's pager going off quite a bit, and him needing to "make some calls." When Lydia realized her predicament, she went off to find George in Boston. We've seen all of that; no reason to revisit it.

Of course, a mercenary who tried to dupe a 14-year-old into some liaisons so he could make a lot of money was not going to own up to his responsibilities with a nearly 17-year-old for free. Mr. Bennet would forever think it was his brother-in-law Teddy who came up with a sort of dowry that was big enough to convince George to troth Lydia and make "honest people" out of the both of them. Okay, neither of them was honest at all, but they were married anyway.

The truth is that it all came down to Darcy in the end. When he heard the news, for he was actually with the Gardiners and Lizzy when they found out, he knew exactly where to go. He and Teddy went straight to Boston where he knew he would find George in one of his old haunts in Brighton, which, as we know, is where the Forsters were. Not remotely a coincidence. He gave George the money that would have been used for his tuition at Mansfield all in one lump if he married Lydia in a civil ceremony right away. They had it all worked out so that by the time Mr. Bennet arrived, he could grant his consent for the wedding. Bizarrely, the age of "consent" in Massachusetts was, and still is, 16 but, one can't be married without parental permission of a parent if one is under 18. Really? Wow. They all agreed to keep this payment information quiet, but Teddy told his wife, who told her niece because she was on Team Darcy, and thought this would be a good way to show her niece that he wasn't the troll she thought he was.

It turned out that he blamed himself for not telling Lizzy about George's wickedness sooner, and if he had, maybe Lydia's "honor would have been protected." Lizzy found this out in a roundabout way in a letter from her Aunt Gardiner who was "sworn to secrecy" but opted to hold the information in for about 15 minutes before she wrote it all down and sent the information to her niece. When Lizzy read the letter, she was absolutely sure Lydia's "honor" had not been lost to George Wickham, and while she found the gesture thoughtful and heartfelt, she was still annoyed that he would think of any woman that way.

Sure, Lydia was clearly seduced, and George was a villain, but Lydia had "the talk" and knew exactly what could happen. She wasn't as strict about taking her birth control pills as the rest of the Bennets, save Mary who didn't take any because she knew herself well enough to know she wouldn't need it. Even if she had been good about taking them every day at the same time, which she absolutely was not, Jane and Lizzy, who were the givers of "the talk" to all three of their younger siblings shortly after Mary turned 15 and just after Kitty started her period, always told them to make sure to use two forms of birth control. Clearly, Lydia didn't always listen, and thus, she found herself with child and married.

Mrs. Bennet was over the moon with happiness regarding the end result because Lydia, the tallest and second prettiest of her daughters, was married to a soldier of fortune. Did she know what that meant? Likely not. However, she was most excited that they did the right thing by getting married because that is what "good girls do" when they are about to become mothers. As you can imagine, Dear Reader, that statement went over like razor blades in Halloween candy with Lizzy and Mary. She cared because Lydia was going to make her a grandmother. She liked being a mother, but she really longed to be a grandmother. Grandparenting seemed much easier than parenting. She could spoil them without regard. Yes, Dear Reader, she spoiled Lydia without regard, and Lydia found herself married and pregnant as a teenager. Mrs. Bennet was never going to let logic get in the way of a great idea she had.

Like her husband, Mrs. Bennet assumed that her brother did some kind of magic voodoo. While she knew Lydia was "a catch" and would look amazing at a military ball, or at any event really, on his arm, and she knew that they would have the most "adorable" children, she also knew that men who wanted to spend their time soldiering didn't always want to have families. There must have been some sort of financial incentive for George to decide to "settle down."

She knew she could never pay her brother back, but she was fine with it. If the roles were reversed, she would have done the same thing. He was family, and he was rich, and isn't that what "having a rich baby brother is for if not to help out his poor older sister and his favorite niece?" Was Lydia his favorite niece? She was not. Did he have a favorite? He did. Can you guess who it was and still is? The answer is in these pages. Would Mrs. Bennet be shocked to find out? She would. Will she ever figure it out? She shan't be bothered to think more about it. She is a grandma after all.

So it was that just over a week later, at the end of the first week of April, after Mary received her acceptance to Yale but held firm and rejected the offer, Lydia and George showed up for dinner at Longbourn just before they headed to London for his next assignment. None of them had ever left the country, and so, unsurprisingly, Lydia didn't have a passport. Because George worked for people who could make things happen, the two of them honeymooned in Miami where they could get a same-day passport for Lydia. It was a lot of paperwork and took almost a whole day of waiting in line. Did she complain loudly and try to use the fact that she was pregnant to her advantage? Of course, she did. Did it work? No. No, it did not. The State Department does not treat anyone differently. Chaos would ensue, and nothing good comes from chaos at a State Department office.

They were due to arrive in time for lunch, but unsurprisingly, they didn't arrive until almost dinner. They hadn't called to say they would be late, and so lunch was a war of attrition with the four remaining Bennet sisters and their mother. They sat at the table with the food that was supposed to be their Easter Lunch in a few weeks, nibbling on Mary's homemade dinner rolls while trying to keep themselves from filling up on bread while also keeping their stomachs from growling. The food had all been placed inside Corning Ware with lids to keep it warm, but nothing lasts forever, and while the food wasn't going to spoil, it wasn't going to be hot for much longer. She kept saying, "They'll be here any moment" for well over an hour, and Mary took it upon herself to go pile up a plate of ham and veggies for Kitty, who was beginning to look wan and was getting a case of the shakes.

With the dam broken and Kitty shoving a whole slice of ham into her mouth, Lizzy said a six-letter, two-word phrase that will not be repeated here and started serving herself. Mr. Bennet, trying not to laugh, "coughed" into his napkin until the "fit passed," and he too served himself. He did tell his wife that the food was delicious, and if it had been Easter lunch, it would have been so good that First Lady Lucas would have been green with jealousy. He always knew what to say.

"Well, it will be lovely to take them out to dinner, won't it? We can show off the happy couple around town. Isn't that right, Husband?" she said as she started piling some food on her plate. "I just hope they are fine. They must be fine. We would have heard something if something was wrong, right?"

"Yes, of course, dear."

The phone rang, and as is the way, on the fourth ring, Mary answered, still not having had more than one bite from her corn on the cob. "Longbourn, how may I help you?"

"Is that you, Mary?" Lydia was shouting from what appeared to be a wind tunnel. "You'll never guess where I'm calling from." She didn't wait for Mary to guess, who didn't want to guess, didn't care, and wanted to get back into the dining room to eat. "I'm in the car. Isn't it just a scream?" She paused for there to be a huge sound of surprise and/or joy.

However, it was Mary, not their mother, who answered, and Mary read enough to know how much a car phone cost and how much they cost to make a call. She wasn't impressed, didn't care, and wasn't surprised that Lydia and George would spend money on something so stupid, nor that they would call just to show off that they had the thing. "Oh, I want to scream all right."

"What's that? Speak up, Mary! We have the top down."

Mary looked outside at the thermometer that hung outside the window. It read 52 degrees. She shook her head. She had a lot of options. She opted to ask a question. "If you had the car phone, why didn't you call to tell us you'd be late for lunch?"

"Why, that's what I'm doing now, you sourpuss."

Mary inhaled and held her breath. Lydia had never once, in her entire life, playfully called her a sourpuss. Whatever this was, Mary didn't like it. She let it out slowly.

"I'll get Mother. She'll care." She would have liked to have dropped the receiver on the floor, but the noise on the other end was such that she knew it wouldn't have caused the desired effect. She placed the receiver on the top of the phone and walked back into the dining room. Before anyone could ask, she said, with as flat an affect as possible, which as we can all imagine Mary Bennet can flatten some affect, "Mother, it's Lydia for you. She's calling from a car."

"What!?" Mrs. Bennet jumped up from her seat. "Is she calling from the future?" She laughed at her own joke and pushed Mary out of the way to get to the phone.

Mary, who was not in the way and thus did not need to be shoved, took and held another big breath. It was moments like this upon which Mary would reflect later in life as she drank a glass of wine or a finger or two of scotch at the end of a stressful day that she wondered if she and her mother would have gotten along much better had Mary drank as a teenager. She shoved a huge slice of ham in her mouth before she even sat down so she wouldn't be asked to answer any questions.

It wouldn't have mattered because no one asked. Lydia was no longer there and wouldn't be there, and the transition was not only not traumatic, it was a bit of a relief. It wasn't until just then, as they all thought the same thing Mary did, which was, "Why wouldn't she call from the road if she had a phone the whole time?" Collectively, they realized that while they would always love Lydia, and they would even miss her from time to time, especially when the cat walked on the piano keys, she spent 17 years trying to get as far away from all of them as possible, and she finally got her wish. She had essentially already moved on from them, so the best thing for them to do was to move on as well, and so they did.

Thus, she finally arrived in a Mustang convertible and made a huge spectacle of herself and her wedding ring and her pregnancy, even though she still wasn't showing. She made a bigger spectacle of herself during dinner in town in front of anyone who walked by. When dinner was over, she departed from Meryton without returning to Longbourn. Mr. Bennet hadn't even asked for the check yet, but they were at risk of missing a flight in Hartford, so they had to leave "right away." Mrs. Bennet sobbed and sobbed with joy and misery and asked her sister over and over what she was going to do without her "special girl" in front of her other four daughters who were sitting at the table with her. Aunt Phillips knew the right choice was not to say anything because her sister was in the middle of a grand performance of her own, and so, she rubbed her back and asked the table if they wanted dessert. They did.

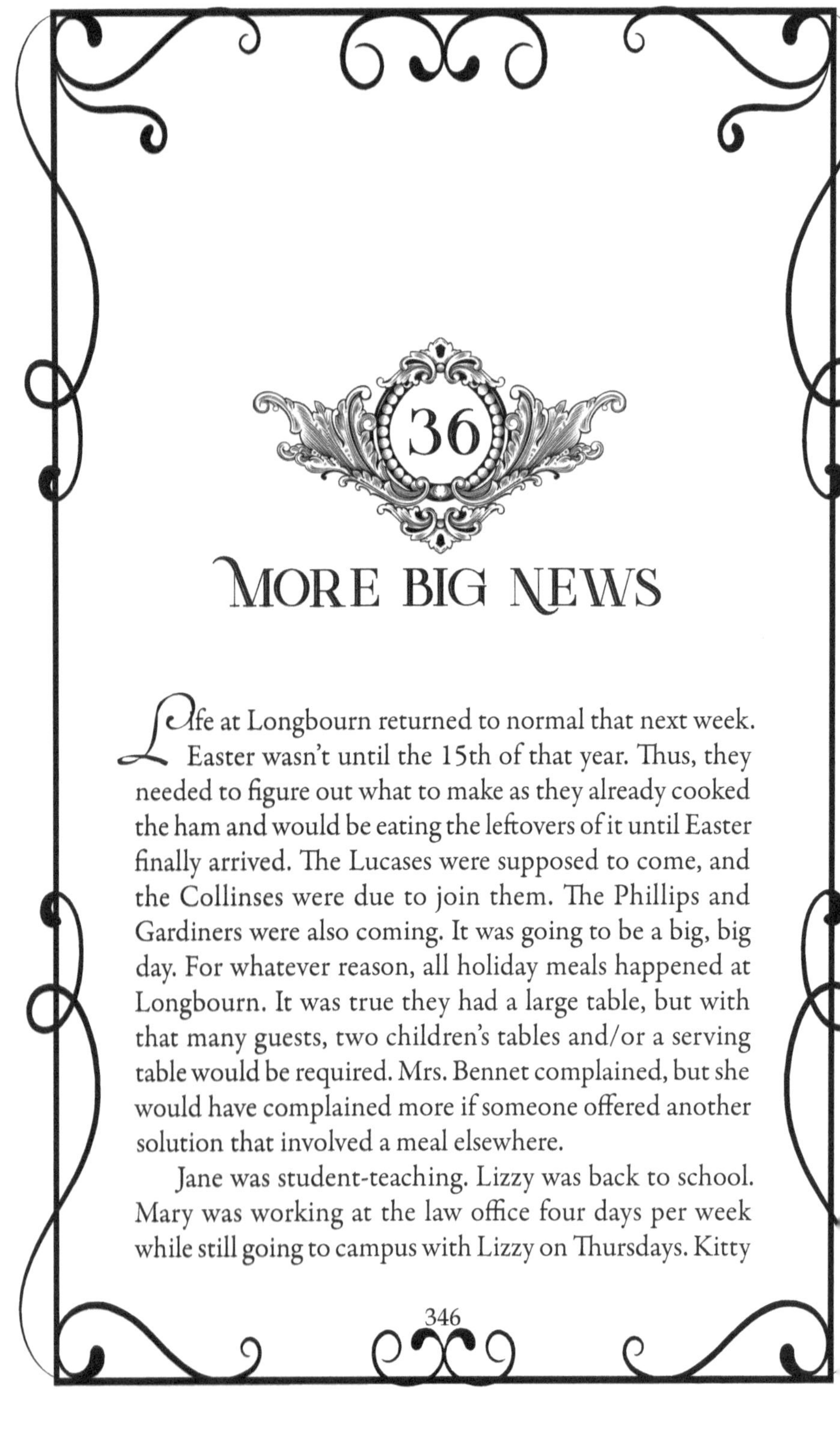

36

MORE BIG NEWS

Life at Longbourn returned to normal that next week. Easter wasn't until the 15th of that year. Thus, they needed to figure out what to make as they already cooked the ham and would be eating the leftovers of it until Easter finally arrived. The Lucases were supposed to come, and the Collinses were due to join them. The Phillips and Gardiners were also coming. It was going to be a big, big day. For whatever reason, all holiday meals happened at Longbourn. It was true they had a large table, but with that many guests, two children's tables and/or a serving table would be required. Mrs. Bennet complained, but she would have complained more if someone offered another solution that involved a meal elsewhere.

Jane was student-teaching. Lizzy was back to school. Mary was working at the law office four days per week while still going to campus with Lizzy on Thursdays. Kitty was finishing up her junior year of high school and preparing to take her SATs. She was playing a lot of soccer, and her team was undefeated. The number of scouts seems to increase with each new game. No one really talked about it because they didn't know what it meant. Was Kitty going to play soccer at the next level? Was she really that good? Maybe? Who could know?

One evening after dinner, while Mary was helping her mother clean up the dishes, and while Jane was in the library with their father, and while Lizzy was spreading out her books on the dining room table so she could outline a research paper she had due for her feminist theory class, and while Kitty was kicking a ball against a barn because the patch of grass where she normally spent time running drills had been given over to the new construction, the phone rang.

Mary, whose hands were elbow-deep in the water, looked at her mother, who was wrapping the leftovers in plastic wrap. Her mother looked back at her as the phone rang for a second time. Why she did this to Mary all the time will forever remain a mystery. She only ever did it to Mary. When Mary wasn't home, she was perfectly capable of answering the phone herself.

On the third ring, Mary grumbled, "Fine." She pulled her hands out and grabbed a towel. That was all it took. Her mother, with a smirk on her face while making direct eye contact with her daughter, answered the phone. She didn't need to win; she just needed to know that she could.

"Longbourn, how may I help you?" She paused. "No, this is her mother." She paused and looked at Mary who had put her hands back in the hot water. She smirked again. "She's right here." She put the receiver on her chest. "It's for you." Okay, maybe she did need to win, and/or maybe she was hurting from the loss of her favorite daughter and was angry that the rest of the family didn't seem to miss her, or maybe she just liked being vindictive, although odds are it is not the latter, as we know Mrs. Bennet isn't a monster; she just plays one sometimes.

Mary closed her eyes and inhaled. She removed her hands from the water again, dried them *again,* and walked over to take the phone from her mother. "Thank you, Mother." It might have sounded like a different word that ended with a "K" that proceeded the word "you" if you closed one eye and turned your head to the side, and you felt guilty for being a bit mean and vindictive for no reason and thought that is what you would have said if you'd been Mary Bennet in that exact moment. However, it is a fact that she did say the words "Thank you, Mother" and not the other thing that Mrs. Bennet heard. While lots of children will utter that two-word phrase to or about their parents at one point or another in their lives, Mary would never do it. She may not have always liked her mother, she certainly didn't care for her that day in the kitchen, but she felt that it would be too disrespectful, and everyone always thought Jane was the best of them. Maybe not.

Having heard what she heard, Mrs. Bennet stormed out of the room to "tell on" Mary. Exactly what she thought her husband would do to a fully grown woman to whom she was just mean for no reason and who didn't actually do or say anything untoward remains to be seen. Suffice it to say, she was getting ready to barge into the library, where other big news was happening that would most assuredly usurp Mary's big news which she was about to receive.

Having no idea who it could possibly be, knowing that it wasn't Aunt Phillips, to whom her mother would have spoken at length, or Charlotte or First Lady Lucas to whom she would have said something disparaging in the form of a joke, it was obvious that the person on the other end was a stranger who thought it was possible for Mary Bennet and her mother to sound the same. Truth be told, much to Mary's chagrin, they did sound quite a bit alike. "This is Mary Bennet."

"Hello there. This is Anne de Bourgh." Her voice had no trace of a New England accent or any accent at all; it was as though she was born to read the news.

While Mary knew who she was as she had heard the name said enough from Reverend Collins, and Lizzy spent plenty of time with her when she was in Rhode Island, her brain couldn't connect that it was the same person. So she asked something dumb because she didn't know what else to say. "From Rosings?"

"Well, yes, but I'm not calling in that capacity."

"Oh?" Again, not her finest verbal achievement.

"No. Not at all. I'm actually calling on behalf of Mansfield College."

Mary's tongue turned to glue and stuck to the roof of her mouth. She could hear her heartbeat in her ears and started to sweat. Puberty hadn't treated her this badly. She reached for the nearest unwashed glass and drank whatever was in it. Thankfully, it was diet soda, not her grandmother's tincture, which her mother had taken to having nightly ever since Lydia left. The whole thing only took seconds, and Anne de Bourgh didn't even notice, so by the time Mary had full control of her body, she said, "Really?"

"Indeed. I've been granted the great honor to let you know that you have been selected as a finalist for The Mansfield Gift for the forthcoming academic year. Congratulations."

Mary's knees buckled, and she put her back against the wall and slid to the floor. "Thank you for this incredible news, Ms. de Bourgh. I am speechless."

"Yes, well, the honor is mine. When I was at Mansfield, I was always in awe of The Gift winners."

"Really?" she said again, but what could be a better response? Nothing.

"Absolutely. We all sort of knew the process it took to be awarded The Gift, but until now, I didn't know exactly what it took. Now that I know, I'm even more impressed."

Mary just nodded. We've all done it. Don't judge.

"Because I am one of the nearest geographic alumni, I've been asked to conduct the face-to-face interview. If possible, we like to have potential Gift winners interviewed by past Gift winners, but sometimes, in an effort to do in-person interviews, other alumni are called upon. People from all around the world apply for The Gift, and so the committee feels that being able to see the person's face has some relevance."

"What about..." Mary began, but Anne was already one step ahead of her and cut her off. Not in a rude way but more in a time-saving way. Not that she was in a rush either. More in a syncopation, finishing off one's sentences, way.

"Yes, I thought the same thing. I let the college know about the unique circumstances of our family connection, and they felt it was proper because we've never actually met and because they know I would never allow that to matter when it came down to it. While it will be very nice to meet you as Charlotte has nothing but lovely things to say about you, I will conduct the interview objectively."

Mary nodded at this, but this time had something to say. "I would expect nothing less, Ms. de Bourgh."

"Anne. Please."

"Yes. Okay. Anne."

"Wonderful. Now that that's settled. Could you do it on Saturday the 21st? I would like to do it as soon as possible, but I'm unable to get away during the week, and with this weekend being Easter, I know that you will already have quite a houseful."

Mary, who had nothing planned on any weekend ever, didn't need to consult her calendar. "Yes, of course. The 21st will be perfect."

"OK. I have your address here, and I can get directions from Charlotte. Can we say 10 in the morning?"

"Yes. 10 on the 21st. Do I need to do anything special?"

"Do you have a space for the two of us to speak privately for a while? Just the two of us?"

Mary thought if there was ever a time for her father to give over his library to her, this was it. She could always use the law office as a backup. Either way, she would want Aunt Phillips to keep her mother busy the whole day. "Yes, I can make those arrangements."

"Perfect. In the meantime, you will be doing two phone interviews as well. One will be with one of The Gift advisors, my favorite history professor, Dr. Allen, and one with the director of admissions, Ms. Flack. Ms. Flack's administrative assistant, Mr. Joseph, will call you on Monday to schedule those. You will need an hour uninterrupted with those. Will that be a problem?"

"No. Not at all. I'm working on Monday. Could I give you the number so that Mr. Joseph can call me there?"

"Of course. Will your employer mind? I wouldn't want to get you in trouble by making personal calls at work."

"I work for my aunt and uncle. My aunt might be the only person in my family who is excited about this for me, so she will absolutely not mind."

Mary and she worked out the rest of the particulars, and Mary thanked Anne profusely for the amazing news and told her she looked forward to meeting her and all of the other things one imagines one would say at the end of a call of that nature. When she was sure Anne had hung up, Mary set about climbing back up to a standing position. She placed the receiver back on the hook and looked around the kitchen, trying to capture the whole event in her mind so she could go into the library and tell her family all about it. She wanted to capture it all just as it happened. She even wanted to remember the way her mother acted when the phone rang. She wasn't much of a storyteller, but she wanted to be able to tell it with the proper build-up so that when she got to the big reveal, she could take their collective breath away.

Before she could take one step, her mother came rushing into the kitchen and shouted, "Jane and Bingley are getting married!"

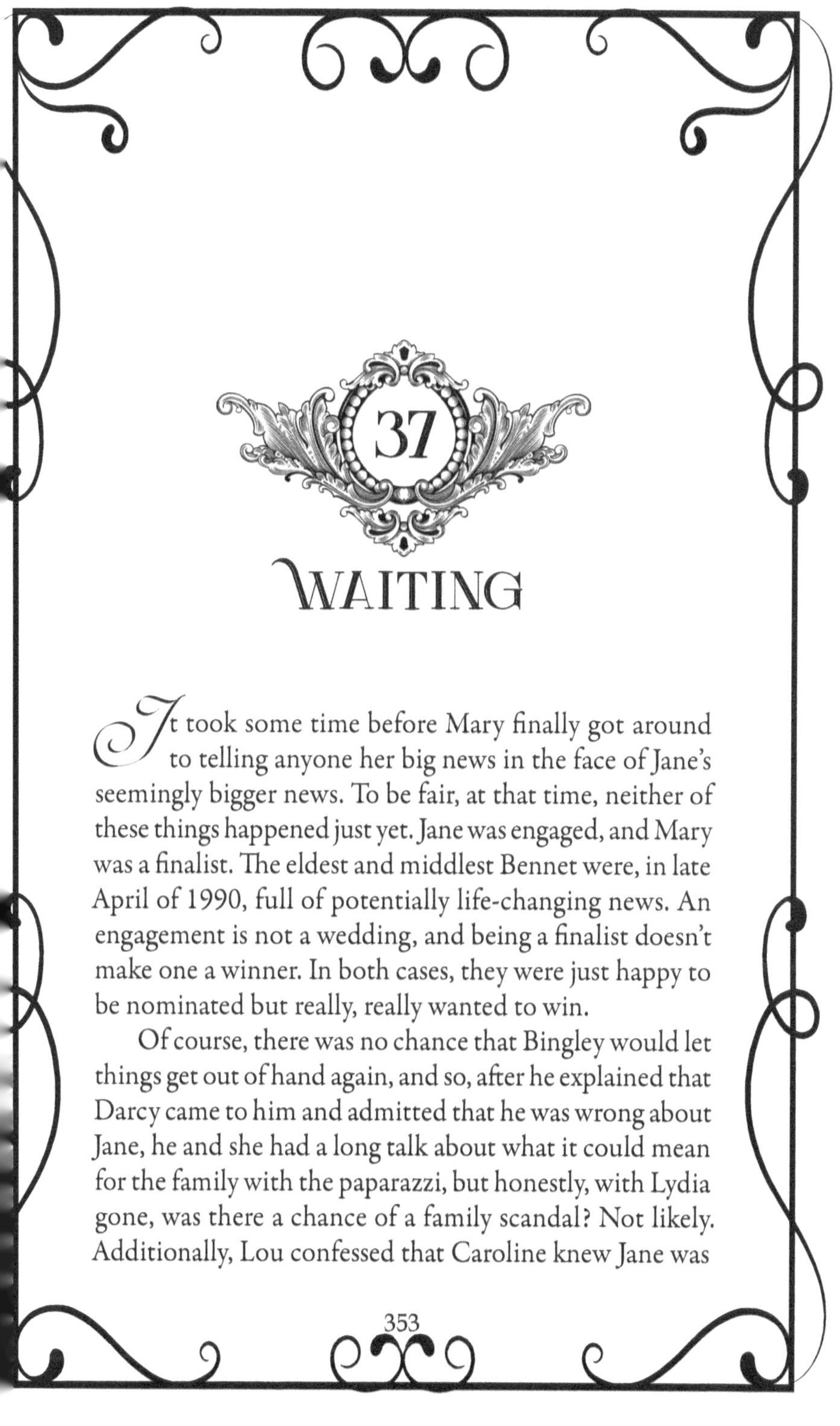

37

WAITING

It took some time before Mary finally got around to telling anyone her big news in the face of Jane's seemingly bigger news. To be fair, at that time, neither of these things happened just yet. Jane was engaged, and Mary was a finalist. The eldest and middlest Bennet were, in late April of 1990, full of potentially life-changing news. An engagement is not a wedding, and being a finalist doesn't make one a winner. In both cases, they were just happy to be nominated but really, really wanted to win.

Of course, there was no chance that Bingley would let things get out of hand again, and so, after he explained that Darcy came to him and admitted that he was wrong about Jane, he and she had a long talk about what it could mean for the family with the paparazzi, but honestly, with Lydia gone, was there a chance of a family scandal? Not likely. Additionally, Lou confessed that Caroline knew Jane was in New York and kept it from him. It was a whole thing. It isn't their story, so we shan't dwell on it, but suffice to say, Bingley forgave his family, because of course he did, and thus Jane forgave him because of course she did.

They had a celebratory dessert that evening as they planned the wedding that they wished to have performed as soon as Jane's student teaching was over in early June. It didn't give them a lot of time, but neither of them wished to wait any longer than necessary. Jane and Bingley wished to take a summer honeymoon, and Jane could come back to Meryton as she already accepted a position at the Meryton public schools contingent upon her graduation.

Bingley decided to just buy Netherfield outright by making an offer the owners couldn't refuse, thus allowing Jane the opportunity to walk to school each morning as she had been doing during her student teaching. Those Bennets really loved to walk, and Jane really loved teaching. The trip from Meryton to Hartford wasn't bad at all, and Bingley wanted to be wherever Jane was, and so, Meryton would be his future home, and that was that. It wasn't really even a question.

Bingley promised Mary that she could have free reign over the library, and he promised to give her a key to the side door to the library so she could come and go as she saw fit. He told Kitty that she would be able to come and use the lawn anytime she wished so she could run drills, kick balls, or do whatever it was soccer players did. He was a male American in 1990. He knew very little about soccer except that it looked exhausting and hands were not allowed.

It was only after the dishes were cleared for the second time that evening, and Bingley was sent home late, late in the evening, and Lizzy and Jane had retired to their room to talk in private and giggle like little girls, and Kitty had passed out from exhaustion and a sugar crash that Mary found her way into the library to tell her father about the phone call with Anne de Bourgh. It was very late, and Mary had to go to work in the morning. She and he could talk more about it in the morning over breakfast, but she just wanted him to know. He was genuinely happy for her and told her so. There were no hugs or shouts of jubilation as that was not the kind of relationship they had, but he smiled so broadly that it reached his eyes, and that was how Mary knew he meant it.

Mary's news spread through the Bennet family slowly the next morning at breakfast long after Mary and her father spoke more about it after they had their coffee and read the paper. Tradition is tradition, and they both felt that maybe their quiet mornings were numbered, and they wished to soak in as many as they could before they were over. As each member of Longbourn found out, each of them had a different reaction. Jane felt terrible for grandstanding with her news. Lizzy was quite pleased and offered to help do mock interviews and to give any inside information on Anne. Mary accepted the former and rejected the latter. Kitty had a mouthful of oatmeal seemingly the whole time. Mrs. Bennet, still buzzing from the high that Jane was marrying rich and staying in Meryton, said something non-committal and hand-wavey that made Mary think that either she didn't care, didn't listen, didn't understand, or maybe even all three.

Mary told her aunt the news the next day at work, and she gave her niece a hug and had an extra spring in her step the rest of the day. She took Mary to a celebratory lunch at the diner where they game-planned and strategized what they thought the interviews could possibly be.

Later that day, as promised, Mr. Joseph called and arranged for Mary to do her phone interviews with Dr. Allen and Ms. Flack the following week after Easter but before her meeting with Anne. They agreed to conduct the phone interviews while Mary was at the law offices when her uncle was in court so his office would be empty. She resisted the urge to ask when the final decisions would be made because she knew they would happen when they happened, and there was nothing she could do to make it come sooner.

Patience is said to be a virtue, and thus, Mary Bennet spent ten days in April of 1990 becoming one of the most virtuous people to ever be born in Connecticut. Harriet Beecher Stowe was born there, so let's not pretend that anyone could ever pass her on the virtue rankings, but being mentioned in the same paragraph as her means something, so now that Mary Bennet has officially been mentioned in the same paragraph as Ms. Stowe, the honor is eternal.

Mary could have skipped out on her trip to CCSU with Lizzy that week because the law office and the college were closed on Friday due to it being a Christian holiday. Not that the Phillipses were particularly devout, and yes, CCSU was and is a public school, but some things are just ingrained, and so, things closed on Good Friday. She would be missing out on a day of work by taking the trip, but she had amassed quite a nest egg, and she wanted to take Lizzy up on her offer to work on mock interviews. One hour in the car each way gave them ample time. Some things are priceless, and for Mary Bennet, one of those things is, as we know, preparation.

When Easter finally arrived on Sunday, Mary, like her sisters, helped make the big meal, which was just a do-over of the meal they originally planned because it wasn't their guests' fault that Lydia had a shotgun wedding and left the country and that Mrs. Bennet decided to make her youngest a big meal that she skipped anyway. Yes, Dear Reader, that means that the residents of Longbourn had all the ham they could ever want for nearly a month. Most people, even those who like ham, don't want that much ham all at once. None of them had a hankering for any for many months to come.

The main topics of conversation unsurprisingly had nothing to do with Jesus rising from the dead. Instead, 50 percent of the conversations focused on Lydia's sudden "situation," her marriage, and her trip to London. The reason this number was so high may or may not have had a lot to do with Reverend Collins' long, convoluted prayer about the joys of marriage, the beauty of children, and the fact that his uncle and aunt could not be blamed for Lydia's actions even though the bible has a lot to say about parenting and how Lady Catherine de Bourgh raised Lady Anne de Bourgh to be a near saint. It was uncomfortable, and it was only when Charlotte said "Amen" as he took a pause for a long breath that moved it along.

Roughly 40 percent focused on Jane's engagement and upcoming nuptials. Jane hated being the center of attention, but weddings are about the bride, so she had no choice. Another 8 percent was taken up by the Gardiner children doing cute things, and everyone saying "aww" or something similar. Perhaps 1 percent of the conversation was about the meal, and 1 percent was dedicated to Mary's upcoming interview with Lady Anne de Bourgh initiated by Reverend Collins and ended by Charlotte. While this isn't Charlotte's story, she is a hero.

On Tuesday, alone in her uncle's office with her aunt staying in the office to answer any calls, Mary did her interviews with Ms. Flack and Dr. Allen. Ms. Flack's interview was more about Mary's readiness to move across the country and live away from her family. Mary was unprepared for that line of questioning, but she felt she had been preparing to move out for 18 years, so she was able to answer with calm assurances to Ms. Flack that homesickness wouldn't be a problem, and self-reliance was a skill she possessed. She was, after all, conducting the interview from her place of employment, where she'd been working since she turned 15.

Dr. Allen asked a lot of academic questions, and it was here that Mary shined the brightest. He was a historian, and having that knowledge in advance gave Mary the chance to rifle through her notes that would later become her thesis and have a long conversation with him about how the teaching of history could be transformed into a more interactive experience for the students to make them more interested. They went over the allotted time by 45 minutes. They would have gone longer if Dr. Allen didn't need to teach a class.

Mary, buoyed by the whole experience, walked home that day feeling so good that when her mother made a crack about Mary needing to get her hair done before the big interview that weekend, she didn't even bother to respond. She simply ignored the remarks, and thus, her mother turned her ire onto Lizzy about something or other. If Mary had known all along that simply ignoring her mother was an option, her life might have been much simpler, but given the chance to change it, she wouldn't have. Fending off her mother's verbal attacks was part of what made her who she was, and she was a person who felt like she was one good interview away from moving to the Midwest and her future.

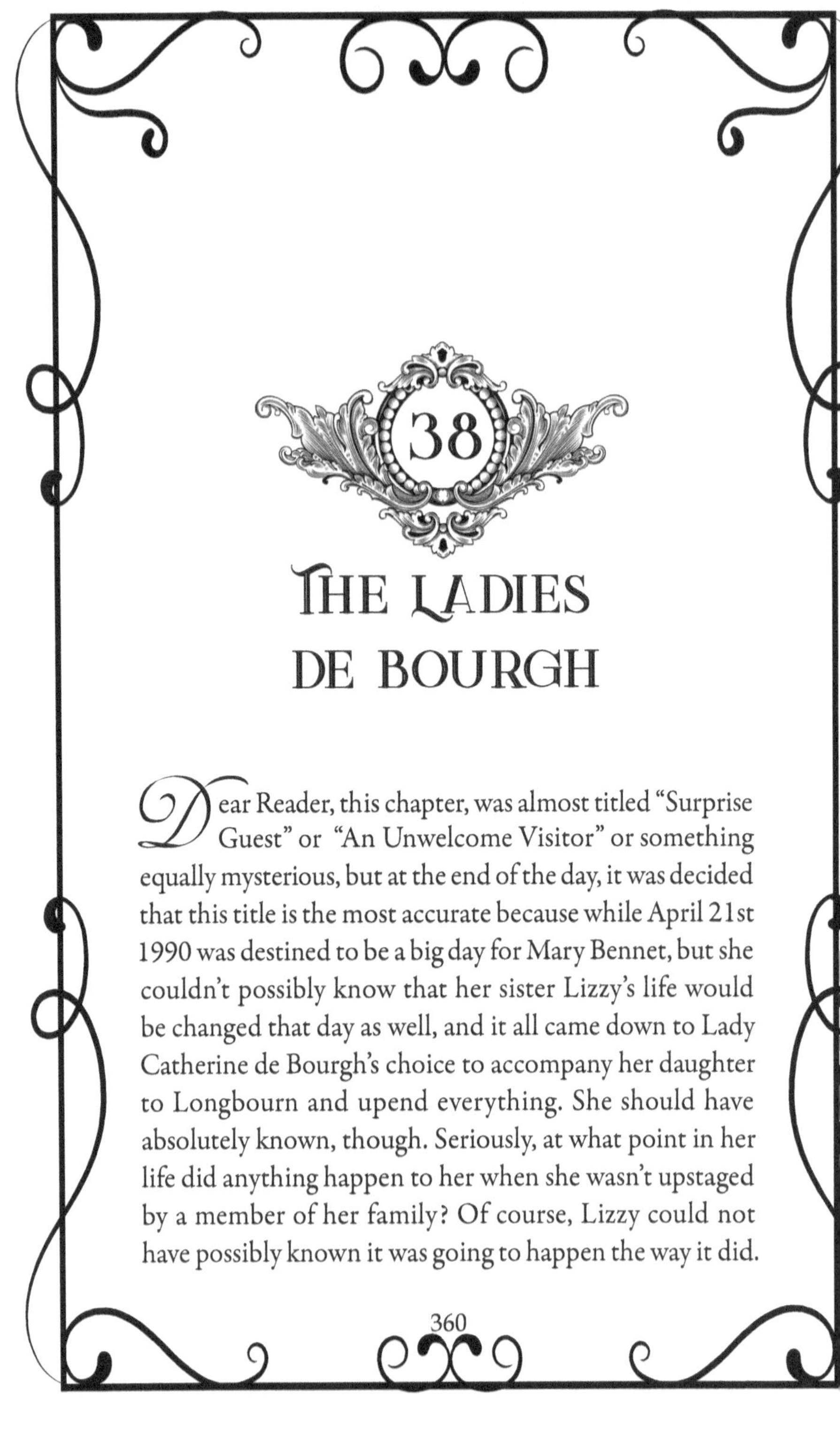

38

THE LADIES DE BOURGH

*D*ear Reader, this chapter, was almost titled "Surprise Guest" or "An Unwelcome Visitor" or something equally mysterious, but at the end of the day, it was decided that this title is the most accurate because while April 21st 1990 was destined to be a big day for Mary Bennet, but she couldn't possibly know that her sister Lizzy's life would be changed that day as well, and it all came down to Lady Catherine de Bourgh's choice to accompany her daughter to Longbourn and upend everything. She should have absolutely known, though. Seriously, at what point in her life did anything happen to her when she wasn't upstaged by a member of her family? Of course, Lizzy could not have possibly known it was going to happen the way it did.

She had done everything she could to make sure the day would go off without a hitch.

Kitty had a game that morning, and so Lizzy made sure that everyone was packed and ready to go early. Generally, they all walked out the door cutting it close, but games in club soccer rarely started on time. Lizzy wouldn't have any of it, and she herded the family up and got them out the door with plenty of time to spare. It took a lot of doing, and Mrs. Bennet was the most difficult, but when Lizzy promised her that she would take her out to brunch after the game, she brightened up and went without a care in the world, or in fact without acknowledging that it was Mary's big day, and when her husband stopped by his own library to say goodbye to Mary, she shouted at him that they were going to be late, which they most assuredly were not.

Thus, at 9:30, Mary found herself alone at Longbourn. It was the first time in a long time that she could ever remember being totally alone in the house. She wandered around, looking at everything in the silence. Her room, which still had three beds, although Lydia would never sleep there again, looked and felt different without the press of bodies as Lydia's tall, lanky frame took up so much space and the sound of Kittys' jittering legs filled every second with noise. She walked through each room, remembering moments of her life. In each memory, she was either a spectator in some big production of her mother's or a reluctant participant in some event spearheaded by Jane. It sounds much sadder than it actually was.

Like everything, Mary knew that it was that life of being the middlest and most overlooked child that afforded her the chance to sit, observe, read, write, and think. Had she been born into a different family, one where her mother wasn't so critical, or where her sisters were not so combative or sweet, depending on which sister and which day, or where her father had given out hugs instead of books and lectures and knowledge that maybe she would be waiting patiently, having surely moved up to number two on the most virtuous Nutmegger ever list. Of course, we know that nature and nurture would forever be part of Mary's ongoing lifelong research and that the final thirty minutes before Anne's arrival were often included in her contemplation.

At 9:55, the doorbell rang, and Mary, who had been waiting for that moment her whole life, pushed her glasses up on her nose, took a breath, and answered it. As you know by now, Anne was not alone, but Mary didn't know, so she was shocked to see two people standing at her door, not one. It could be argued that some people can look at their parents and see themselves in the future's mirror. That was most certainly the case for Jane Bennet. Her mother never quit looking like Miss Connecticut, and Jane, who never had the inclination to be a beauty queen, could have been. The same was true for Anne de Bourgh and her mother.

When Mary opened the door, she saw the exact same person except one was aged 50 and the other was 25. Lady Catherine, like Mrs. Bennet, was a woman who at 50 could easily pass for 30 when she wasn't with her doppelgänger child, but when standing next to her, one could easily see who was from the same clan but from an older vintage. Shocked by her surprise visitor and most unwanted guest, Mary stood mute, a smile plastered on her face, unsure of what to say or do. She looked from the elder de Bourgh to the younger. One's face was angry and clearly demanding while the other was embarrassed and regretful.

"Where is your sister? Ms. Elizabeth Bennet? I demand to speak to her at once!" Lady Catherine bellowed as she pushed her way past Mary and into the empty house.

"I... She..." Mary was trying to get her brain to catch up to what was happening. She turned to watch Lady Catherine storm into the dining room as though she owned the place.

"I'm so sorry," Anne was saying as she came in behind Mary and closed the door behind her. "She promised she wouldn't do this. I should have known better."

"MISS BENNET!" Lady Catherine was shouting from the kitchen, out of sight, but not out of earshot. "I demand an audience. Get out here NOW!"

Mary turned back to Anne, opting to talk to the member of the de Bourgh family who seemed most rational and open to hear her. She said, "She's gone. They're all gone. My sister Kitty has a soccer game today, and they are there."

Anne nodded. "Please forgive me," she said to Mary right before she shouted, "MOTHER, STOP!" Lady Catherine was pounding her way back into the entryway, having seemingly gone through every room in the house. Amazingly, she stopped and looked at her daughter, who may or may not have raised her voice like this at her mother before. We shall leave it to you to decide, Dear Reader. "She's gone. She's at her sister's soccer game."

Lady Catherine looked past Anne at Mary and demanded, "Where?"

Mary, unable to comprehend why this short, screaming woman wanted her sister so badly, did what any of us might have done; she just said the truth. "At the high school. They play at the high school."

Lady Catherine nodded and said, "I can find it." She pushed past Mary for the second time in five minutes and was out the door that she left open behind her for the second time just as the clock struck 10.

Anne dropped her head and shook it. She muttered something that Mary couldn't hear. Mary didn't need to hear it, nor do we need to hear it, Dear Reader. It is evident what kind of sentiments Anne was mumbling under her breath. She started walking forward to pace in a small circle and mutter, head dropped, eyes clamped shut, and her hands balled into fists, which was, unbeknownst to Mary, Anne de Bourgh's go-to anger mitigation strategy.

Of course, Lady de Bourgh was so used to living in a palace or something very much like one that she wasn't prepared for what her mother would certainly call detritus but what normal people would call the cluttered living of a house with a big family. Lydia being gone removed only one or two things that were normally left lying about along the wall in the entryway, but the truth is, several pairs of her shoes were still there as though they were expecting the youngest and most mercurial of the Bennet sisters to show back up at any moment as though she never left.

So it was that Anne, flummoxed and frustrated, tripped over some ice skates and fell unceremoniously forward. In a fall, the thing to do is to tuck one's arms in and try to roll, letting one's backside absorb the fall at best or one's shoulder at worst. However, humans who are not athletes are rarely taught how to fall correctly, and thus, when falling forward, they put out their hands to catch themselves. It was just what Anne did, and a second later, she found herself, having only just arrived at Longbourn facedown with a wrist injury, wailing in pain.

Mary saw the whole thing happen in real-time, and as one does when one watches someone else fall, she was lurching forward as though she would be able to be helpful in any way. Thus, by the time the whole event was done, Mary was on her knees next to Anne shouting her name, which wasn't necessary but was again, human nature. Shouting in a crisis never helps.

Anne rolled herself over on her back, and the noise she made turned out not to be a wail but a laugh. She held her right wrist against her chest with her left hand, pushing it firmly in place as her body wracked with a kind of laughter Aunt Phillips would have called hysterical, only to be chastised by two of her nieces.

Emotions swing on a pendulum, and Mary was caught up, and so she slid off her knees onto her backside and started laughing as well. Two women of two overbearing, demanding, and enraging mothers allowed themselves the time to let it all out. Either one laughs or one cries or one writes blank verse in a diary while grinding one's teeth. Everyone forgets about that third option, but it is a really good one.

They laughed and laughed on the dirty entryway for longer than was entirely necessary. When one of them started to stop, the other would catch her eye, and it would start all over again as is the way. It isn't called infectious laughter for no reason. If it were caught on film, viewers would look at their watches halfway and think that the editor needed to step in.

After they finally petered out, Mary stood up and reached out her hand. "Let me help."

Anne nodded and, keeping her right arm tight to her body, gave her left hand to Mary, who first pulled her from her back up to sitting. Anne looked up at her, bracing herself.

"One, two, three, go, or one, two, threeeee?" Mary asked.

"On go. I need the extra second."

Mary nodded. "One."

"Two," Anne said.

"Three," Mary countered.

"GO!" they both shouted, and Mary clamped her other hand around Anne's wrist. Within seconds, they were standing nose to nose, smiling at each other. Both of their glasses were askew, their hair was disheveled, and they were covered in floor dust, looking very much like they were about to do a bit where they pretend to be each other in a mirror.

Dear Reader, in another book, you might expect this to be the moment where Anne and Mary fall into a passionate embrace. This is not that book, and Mary isn't that character. She didn't suddenly become someone else so near the end of the book. That would be disingenuous and false, and this is certainly not one of those books. There is personal growth, and then there is nonsense and buffoonery.

Sure, if Mary were a person who found women attractive, one might assume Anne de Bourgh was her perfect match, but she wasn't and isn't, and get your mind out of the gutter. Anne was there to do a college interview. Remember? Plus, Anne is a professional philanthropist of high moral standing and would never use her position of power to begin a relationship anyway. Sheesh.

Mary straightened her glasses. She took one step back. "I'll get you some ice and a wrap. We should go to the hospital. We'll have to take a work truck, I'm afraid."

"Oh, the ice and wrap will be enough. We don't need to go to the ER."

Mary was already walking toward the kitchen. "Nonsense." The jovial tone was now gone from her voice. She was back in control and had a task. "Come sit." She pointed at the dining room table. She just expected Anne would do as she said, so she put ice in a baggie and wrapped the bag in a towel. She went into the bathroom, grabbed a few painkillers from the medicine cabinet, and dug under the sink to get the same wrap that they used on Jane earlier in this tale.

She came back into the dining room to see that Anne had indeed listened. She set everything on the table next to her patient and went back into the kitchen to fetch a glass of water. She brought it back in and set it on the table in front of Anne. "Right," she said as though mending injuries was something she did every day, which it was absolutely not. Within three minutes, Anne had ice on her wrist, wrapped up tight so it couldn't slide off, and painkillers in her stomach. Mary pulled the pencil out of her hair and a notebook out of her back pocket and wrote a note addressed to her father. It explained the situation. She tore out the page and took it to his desk. She came back in and asked, "Ready to go?"

Anne nodded, and by 10:20, they were driving down Longbourn's dirt drive headed toward West Hartford and the nearest emergency room. They chatted like old friends or new friends but not people on a first date no matter how much people might want that. The subjects were vast, and there were no bounds. They talked while they drove and while they waited and while Anne was checked in and X-rayed, and while she was given a splint, not a cast as it was just a severe sprain, not a break, and while they drove back to Meryton, and when they stopped at the diner for a late lunch, and when they finally, many hours later, pulled into Longbourn. It was only when Anne noticed her own car was not in the drive that she was pulled back into reality from what, save for all that happened before the wrist sprain, had been an excellent day in Connecticut.

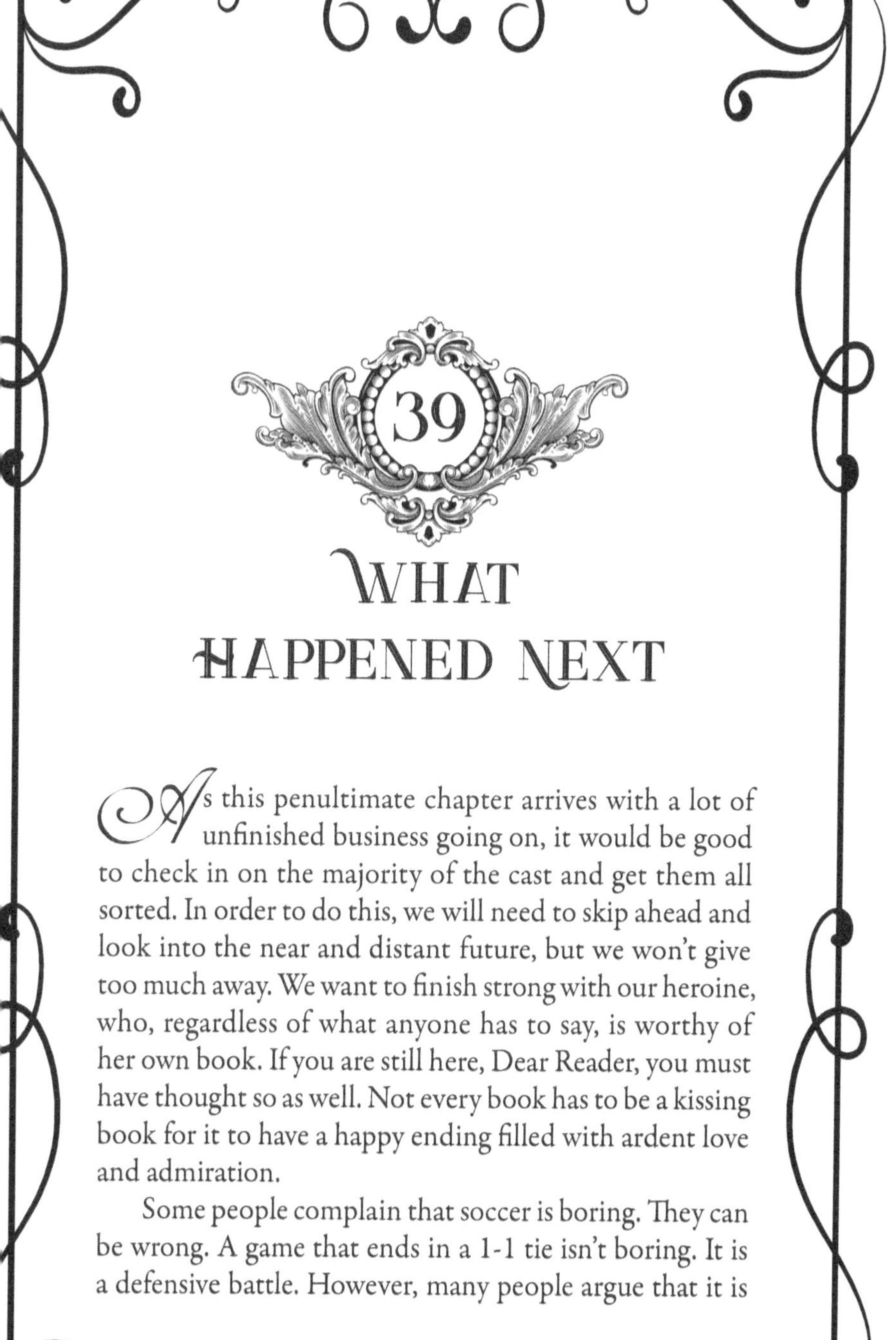

WHAT HAPPENED NEXT

As this penultimate chapter arrives with a lot of unfinished business going on, it would be good to check in on the majority of the cast and get them all sorted. In order to do this, we will need to skip ahead and look into the near and distant future, but we won't give too much away. We want to finish strong with our heroine, who, regardless of what anyone has to say, is worthy of her own book. If you are still here, Dear Reader, you must have thought so as well. Not every book has to be a kissing book for it to have a happy ending filled with ardent love and admiration.

Some people complain that soccer is boring. They can be wrong. A game that ends in a 1-1 tie isn't boring. It is a defensive battle. However, many people argue that it is boring and wish it were more like hockey and had more fights. This was truer at the time this tale takes place when the Whalers were still in Hartford. Thus, we can forgive some people for getting excited for far too long about what happened the day that the de Bourghs arrived in Meryton. For decades, people would start the story by saying, "You know how people think soccer is boring and would be better if it were more like hockey..." and they would end, "I never thought I would see it at a girls' soccer match, but..."

The versions of the story told were not all inaccurate, but they were not entirely accurate either. The game was finished, and Kitty's team remained unbeaten although it was a nil-nil tie, not a win. It didn't matter though; they would ultimately be crowned champions in a 4-0 beatdown that would, of course, remind people of the verbal beatdown Lady Catherine de Bourgh suffered at the hands of Lizzy Bennet that day.

The short version is that Lady Catherine had gotten wind that Darcy was in love with Lizzy, and she wasn't thrilled about the union. While she had given up on the idea that Anne and Darcy would end up together, she wasn't about to have that "mouthy girl," as she had taken to call Lizzy after her first visit to Rosings, in "her family." It didn't matter that Darcy was not actually her nephew, and all signs point to the fact that had his mother been alive to meet Lizzy, she would have liked her very much. Lady Catherine de Bourgh was just not very nice.

Lizzy didn't like being told what to do by her own mother, and she certainly wouldn't be told what to do by someone else's mother. Lady Catherine ended up storming away, shouting expletives and kicking up dirt and rocks under her tires as she drove away straight back to Rosings, forgetting all about her daughter, and without knowing that she was, at that moment, in a beaten-up pickup truck on her way to West Hartford. Of course, Lizzy's feelings about Darcy had managed to come around. He and Lizzy took a walk after he arrived later that evening to apologize to the Bennets for his "aunt's" behavior and to pick up Anne, who called him to let him know what happened. On that walk, Lizzy let him know that she loved him in return.

They would not be married for many years as Lizzy wanted to finish college and go to grad school and see the world both with and without him, which she certainly did, and she would ultimately end up as an editor at a feminist magazine of some renown. They did serve as best man and maid of honor in Jane and Bingley's wedding which was held in early June of 1990 on the grounds of Netherfield. It was actually beautiful, even though they agreed to let Reverend Collins do the ceremony because Charlotte promised she could get him to keep it tight. She made him practice doing the whole thing in 15 minutes, which meant, of course, that it only took an hour. No one minded.

Lydia arrived, six months pregnant, and tried to make the day about herself because of course she did. Her mother was torn because she too wanted to show off her soon-to-be grandchild, but she also wanted to remind everyone she was the mother of the most beautiful bride in the history of Meryton. It was a conundrum for sure. We shall leave it to readers to decide how it went and what Lizzy had to say about it all.

Mr. Bennet's plan to turn Longbourn into a farm-to-table rustic resort was a rousing success. It took a bit longer than he would have liked, but they opened up the restaurant first, which managed to have excellent coverage in several of the Darcy-owned publications which helped raise the profile. Nepotism is a thing; let's not pretend it isn't. It really all depends on how it is used in the end. In this case, it was done lovingly and in a way that helped not just the Bennet family but the residents of Meryton. The articles brought people in from New York and Boston and of course Hartford and Providence, and eventually, when the cabins went up for rent, the waiting list was several years long. Longbourn would remain the biggest tract of land in the county as well as the biggest employer. The rest of Meryton remained mostly unchanged, save for some technological updates as time went on, but legend tells of how the weird guy from Maine who funded the local library and the former Miss Connecticut saved the town from urban sprawl. Some legends are true.

Reverend Collins' blind faith in his "uncle" paid off so well that he managed to form his own charity wing of the Rosings Foundations where he gave out low-interest loans to low-income entrepreneurs to start up their own small businesses. Okay, yes, let's not pretend this all wasn't Charlotte's idea, after all. Of course, it was. If anyone was born to do charity work, it was Charlotte Lucas Collins. She'd been working for others her entire life. It was called Collins Cares. It changed the lives of thousands of New Englanders. She would go on to have a feature written by her best friend in said feminist magazine. She framed the cover, and it hung behind her desk for the rest of her days. She and Reverend Collins never did have children, but neither of them felt that they had an empty life.

What of Kitty, you may ask, Dear Reader? Well, believe it or not, what happened to her actually has a lot to do with what happened to Mary. Thankfully, you only need to turn the page to find out what happened to both of them.

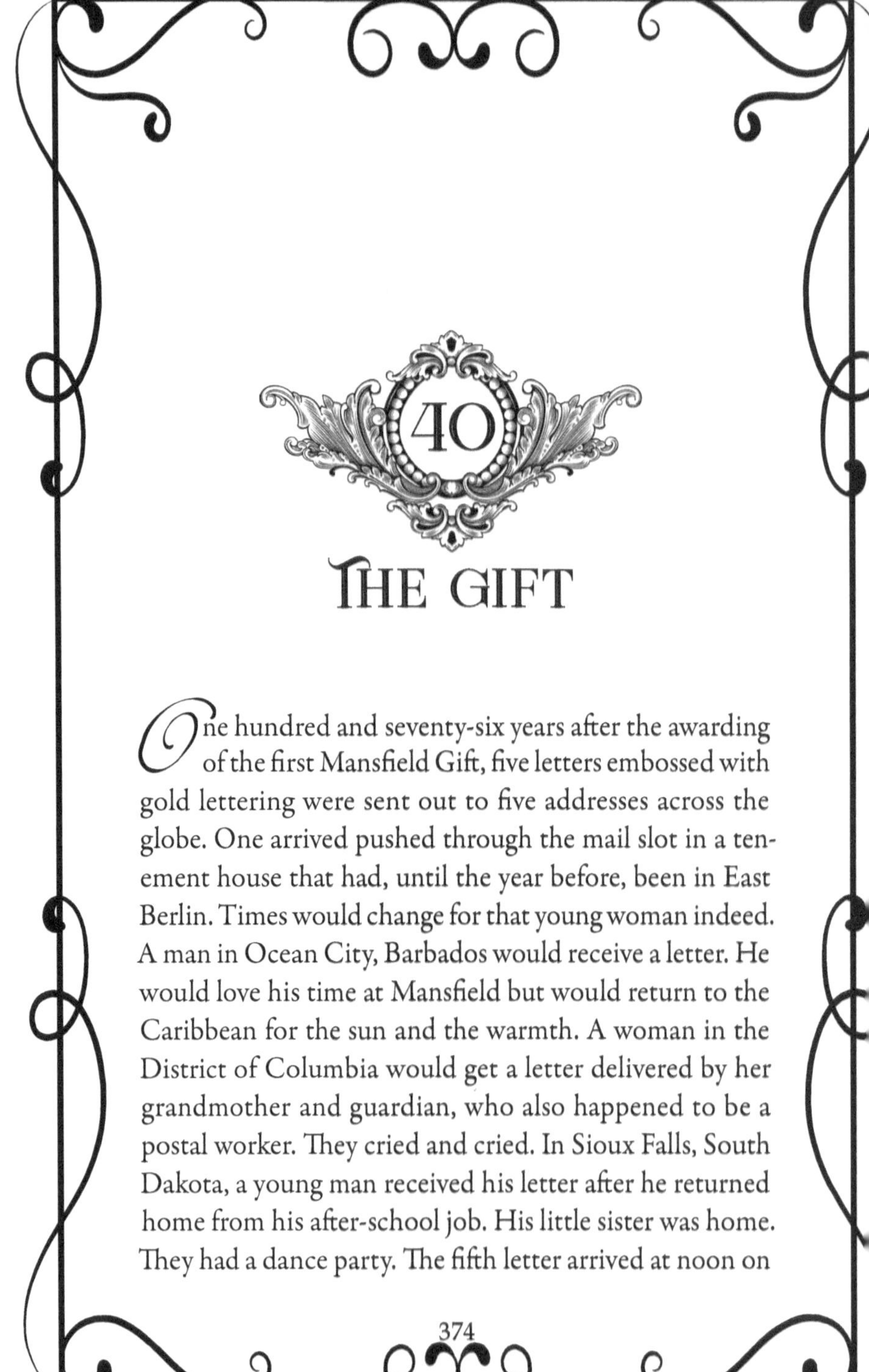

40

THE GIFT

One hundred and seventy-six years after the awarding of the first Mansfield Gift, five letters embossed with gold lettering were sent out to five addresses across the globe. One arrived pushed through the mail slot in a tenement house that had, until the year before, been in East Berlin. Times would change for that young woman indeed. A man in Ocean City, Barbados would receive a letter. He would love his time at Mansfield but would return to the Caribbean for the sun and the warmth. A woman in the District of Columbia would get a letter delivered by her grandmother and guardian, who also happened to be a postal worker. They cried and cried. In Sioux Falls, South Dakota, a young man received his letter after he returned home from his after-school job. His little sister was home. They had a dance party. The fifth letter arrived at noon on

Saturday, May 5th in the mailbox of a farm within walking distance of an unremarkable village in Connecticut.

Mary had, much to her chagrin, been mail-watching for a week. Each day, the mail would come, and she would be home, having taken her lunch from the law office, where she'd been working full-time since the interview was over. She would see the carrier fill the box, and she would ungallantly run out to the box, only to find it wanting. She knew she would find out the final decision about The Gift no later than May 10th. Finalists who did not win The Gift were sent out typewritten form letters in regular envelopes the week before. They were very nice and let the students down gently. They were reminded that that year there had been 3,376 applicants, and thus, making it to the final round was quite an honor. There is no reason to get into that because Mary didn't get one of those letters. She won The Gift, of course, but she didn't know that yet.

So, on that Saturday, just as Kitty was setting the table for lunch, while Jane and Lizzy were working out final wedding plans, while Mr. Bennet was in the library with Mrs. Bennet as she was upset about some slight she was sure First Lady Lucas had made earlier that morning and he was only half listening as he heard Mary close the door and head out to the mailbox, she opened it, and as fate or luck or magic would have it, there was only one letter delivered that day, and it happened to be an envelope addressed to her. She opened it standing right there at the edge of the road. It read:

Dear Ms. Bennet, on behalf of Mansfield College, it is my honor to present to you one of the five annual Mansfield Gifts. As you know, this gift is the most prestigious honor that can be bestowed on any student at

Mansfield College. Every year, thousands of applicants from all around the world compete for one of these five spots. Clearly, your hard work and dedication have been rewarded.

Enclosed are the documents you will need to send back to accept The Gift and begin your registration for Fall classes. Congratulations. Welcome to the Mansfield Family,

Dr. Goddard, President

Mary Bennet was never much of a dancer, she was a terrible singer, and she was a worse piano player. When The Smiths put out *The Queen is Dead*, she could have been made to believe that the line about Morrissey's piano playing being worse than his singing could have been written about her instead of him. Of course, we know she loved music, and her head, while not a jukebox, was packed with melodies. After she read the letter for the second time and folded it up carefully, she could not help but think of a song, not from *The Queen is Dead* but by the band Queen. She began belting out the lyrics, and by the time she opened the door, she was shouting that she was the champion of the world and was, for all intents and purposes, doing an interpretive dance.

Her father, hearing the lyrics and, of course, knowing the song because he was a person in the world, who was not much of a runner, was running past his wife and into the entryway, shouting along. While he and his middlest daughter rarely hugged, if there was ever a time for it, it was then, and so they did. Lizzy, Jane, and Kitty soon joined in, and the entryway to Longbourn became, for a short time, a karaoke palace. Did Mrs. Bennet join in the fun? That is up to you to decide, Dear Reader.

The elation lasted all night as phone calls were made, both local and long-distance. The final call of the day was the second call to Rhode Island of the night. Anne admitted she already knew the results, but she was sworn to secrecy. While it had been an unorthodox interview, it had been the most thorough one in the history of The Gift, and obviously, Lady Anne had been so moved to recommend Ms. Bennet, who, now that the secret was out, had top marks from all the interviewers, and Dr. Allen volunteered to take Mary on as an advisee.

The paperwork had been filled out, and Mary wrote the first of four checks she would pay to Mansfield College in the next four years to cover her room and board for the year. She couldn't mail it until Monday, and she wanted to hand it to the Postmaster herself, just as she'd done with her application, but she wanted it done so the first box on her mental checklist could be ticked off.

That evening, after more hugs and promises to Aunt Phillips to go school shopping, and congratulations from everyone she ever met, except for Lydia, who was in London and was actually asleep when her phone rang, and who was likely to make it about her anyway, Mary found herself in her bed on her stomach, writing furiously. She was thinking about all the things that led her to that moment in time and what it meant for her and her father and their relationship, which, of course, got her thinking about the rest of her family and what it would mean for them to have her so far away.

Mary would be, of course, on a very tight budget, and letters, not phone calls would have to do for communication. She knew her father would write as would Jane. She thought that Lizzy would mean to write but would be so

busy that she likely wouldn't be a great pen pal. She knew her mother would "send her thoughts" through the letters she would receive from her father. While this place, these people, were part of her, she was excited to be away from them and to make her own mark on the world, but she didn't want to forget them. She didn't, if she was honest with herself, which she always was, want them to forget her. Lydia already had. She'd never really known her anyway.

She wanted to be her own person and to live her own truth while never, ever losing touch of what made her who she was. Lizzy and Jane had never once complained that she was so obviously not interested in boys or girls or romance at all. They never made fun of her or made her feel less than or broken. Her strange little home school, reclusive, cut-off existence had actually been the most freeing thing that could have ever happened to her. Had she gone to public school, her brains, her demeanor, and her asexuality would have certainly put a target on her back.

At the Bennet school of life, as oppressive as it could sometimes be as the school Marm was a bit of a handful, Mary Bennet thrived. She discovered her own life and became her own person, and while it seemed that her parents were trying to hold her back, and of course, they were a little bit, they were giving her the chance to find the truth she needed to find. It had been the case for all of them actually. They all had, really, even Lydia, who, let's face it, was doing exactly what she hoped she would be doing. She was living a grand life in a foreign country.

It was then, in that quiet moment, writing in her bed that she realized the thing she wanted to do with her life. It was right in front of her the whole time, of course, as things like this often are. She wanted to be the person who could give to others what had been given to her. Sure, she didn't know exactly what it would look like at that time, but she understood then, that the universal truth was that each person in the world should be given the chance to find out exactly who they wanted to be, but not every person was going to have the life that she had. They would need a person in their corner to ask questions, be supportive, and challenge them.

Once a person discovers her mission in life, there is no reason to wait to live it. She sat up and turned on the lamp next to her bed. She knew Kitty was quite obviously awake because, surprise, Kitty was the one who talked in her sleep. She cleared her throat, and she did something that no one had ever thought to do before. She asked Kitty what she wanted.

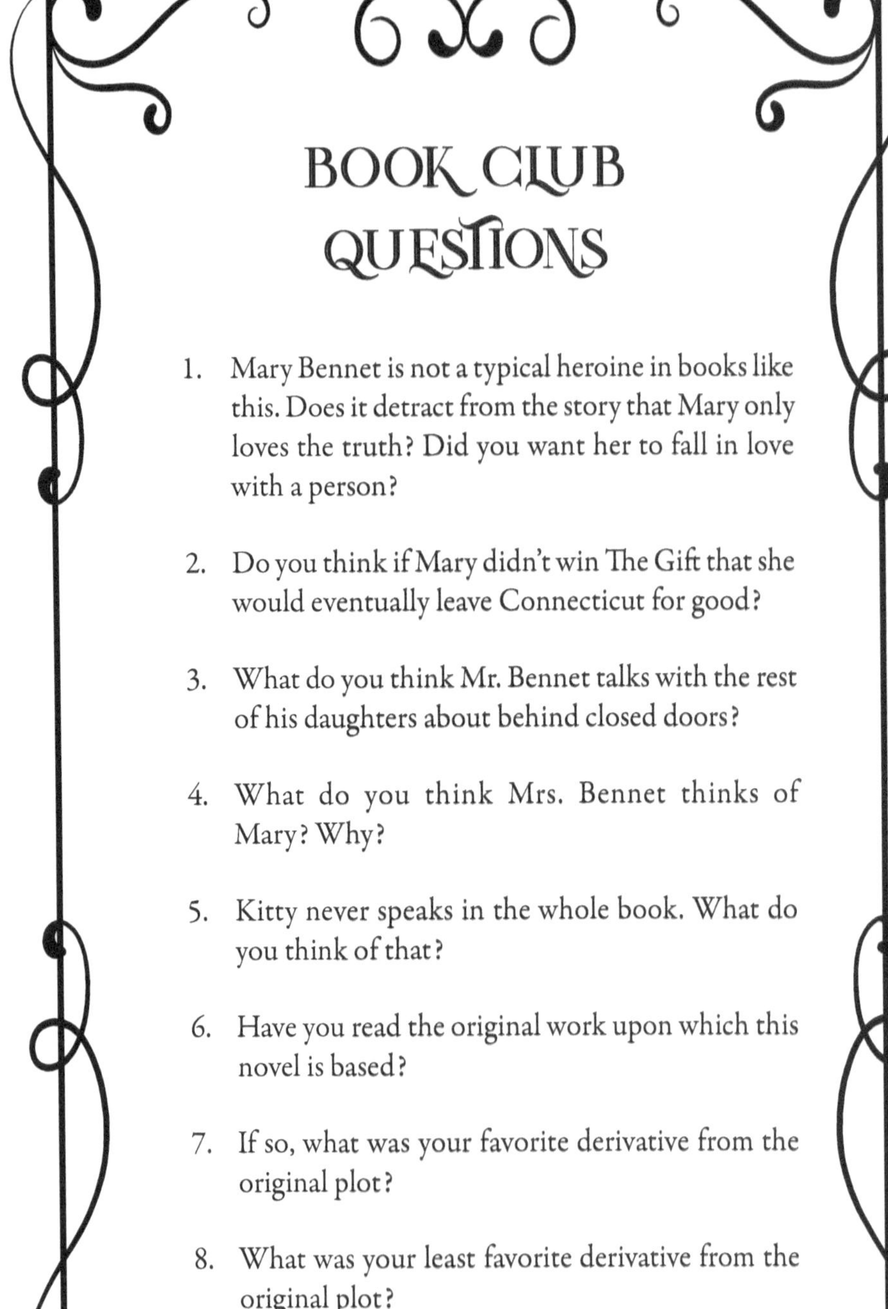

BOOK CLUB QUESTIONS

1. Mary Bennet is not a typical heroine in books like this. Does it detract from the story that Mary only loves the truth? Did you want her to fall in love with a person?

2. Do you think if Mary didn't win The Gift that she would eventually leave Connecticut for good?

3. What do you think Mr. Bennet talks with the rest of his daughters about behind closed doors?

4. What do you think Mrs. Bennet thinks of Mary? Why?

5. Kitty never speaks in the whole book. What do you think of that?

6. Have you read the original work upon which this novel is based?

7. If so, what was your favorite derivative from the original plot?

8. What was your least favorite derivative from the original plot?

9. Have you read the first books in this series? If so, did you like the Easter Eggs and nods to that book? If not, are you interested in going back and reading them?

10. If you have read the first two books, you know where Mary ends up. Are you interested in finding out what her journey was like getting there after she leaves Longbourn? How do you think she ends up in such a high position at such a young age?

11. This book, and all the books in the series, tries to diversify the cast from the original novels. Do you think that this works?

12. If you are familiar with the original novels, do you think that Austen opens the door for this kind of diversification? Are these kinds of characters already in the subtext of those books?

13. There is a running soundtrack through this book. Did you listen along to the playlist? Did you like the music? Was there something there you never heard before but wished to explore?

14. Who do you think the narrator is?

15. Do you like having the narrator jump in and speak directly to the reader? Why or why not?

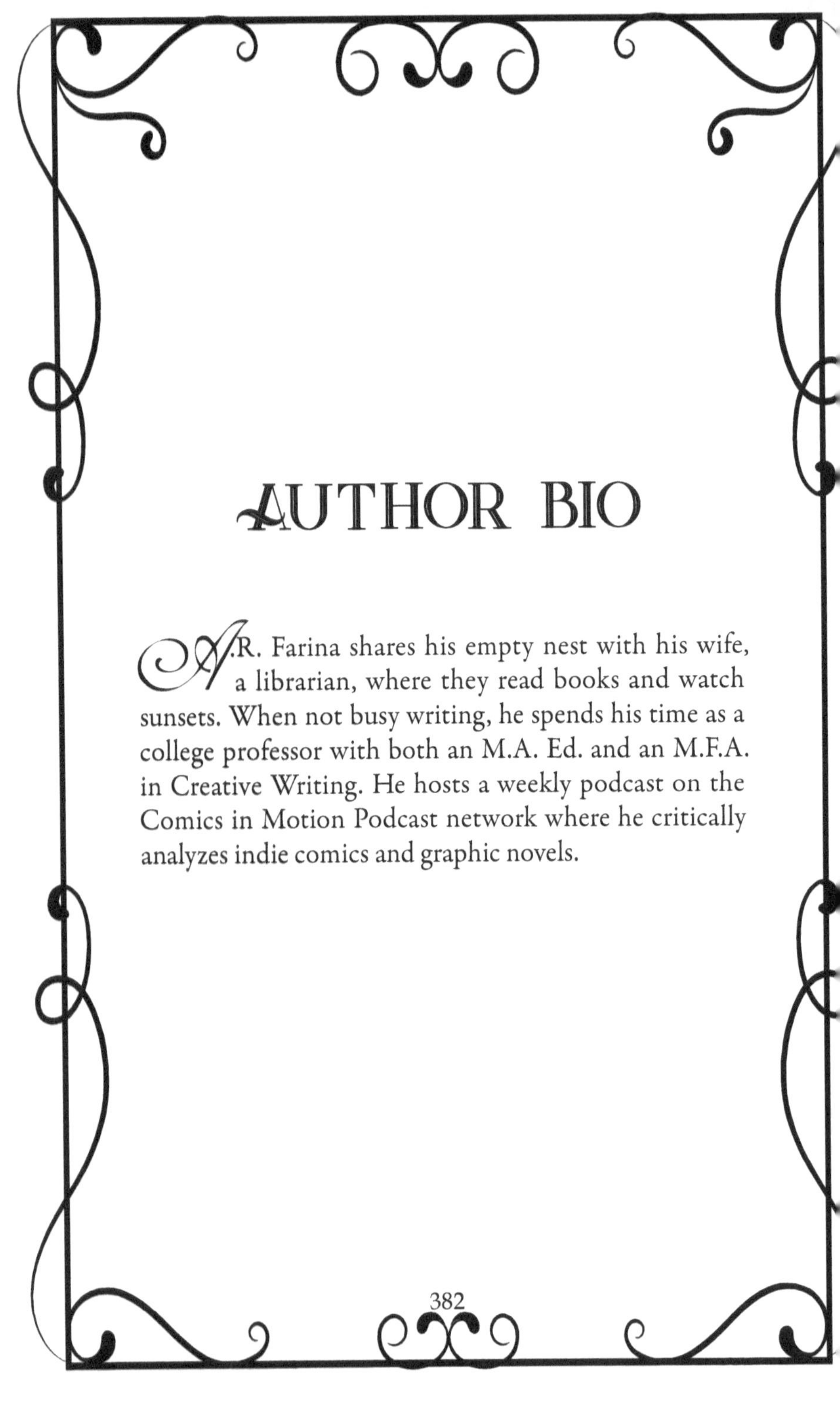

AUTHOR BIO

A.R. Farina shares his empty nest with his wife, a librarian, where they read books and watch sunsets. When not busy writing, he spends his time as a college professor with both an M.A. Ed. and an M.F.A. in Creative Writing. He hosts a weekly podcast on the Comics in Motion Podcast network where he critically analyzes indie comics and graphic novels.

Discover more at
4HorsemenPublications.com
10% off using HORSEMEN10

www.ingramcontent.com/pod-product-compliance
Lightning Source LLC
Chambersburg PA
CBHW030105310726
48970CB00004B/1149